j. kirsch

Sharp Edges
Published by Blueberry Beans Publishing
Mansfield, OH, 44906

ISBN: 979-8-218-18623-4

Front cover design by ©J. Kirsch
Front image by ©oleschwander/shutterstock.com
Publishing logo by © Kathryn Recker
Author photo by © Brooke Smith/Enchanted Exposures

DEDICATION:

To those of us living in the shadows, chasing the sun.

WRITTEN FOR:

Jeff, because I promised you a new painting. Never thought it'd be done in words instead of oil or acrylic. I love you. You saved me. One step, one day at a time. I'm so proud of you.

ACKNOWLEDGMENTS

First off, I want to thank my wonderful husband, Cole, who's tolerated my spaced-out-into-another-world mindset for the last three years. I love you, BooBerry. Thank you for the love and support, and for sharing yourself with two other guys.

To my loving family: my supportive, beautiful mother, Sheri, and to the dad who stepped-up, Steve. To my hardworking father, Don, and the loving mom who also stepped-up, Laura. To my grandparents and uncle in heaven, and to Grandma Frye.

To my crazy, intelligent, handsome brothers, Jeff and Brian, for giving me *the most amazing, wild* childhood a girl could ever ask for! You both inspire me to be better. Thank you for your loving words of wisdom over the years.

To the other two in the Triple Moon: Brooke and Bobby. Over twenty years of friendship, and still counting. Look how far we've come. I love you!

To my friends, who listened to me ramble on… and on… and on about *Jessike* and my writing struggles. Sara Jo (I sure do miss our cigarette/coffee writing days in Florida), to Kat, who fell in love with *Jessike* just as much as I did ("Overpass Graffiti!" I love you so much!). To Nick, Julie, Kristie, Dylan and Joy. To Mychal, who helped birth the POV of Addiction—if not for you, this book wouldn't have happened—and, of course, to my second favorite ship, *Myikki.*

To my beta readers I've lost track of over the years. Thank you for making the story stronger.

To my Barnes & Noble Family: Aileen (The Queen), Laura (my bat-loving friend), Michelle (my Work Wifey), Elly (my fellow sarcastic B), Nate (you're still cute as a button!), Grant (DO YOU HAVE TIKTOK?!), Denny, Nancy, Erin, Chris and Jessee, Brayden (I'm still your Other Mother), Lilly Pad, Dylan (still glad the floor took me out instead of you haha!), Gabby, sweet Emma, Theresa, Kelly, Hannah and to everyone else I may have forgotten, there's been a lot of us over the years.

To the awesome, talented artists and writers/poets who contributed to this book: Dave Porter, Elly Evans, Michelle Mease, Kayla Guerrero, the AH-MAZING Matthew Keeton for all the badass artwork you've done for me for promotion, and, of course, to Scooter Ward of the band Cold for allowing me to use the lyrics to "Wicked World" in Part Three. You've always been a huge inspiration to me, and it was an honor to have you as part of this indie project.

To all the musicians/artists who kept me company for the last six years while writing this novel: Linkin Park for the initial title/inspiration, Cold, Asking Alexandria, Tool, A Perfect Circle, Matt Maeson, HIM, Ville Valo, Ed Sheeran, Calum Scott, Coldplay, U2, Slipknot, Dead by Sunrise, Parachute, Snow Patrol, The Fray, The Script, Rihanna, Incubus, Avenged Sevenfold, Lifehouse, Third Eye Blind, Staind, The Offspring, Puscifer, Faith in Failure, and many, many, many, many more.

Lastly, to those we lost to overdoses and suicide, to those in recovery, to those in active addiction. We hear you. We see you. You are loved.

IMPORTANT
AUTHORS NOTE
PLEASE READ BEFORE... READING

We live in a society where topics such as addiction and mental health are widely misunderstood. Because of the misunderstanding, the conclusion everyone jumps to is *romanticizing.* I'll be upfront with you just so we're clear: when I was an addict, the most romantic part of my life *was* the *drug.* It was the rush, the hunting down dealers, living on the edge of danger. Addiction isn't black and white. Believe it or not, but when I was an addict, I was still doing everything everyone else was doing: working, falling in love, hanging out with friends, putting my jeans on one leg at a time, just like you, but when all else failed, I still had my drug who, in the end, became my friend *and* lover.

This story won't be relatable to everyone. It may not even be relatable to most. However, 95% of the stories/situations you're going to read were taken from real-life persons whether via bluelight.org or my friends, family, strangers, and myself. I interviewed multiple active and recovering addicts. I suffer from depression, have had three miscarriages, and saw addiction from both the inside and outside. They say to write what you know, so I did.

This story may contain a romance, but it's not romanticizing in the way many people use the term itself. I'm being *honest.* I'm being *raw,* and if you don't think that you can't fall in love with addiction, then perhaps this book isn't for you. I'm not trying to be arrogant. I'm trying to save your time. This story isn't for everyone. I wrote this for closure from my own addiction and mental health, and for those close to me.

For those of you who do understand where I'm coming from: *Thank You.* I see you, I hear you, and I love you.

One step, one day at a time, my friends.

We do recover.

CAUTION

This story contains strong language and sexual content.

If you or someone you know is suffering from drug abuse/use, addiction, suicide, depression, miscarriage, eating disorders, parental emotional/physical abuse, and self-harm, please reach out and contact these hotlines:

National Child Abuse Hotline: 1-800-422-4453
National Center for Missing and Exploited Children: 1-800-222-5678
Depression Hotline: 1-630-482-9696
National Domestic Violence Hotline: 1-800-799-7233
National Association of Anorexia Nervosa & Associated Disorders: 1-847-831-3438
National Human Trafficking Hotline: 1-888-373-7888
The National Sexual Assault Hotline: 1-800-656-HOPE
National Runaway Safeline: 1-800-RUNAWAY
Covenant House: 1-800-999-9999
Self-Injury Hotline: 1-800-366-8288
Crime Victims Hotline: 1-866-689-HELP
Alcohol Abuse and Crisis Intervention: 1-800-234-0246
Alcohol and Drug Abuse Helpline and Treatment: 1-800-390-4056
The Drug and Alcohol Addiction Resource: 1-800-390-4056
Alcohol Hotline Support and Information: 1-800-390-4056
National Suicide Hotline: 1-800-784-2433
National Suicide Prevention Hotline: 1-800-273-8255
National Suicide Prevention Text Line: 1-800-799-4889
LGBT Youth Suicide Hotline: 1-866-488-7386 or Text “Trevor” to 1-202-304-1200
The Miscarriage and Abortion Hotline: 1-833-246-2632

We are not stats or statistics.
We are the uprising profit of the pharmaceutical and government's addiction to greed.

SHARP EDGES

INTRODUCTION

We don't need a proper introduction.

I'm all around, whether you choose to see me or not.

But I'm here.

And I disguise myself well.

I'm with the scantily dressed girl on the streets and the driver in the car who'll pick her up and use her for the few bills. She'll be rewarded for her midnight services. I'll comfort her when she's reminded of what she's become. Unwanted. Forgotten.

I replenish the father of three with his fourth glass of whiskey as he and the wife argue about his overtime work hours that can be better spent with the family. I doze off with him in his office, the glass tipping from his hand and bursting onto the floor. I am the drumbeat of his own self-loathing.

I'm the stay-at-home mom, sleeping too late and waking up too early, and swallowing her child's ADHD prescription.

I'm the reflection of the teenage girl in the mirror, poking her ribs and pinching her belly. I'm the fingers down her throat, and the food spat into the napkin. "Not good enough," I tell her.

"Never, ever good enough."

I order into a speaker, "A number twelve, extra-large, and a diet coke." I'm the inclining scale numbers, labored breathing, and aching joints.

I shiver with the strung-out homeless man under the bridge.

Yes.

I am many, many things:

The bean water in your coffee mug.
The sugar in your candy.
The razorblade to your skin.
The result of you giving head to a loaded gun.
The people clustered around a Las Vegas gambling table.
The devil on your shoulder.

I'm your shakes, chills, constant trips to the bathroom, the acid lump in your throat, the heated spoon, the tightened tourniquet, the needle sinking into your veins.

I'm the perpetrator of your relapse.

I'm why your friends cut ties; why your family commits you.

I am ADDICTION.

Everyone has their own VERSION OF ME.

How do I get here?

Sometimes I'm born into your family. Other times, I'm invited to dinner. It's up to you to decide if I will stay for the night, a week, years, or a lifetime.

I am an immortal god to be fed and worshiped. Your

destruction, your weakness, your descent, your *death* are my *ultimate* goal.

I am always with you, relentless, and patient.

Can you hear me?

Can you see me?

I'm here.

I'm not going away.

Two teenagers on a blood-saturated porch were strangers until two weeks ago.

It's your typical Dickens' tragedy:

One grew up in the lavish Richland, Ohio, middle-class area known as The Golden Suburbs, a pretentiously perfect population with paved roads and cookie-cutter houses. I was there when he found his sister in the bathroom with a needle in her arm. I was the blown veins under her skin. I was his broken screams.

The other was raised in the inner-city streets of the ROY G BIV. Over the years, he made right with the middle-aged men wasting away their days drinking cheap American beer in their driveways. He shared his joint with the twelve-year-old girl next door colored black and blue by her father's hand. This was home and gunshots never fazed him.

Their encounter is my doing, although they don't know it *yet*, for I am never without an itinerary.

It all started in mid-July.

Mike was working at Blueberry Beans, a small coffee shop attached to the Indie Pages independent bookstore inside the Richland Mall. It was his third day on the job, and his manager, Jazz, a quirky girl with wild, curly black hair and dressed in goth apparel and high boots, was instructing him how to operate the steamer. Mike may be shy and awkward, but he wasn't dumb. He mastered it on the first go.

As he was practicing steaming nonfat milk for a cappuccino, a group of four guys close to his age approached the café, three of the four jabbering about cars and engines.

"Hey there," said a baritone tenor.

Mike glanced up and came face to face with Jesse Harris.

"S'that the steamer foggin' up the room?" He skimmed Mike up and down. "Naw, it's just you."

Milk spluttered from the pitcher onto the ceiling. Jazz ran over and stopped the machine, laughing profusely.

"What the hell, dude? You were doing so well! Distracted?"

Jesse gave him a coy smirk. "Dang, I do like my baristas like I like my coffee—tall, creamy, and Italian."

Jazz rolled her eyes. "Get outta here, Jess."

"I'm a payin' customer, Jazzlyn," he said, still stuck on Mike. "You're new here. Ya moved in across the street from me, didn'tcha? Indigo?"

Mike nodded.

Jesse hummed and looked at Jazz. "Usual, Jazzy."

"I'm not giving you an IOU this time."

"I got money."

She rang him up, ripped the order sticker out of the printer, stuck it to a plastic 22 oz cup, and handed it to Mike.

"Upside down maple drizzle macchiato, light ice, extra maple, extra shot of espresso. Got it."

He spun to the syrup bottles and stopped short when Jesse said, "Make it *extra, extra saucy*, wouldja?"

"Jesse Harris!" Jazz snapped. "Don't fluster the newb!"

Mike wiped his brow and squirted flavoring into the cup, averting his eyes from the ones searing into him as he returned to the espresso machine.

Jesse rested his elbows on the counter. "Am I flusterin' ya?"

"No," he lied. "You're just a customer who knows what he wants."

Jesse's aura twinkled.

"Damn straight. I'm lookin' right at it."

Mike completed the drink with shaky hands, slid it on the counter, and tried to look elsewhere as Jesse sipped. He smacked his lips and stared quizzically at the beverage.

"Yo, this is cold."

"You ordered an iced coffee," said Mike, almost defensively.

"But you made it. It should be *scorchin'* hot. Oh, shit! I *am* flusterin' ya," he said, noticing Mike's red-tipped ears and cheeks.

Mike cleared his throat. "How many one-liners do you have?"

"A-*latte*," he answered, and, their eyes deadlocked, Jesse leaned in for a whisper. "As much as I've been enjoyin' our nightly starin' contest, I'm *literally* across the street, and I don't bite."

"What if I do?"

"What? Bite? Ha. I hope ya do. Wanna show off my scars when I tell people how ya sank your teeth into me."

Don't be daft, Michael. He's not flirting with you. He's making fun of you like all the kids in school did.

"See ya tonight, Mike. Midnight, on the dot."

It's true.

Midnight. Every night. On the dot. Mike and Jesse came out onto their porches; Mike sat and drew in his sketchbook; Jesse stood, one ankle crossing the other, hip on the porch post, and merely *stared.*

Tonight is no different. Jazz cautioned Mike that Jesse was bad news, and the conversation orbits in his head as he drinks in the sight of the boy across the street.

"We're best friends. We have been since the ninth grade, but that's not the point. I can be friends with him and still warn against his dumbass. Stay away, Mike."

"Wasn't planning on befriending him, Jazz. I got enough on my plate."

It wasn't a lie.

Totally.

Staring wasn't off-limits.

Staring wasn't dangerous.

"Stay away, Mike." Her admonition was defacing his midnight stare-down.

"Damn it, Jazz," he curses and lights a cigarette. Seconds later, Jesse does as well.

He knows his boundaries. He doesn't care for people regardless of their captivating dimpled cheeks and suave talk. Forget the long, lean legs and the muscular limbs constructed from years of doing street sports Jazz called "Parkour" and "Freerunning." Mike had to google it because A: what in the actual hell was Parkour? and B: Jazz informed him that Jesse was semi-YouTube famous for his Parkour videos. Locally famous, seeing as he never raised enough money off his channel to escape this hellish town.

This is Jesse? Mike wondered, fascinated as Jesse ran in different environments, climbing over walls, jumping from building to building and up trees and over railings and flipping, kicking, spinning mid-air as though he were some godly-strength, humanoid Spider Man.

And you get winded walking up the stairs. Give it up. You're so dull.

Jesse waves as an invitation, and I scoff as Mike stands and sets his sketch pad on the swing.

Really? You? Michael Sinclair, who couldn't make a single friend his entire school career, is going to march across the road and, what? Hang out with YouTuber, Parkour Jesse Harris? Sit your ass down before you embarrass yourself.

He senses the pending storm—rain, thunder, and something else he can't quite place.

Danger.

Jesse lightly shrugs, steps back into his house, and as soon as he does, Mike hears three voices getting into what sounds like *the* most heated argument since his parents split.

I'd hate for you to become the neighborhood snoop. Best to call it a night, yes?

Mike sighs, defeated. He crushes his cigarette butt into the sand-stuffed silver can and, at the door, spins around, forgetting his sketchbook and phone.

Jesse's family continues to feud, giving Mike pause. I push him along.

You can't help him. Go inside. I'm trying to protect you. He doesn't want to be your friend. He'll use you just as all your other "friends" used you. Remember them, Mikey? Remember what they did to you? Some friends, huh?

Mike shoves his cigarettes into his hoodie pocket and shivers as the rain and wind pick up. Two more strides and he'll reach the door, and on step one, the first—*BANG!*—erupts, notching him back on a historical timeline when pirates sailed the high seas and fired their cannons.

Still, he knows time travel isn't possible, and Ohio certainly doesn't have seas.

It's thunder. Only thunder.

BANG!

BANG!

BANG!

Mike ducks and covers behind the SUV, waiting for another pirate cannon—*BOOM!*—that doesn't come. Jesse tumbles out of his house, and a man noticeably bigger than them chases him.

Mike takes off, crossing the road, and collides with Jesse.

"Get outta here, man! Please. Go home. It's not—"

BANG!

Jesse grasps his stomach and buckles, his deadweight dragging Mike down with him.

"*Shit, shit, shit....*" Mike presses his hands on Jesse's wound. "Stay with me."

Jesse, his breathing laborious, clamps his eyelids.

"P-p-poc..."

"What?"

"P-po-cket."

Mike frisks him and finds the cellphone, bypassing the code to reach the SOS button, and he can't fathom what had happened, but is able to tell the operator Jesse's been shot and requires an ambulance ASAP.

"Is anyone else hurt?" asks the operator.

Jesse tugs on his arm, and Mike huddles in to listen.

"He... he... he kill... killed my... ma."

"*Fuck.* Yes, there is. A female. Please hurry."

The operator instructs him to keep Jesse awake.

"Stay with me. You're going to be fine. Don't close your eyes. Stay awake. Stay with me."

Gunshots. Blood. *So much blood.* He unzips his hoodie and drapes it over Jesse.

Mike relates the scene to a horror flick. I'm sure you've heard the overused plot: a bunch of reckless teenagers are camping out in the middle of BFE. The girl notices the killer in a hockey mask, and she bellows as his machete slashes the tarp, but her boyfriend *keeps* pounding her because getting your dick wet (courtesy of me) is of more importance than fleeing the murderer.

Jesse's the girlfriend, and the residents of Indigo Street are the neglectful, horny boyfriend. House lights illuminate the road; heads emerge from curtains and open doors, though nobody helps the guy who's practically dying just feet away.

Mike, far from courageous, can't say where his newfangled bravery flourished from when he took off *towards* the screams and gunshots. His older sister, Charlie, has called him a "pussy" since he was old enough to understand insults. Courageous boys don't cry after finding their sister overdosed on the bathroom floor. Courageous boys don't bruise their knuckles from punching a wall because kids at school called their sister "Maddy the Addy." If Mike had a reaction scale, he feels the *human* end would outweigh the *pussy* end. Reading Baudelaire in braille was, still is, easier than swaying Charlie differently.

Jesse jolts from Mike's nudge.

"I'm sorry. It's me. Just me. I'm not going to hurt you."

Of course not, Mike, that's my job.

"Stay awake. Stay with me."

Their eyes meet black ink to amber honey, an intoxicating, explosive oil and fire cocktail. Eye contact is an essential form of communication representing trust and respect and motivates Jesse to trust Mike, not just now, but also in the coming months.

"Don't hate me," says Mike, "but I have to do this."

He pushes down harder on the bleeding lesion, and Mom

appears as Jesse wails.

Mike rests his forehead on his. "You're losing blood. I gotta stop it." He looks up. "Where the *fuck* is the ambulance?!"

"I didn't do it."

"Do what?" he asks, smearing the blood his thumb tries removing off Jesse's cheek.

"Ma… I didn't… kill her…"

"I believe you."

Mom sits beside Mike, his plaintive expression searching for an answer. Nobody has answers except Jesse, but he's bone-stiff, saying and hearing nothing, Mike's fingers grazing his bloodied hairline being his only consolation.

Piercing alarms, police vehicles, ambulances, and fire engines busy the roadside. An officer forces the paramedics aside, and Mike does a second and third glance—the likeness between Jesse and the cop uncanny. He addresses him as "son" and asks the questions we're all too mortified to ask:

"What happened? Where's your brother?"

Jesse whimpers.

His dad jogs into the house.

Mike scans the red and gray-spattered cream living room walls, or at least he *thinks* they're cream.

Two paramedics lift Jesse onto the stretcher and hook him up to oxygen and materials to slow the bleeding, his horrified gaze blinking at Mike.

"Don't leave me. Please."

Mike squeezes Jesse's hand and walks in time with the

paramedics moving him into the truck.

"Don't worry," Mike says. "You're safe. I promise."

You promise? You can't even keep your family's rickety levee composed. How do you expect to maintain his?

He has no explanation. All he knows is he'll lose his mind if someone harms Jesse, and we're all aware of the sort of damage one's capable of in the absence of sanity.

Mike recounts to Paul Harris, Jesse's father, how he was about to go inside when he heard the arguments and gunshots; about Jesse being shot by....

"His brother? He ran down Violet Street." He breathes uneasily. "His brother killed their mom."

I've been idle, documenting the wrought scene, and Jesse shoots me the evil eye. *Don't look at me like that. I'm not the crook behind your mother's death.* Not entirely. I was the meth in his brother's veins, and my influence persuaded him to pull the trigger *four* times.

Paul sighs. "Are you okay? Are you hurt?"

"I'm fine," answers Mike. "Shaken up, but not hurt."

"Alright. I'm going to need you to come down to the station at some point tomorrow to give a statement."

Mike sidesteps the cop cars and joins Mom at the end of their *new* driveway, his reflex to my hands on his shoulders like ribbons cascading down his vertebrae.

The ambulance's taillights shrink and fade, as does Jesse, and Mike's left asking himself: *for how long?*

Not long at all, Mike, not long at all.

PART ONE

Jeff then said, "There are two things that can happen if you continue down this route.

One: all your creativity will vanish. Everything you love to do—writing, painting, creating—will disappear completely the longer you are an addict. You will be so engrossed in your high that the desire to create will become covered by this addiction and you'll never get it back.

Two: Everyone you love, everything you care for, will slip away because you won't have time for anything or anyone other than the addiction. You will spend your days high, chasing your fix, or dope sick.

"You have to make a choice. Do you want to be the Jessica who is sober, creating things, loving, and spending time with her friends and family? Or do you want to be Jessica the Addict: the self-absorbed person not caring about anything or anyone else other than her next fix? Do you want to spend your hours chasing down a high or chasing down more important things?"

What he said hit me, and it hit me hard. We hung up the phone after two and a half hours. I was offered another Oxy. I wanted it. The Stalking Butler said, "One more won't hurt you. You can stop after this."

Jeff said, "Don't do it. Once you start, it's hard to go back. Remember who you are and who you're going to be when all of this is over. Happier. Healthier. Don't listen to the voice. It's not there. It's not your friend. You're stronger than your monster. You're bigger than this drug."

As hard as it was to do, I turned it down. It stared at me from the ottoman, where it sat on the glass chessboard. My boyfriend said he wouldn't judge me if I wanted it just one last time. I almost caved. My heart raced. My hands shook. My eyes cried.

"No," I said, "take it out of the room, and don't tell me where it is. I'm done."

I'd end up doing drugs for another eight months after this journal entry.

—Taken from the Author's Personal Journal
Thursday, November 5, 2015

ONE
Studying the Light

I am a thing to be feared.

I'm not as fearful as ***Death***, but I should be. Without my supremacy, ***Death*** wouldn't be as profitable as he is. He won't go out of business. He'll just struggle to pay the rent.

Despite popular belief, I assure you there's truth to what's said about my choice of victims. *I* choose *them*, not the other way around, and I'm not overly picky, either. Young. Old. Poor. Rich. It makes little difference to me so long as I'm fed, loud, and strong.

Teenagers, on the other hand, are a personal preference. These ripe, confused, delicate young pups lilting on the cusp of life; still naïve enough to find some hope in a world that's yet to betray them. It's almost sad how easily I can convert them, especially when they're pissed-off loners, much like our star of the show, Michael Sinclair.

From the outside looking in, he isn't that different, nor the same, as the next teenager. After all, aren't we all unique and the same in subtle ways? Even if he's more "privileged" than Jesse Harris, will they still not find common ground where they can sympathize and relate? It may not seem feasible at first.

If I'm to jump straight to the present, you won't fully grasp how Michael Sinclair's past shaped him into an oblique, sharp edge.

Come, take my hand, and let's journey back in time. I can't guarantee your safety since nobody understands my influential power until it's too late.

Mike, eight years old, perches on the concrete veranda connected to a spacious two-story house on First Avenue, one of ten streets within the suburban countryside of Richland, Ohio. I've been a member of the family for seven years. My stamina hasn't yet peaked, and I rest my weary bones beside him.

Ah, the Golden Suburbs, every soccer mom's wet dream. Vibrant grassy lawns, wrap-around porches built on houses two or three stories tall, community-watch meetings and mid-afternoon gossip brunches with the other stay-at-home wives and mothers; sunhats and sundresses and suntans aplenty. Maddy, his oldest sister, joked to Michael that their lives were taken out of an episode of *Desperate Housewives* because no matter how "Stepford" the families in the Golden burbs appeared to be on the outside, they're "just as fucked up and messy on the inside."

Naturally, this made little sense to Michael until he got older. His childhood *seemed* average. He spent his summer vacations in the pool in their backyard, feeling weightless as he back flipped underwater, the *whooshing* sound drowning out the terrible boy-band music Charlotte played from the boombox. She sipped diet coke while sunbathing, her body slathered in baby oil and tanning lotion.

Charlie gained the more unflattering traits where DNA was concerned. Although the pure definition of *drop, dead gorgeous,* she was sandy-haired, gray-eyed, and pale.

"How is it you stay tanned in the wintertime, and I turn into an undercooked pastry?" she'd snarl at Michael as if it were *his* fault she ended up being more Scottish-German like their father and less Italian like their mother. "You're not popular. You're not a school athlete. You're a freak of nature, and nobody likes you, so why do you get good skin genes? You eat nothing but sugar and not a pimple in sight! *Freak.*"

Charlie put the—*pop!*—in "popular": head cheerleader, top of her class, slim and tall, and homecoming queen two years in a row. She wasn't the queen bee, she was the entire hive, and people swarmed to her as such. The first time he watched *Mean Girls*, he compared Charlie to Regina George—always snobby, always the victim, and fake. *So fake!* She was that girl who complimented another girl's wardrobe and then, as soon as she walked away, said something remarkably diametric, like, "Where did she get that dress? Off her dead Grandmother?"

It's difficult to say how or when Charlie became a pom-waving megalomaniac. Maybe it goes back to Maddy's comment about how the Golden Suburbs were *perfectly perfect* until the lights went out and the doors locked for the evening. Not everything is what it seems. A picture-perfect family who walks with impeccable posture, says all the right things, and wears designer clothes isn't better than those who shop at thrift stores or are visited by the cops or Children's Services in the rougher parts of Richland. It's not so much that the Golden Suburbs were *better*, but better at *hiding*. Camouflage. Smokescreens. Yes, that's it. The Sinclairs owned the name-brand smoke and mirrors.

Leon Sinclair relaxes in his patio chair, reading the Sunday paper, his Marlboro Red occasionally tapping the glass ashtray.

Look at Mike: shy, misunderstood, even at a tender age. In other words: *the ideal victim*. The pencil in his left hand copies onto paper a bluebird high on an apple tree, his stomach churning from the smokey stench of his father's cigarette. He frequently wondered what was so attractive about smoking. According to the DARE lady who spoke at the school assembly, they were cancerous. Maddy would end up being a smoker, too.

Leon, disgruntled, goes inside to answer the phone, providing Mike time to contemplate his next move. He sets his sketchpad down and checks both ways. The coast is clear.

He skulks to the ashtray, sucks in a single lungful of smoke, then quickly learns what a mistake *that* is and throws up at the side of the house.

When he's sixteen, Maddy will move to Florida in four months, and Mike, in two more years, will move to the ROY G BIV, where he'll meet Jesse Harris. I'll have been with the Sinclairs for fifteen years. I'm stronger, louder, and very much present, but I have yet to take on a physical form.

As their metal shovels slice into thick snow, Maddy asks if Mike wants to go on a drive with her later in the afternoon, and he answers yes instantly. It's been three years since the "Bathroom Incident," but they've never spoken about it. He's not sure whether she's embarrassed that her baby brother found her strung out on the floor or if they just don't want to admit that their seemingly optimum family is really rather sooty. Spending quality time together gives him the belief they'll be able to clean up their dirty history.

Little does he know as long as I'm here, it'll *always* be dirty.

She steers onto Amoy West, the wintry breeze outside and the artificial heat inside the blue Nissan mingling, her window cracked so she can flick her cigarette ashes. She expresses her excitement about starting anew in Florida, and although he understands why she has to go, it doesn't make it any less distressing.

She can escape her environment, but she can't escape me.

"What's new with you, kiddo? Got yourself a hot girlfriend yet?"

Laughter flares from the passenger's seat (Mike) and the backseat (me). Who wants to date the younger brother of "Maddy the Addy"? Not a soul, that's who. Afraid he'll hurt her feelings, he says he isn't interested in anyone, and she hums a *that's too bad* sort of hum.

"What about school?"

Mike loathes Cougar High School. While teenagers twist the facts to be dramatic, when he claims he has *zero* friends, it's *not* a stretch. I'm there when he eats lunch alone at the corner table, avoiding eye contact and never asking or being asked about weekend festivities. He doesn't fit in with the goths, preps, nerds, and jocks. HA! The *jocks!* That's the *last* group he belongs to, Leon likes to remind him.

When he doesn't answer, Maddy changes the subject to art.

"I have this teacher, Mr. Steele, and he's a complete tool. I don't even enjoy drawing anymore. He says I ain't talented," says Mike.

Mike hates Mr. Steele. I love him. He's one of the countless diggers contributing to the hole leading to an abyss where I'll be waiting.

"Are you kidding me?" Maddy shrieks. "Mr. Steele can suck a fuck! Don't listen to that jackass, ya hear me?"

If you can't guess by now Mike's minimal support system, I'll break it down for you.

Leon saves his praises for Superstar Charlie Sinclair. Rarely will you witness her receiving Leon's verbal backlashes. Then there's Mom, a woman who invariably pelts in Leon's shadow. Maddy shuts herself in her basement bedroom, distant and cold, coming out only to go to work, school, or to scope out *me.*

According to him, Maddy sticking up for Mike is the most *incredible* feeling *ever!*

"It's kinda hard to be optimistic when Charlie's our sister."

Maddy agrees she used to feel the same way. Born clever, Charlie solved at an early age what it took to attain Leon's validation: talk about sports, compliment his haircuts and achievements, and ask about his day.

"Gotta give the girl credit. Charlie worked hard for it. She's been an honor roll student since kindergarten; accepted to OSU, Bowling Green, and AU, all free rides. She brought home nice guys,"—she raises an eyebrow at Mike—"quarterbacks."

"Dad's ultimate hard-on."

Maddy laughs. "Right on, bro! I mean, she did everything right. Not saying you did anything wrong. I'd say you've had it the worst: waking up at 3 AM to shovel snow, five to mow the lawn, six to dust books. It's like Dad planned these things years in advance, but you're a smart kid, Mike."

"*Pffft.* Tell that to my GPA."

"GPAs aren't jack. Your worth has nothing to do with numbers designed by corrupt systems whose crucial goal is brainwashing the youth to conform to their government-controlling bullshit corporations. (Try saying that three times fast.) Your grades are obviously important, but you're not dumb. You're like me—"

"Not book smart, but smart in the topics we're passionate about."

She clicks her tongue. "*Exactly.* You're the only person I know who can pass a stranger on the street, go home, and sketch them down to their freckles. If that's not smart, then I'm Mother Teresa, and we both know I'm no nun."

Maddy has a point, and I wish she didn't. Her encouragement will only weaken me. Nevertheless, her words that should've flown him to Pluto falls into an emptiness he, with Leon's assistance, spooned out over the years, his father grilling his ego until there'd been no ego left. It's in that cavern where I constructed a home for myself.

Mike's low grades resulted in Leon enrolling him in summer school. His grades will never be above average, and average won't do. If it's not an A+, it damn well better be an A++, and Superstar Charlotte set the bar high with her outstanding academic achievements.

Maddy gestures to her Camels and winks. "I won't tell the 'rents."

He doesn't reach for them. We're not quite there. However, he'll prefer her chocolate-flavored Camel Golds over Leon's stale-raisin Marlboro Reds.

"Teachers can be bigger bullies than students." She goes into a story about how this boy, Daryl, groped her in the hallways. Amanda Gross—"*Absolute* bitch, *totally* lived up to her last name"—told their homeroom instructor Maddy and Daryl were making out by the lockers.

Their VERSIONS OF ME were in the classroom holding hands with Daryl and Maddy, and that night, I paid Amanda Gross a visit disguised as a shiny razor blade.

"The teacher said the boys would think I was easy if I kept acting like a slut."

Mike's jaw drops.

I brush my shoulder off.

"She called you a slut?!"

"Yep." She pops the *P*. "And that year, fifth grade, they were breaking us up into periods, right, so we could adjust to junior high school. We had four teachers, and all but one *hated* me. Can't tell you how many times I came home from school crying. One of the worst years of my life, bro. All I'm saying is, don't listen to anyone but yourself. People are shit. *Period.*"

"Did you tell Mom and Dad?"

She shoots him a look as if he'd invited the Pope to a demonic dinner party.

Frozen snow crunches beneath rolling rubber down Claire Road, a street rooted in the middle of cornfield country. Trees line the path, naked and covered in icicle crystals like an old man's whiskers.

For the last twelve years, a VERSION OF ME has been infesting the trailer she parks in front of. Broken toys are scattered about the property, and there's a swing set minus one swing, its color a shocking red once upon a time judging by the jointed and disjointed batches of paint and rust. Flowerpots dangle from the porch hinges, their plastic baskets lifeless. Will they bloom in the spring or stray as carcasses of their once lively prime time?

"Back in a jiffy, Mikey."

Mike and I stay in the car, and Maddy and her VERSION OF ME tram up the walkway. Maddy knocks on the screen door and rubs her arms, springing in place. The man who answers matches his home: scruffy, dingy, and desperately needing a facelift. He directs his finger at Mike, and Maddy flicks her wrist as if to say, *don't worry about him.*

They go inside.

Mike isn't as gullible as he lets on and is thoroughly aware of what's going down in the trailer. If Maddy brought him here when he was ten or eleven, he'd presume she was visiting a friend, picking up a CD or another identically stupid object.

We crave such innocence. Naivety is a vastly distributed steroid in my cabinet of persuasions.

Mike punches the glove box, shakes his stinging knuckles, and grabs the Camel Golds and the purple Bic in the cup holder. My mouth to his ear, I perform my magic show.

It's just a cigarette. Everyone smokes. It's not a big deal.

Nicotine terrorizes his unmarked lungs, and he sinks into the plush seats, his nerves melting like chocolate under an Arizona sun with every drag.

Maddy buckles in.

He initiates an investigation.

No changes in pupils.

No sweats.

No droopy eyelids.

She's sober.

For now.

She shifts the car into reverse.

"Douchebag in there owes me money for—"

"Don't lie to me. You took me on a drug run."

She brakes, shuts her eyelids tightly, then checks the streets, her colorless hands squeaking against the leathered steering wheel.

"I'm sorry, Mike," she whispers. "I don't mean to be this way."

Don't be angry, Michael. It's not her fault. You'll both run to your rooms when you get home, and you'll cry into your pillow as she pulls me from her pocket, shreds the cellophane, and burns my sugary substance into liquid gold. She'll inject it from a needle into her tapped vein and nod out painlessly, whereas you'll be listening to the ceiling fan, wondering how much you can withstand before breaking.

You don't see it, but you will. For now, all you see is my death grip turning your sister blue, and all you hear is the gritting crack *of the Sinclair Family Levee.*

TWO

Ever-Glow

The night Jesse's brother took off, and after Jesse's gone, the windows staring back at Mike and Mom implore to be freed from the massacred nightmare that had occurred. Mike thinks Jesse would be pleased if he doused the place in gasoline and torched it to oblivion.

Mike fishes the SUV for his unopened pack of cigarettes, catching Mom's (understandably) disapproving side stare. A second look overwrites the previous one, the one he saw the night Maddy overdosed on the bathroom floor. Mothers don't want their teenagers to smoke, but he remembers when she said she'd rather he be open about it than go behind her back. Besides, she let Maddy smoke in her teenage years.

Mom asks for a cigarette, and he's surprisingly unsurprised.

Me? Why, I'm overjoyed. Marie hasn't a VERSION OF ME. I've tried. It takes a strong-willed person not to fall for my jurisdictions. Don't get too excited. She may not have an addiction. She has an *entity* you'll meet in due time.

They watch as the coroner drives deceased Margaret Harris out of the ROY G BIV and to the morgue.

The police yellow-tape 245 Indigo Street, ratifying it as an official crime scene.

"My sweet boy. I'm sorry you had to see that."

Mike drags on his Camel. "Me too. I hope he's okay…."

"You're lucky you weren't hurt, too. I don't… I don't know what I would do if I lost you." She hugs him tight. "I love you, Michael. You should get some sleep."

She pecks his cheek and heads to bed. Sleep won't come. She'll toss and turn, the mental footage of her baby blue daughter forever tormenting her peacefulness.

Mike and I don't sleep either, preferring to sit on the top step of the weathered porch, scraped and textured by old and new paint. Was it originally white? Yellow? Tan? He flips his bloodstained hands. *So much blood.* It's on his shirt, his jeans, his mouth. He should wash it off, but the traumatic evening has him stuck to his seat.

With a sketchpad on his knees, his mind becomes a bumbling cathedral designated for troubling thoughts. Was it Ernest Hemingway who said writing's easy? "All you do is sit down at a typewriter and bleed." Mike's not a writer. Artists don't bleed. They create fantastical worlds in which bleeding becomes an extinct and unnecessary pastime, and Jesse's the sole subject as he puts graphite to parchment.

I err off into the dark and permit him a perishable taste of serenity.

I'll be back.

I *always* come back.

I'm sure you're pining to meet Jesse again, as am I. The two of us are well past our expiration date for a one-on-one.

First, we must skip backward if we're to progress.

Mike's almost eighteen, and it takes six weeks to pack up their old house. He had plenty of time to accept his adjustments and say farewell to the First Avenue home. He'll miss the wood floors and the scenic view overlooking luscious woodlands. Three months before the move, Leon and Mom sat Mike and Charlie down at the kitchen table, the word "divorce" hovering heavily, and even then, it hadn't hit him, not like it did when the outcome of the separation hammered into him like a rusty nail to the heart.

Taking one last look at the house, maybe leaving wasn't all that bad. Childhoods should be simple and fun. Although Michael wanted his childhood to be an even-flow, it was more of an electrical circuit with the tiniest disconnect, creating the largest eruption in the history of family histories. And this house held it all. Every memory. Every overdose. Every screaming match.

Thinking back on it now, how did the levee first *crack?* Maddy and her drug addiction? Charlie and her big-headed snobbery? Michael's inward struggles? Their parents' separation? Those scenes, all those godforsaken heroin-filled needles, snarky insults, and 3 AM punishments, would lead him to the other side of town, to Indigo Street. When did it all go wrong? How could Leon leave their beautiful, soft-toned, delicate-as-lace mother?

"It's time to go," she says.

Make yourself comfortable in the family SUV, the only expensive materialistic possession she won in the nasty divorce settlement, not that it's any prize. They've owned the van since Mike was twelve, and the silver paint is corroding and peeling. The engine has this *click, click, click*ing sound indicating it's in dire need of an oil change too long overdue.

My heartfelt apologies for the tight squeeze. My sister's along for the ride. Isn't Madame spectacular in her jade, corset dress, and crimson lipstick? She's positively prepped to own the night, do the cancan, and auction off her ladies.

She whispers in Charlie's ear, and you blush when Madame directs her seductive gaze your way. No reason to be bashful. She has that effect on people.

It's 1 AM and quiet aside from the *clicking,* the Golden Suburbs twenty miles behind us, and we're smack-dab in the cesspool of downtown Richland, the contrast otherworldly. The roads are bumpy from the potholes the taxpayer's money should go towards fixing but aren't, and the stoplights appear to be the only functional lights, the storefronts either dark or sporting neon open-and-closed signs.

As diverse as we are, we're all pondering the same thing: *what the hell is Mom thinking?* They left the flawless suburbs for *this?*

We can doubt Mom's antics until we're nose-deep in maggots; it won't change the circumstances, nor will we condemn her for her choices. We might've sprung from challenge to challenge and underwent the bruising after-effects of those alterations, but we haven't been bitch-slapped by them as severely as Marie.

Mike's head against the window, he dubs Downtown Richland a trash and homeless, sullied eyesore. Streetlight hues—orange and white, red, green, yellow—luster inside peppered water droplets on the glass. *Rain*. How cliché. Only happy stories with happy endings begin with sunshine.

In the meantime, with his headphones on, everything's a-okay. One song shifts into another on his iPhone, and the SUV passes an alleyway lit up by a street firepit. He's befuddled by the men and women gathering the flames, their ages widespread, their jeans and sweaters grimy. Is the July rain cold? How would he know? He's in the warm, protective car, the woman at the wheel just as warm and protective. He has no grounds to be crass in terms of his entitled life.

The watered-down woman in the backup mirror is someone he's grown to admire and who has an impeccable gift for turning low self-esteem into confidence and ugliness into beauty. The years have beaten her—still stunning and radiant, though undeniably dimmed. She catches his eye in the mirror, and they smile—quite a feat given their somber situation.

Mike unlocks his phone and texts Maddy.

Hell's bells, Mike, I wish you wouldn't cling to her like shrink-wrap.

(Maddy): Hey, bro! I'm good! Just got home from work. You guys at the new digs yet?

What sort of backward establishment is Smoke N' Bones to have Maddy working past midnight?!

Oh, Mikey-boy, you've got a lot *to learn about jobs.*

A *gang* goes by at the stoplight; the men dressed like clones in their baggy jeans, white muscle shirts, and bandannas knotting biceps, left ankles, or skulls.

"Jesus," complains Charlie from the front seat, "please tell me we won't be living next to *them.*"

Mom focuses on the roadways after a brief once-over. "No, dear, I've met our neighbors, and they're lovely. Mrs. Jameson lives next door. Nice lady; a widow. She lost her husband last year."

"Gee, Mom, looks like you'll make a friend after all. You two have *so much* in common already!"

Ouch.

Don't worry. Mike will snap back in no ti—

"Shut up, Charlie. Why do you always have to be such a bitch?"

"Michael Alan!" says Mom. "Language!"

"But she—"

"Drop it, Michael!"

(Mike): No. Not yet. I still don't understand why we're moving in the middle of the night. Mom's lost it. And there's like... gangs here.

BUZZ!

(Maddy): It's the ROY G BIV. Mom doesn't want the neighbors to see what you're moving into the house. Robberies happen that way. And really, Mike? Gangs? There aren't gangsters in little ol' Richland, just wannabe thugs.

(Mike): Yeah. Remember the LKY?

What a *hoot!* If not for me, those "thugs" never would've met. What a shame half of them are now locked up; just one of my inevitable consequences, and I'm with them as they trade, sell, and use drugs inside prison walls.

(Maddy): LOL! Little Kentucky? Those dudes were a joke!

You should talk, Madeline.

(Mike): Shit, yeah, they were.

You too, Michael.

Deep into the central city, we enter what the locals consider the "ghetto" of Richland, but it's not the sort of "ghetto" you picture upon hearing the word itself. Sure, the ROY G BIV is, credibly, as hazardous as any other impoverished urban district. Ohio is famed for corn, farms, Cedar Point and the Rock and Roll Hall of Fame, any brutality scarce apart from *The Cleveland Torso Murders* or the *Piketon Family Massacre.* Furthermore, Richland isn't as congested as Cincinnati or Cleveland, nor as violent as the neighboring cities such as Chicago, Detroit, or Baltimore. Remember, the ritzy, silver spoon-fed *locals* termed the region. I'll bet money on how many of them have stepped a Gucci toe into an *actual* ghetto.

Mike expects—*we expect*—for ROY G BIV to live up to its street abbreviations. We hope for spirited painted Victorian houses—canary yellows, sky blues, and Easter greens—and manicured, lush lawns, bird baths, succulent trees by the rows, and end up with a figurative kick in the gonads.

Chapped sidewalks, spray-painted profanity, and racist symbols on stop signs and buildings (all done under my influence) can be seen in the midnight shade.

"Isn't 'Langer' a Jewish name?" Charlie asks, and Mike pauses his music.

"I believe so," Mom answers. "Why do you ask?"

"There's a swastika painted on their front door," says Charlie in reference to Langer's Family Convenience Store, a small, white building with two gas pumps and a parking lot that, on a good day, could fit five cars.

Mom sighs. We all do.

"Oh, dear."

"Sure can't wait to walk *these* streets at night."

Madame applauds.

Mike snorts. "Be polite and give your pimp a two-week notice."

I lower Madame's direct, open hand at Mike. *Calm down. You're not going anywhere, anytime soon.*

Charlie whips around in her seat. "*What* did you just say to me?"

"Michael!" snips Mom.

"Suck it up, Charlie! You're going to OSU. Why do you care?"

"Shut up, Mike! Nobody asked you!"

"KIDS!"

"And nobody asked for your shitty comments!"

"Screw you, you suicidal freak!"

"ENOUGH! BOTH OF YOU!"

"But Mom—"

"Michael! Hush! You two apologize right now, then not a peep until we get to the house. Understood?"

"Yes, ma'am," they mumble and apologize half-assed.

(Mike): I wish you were here. I hate this.

BUZZ!

(Maddy): You'll be fine. Just keep your nose clean and your head up. Everything will be alright. Love you, kiddo.

(Mike): Love you too, Madds. Miss you.

Mike and I gag at our *new* driveway because, sadly, Charlie's right. The place is a *dump,* as in somebody may as well have taken a bare-assed squat on the patchy lawn. At least Mike won't have to mow, but that's a story for another time.

The third house on the left on Indigo Street seems *sinister.* The porch lights flitter orange, and the bowed stairs leading to the front door are as old as the siding and roof. A silver chain-linked fence with a broken gate separates their property from the neighbors.

The moving truck arrives, and Mom hops out of the van, Charlie following suit, Madame's jade dress *twirling, twirling.*

Mike thinks she'll go straight to sleep or phone a friend to bitch about the house.

She won't.

She'll sneak out to meet Devon Sanders, the notorious "bad boy" waiting for her in his daddy's sleek, black Corvette on Green Street next to Junkies Playground.

Scandalizing? Not in the slightest. No discrimination to see here. My family tree, deep-rooted from the same trunk and branching out into our unique, unhealthy habits, is extensive. There's a VERSION OF ME to accommodate everyone's special fix.

We're everywhere.

We're in everyone.

You keep us immortal.

Later in the evening, Mike provides enough room for the movers to do their jobs without interruption on the stairs, and he rummages through his backpack for his sketchpad and Camels.

A pencil in his left hand and a cigarette in his right, his brain allows the graphite to do the thinking for him. What kind of future awaits him now? He should be running into the house to see what his room looks like, but the excitement isn't there. It won't be the room he grew up in with the bay window. The walls won't be bright red, and the carpet won't be squishy as marshmallows on his heels and toes.

Rain gobbles up his flicked ashes. Anemic, I sit and compel him to light another smoke, so he does. Mom instructs the movers where to set the furniture and television inside the house. Mike finds his headphones and shuts out the world, M Shadows singing to him about how we're all victims of a crime, and, with the song acting as some inexplicable siren ballad, the house across the street comes to life, two yellow globes blinking on like owl eyes...

...and fate commences.

Mike tries his hardest to pretend he doesn't notice.

And fails.

It's rather suitable, seeing he's been a failure his whole life.

Lightning flashes like a camera on the boy across the street against his porch post. He crosses his ankles and flicks his Zippo—the stormy breeze wafting the cigarette smoke, and he's *unapologetically* staring at Mike. What's the term I'm searching for here? Leering? Sounds creepy. Gawking? Sounds like something a bird would do. Inspecting? Inspecting isn't too far off, I suppose.

They stare… and stare… and stare… curiously…

What's got you so… so… captivated?

Mike smiles.

He looks away (only for a second) and writes on a blank page:

The Boy Across the Street

THREE
Stargazing

How regent the empowerment of a single person—a single name—can reign over one's submissive psyche.

Jesse Harris, Jesse Harris, Jesse Harris…

He's the key factor in Mike's sleepless nights.

It'll be nine days after the murder until they reunite.

This being said, we'll reverse two weeks.

If you were to ask Mike, this is where the story *truly* begins. While we'll hear more about the sinister house, Indigo Street, his father's hidden agendas, and Charlie jail-breaking out of her bedroom window late at night, none of it is remotely as important as this.

Mike graduated a year early, and finding a job became his primary goal, mainly because his family's finances suffered when his father divorced them for a younger, perkier woman. "Younger" is an understatement. Carol graduated three years before Maddy.

Yeah.

Disgusting, we know.

Anywho, enough about that POS.

The story.

This is where the story *begins*: in this tiny coffee shop inside a tinier independent bookstore inside a gigantic mall drowning in the recently broken economy. He originally applied for the bookseller position, though he knew just as much about books as he did about espresso. Maddy's obsessed with reading. Whenever she misbehaved, Leon locked her books in a gun cabinet equipped with a digital passcode in the master bath. She'd go about the house reading the back of cereal boxes and instruction manuals to get a taste of the written word.

When it was time for the interview, three other booksellers already filled the positions, but the café, Blueberry Beans, urgently needed a barista.

In the days leading up to Mike over-steaming his pitcher of skim milk, Jesse and his friends visited the bookshop many times, hanging out in the sci-fi and graphic novel aisles. They recognized each other from living across the street and their midnight staring, and more staring transpired in the store as Jesse came and went. Why they never formally introduced themselves can be filed in the mystery section.

Mike never would've spoken to Jesse if not for the job. *Maybe.* Destiny had other things in mind. They would've met that fateful night when Jesse's mom died. Ugly, yet factual.

That fateful night was nine days ago.

Mike wraps up his last shift for the week.

"Excited to have four days off?" Jazz asks.

He didn't expect his boss to be a year older than him. She's quick, intelligent, and entertaining, which is helpful as they spend eight hours together three days a week.

"I guess."

"Worried 'bout Jesse?"

"I barely know him."

"True, but I bet the situation was traumatic for you. They still haven't found his brother."

The WANTED poster on their corkboard shows twenty-four-year-old Daryl Harris, the same age as Maddy, six-foot-two and a hundred and sixty pounds. He and Jesse have the same dimples and almond-shaped eyes, pale complexion, and blonde hair, but Daryl's *rough,* his face covered in pockmarks and scars, and the tattoo on his neck can't be distinguished in the photo.

"How'd it go at the station?"

"It was... terrifying." Mike laughs. "I was a nervous wreck, but they just asked me the basic questions like time, date, and stuff. I was there for maybe a half hour. I was gonna visit Jesse, but the cop said he wasn't allowed visitors at the hospital. He's also a person of interest because they can't prove who killed their mom without Daryl. Is that... will he go to prison? Have you talked to him?"

"I haven't."

Jazz's VERSION OF ME, a veiny-eyed Goblin chilling on her shoulder in a Wise Ace position, gives me two thumbs up. What the hell? Never in all my years...

"My boyfriend, Eli, is tight with Jesse and he hasn't heard from him either. I'm sure this is a lot to process. Daryl's not a good person. He was abusive as all get-up to Jesse. It wouldn't surprise me if he hit their mom, too. What sort of sick fuck kills their mother, y'know?"

"You believe Jesse didn't shoot her then?" asks Mike.

"*Hell no.* Jesse's a hardcore mama's boy. Everyone knows it. And what? He took Daryl's gun, shot himself, and gave the gun back? Our PD needs to polish their investigation skills."

Mike finishes his daily tasks, restocks the bakery case for the morning, and runs a cleaning cycle for the espresso machine, lovingly nicknamed "Rosie." He clocks out for the week and Jazz pats him on the back.

"Chin up, buddy. Jesse's tough. He'll get through this, believe me."

7:55 PM

Mom and Mike talk about their day over turkey and grits during dinner, and the short, childlike shadow waves at me in the kitchen corner.

Mike takes his spot on the porch stairs after loading the dishwasher, the overhead light droning worse than a weary housefly, and the fulsomely odorous cannabis and cigarette air has him grumbling. If he concentrates, he might trick himself into smelling suburban lavender and apple blossoms.

Notta chance.

Giving up on his useless reveries, he centers on his sketch, his hand and colored pencils materializing Jesse. For three days, he's drawn his interpretations of who Jesse is, striving to obliterate the image of the boy decked out in gray and crimson.

Nine pages. He's filled *nine total pages* with gray-scale and full-colored drawings of a happy, dimpled-smiling Jesse Harris, as if *anything* could bring him happiness after *that.*

He mulls as I mope—distant, weak, impatiently awaiting my reclaiming invitation.

I'm so bored!

'What're you doing right now, Jesse?'

I tilt my head. Mike seldom cares about what other people do and doesn't want an additional person invading his comfortable isolation, Jesse included. Who's to say he'll even see Jesse again?

We know he will. If not, there'd be no tale to tell, and I'm an absolute schmo for juicy, catastrophic stories. Hell, plotting them is my forte.

Mike blends his work with his tortillon and, satisfied, flips to a blank page (*Arrrgh! I said I'M BORED!*), lights a cigarette, and outlines his next piece. I'm intrigued as black and green DC sneakers cut into his field of vision, interrupting his artistic utopia I'm unauthorized to enter. Mike thwacks his book shut, his gaze traveling up Jesse's ripped skater shorts, white t-shirt, and lopsided grin.

"Hey, didn't mean to startle ya. Remember me?"

'You're kind of unforgettable.'

Don't say that out loud, Mike.

"I do. Hi, Jesse."

His hyperactive VERSION OF ME, Twitch, runs in circles, and his left eye, markedly smaller than his right, has a severe case of the tremors. He's tweaked out, jittery, and, my God, *loud!* He won't stop laughing, and it's not a cute laugh. It's... how can I word this? Like a rabid hyena on crack. And when's the last time he bathed? *Nauseating!* Twitch is irritating to boot, yet we could do wonders as colleagues.

"You look busy. I can leave. Didn't mean to bother ya."

"You're not. Please, sit." Mike says, sliding to clear a space on the stairs.

Jesse peers at the cul-de-sac, nibbling on a silver hoop pierced into his bottom lip, and in one-point-five seconds, Mike fixates on it. Has it always been there? How'd he let that detail go unperceived?

"Ya sure?"

"Of course."

Mike and Jesse pore over one another as if I'm not here; as if Twitch isn't screeching and flailing his arms like an ape flinging dung.

"Suppose I should formally introduce myself: Jesse Harris."

They shake hands, the porch light short-circuiting.

"Michael Sinclair. Nice to meet you."

"The pleasures all mine, Sinclair."

Mike reflects on the old saying, "ignorance is bliss."

He's never encountered blissful ignorance. Due to his unbeknownst ignorance, he's about to, and blissfully so.

Jesse's incidental company binds Mike into hypnosis—not a speck of blood or gray matter in sight; his glacier hair packed down flat.

Their knees bounce as they smoke their cigarettes.

"You didn't have to do that," Mike says about the gifted pack of Camel Golds next to a box of Salem Menthols.

"Yeah, man, I did. Gettin' ya a pack of smokes was the least I could do for helpin' me."

"How did you know my brand?"

"Jazz told me. And I apologize if I came off... *needy* that night. You must think I'm the biggest freak on the planet."

Pretty sure you wear the freak-crown, Michael.

If a stranger had comforted Mike after seeing his mother killed in front of him by her son, he wouldn't have said no.

"I don't think you're a freak."

I think they're both freaks.

Why else am I here?

Twitch is off somewhere, braying his hyena laugh.

"Not what I had in mind when I toldja to come to my house." Jesse chuckles, his shoulder bumping Mike's.

Was that supposed to be funny?

"Uh..."

"Sorry. Dark humor. Not always a good icebreaker. Here, this is yours." He places Mike's folded hoodie on his lap.

That night, Mike recalls washing his crimson tie-dyed shirt and skin. It'd been upsetting to hear the swirling, coral-colored water as if the only part of Jesse he held wasted away in a drainpipe.

"It's clean. Washed it three times."

"You could've kept it." Mike moves the hoodie and sketchbook (*finally!*) away from him.

"Naw, man. It was cool to lend it to me, though. I owe ya. *A lot.*"

"Seriously, you owe me nothing. How're you holding up?"

He spins his cigarette leftward. "Doin' a lot better than Gabe and Rachel."

Gabe and Rachel are the well-known bickering couple on Indigo Street. She lectures him to, "man up and get a real job," and he orders her to, "put your tits back in your shirt!"

Jesse chortles. "I'm sure you've heard them fightin' on the daily. Gabe's chill, but she's a *loon,* yo. She's got three kids. Notta one of them Gabes. She says the youngest is, but I think it's a ruse."

"How do you know so much about them?"

"Been livin' on this street for ten years. And Gabe grows the *best* weed in town; *legit, sticky dank.*" Jesse's nicotine breath fogs Mike's cheek. "Been buyin' off him for a while."

"Isn't your dad a cop?"

"Yeah. So?"

"How do you get away with smoking weed?"

Zip it, Mike!

Jesse, mouth thin, puckers his forehead.

"Shit," says Mike. "I'm sorry. I—"

We stare at Jesse's hand on Mike's knee.

Bizarre.

Twitch climbs a tree.

"Don't apologize. Dad has his own family to worry 'bout. I'm just the screw-up who comes 'round for birthdays and holidays."

"When did your parents split?"

"I was eight. He left for another woman."

Mike snorts.

"Familiar story?" Jesse darts him an amused sideways glance.

"Too familiar."

"Lemme guess, she has bleach-blonde hair, fake tits, an orange tan, belly piercin', and is fifteen years his junior?"

"*Dayum!* Were our fathers separated at birth? Scarily accurate, except Carol's a brunette."

"Carol, huh? That name's trouble."

Their throated laughter dwindles into chuckles, and Mike cranes his neck and stews, the city lights obscuring what should be an inky sky twinkling white.

"Somethin' wrong?"

"Miss the stars. Too much light pollution here."

Jesse jumps to his feet. "Let's go. C'mon, trust me."

Twitch and I tromp after them onto Orange Street. *Whew!* Once Mom discovers we're out, we may end up on an episode of *Serial*! We come upon a sepia condo with black shutters and a single white garage light.

"Who lives here?"

"My aunt, but this piece of junk"—he raps his knuckles on the hood of the white Honda Civic—"is mine."

Twitch sticks his head out the back window, his slobbering tongue flopping from the side of his mouth.

"Mom's gonna murder me."

"She worried 'bout her baby boy hangin' out with a deadbeat from the ROY G BIV?"

Damn straight she is! I'm not. This is getting interesting...

"Curfew."

"Yo!" he says. "How old are ya?"

"Seventeen."

"It's summer. Curfew ain't 'til 2 AM."

"I should text her."

"Sure, man."

BUZZ!

(Mom): You should've told me before you left. We don't know Jesse. Be careful. Don't do anything stupid. Back by two. We'll talk later.

"How'd it go?"

"Told me not to do anything stupid and to be back by two."

"Eh, she's right. You should stay away from me if you know what's good for ya."

"Leon says I wouldn't know what's good for me if 'good' shoved a foot up my ass and called me 'Daisy.'"

"Da hell? Who's Leon?"

"Sperm donor."

"Whadda dick." He scans Mike from knee to hairline. "You're quite the square, aren'tcha? Not from the ROY G BIV. Golden burbs?"

"First Avenue. How can you tell?"

Jesse whistles. "The *real* yuppie side. Sperm donor work for NASA? And nobody just *moves* to the Rainbow. You don't wind up there without reason, y'know. It's the last resort. Also, you're wearin' a polo shirt and khaki pants, the very uniform of suburban life. Didja move to Indigo 'cause of your parents?"

Mike picks at his fingernails. "Something like that. Mom's a biology professor at Ashland University, and Leon works for the Steel Mill."

Memories arise from the minor mention of the factory: Leon's forest-green coat on the rack in the hallway, the oil and metal smell so potent we pinched our nostrils while walking past it. Recollections of Mom in the kitchen preparing Leon's lunch and kissing him before he left for the second shift, or third, or first.

"No shit? My ma worked there for a bit. Had a nasty fall that left her semi-paralyzed for a couple of years."

"Dang, dude. I'm sorry."

"All good. That woman taught *herself* to walk again even after the docs said she never would. That's how much of a badass she is." He swallows. "*Was.*"

"*Is,*" Mike confirms, and Jesse smiles.

"You're an alright dude. For a square, that is."

"Nice."

"Just joshin' ya."

"So, where are we going?"

"Issa surprise."

Super. Surprises are building blocks to his anxiety-made skyscraper. Tonight, he'll let this one slide. In Mike's mind, Jesse's an element of surprise all on his own and the farthest thing from an anxiety block.

Passing cow pastures and a trailer park, Jesse stops outside the beanfields in Greenwich, the stalks brushing our legs as we stroll in the midsummer night. Twitch, screeching, zooms off to… ah, who cares?

We lie on the knoll, enveloped in the beanstalks.

"Wanna swig?" Jesse shakes a glass bottle.

"Where the hell did that come from?"

"You're not as observant as I thought. Whadja think I was grabbin' from the trunk?"

"Not alcohol."

"It's vodka."

"Alcohol."

"Potatoes."

Mike laughs. "Alcohol."

"No? Eh, more for me."

"Gimme that."

Cigarette butts accumulate as they share the vodka, the flashing fireflies making it difficult to decrypt bugs from stars.

"Is this whatcha wanted to see?"

"It's perfect. Thank you."

"My pleasure."

Mike searches the glimmering skies for dippers and zodiacs. "Do you ever feel like we're in an alternate reality? Like you and me right now, but we're in another realm, infinite years away? What if we're on the moon looking at the earth? Or a distant planet?"

"Hot damn, dude. How drunk are ya?"

"I'm not drunk. I'm serious. You don't think about stuff like that?"

"Not 'til tonight. I like science, but, naw, I haven't thought 'bout it. I like the idea of us layin' on the moon. I'm sure we've met in multiple universes and lifetimes. Can I ask ya somethin' now?"

"Depends."

"Why didn'tcha just come across the street? Y'know, all them nights?"

Mike falters. "I… I don't really have an answer for that."

"It's okay. I'm sure it'll come to ya."

Well into the witching hour, Mike discovers their common ground is vast, regardless of growing up on different sides of the metaphorical river. Shitty fathers. Addicted siblings. Sweet mothers.

"Are you good to drive?" Mike asks as they pack up.

"You really are a square, aren'tcha, Sinclair? HA! Sinclair Square! Square Sinclair!"

"Hardy-har."

"I'm good to drive. Not even tipsy. See!" He walks straight, taps his right index finger to his nose, and then his left, right, and left.... "Oh! *And!* This is even better!" He inhales and, in one breath, recites the alphabet. Backward. Without a glitch.

"I couldn't do that with the alphabet in front of me! You're something else."

"I've been told."

Mike defines Jesse as a rockstar with a traveler's soul—ungrounded, untamed, following fate's paved avenue, and his oozing sex appeal would make him a rarity among suburbanites. He can be sweet, polite, and soft-spoken one moment and a loud-mouthed punk the next. If a tabloid reporter were to jump out of the bushes, Jesse'll either pose like an underwear model or bash the photographer's brains in with his own Nikon.

Jesse shows confidence. Mike's a sloucher.

"Sinclair's don't slouch," Leon would scorn. "We stand tall and proud. Shoulders back and head held high. Dignity, Michael, show some *damn* dignity."

Moreover, if you're to pass Jesse on the streets, he isn't someone you'd disregard or duel, and his you're-dead-to-me glare will have you running scared back to the womb if you wrong him.

Conversely, he'll treat Mike earnestly as they unearth the world—*their* world—like two toddlers thirsting for knowledge, and Mike won't have to be the baby brother of "Maddy the Addy" ever again. He can be Michael Sinclair. *Valuable.*

I'll make them both feel invincible.

Jesse and I will be a fever Mike won't want to break, our heat unleashing qualities in himself he never knew existed. Akin to most illnesses, the side effects are harmful, and it won't be up to us to dictate how long he'll stay ill.

He'll welcome it.

He'll die for it.

He'll die for us.

FOUR

Blinded By Your Light

As one can't stop thinking of the other, they go to the beanfields for two days, try counting the stars, and laugh when they can't.

It feels good to laugh.

It'll be short-lived.

I have a way about me.

I have a way of destroying happiness.

Mike perceives himself as an impenetrable conundrum, but his fortress degenerates one pebble at a time on the third night in the beanfields. Jesse wants to be around *him*, talk to *him*, and get to know *him* out of sheer interest. Nothing more, nothing less.

"Still surprised your ma hasn't talked to ya yet."

"Me too. I think she's saving it for when I royally fuck up. Like, *hours* past curfew."

"Why the strictness? It's summer, you're graduated, and you gotta job."

"It's not her. We've been through... some *tough* shit. Not as tough as you."

"It ain't a competition. Life is life. Our own wars may be small to others, but they're huge to us 'cause they're happenin' in our own little worlds." His dense exhale reaches the galactic heavens. "At first, Daryl was dealin'. Just dealin'. Ma couldn't pay rent. We never had food in the house. Daryl wanted to help, and growin' up the way we did, didn't leave a lotta options. We knew Daryl was dealin', just never said anythin'. It'd been only a couple of months 'til he started usin', snortin', and shootin' up his stock. Shit went sour pretty damn fast."

The classic "gotta test the product first" scenario. Daryl Harris was a glutton for punishment, and his distinctive darkness made it ridiculously easy for me to reel him in on his twelfth birthday with a joint-baited hook. I hate to debunk your "marijuana is a gateway drug" fallacy. Who better to disprove it than me? I've seen firsthand who's to blame for the "gateway," and, trust me, he's far more cunning than I, bar-none.

Mental Illness wanders as shadows and is as much of an immortal parasite as yours truly. He's inside you, your mother, brother, sister, friends, child, and lover. It's not your fault you can't see him. You're used to seeing shadows—yours and others—daily. It takes those imprisoned in the darkness waiting for the sun to assimilate his presence.

Jesse speaks of Daryl as a girl speaks of her cheating ex-boyfriend, and Mike's enlarged heart begs him to volunteer empathy. His brain objects—*No! No! You've made a friend! Don't screw it up!*—when he contemplates reciprocating Jesse's willingness to open up. The heart belittles him when the brain pegs victory.

Selfish Sinclair. Wise choice.

Flipping onto their sides, breath passing breath, Mike experiences the lore of butterflies. Scratch that; they're pterodactyls. He figures he should back off and give Jesse space. Friends don't touch. Friends don't lie in beanfields in the middle of the night gazing at the stars and each other.

Jesse settles in closer, their knees touching and pupils visible in the moonlight. Twitch and I become ghosts, which is *unacceptable,* and since Twitch is an *utterly degenerate fool* who won't do his duties, Jesse grimaces when I shout, *YOU CAN'T IGNORE US FOREVER! And where's the vodka? This night is boring!*

I'm at a crossroads: either I cold-shoulder their proposing relationship and writhe in weakness, or I take an axe to Mike's chest, shove his bleeding heart into Jesse's hands, and redeem authority.

Ultimately, the choice is a no-brainer, and I continue whispering my taxing, slick doctrines. In his defense, Jesse has over-compensated, and it's about time Mike does, too.

"I know it's probably impossible to believe, but you *can* trust me." Jesse flattens the blockading bean plants between them. "I won't judge ya. What could be worse than my tweaked-out brother?"

Go ahead, Mike.

"Where do I even begin?"

"Wherever you want."

Mike mentally checks off the circumstances contributing to

the rifts in the Sinclair Family Levee, finding it strange how it requires an army to build such a levee a lone soldier can annihilate.

I know you'd rather be drawn and quartered than talk, but you can't keep it bottled up.

Go where it all began.

Open with whom sent me the key to your dark kingdom.

"When I was seven, Leon taught me two things…."

FIVE

(Ultraviolet)

1: Boys don't cry. EVER.

Seven-year-old Mike and his family are outside watching an orange and hot pink swirling dusk. Charlie, the brat she is, shoves Mike off the porch railing where he sits, and Charlie's random abuse shocks Maddy and Mom, but Leon remains stolid until Mike dives into Marie's bosom, weeping.

"Leon! We need to get him to the hospital!"

"He's fine, Marie. He's just being a sissy."

"I'm serious. He's bleeding."

"Boys bleed. It isn't my fault he can't handle it. He should man up."

"He's seven!"

"Get inside, Michael. I'll patch you up."

Leon carries him into the bathroom, shuts the door, and looms over Mike like a giant to a flea, shouting, hitting the wall, demanding Michael to…

Stop crying.

Stop crying!

"DAMN IT, MICHAEL, STOP CRYING!"

Marie rushes him to the ER, his head wound requiring six stitches, and the nurse gives him a lollipop for being such a *brave* young man.

Michael never cried after that day.

Michael wouldn't talk after that day.

Michael became a problem after that day.

2: To be the absolute best is expected of yourself and anyone you bring into your life; people who'll enrich the Sinclair family name, not tarnish it.

I've been with the Sinclairs for six years, and we can thank Leon for that. If it hadn't been for him opening the door, there's a fifty-fifty chance I may or may not have been adopted.

Leon tries morphing his only son into a younger version of himself several times. Because they don't look alike (which we're sure displeases Leon enormously), Mike acquiring Marie's onyx irises, olive skin, and curly ebony hair, Leon finds an alternative means of cloning him. AKA: athletics.

Leon was the team captain of his high school football team, his abilities legendary even today, his jersey, photos, and trophies posted in the Cougar High corridors near the gym. He met Marie via mutual acquaintances during his senior year at an away game. When she showed him her positive pregnancy test two months after graduation, essential family obligations scrapped his dreams of attending OSU to play professionally.

Leon and Mike play baseball in the backyard and the batting cages from ages five to seven, and accept that Mike isn't cut out for the minor leagues or any other sport. Leon tosses that strategy (baseball puns, anyone?) in favor of another.

Their two-acre property includes peaks and valleys that are canyons and craters in Mike's youthful imagination. For an entire summer, seated on Leon's knee on the lawn mower, he switches the speed from turtle to rabbit, and they soar over the hills. Mom and I stand at the kitchen window, the poor lady suffering the mini-panic attacks induced by a concerned mother.

Leon teaches his son the machine's fundamentals: how to gas it up, wait for the *click* of the cap, start the engine and pull the lever to activate the blades.

Big whoop, right? Leon isn't the first or last father to mow the lawn on a summer's day, and sure, it sounds logical to a normal ear, but as we've learned, the Sinclairs aren't your typical family. Marie moved her kids to the ROY G BIV in the middle of the night on a *Thursday*. If that doesn't cut it close to the *not-odd-at-all* edge, then I should end the story here.

Mike enjoyed bonding with his father back then. Now he'd rather bond with a starving rattlesnake. After he mows the lawn for the first time, he skips proudly alongside Leon to the Richland General Store to pick out his ice cream cone reward.

He awakes with the sunrise, shovels his breakfast, and begins his days on the John Deere for the rest of his years under Leon's thumb. He wasn't bothered by it for the first few years. On the mower, he could listen to music and not Charlie's insults and tattletales:

"Mikey won't stop looking at me!"

"Michael won't give me the remote!"

"Dad says you're adopted!" (We don't doubt it.)

Mr. Sherman, the pleasant elderly man two houses over, is as perfect as perfect gets in the suburbs. In the springtime, Mike smells the scents of his thriving gardens: strawberries, tomatoes, peppers, roses, lilies, and daisies. He'd bring the Sinclair siblings candies and sodas for their birthdays, and Marie put his renowned blueberries and strawberries into baked pies and preserves.

Mike's distaste for the geezer has little to do with his good intentions or his grass-mulch trousers and suspenders. Mike idolizes Mr. Sherman, even drawing the hunchbacked man as he prunes his gardens like Quasimodo tending the bell tower.

What's the reason? His *yard.*

It sounds childish, but bear in mind Mike *is* a child, and as we all know, children take everything to heart.

I spent years trying to con Mr. Sherman to no anvil, and it tickles me pink when Mike comes to detest him. It'll do me no favors if he keeps flooding Mike's mind with positive reinforcements.

I'm sure you've seen the White House lawn (*I know I have!*) and those super-posh government buildings (*I've seen those, too!*) and fancy hotels (*also those!*). Ever notice how their lawns have *perfect, straight* lines? To spare us some time, I'll say, compared to Mr. Sherman's lawn, those other lawns are as sloppy as unsupervised preschoolers going ham with fingerpaint.

These become Leon's expectations of his adolescent son.

And you betcha he'll learn to do it perfectly, if not as perfectly as Mr. Sherman.

Jesse listens attentively to how Leon scammed their father-son bond into child labor.

"I remember this one time we had a dry season. No rain, and everything was dead. He made me get up at 8 AM every morning to mow. Kept me out there for hours, saying it wasn't good enough when there wasn't anything to cut. He wouldn't give me water or sunscreen. I ended up dehydrated, throwing up for the rest of the day, and I had these *gigantic* sun blisters on my arms and shoulders. I wasn't allowed to swim until all the sticks were picked up out of the yard and into the burn pile, and Charlie would come behind me and toss the sticks from the pile back into the yard. If I tattled, I was sent to my room without dinner, or he'd wake me up at 3 AM to dust the family library. My mom's a big reader, so we had *thousands* of books, and he'd have me rearrange them into alphabetical order and subject, then he'd take them down and make me do it again."

"*Geez.* But why?"

"Dunno. Maybe he was trying to make use of me? Make me into a '*man*'? Or maybe he just hated that I wasn't like him. And it's stupid when it's said out loud. Oh, no, I had to do *chores.* Poor, pitiful me." He chuckles. "That wasn't the issue. The issue was I knew he did it because he hated me. I tried so hard to please him; to make him proud, but nothing ever worked. So, I just gave up or acted up.

"When I was twelve, Mom and Leon were grocery shopping,

and I was mowing. It'd been raining for days, and the grass was a good six inches tall. I'd *had* it with his bullshit, and I did something that I *knew* would get me into trouble but didn't give a shit."

Jesse inclines, wild-eyed. "Whadja do?"

Mike and I teeter. "I made a crop circle."

We partake in Jesse's side-splitting reaction.

"Shit, man, that's brilliant! What'd Leon do?"

"He woke me up from a dead sleep to re-mow the lawn."

It's a half-truth. He doesn't want Jesse to think of him as the freak he's been identified as, and he's an honest person, yet he leaves out that after Leon asked why he'd done it, Mike answered sarcastically, "I guess the aliens abducted me."

Leon's icy glare lanced into him. "Why would aliens waste their time on you? You little shit. They want intelligent, useful boys. *You?* You're *worthless.* You're not worth the human race, much less the extraterrestrials."

Mike never forgot how Maddy's giggles stopped or how Charlie (*Charlie!*) gasped. He threw himself onto his bed and cried into his pillow, wishing Mom would comfort him, and we realized Marie chose Leon over Mike for the first time.

Maddy soothed him later that evening.

"He shouldn't have said that to you. You're not worthless, Mikey. How many boys your age can create mathematically accurate crop circles?"

As for me? I told Mike he was to blame (*must keep digging the pit*). To see the reverberating vein in Leon's forehead while pointing to the yard in an uproar—"It looks like an alien came down and left behind a goddamn cryptic message!"—had me doing Twitch-style cartwheels.

Crack went the Sinclair Family Levee.

Another hole was dug.

My muscles were strengthening.

"Leon sounds like a real asshole," says Jesse.

"You have no idea."

Jesse has no idea? Are you sure? A tarnished family, addicted siblings—is that not kismet binding you two?

What an uncongenial upbringing they had—sidestepping in their homes, afraid to breathe incorrectly, nervous as to what sort of mood Leon or Daryl were in. What if Jesse had been there when Daryl was withdrawing, just as Mike had been there with Maddy?

"You're not to help your sister. She didn't need our help becoming an addict. She doesn't need our help getting clean," Leon unjustly stuck Mike between house rules and his sick sister.

Did Jesse, like Mike, break the rules to help his brother as he had for his sister? Mike couldn't snub her agony; act as if it wasn't happening in their *perfect* household. Jesse probably knows better than most the entailments of being a Sinclair, and Mike's inability to be candid with him is his problem, not Jesse's.

What's the deal, Mike? Afraid of rejection? Afraid of losing him? You forget about the levee when he's near. Don't let the bleak strokes of your past wager your friendship.

He believed Charlie when she said he'd become overweight

and pimply if he kept eating and drinking the hot dogs and milkshakes Maddy brought home for him from her job at the ice cream parlor.

He's aware of his shortcomings: his button nose and too-large eyes, the scar above his left eyebrow, his pimple-free skin dried and cracked in the winter seasons, and he's self-conscious about his curly hair and two crooked front teeth.

Right here, amongst the beanfields and fireflies and Jesse's amber gaze, a place his own will persistently end up, he's never felt more attractive.

"I could stay here forever. Everythin' is just so... *beautiful,*" Jesse speaks at Mike, *not* the celestials. "I know we barely know each other, but... I dunno. It feels like I've always known you. Maybe you're onto somethin' with the alternative universe idea. Kindred spirits."

Mike's burning epidermis could set the fields ablaze. Having always been squeamish towards physical contact, he's baffled as he deliberates holding Jesse's hand and how it'd be as natural as breathing.

Baffling, indeed.

I'm too weak to care.

SIX

Light My Way

"S'that Charlie?" Jesse asks about the girl on the porch swing at the Indigo residence. Madame pirouettes the stretch of the patio, her jade gown spinning.

"Yep."

"She looks like she has Triple-A."

"Car insurance?"

"Nah, spaz. Triple-A: Arrogant Ass Attitude."

Mike and I laugh.

"Right on. I should get in there."

"Will I see ya tomorrow?"

"I hope so."

Jesse reciprocates Mike's smile. "Me too, Sinclair. G'night."

"G'night, Jess."

Jesse pulls out of the driveway as Mike ascends the steps.

"You're in for it," Charlie sings.

"Screw off. I'm home before two."

"That's not why."

Fantastic, that can only mean one thing...

Mom's at the kitchen table in her pink robe and matching slippers she's had since Mike's tenth birthday. She crosses her legs, her right foot kicking to and fro.

"Sit," she says.

We do.

Charlie dawdles in the hallway, and I'm fixing to slug the smugness clean off her pretty face. Madame flicks her paper fan at me and resumes to do the cancan.

Countdown to interrogation: three... two...

"Where were you?"

Nailed it.

"A beanfield in Greenwich."

"Doing what?"

"Sucking dick," Charlie mumbles.

Madame giggles.

Mike and I shank them with coffin-nailing scowls.

Mom kneads her temples. "Charlie! To your room!"

She and Madame eavesdrop from Charlie's doorway.

"We stargaze," Mike answers. "You know I love the stars. The light pollution out here is garbage."

He shouldn't have to explain himself since it's general knowledge he and Maddy spent sultry summer vacations floating in the pool, the humidity and chlorine cardboard thick as she educated him on astronomy, the zodiacs, and planets. The suburban region matured in his mid-teens with shops, a racetrack, and a military airport, and the constellations, unlike their conversations, washed-out. No matter. Their sibling connection was a more prosperous currency than the stars themselves.

He zones in on the womanly hands before him and the indentation where her wedding ring used to be. Soft, ladylike hands exuding childhood serenity. Jesse's slim, callused fingers felt like slippery plastic and electrified Mike's electrons into a stimulating boil. Both sets of hands provide security, and he can't favor one over the other.

"Michael?"

He lifts his head. "Yeah?"

"Sweets, it's great you're making friends, but, well, you've been gone an awful lot lately, and I appreciate you for coming home on time, but I'm a little uneasy with you spending time with someone you don't know."

"Isn't that how friendships work? Hanging out? Talking?"

In his thoughts, he's sashaying about the house in a manic phase, crying out, "I made a friend, I made a friend!"—his inky black eyes becoming rusty brown. The pubescent response is tolerable as he's spent too much time behaving years beyond his age. He spills to Mom his and Jesse's commonalities, like movies, insensitive fathers, and addicted siblings, and, ending his spiel, Mike's breathing hard and Marie's hardly breathing, her posture and mouth fraught.

"You've told Jesse about Maddy?"

Mike tears at his fingernails. "Erm… not quite."

"Meaning *what,* Michael?"

"I haven't… I haven't told him anything about her. He doesn't even know her name. I'm not ready for him to know yet. It seems irrelevant right now."

Her troubled brow ages her face. "You *plan* on telling him?"

"When the time is right. He's been honest with me. I trust him, and you know how I am; I trust nobody."

"Mike," she says, her maternal tone having the light in his eyes darkening, "do you remember when you got that pocketknife for your birthday?"

Do we remember?! The Swiss Army Knife was a big deal, as Mike wasn't entrusted to butter his toast, and you can find its lime green wrapping paper in his desk's lock drawer.

"What did we say about the knife?"

Ooo, splendid! I know where this is heading!

Mike groans. "Never to run with the blade out or point it at people."

"That's right. You didn't run around with sharp edges when you were eleven, and I expect the same now."

"I didn't run around with *anyone,* and Jesse's *not* a pocketknife."

"His brother's a meth addict and a murderer. You're under my roof, and you will abide by my rules. I can't have you associated with people like Jesse."

Here it comes. Mike's flushing. His fists clamp.

Mom flinches as his chair *CLUNKS* to the floor.

What a treat! He's never berated her.

"People like Jesse?! You wanna talk about people like Jesse? How dare you judge him in the same *disgusting* way everyone judged us! How many friends have you lost because of our family's reputation?"

"We've never killed anyone," she retorts, unruffled.

"You mean to tell me Maddy didn't watch her best friend die from an overdose because she was too *strung out* to call the ambulance?"

"Michael!"

Now she's ruffled.

"We're not murderers, but you're in denial if you think we haven't been close or worse! Do you know why I don't have friends?"

Oh! I do! I DO!

"Because I'm a Sinclair. Jesse doesn't care! He's a good guy and for you to judge him because of Daryl's crimes is unreasonable and *so* not like you, Mom!"

The room, omitting Madame *twirling, twirling* in the hall, goes torpid. Expressionless, Charlie stops in the hallway, and Mike huffs and puffs like a wolf against a brick house he can't blow down.

"You're right."

Huh?

"What?"

"You're right. I was quick to judge him. I didn't like being ridiculed for Maddy's addiction, and I shouldn't do the same to him. I'm sorry. I was wrong. He obviously means a lot to you, and I'd like to get to know him better. Invite him over for dinner tomorrow night."

Seriously?

"For real?"

"Really."

Mike puts the fallen chair back into its upright position, embraces Mom, and apologizes for yelling. She wonders how he got to be tall and where the years went, suggesting he needs a haircut.

"It took months for it to reach my shoulders!"

"Just a trim, sweets."

"*Fiiiine.* I love you, Mom."

"I love you, too."

I need to rest.

A mother's love for her child is the guillotine to my beheading.

(Jesse): I don't mean to be annoying.

(Jesse): I hate being alone.

(Jesse): Can I stay with you tonight?

Mike re-reads Jesse's texts while in his tiff with Mom, the words etched into memory, safely deposited into a heart-shaped lockbox.

He types.

He re-types.

I slump at the desk. *Teenagers.*

The *PING*ing text serves as the prelude to their genesis:

(Jesse): I feel safe with you.

I shake my head at the ceiling. *Cheesy.*

Mike finalizes his message and pushes SEND without

reservation.

(Mike): Family is asleep. Right side of my house. Second window on the left. I'll be waiting.

Do you hear that? His

thump,

thump,

thumping heartbeat?

Do you feel that? My marrow *cracking* like the Sinclair Family Levee.

SEVEN

We'll Shine, Crazy Diamond

An orange cylinder burns between them as they kneel at the raised window. Mike has a knack for distinguishing the spunky cannabis aroma from cigarette smoke after uncovering the bongs in Maddy's room and the joints in her Camel Gold packs. I regain my wind and stand behind Mike to inspect the burgeoning spectacle.

Twitch lollygags in the grass.

You're useless, Twitch!

"Thanks for lettin' me stay tonight," says Jesse.

"Mi casa es su casa. Besides, insomnia blows."

"Mm." He nods and… and… offers Mike the *'tangerine glowing thingamabob!'* Yes! Gates open! Christ has risen! Mike... Mike…

"I'm good. Don't wanna smoke up all your shit."

Son of a witch's tit, *TAKE THE JOINT!*

Jesse's playful smirk has me smitten. "Mi ganja es su ganja."

Come on, Mikey! You're about the last person in the tri-state area to smoke weed! It'll help you sleep! It'll silence the voices in your head! All those menacing, taunting voices reminding you you're a good-for-nothing son, an abomination, a loser, a freak.

Do it.

Do it!

DO IT!

Inhaling a mega-hit, Jesse shrugs and flings the roach over the fence.

BLAST! We were so close! We could practically taste it!

Oh, well, there's always tomorrow.

Mike shuts the window as Jesse climbs inside, and they stand an arm's length apart. Twitch prowls the room, sniffing soiled laundry in the hamper, gathering and putting down incongruous items, snapping the lamp on and off, and trampolining on the unmade bed.

Jesse also examines the room: the HD TV tucked in the right corner atop a three-drawer dresser and the full-sized bed. Mike's art desk is beside the window, close to a tall fan. They're able to navigate amid the clutter—canvases, books, trinkets, and art tools stacking the perimeter, TV stand, and desk. Two candles on the dresser offer light and disperse mint and cinnamon.

"Nice room, or what I can see of it." He points to the posters tacked to the robin blue walls. "You really dig nineties alternative rock, don'tcha?"

"And nu-metal."

"Is nu-metal still a thing?"

"Probably not." Mike sniggers. "My sister made me lots of mixed CDs growing up, and she was into that sort of music. You're into nineties clothing, aren'tcha?" he asks, surveying

Jesse's skater shorts and muscle tee.

"Touché. I don't get how people can skate or run in skinny jeans. Function before fashion."

"I'm not complaining."

"Neither am I."

Jesse's ardent gaze warms Mike's ears.

"Your eyes are like golden suns."

Jesse opens his stoned eyelids wide.

"The... ahem... candlelight," Mike mumbles, stumbling foot to foot in tiny circles and grabbing the remote. "Movie. Wanna watch a movie?"

"Can it be a horror movie?"

"Psh, dude, horror or go home."

They sit side by side on the mattress and load *Netflix*, their what-to-watch roster outnumbering the what-not-to-watch.

"*Donnie Darko?*"

"My favorite."

"Ah! Same!" His shoulder bumps Mike's. "'Why are ya wearin' that stupid bunny suit?'"

Mike grins. "'Why are you wearing that stupid man suit?'"

Chuckling at their Frank the Bunny and Donnie Darko parody, Mike clicks SELECT.

Halfway into the opening credits, they lie down, Mike's feet dangling over the foot of the bed while Jesse's prop up on the headboard. From the desk, what's left of my sanity is rattled by Twitch's hyena cackling as he removes clothing from their hooks inside the closet. This kid needs to be taken down by *several* hundred notches.

Jesse lays his head on his angled arm, his palm facing upward, and Mike reads the lifeline, heartline, and destiny line on Jesse's palm just as Maddy taught him, and laughs to himself.

"What's up, Chuckles?"

"Nothing. My oldest sister is Pagan… whatever the hell that means. Tarot cards, pendulums, gods and goddesses, that sort of thing."

"Why's that funny?" Jesse asks, the television screen tinging his face cyan.

They look at each other, their noses touching, and Mike's stomach conducts clumsy handsprings as miniature tsunamis, like lightning striking an ocean, rebound inside his stomach.

"Her being Pagan isn't funny, but when I was thirteen, she made this pentagram on her bedroom floor with salt, and Mom walked in on her meditating in the middle of this salt circle and *flipped*. I don't know if she was pissed because she seasoned the carpet or because she was doing witchcraft in the house."

We're all laughing (by now, you should know Twitch is howling).

"What happened after that?"

"Mom and Leon forced her to volunteer at St. Pete's, the Catholic church on Park Ave."

"I bet she hated that."

"You'd think. She and her friends took these yearly camping trips to Hocking Hills, and she missed out on it that year, dishing out food to the homeless."

"She *wasn't* mad?"

"No. She was too busy smoking weed behind the church and banging an altar boy in the confessionals."

"Man, she must be a *real* badass."

"She is."

She's not *nearly* as badass as she used to be.

"She live here?"

"Florida."

"Why'd she move?"

Mike's chest contracts.

She moved to get away from *me*.

He's not ready to admit it to Jesse. Not sure if he ever will be.

"She wanted to get away from here."

"Don't we all?"

"I do, that's for damn sure," Mike *truthfully* confesses. Ohio holds onto bad memories like he holds onto Jesse's friendship. Ohio can't let go, and neither can he.

They talk daybreak out of slumber, blowing smoke out the window and exchanging cigarettes and stories. I lounge on the floor, and Mike doesn't acknowledge me, just as Jesse doesn't acknowledge Twitch ripping pages from Mike's sketchbook and creasing them into paper airplanes.

Do your job!

He pokes his tongue out at me, and a paper jet boomerangs off my forehead. He claps his hands like a wound-up monkey toy with crash cymbals when I crumble it and chuck it at him.

You're hopeless, Twitch!

"I get why you can't sleep. Wanna talk about it?"

A valiant question, Mike. What sort of person would you be if you hadn't asked?

Jesse swings his feet back and forth on the headboard.

"I see it all the time," he begins, the faint periwinkle shades of dawn splashing along the ceiling. "The gun in Daryl's hand, the blood, the pieces of... *brain* explodin' everywhere. Dang, I can still smell it and feel it. I was screamin' when it happened, and it got in my mouth and... and...."

"I'm sorry, Jesse. I wish I knew what to say. I can't even imagine."

"You and me both. Daryl was... he just lost it. He and Ma were fightin' over money. They were *always* fightin' over money. Daryl's stolen Gram's fine china, Ma's jewelry, and we'd gone through, like, ten TVs. He stole my Xbox both times I replaced it."

Daryl and I had *loads* of fun.

"Why?"

"Needed the money. He was usin' more than he was sellin' and ended up owin' his suppliers. Shit was a nightmare whether he was dealin' or usin'. I can't tell ya how many times our house got shot at. We got threatin' phone calls durin' all hours of the day. One night when he was hardcore tweakin', he tore our walls apart with a sledgehammer 'cause he said the government or police or whoever wired the house.

"The night all the shit went down, Ma wouldn't give Daryl the car keys 'cause she was afraid he'd pawn the car for money. He got angry, started yellin' at her, kept sayin' Grams was in the kitchen cookin' dinner, but she's been dead for seven years. He started goin' on 'bout how Ma and I were workin' with the undercover cops to bring him and his dealers down.

"He went after Ma first, had her choked against the wall, her toes off the ground, and all I could think was: '*fuck*, he's gonna kill her!' I jumped on him, and we fell to the floor. The rest is a daze. I know we both got some good punches in. Before I knew it, he was above me, kickin' me hard in the stomach, and I was throwin' up blood. Then it just went so... *still.* Ma had a gun to Daryl's head. I didn't even know she owned a gun. When I told Dad all this, he pointed out Ma had been married to a cop for nine years. Guess we always had guns in the house.

"She told Daryl to get out, or she'd shoot. I don't know if Daryl believed her. I don't know if *I* believed her. Daryl acted like he was gonna leave, but he punched her in the face, stole the gun, and the first bullet hit the ceilin'. Then..." Jesse breathes out, going blank, then blinks at Mike like he's the first living thing he sees after falling from outer space. "Sorry, Sinclair."

"For what?"

"For puttin' all my sob stories on you."

"I'd say this is far from a 'sob story,' wouldn't you? You can talk to me about whatever you want, whenever you want."

Jesse expresses his gratitude, his half-smile fleeting.

"Wanna know the worst part? It took *days* to convince Dad I wasn't the one who killed Ma. I loved her, Mikey. She was my world. I almost died tryin' to protect her. What the fuck, ya know? Why would I shoot myself? *Bullshit.* One of Daryl's little druggie bastards confessed he helped Daryl plan the whole thing out."

"What do you mean?"

"He premeditated Ma's death. The gun wasn't hers. It belonged to one of Daryl's dealin' partners, and they're helpin' him to hide, too. Not even the dude who ratted knows where he is. And I still don't have answers. Still don't know why he had to kill her. Only thing that makes sense is the life insurance. She had both of us down as the beneficiaries. I dunno, Mikey. The world's on fire." He stops for a second and asks, "This isn't weird, is it? Me stayin' over?"

Will he come off weird if he says it isn't weird? And admitting Jesse's his first real friend will make him even weirder. Mike concludes he's a weirdo either way and is left to decide which of the two excuses seems less pitiable.

"Honesty is the best policy," Mom would say.

"It's a little weird, but not because of you," he promptly clarifies. "I've never been close to someone before. I didn't have friends, been invited to parties, or spent the night at houses. You're the first person to spend the night with me. I'm a loser."

"I'm honored to be your first. You're not a loser. I'll be your friend."

"Thanks, Jess."

"My pleasure. Y'want me to sleep on the floor?"

"Floors suck."

"Ya ain't wrong. Wanna go somewhere with me tomorrow?"

"Where?"

"Just say yes."

Mike smiles. "Yes."

EIGHT
Flicker

The bunch of "thugs" wearing muscle shirts and bandannas we saw on the move to Indigo appear again the following day on Blue Street. Jesse tosses an arm over Mike's shoulders, juts his chin at them, and they turn onto Violet Street.

"You know them?" Mike asks.

"Sorta. They're nothin' to be afraid of, not when I'm 'round."

The deserted skatepark—a silver and teal concrete jungle—is set under rain clouds floating across platinum skies. We'd previously gone to Jesse's aunt's house to pick up his skateboard, and now he throws it on the ground, declares, "This is what I do for fun," and kicks off, the wheels grating on the asphalt.

From the park's grassy section, we watch Jesse and Twitch perform stunts we aren't familiar with. On a ramp designed like a tidal wave, they kick, flip, jump, and roll up and down (a maneuver Mike refers to as "Concrete Surfing"). *Remarkable.* Twitch can perform such tricks professionally but can't carry out his *actual* tricks? Go figure.

Jesse stops and hands Mike his phone. "Mind doin' some

video footage for me?"

"Under one condition."

"Which is?"

"You gotta do some Parkour."

Jesse laughs. "Oh, so you *do* know 'bout that. A'ight, anythin' for you, Square."

He films Jesse, his smile carefree. How long has it been since he's felt this way? In many respects, Jesse's making up for the portions of Mike's childhood joy taken from him by the poaching hands of addiction, hateful words, and nights spent in anguish, bracing himself for yet another drab day. Even if the darkness still surrounds him with each stride, Jesse's sunshine shows him its gracious hospitality.

Reanimated by a brand-new, similarly unorthodox friendship, Mike finds timeless tranquility in another place outside of this world where purple galaxies and endless wormholes predominate.

His shirt sticking to his flat stomach, Jesse takes a breather next to Mike and lights a Salem.

"That was *sick!*"

Jesse replies with a winded smile and reviews the playback. "Didn't know I could still do half this shit."

"I didn't know it was humanly possible to run up a skate ramp and back flip onto the next one and then run across the top of a wooden fence. How the hell did you learn to do it?"

"My brother taught me to skate. We came here all the time. Then one day, I jumped off my board and ran and never stopped.

A lot of it was self-taught, but I did gymnastics for twelve years and took Tae Kwon Do and Kung Fu classes."

"Holy hell! Do you still take them?"

"Naw. I started Parkour and Streetrunnin' once I learned proper balance and built enough muscle. I don't do those much anymore, either. I missed a landin' last year that nearly cost me my brains. Check it." He parts his hair, exposing the scar tissue stretching from the back of his skull to his left ear. "I was in the hospital for three weeks. Gnarly surgery. I get dizzy easily, so it ain't safe to do Parkour for long periods."

"Do you miss it?"

"Sometimes. I miss the runner's high. Sounds crazy, I know. Skateboardin' is less on the body. My goal was to get into the X-Games, then the accident happened, and, well, here I am, skatin' in a dinky ass park in a dinky ass town."

"I'm sorry."

"It ain't so awful." He directs his phone screen at them. "If I'd left, I never woulda met you. Now smile, Sinclair."

Click!

"Funny face!"

Click!

"You okay if I post these? I'll tag ya."

Mike puffs on his cigarette. "I don't do social media."

"*Nothin'?!* No statuses? Tweets? Snaps?"

"Nope. But it's cool if you post. I don't mind."

"Good. I wanna show ya off."

Mike picks at the skin around his fingernails.

"Am I makin' ya all hot and bothered, Sinclair?"

"Get bent, Jess," Mike mutters, grinning.

"Here's my caption: *At the skatepark with my favorite Square.*"

Mike shoves him. "You're an asshole."

He shoves back. "And you're a polo-wearin' square!"

"That's it!"

Their limbs entangle as Mike flicks his cigarette and tackles Jesse. I scurry away, miffed, while Twitch skates on the ramps as Jesse and Mike playfully wrestle in the grass.

They land on their backs, Mike's head on Jesse's shoulder, as they gasp for air and shake mirthfully.

"Gotta say, Sinclair, you may be a square, but you're *my* square."

"Gotta say, Harris, you may be an asshole, but you're *my* asshole."

Jesse hikes an eyebrow. "Kinda kinky."

Mike titters, his thumb rubbing the pulse in Jesse's wrist.

"We have sixty-two likes, and Suzie Anderson says you're 'adorable AF.'"

"Lemme see that." Mike laughs at the profile picture of a plain, blonde girl with an overbite. "Tell her she's sweet."

Jesse types: *Square Sinclair says you're sweet, but, sorry, he's already taken.*

Mike utters, "I hate you."

Jesse's brief snort develops into a profuse cackle.

"Suzie says, 'that sucks because I'd totally tap that.' HA! Suz knows what's up!"

Mike hides his face in Jesse's neck. "Alright, that's enough social media for one day."

Jesse prods Mike's stomach. "You're a sexy square."

"Shut up, man!"

"Aw, I'm sorry. I'll stop."

"Thank God."

"Some call me 'God,' but I'm a humble mofo, so 'Jesse' will do just fine."

Mercy me, they're flirting *again*—slow blinks and tender smiles. *Shoot me.*

"I'm glad you're here, Mike."

"I'm glad you're here, too."

"I smell rain. Should probably head back before it hits."

As foreseen, thunder rumbles, lightning wallops, and it downpours on our walk home. I plot under my umbrella, and Twitch ditches his skateboard to leap in the puddles with Mike and Jesse, kicking water at one another.

Drenched, they hurry into the bathroom and Mike uses a navy towel to dry Jesse's face and neck, their stares and skin glinting.

"My mom wants you to come over for dinner tonight."

"What's she makin'?"

"Pot roast. She always makes pot roast when we have guests."

"Count me in! But I have to meet up with my dad soon. Gotta tie up some loose ends for Ma's funeral."

Both the towel and Mike's mood descend.

"Cheer up. Look at me," Jesse softly says as he cradles Mike's chin, his thumb grazing his mouth. "I'll be fine. What time tonight?"

"Six."

"Alright, Square. I'll see ya then."

After an afternoon nap, he showers and nervously prepares for dinner, crossing his fingers, hoping Jesse's charms will win Mom over.

Mom spoons alps of mashed potatoes, sauteed carrots, and pot roast onto Jesse's plate, his lips rolling past his teeth as she drowns it in brown gravy.

"We'll need to rent a crane to get him out of the house at this rate."

"Nonsense, Michael. I can't have him leaving on an empty stomach."

Twitch raids the cabinets and assembles a drum set with his findings, the pots and pans teeth-grinding. I've been doing this job for millennia, yet people's ignorance toward those like Twitch and me still boggles my mind.

Mom learns Paul Harris has been on the police force for over twelve years, and he and his wife, Anne, have one biological son, Ben, who turned eight last week, and Paul legally adopted Anne's daughter, Jane, three years ago.

"How old is Jane?"

"She's eleven."

"Are you close to your siblings?"

"Not really. Dad separates me from them. He sent me to live with my aunt Iris on Orange Street after Ma passed. They're helpin' me with a down payment for an apartment on Red."

Mom strokes Jesse's arm. Leon also kept his new life and family separate.

The front door swings open, revealing Charlie and Madame, their already skin-tight garments clinging to every feminine curve, and a hot pink bra is clearly seen as Charlie readjusts her white blouse.

"Hello, darling," Mom greets her. "Hungry?"

Charlie sets her eyes on Jesse, her sourpuss attitude transfiguring into a sportive gander. Madame speaks softly in her ear.

"Famished."

Pegging Jesse down like two felines in heat to a tomcat, she and Madame take their seats across from him.

Mike stabs at his meal, infuriated at how his sister's acting like, well, his sister. Jesse either pretends to be engrossed in his dinner, or he's *that* much of a caveman scarfing down one heaping helping after the next.

Mom asks Charlie about her day, and she presumably delves into how she and the *girls* did some old cheerleading routines *just for fun.*

"I was head cheerleader," she tells Jesse.

He glimpses up—"Good for you"—his mouth full of pot roast, ignorant to Charlie and Madame's crucifying glares.

Mike's hand covers his amusement, his foot responding to

Jesse's slight kick before their legs form into a crisscross under the table. Mike has never seen a guy turn down Charlie in the same way she rejected any nerd who dared to approach her in high school.

"It's nice you're staying active," says Mom. "Some girls let themselves go."

"I refuse to become one of *those* girls."

"Better back off *those* mashed potatoes then," Mike suggests.

Jesse coughs on his soda.

"*Excuse me?* Think you're all hot shit because your boyfriend's here?"

"Not tonight, you two." Mom intervenes. "We have a guest."

Charlie points her cutlery at Jesse. "Who invited you here, anyway? Didn't your scabby-faced, meth-head brother kill your mom?"

Madame flicks her wrist, a paper fan opening and flapping.

"Shut it," Mike cautions.

"What? Suddenly it's okay to have murderers in the house? Who're we inviting over for dessert? Crystal Meth?"

"Lost her number years ago," Jesse quips and imitates her patronizing grimace.

"You'll see who Mike really is sooner or later. He's more of a girl than I am. He doesn't have a single friend. Didja know that? Nobody wants to be friends with a freak. Especially a suic—"

"ENOUGH!" Mom grips the table's edges. "Apologize to each other and to Jesse at once!"

"I ain't apologizing for shit!" Charlie spits at Mike. "You ain't nothing but a dick-sucking prick. You wanna know why Dad left us?"

Madame bats her eyelashes and giggles behind her fan. Mike's jaw clenches as tightly as Jesse's grip on his knee.

A hole is being dug as we speak.

"Stop it, Charlotte!" Mom shouts.

"Dad left because of *you!* He couldn't stand looking at your ugly face every day because it reminded him of the mistake he made the day you were born!"

"CHARLOTTE!"

Charlie cuts loose the rubber band keeping Mike and his wits poised, his breaths long and audible.

It's okay, Mike. It's better to unleash the beast than to keep him cooped up.

Ready.

Set.

ATTACK.

He slingshots out of his chair, pushes Charlie, still seated, and Madame steps back, the paper fan at her mouth, and flinches, Charlie's head striking the wall. Twitch pounds on his makeshift drums. My hands crossing on my lap, I recline in my chair, satisfied as Mike's world whitens.

His fist preparing for take-off, Mike's hastily pinned to the ground by Jesse's knees on his shoulders.

"Chill! Calm down, Mike!"

"Let. Me. Go!"

"C'mon, buddy," he says, Mike's face in his hands. "Come back to earth. Follow my breaths." They press heartbeat to heartbeat. "Follow my breaths. In and out, Mikey." Their lungs sync. "… in… out… in… out… in…"

Mike disembarks out of his irate domain and into Jesse's amber irises, universes deep and pledging future sea breeze and serene, mint-green oceans.

"Back in your head?"

Mike, thin-lipped, nods.

"A'ight. Get up and shake it off."

His blood turns to coal as Mom, Charlie, and Madame flock into the corner.

"I'm sorry. I… I don't… I don't know what came over me. I'm sorry, I'm sorry…."

"Get out of my face," Charlie scolds. "You're not my brother. Not by choice."

Mike grabs Jesse and storms out of the house. Mom doesn't ask about their whereabouts, nor will he tell her. Twitch and I cram into the Honda.

"Can we go to the fields?"

Jesse cranks up the engine. "Gotta better place in mind."

NINE

All that Shimmers

We've been driving on Highway 13 for thirty minutes, twenty of them outside of Richland. Chain-smoking, Mike browses the approaching road signs and Jesse's mouth singing along to his heavy metal playlist. Twitch, salivating, smooshes his face against the glass. I curse the Gods.

"What you saw back there? That's not me. That's not who I am."

Jesse mutes the stereo. "No need to explain. You were pissed. It happens. And while I'm totally against hittin' girls, I see why ya lost your shit. Looks like I was right 'bout the Triple-A."

"You hurt her ego," he says, facetiously. "I think you're the first person to turn her down."

"Eh, I can do better."

"Cocky much?"

"Whadda 'bout my cock?"

"Piss off," Mike jests to masquerade his disappointment towards their lack of physical contact, and, at that precise time, Jesse's hand lands on his knee.

Can he read your mind now? Godspeed. It's shambles in there!

The tires slosh through mud, and Jesse parks on the side of a dirt road, Mike's end teetering.

"Get out on my side. That ditch is lethal."

No shit, we think.

Keeping Mike's hand firmly in his, Jesse leads the way into the woods, Twitch skipping in front of them, the sprinkling rain leaving the cool night curious. Mike imagines the trees as a patchwork of green and gold in the daylight as we cross into a ravine, a brook bubbling in the distance, though all that's left now is the blackening tree tops swaying in the drizzling winds.

"Stay close. Easy to get lost here."

Again: *No shit, Jess.*

"You're not gonna like... go all Jason on me, are ya?"

"Say what?" Jesse feigns outrage. "C'mon, I'd go Hannibal—store your beautiful brain in the freezer and mix it into a hearty stew."

Mike makes a playful sideways stride, and Jesse ropes him to his hip.

"I couldn't do that," he says, his nose on Mike's cheek. "Can't let that brain go to waste."

"Hannibal didn't waste the brains. He kept a piece of his victims inside of him forever."

"Only you could make somethin' sick sound poetic."

"It's a needless gift."

"It's an artistic one. I love to hear what your beautiful mind is thinkin'."

Mike bites at his lips and hugs Jesse's waist. Twitch's animated yowl blares from afar as we trudge up and down more hills and evade dead timber on the pathway.

"Fallen tree ahead… mud hole to your right… comin' into water…" Jesse's signals put Mike's fear of being in danger to rest.

Our hike comes to a halt, our pants cleaving to our ankles and arms scraped by thorny shrubs. Mike marvels at the creamy moonlit mansion ahead atop a behemoth mound.

Another hill. *Fan-bloody-tastic.*

"I really need to quit smoking."

"This way." Jesse directs him onward up the property's winding, stone stair footpath.

Mom would take Mike to the Columbus district where the millionaires lived, and he'd feast his eyes on the white-columned colonial mansions, especially this one magnificent property with an Olympic-sized pool.

"They have a water slide!" He sprang in his seat. "You have to climb a ladder to get to the top! Did you see it, Mom? Did you?"

She smiled broadly. "Yes, sweets, I saw."

Those houses were clean, fancy stone or marble and richly festooned with ivy and pastel flowers. While the estimated thirteen-room manor before him beholds its own captivating lure, it still comes off as less than extraordinary and somewhat intimidating. The wings' loose shingles clangor against red brick, and Mower Mikey is eager to cut the neglected high grass into skilled, clean lines… or crop circles.

"Y'could make some bitchin' crop circles out here."

Mother Mary, he can *read your mind!*

"Welcome to the Black Estates. We couldn't find much info on it 'cept that Roger Black built it for his wife, Rose, in the 1990s."

For ten years, in these very estates, I devotedly served their poisoned-obsessed preteen daughter who murdered them and her two younger brothers with arsenic.

Mike's sure the estate was, in its prime, a spectacular landmark in the heart of Ohio, even if the depressed, sobbing windows and lattices signify otherwise. The rickety bone structure rasps from our weight on the moss-covered stairs, every groan and moan retelling its autobiography of surviving years, if not decades, worth of inhospitable winters and hailstorms. Mud, rain, and snow have worn away the paint, and the oak patio squeaks from Twitch's gambol near the wide, double doors, his eye convulsing as Jesse picks the lock with his pocketknife.

"Quit fidgetin', Square. The cops don't come out this way."

"That's reassuring."

Twitch zips inside like a Tasmanian devil.

Jesse closes the doors and stands next to Mike, watching him shine his phone's flashlight on the main entryway linked to the living room.

The interior reimburses its outward façade, and while it may be dirt-infested, dusty and moldy, whoever lived here previous to its abandonment left behind antique settees, typography carpets, and mirrors and paintings framed in either gold or black baroque designs Mike and I learned about in Mrs. Tiller's Art History class junior year.

“Who just leaves this shit behind?” Mike asks, his fingers skimming the Tudor antiquities and black walnut fixtures on his way to a painting hung above the sandstone fireplace.

Jesse accompanies him. “Not sure. We’ve researched this property, but couldn’t really find any answers. The family just seemed to vanish.”

“Weird.”

“And we agreed not to remove anythin' from here. Respect the dead or whatever.

The lady in the painting has dreamy, faraway eyes, her plump pout hinting at the yearning for an unattainable lover. On his toes, Mike reaches out to touch her pale skin, wheat-colored hair piled like a crown, and the sable background. His fingertips trailing the blue ribbons on her breasts and head continue to the feature that’s made her famous: the white silk gown embellished in gold lace.

Mike admires the artwork, whereas Jesse’s enamored with Mike’s wavy hair, upturned nose, asymmetrical lips, the bottom being a smidge fuller than the top, and those luscious, curly eyelashes any stumpy-lashed girl would be envious of.

“Madam Grand.”

“Hm?”

“Madame Catherine Grand, Mistress of the Minister of France, Charles-Maurice de Talleyrand- Périgord. He married her for her Nordic beauty.”

“Vain, much?” jokes Jesse. “How do you know all of this?”

“I love art, and Élisabeth Vigée Le Brun is one of my favorites.

You know she did over a thousand paintings in her lifetime? Talk about impressive. Female painters were almost unheard of in the 1700s. Marie Antoinette invited her to Versailles and loved her work because she portrayed Marie as a doting mother. She did her portraits for four years."

"Six. Six years."

"If you already knew, then why'd you ask? You testing me?"

"No," Jesse responds, his scintillating eyes staring into Mike's. "It sounded better comin' from you."

Mike's amiable smile mirrors Jesse's tone, the floor now as enticing as Madame Grand, his raging-volcano temperature spreading up his cheeks and ears.

"You're so shy," says Jesse.

"Am not."

"Yeah, ya are. You've mud on your face."

Mike swipes at his right cheek.

"Other side."

He tries again.

"Lemme just..." Jesse raises his hand, and Mike withdraws. "I'm not gonna hurtcha."

Swirling vanilla moonbeams stream past the moth-eaten curtains, and patterns of hand-sewn lace overshadow Jesse's face as he caresses Mike like a sultan to his beloved gems.

Dry earth drizzles at their feet and his thumb dips into Mike's cheekbone, their pupils dilating, and it'd be an amorous moment if Twitch wasn't skylarking about the place.

"Got it."

“Thanks.”

“My pleasure, Sinclair,” he says, his right hand moving to Mike’s waist while his left lifts his flashlight upward. “Upstairs is off limits.” He nods to a burgundy-carpeted spiral staircase and the hole in the landing which could lead to China.

“I see. How’d you find this place?”

They settle on the living room floor and Jesse filters through his backpack as he recites how he and his friend, Eli Miller, were ghost hunting one night some years ago—

“Ghost hunting?”

The white flashlights border Jesse’s chin and darken his under eyes. Telling ghost stories in an abandoned house in the middle of the boondocks—is this not a slasher movie preface?

“Ohio’s haunted as hell!” He grins at Mike’s horrified reaction and his words run smoother than chocolate pudding, affirming, “I’ll protect ya from any monsters, Mikey. Rumor is Mary Jane’s grave is 'round here. We never found the grave, but the estates was a good trade, if ya ask me. Here, hold this, will ya.”

My heart somersaults as he thrusts a glass, phallic-shaped object at Mike.

“You just walk around with these things in your bag? Ballsy.”

“Ballsy or stupid?”

Jesse unravels a plastic bag, the vegetal odor virtually whacking Mike sidewards.

Jesse takes the bowl and packs it full.

Twitch wheezes in Jesse’s ear and I pray my Hail Marys.

Mike opens his pack of Camels. Two lighters flick and two

flames designated to two individual tasks dance their ballets. Two leaves from different plants spark and sizzle. Two guys who couldn't be any more different from each other deal with similar issues in two diametrical ways.

Jesse's sunken cheeks bulge out like a blowfish, and the smoke he's holding in explodes from his mouth. He and Twitch laugh maniacally, their coughing fit blanketing Mike in skunky fumes.

Jesse swats the smoke away. "M'bad."

"All good."

Jesse passes him the bowl.

Good boy, Jesse.

"No, thanks."

C'mon, Mikey, you've made a friend, and this, this, *is how you keep one. Sure, he likes you, but if you do this, he'll* love *you.*

Mike can practically see the lightbulb *BING* above Jesse's head.

"Dude! You've never actually smoked before, have ya?"

Funny how Jesse can fluster him with both compliments and obvious observations. Mike picks at his fingernails. He read somewhere a person's survival rate is eight to ten days without water, and he *might* survive dehydration for that long if he hid in the closet to Jesse's right, but he won't last another five minutes in this humiliation.

He's mocking you! He doesn't like you anymore. Fix it!

Mike snaps, "And how old were you when you first smoked weed?"

Dearest Michael, I've been with Jesse for a loooooong time.

Jesse composes himself and scoots into him, their crossed legs now knee-to-knee.

"Ten. That ain't important. I'm sorry. I wasn't makin' fun of you, I swear. Everythin''s funny when I'm high, not that it's an excuse. I didn't mean to upset ya."

You're just a loser, is all.

"I'm not upset. I've just... I dunno..."

"Never wanted to try it?"

"It's not that. Like, yeah, I've wanted to try it. I never felt comfortable enough with someone to try it with."

Liar! You trusted Maddy. I know what you're thinking: it would've been a cruel, selfish request to ask the one person who's been fighting her entire life to get rid of me. Jesse isn't Maddy. Look at him, Mike. He's everything you strive to be—beautiful, carefree, charismatic.

"You can trust me, Mike," Jesse lures us back to reality.

Reality. You ward it off as much as possible: drawing, painting, blasting music to ear-damaging volume. And now you have Jesse. He makes it all disappear, doesn't he? The darkness? He's your sunshine. Don't let him fizzle out.

Jesse's piercing clinks against the green and black swirled bowl. He drinks in a sizable hit, sets the piece down, pinches Mike's jaw, and—*Oh, yes!*—blows it out into Mike's mouth.

We wait...

Wait...

Wait...

It won't come. Not *that* way.

"What?" Mike asks.

"Anythin'?"

"No."

"A shotty ain't gonna do much for ya. Wanna real hit?"

Hell, yeah, we do!

"Does it burn?"

"A tad. Nothin' you can't handle."

You can do this. It isn't all that different from a cigarette. Focus on his brilliant, amber eyes that's had you wonder-struck since the second you met while he presses the glass to your lips. Follow his instructions: plug the tiny side-hole, wait for the crackling fire, release the plug and take it in—

"Slowly," says Jesse.

Leafy vapor chars our lungs and we gag, our Adam's apples plastered in place. Mike coughs into his elbow to prevent the approaching tantrum from bombarding Jesse.

"Hey, Mikey, I think he likes it."

"How original."

They swap the bowl back and forth, emptying it.

"You're gonna be *soooooo* high."

Before Jesse completes his sentence, we feel *it*: a cotton ball stuffed dryness in our mouths and tongues bonded to their roofs; our heads like bobble-figurines on the dashboard of a moving car, our eyelids ten pounds heavier, and we're all as much of deranged, rabid hyenas as Twitch,

laughing...

and laughing...

and laughing!

"Stop swerving! It's making me queasy!"

Jesse crows. "I ain't movin'! You're just stoned!

"I'm not stoned! You're stoned and don't realize you're moving!"

"I'm stoned, alright, but you, my Square, are *blitzed!*"

"You know those conveyor belts at the airports? The ones you walk on? Yeah, that's how I feel right now."

Jesse's entire body shakes, his snorts peppy.

"I need to lie down," groans Mike.

Trading off a Salem Menthol, they stare at the water-stained ceiling plasterwork, and Mike inhales Jesse's fabric softener-smelling shirt and cedarwood body wash coupled with weed, smoke, and dust.

Invigorating, isn't it, Mike?

"Hear that?" Jesse asks regarding the docile aria—crickets, owls, the wind blowing the loose particles of the estate's exterior, and their lightweight breaths. "Nature's silence."

"I hate silence. I can't sleep unless there's sound, like the TV or music. Been that way since I was a kid. What am I supposed to do with all that damn silence?"

Jesse pivots onto his side, head in hand, and gazes down at Mike.

"Does it scare you?" asks Jesse.

"Kinda. It doesn't scare you?"

"Not really. Why's it scary?"

"Because silence doesn't exist. My mind wanders, or I'll remember things; hear voices. I hate the voices. They're so... *loud.* Noise is the only way to shut them up."

"What do they say?"

"Too much."

"I've shown my skeletons. When will you show yours?"

"My life isn't a game of show and tell."

"Not tryin' to play games with ya." Jesse lays back down, his folded arm pillowing his head. "You're so complex. I swear, one moment, your eyes are black as night and brighter than shiny copper the next. I'm just tryin' to figure you out."

"Not much to know."

"I disagree. I think your mind has black holes waitin' to be discovered. You're skittish. You jump whenever I move."

"I'm sorry."

"And you apologize all the damn time."

"I'm… sorry?"

Jesse laughs through his nose and says directly to him, "I just wanna know you, Mike."

"That's what I don't understand. Why?"

"Why do I wanna know you?"

"Yeah."

"'Cause I like you."

"But why?"

"'Cause, Mike, you saved me."

He sulks. "So, it's an obligation. I helped you, and now you feel you need to—"

"Mike," Jesse says firmly, grabbing his hand, "stop. That ain't it at all. It ain't outta pity or obligation. C'mon, cut yourself some slack. I was talkin' to ya even before the… bullshit happened."

"We weren't *talking*. We were… I don't know *what* the *fuck* we were doing, but it sure as hell wasn't talking."

Jesse laughs, then heartily reassures, "Just know it ain't an obligation. I wouldn't have brought ya here if you were just an 'obligation.'"

"This is what you and your friends do? Get high with the shadows in abandoned buildings?"

"I'm a dead-end kid."

"I don't think you are."

"You'd be the first. Dad says I'm on a one-way path to bein' a strung-out junkie like Daryl. I ain't even allowed to be 'round his kids. They're good kids, y'know, and I've nothin' against them, and I get it. Still hurts, though, knowin' your father thinks you're on the same rank as a murderin' tweak."

"If it's any reassurance, I can say from personal experience dads aren't always right about their kids."

"I'd know if you'd tell me more about yourself."

Mike flips the topic. "Where do you think Daryl is? His picture's all over town. You'd think someone would've seen him by now."

"I'm sure his boys got him out of the country. Christ, I'm almost jealous. I wish I could get outta here. Start over."

"Let's do it then. Let's save up our money for a year and dip."

"Ahhh, Mikey, don't tease me with sugary impossibilities."

"Why do they have to be impossible? Where do you wanna

go?"

"As far away from this shithole as humanly possible. Maybe out west? Cali? But not like LA or Hollywood. I hate clusterfuck cities. Someplace north next to the ocean."

They envision daydreams where sunlight ricochets off pale green waters swelling over gray rocks during their morning outings, their ankles washed by sea foam, and the morning mist kissing their skin.

Mike's hand drifts to Jesse's, because to physically feel him chases the darkness away. Jesse sees him and speaks to him, not *at* him. For once, he feels he belongs in the world, existing not as an airborne, transparent outcast. Jesse's seaside future haven is well merited, and Mike selfishly craves to be the one to give it to him. After all, Jesse saved him, too.

"Northern California it is, Jess."

Their fingers intertwine and a realization strikes Mike: it's *not* weird. It is, in fact, as ordinary as breathing.

"You're a dreamer."

"And what's wrong with that?"

Astray in his riviera dreamscape, Mike hears Jesse's response, which sounds oceans away:

"Nothin', Mike, nothin' at all."

As proof I'm not always the sadistic scoundrel I claim to be, I allow them to formulate a future *together* tonight. Besides, California doesn't sound half-bad, wouldn't you agree?

TEN

We'll Glow in the Dark

During the half-hour trip from the estates to the ROY G BIV, Mike muses over how he fell asleep holding Jesse's hand and, in the waking world, wonders if Jesse felt his insecurities seeping from Mike's pores.

I've noticed recent changes in Mike. Old, unkempt, insignificant Michael Sinclair is shackled on the sidelines, and New Michael Sinclair—courageous, confident—performs as a showman. Jesse has aided in this symbolic rebirth, even if he doesn't claim it.

Jesse's singalongs to the music in the Honda Civic calm Mike's formerly anxious mood. With their treacherous levee on the verge of collapse, "safety" was an undomesticated theme in the Sinclair household, and if he could, he'd concrete the car to salvage the safety Jesse grants him.

Meanwhile, Twitch spends the better half of the drive scampering from one end of the backseat to the other, and I think a break from him is justifiable.

Headlights spotlight Mom's crossed countenance, and Mike gulps.

"Dang, Square, you're gonna be a parallelogram once she's done with ya."

"You sound as scared as I feel, and you're not even her kid."

"Gonna get grounded?"

"Most likely. The downfalls of still being seventeen."

"I'm sorry, Mikey. This is all my fault."

"You didn't attack my sister."

Jesse shakes his head. "I'm just bad luck."

"No, you're not."

Their fingers lace.

"It's not your fault, alright? But I should go before she grounds me to my thirtieth birthday."

"Suppose this is when the carriage turns back into a pumpkin, huh, Cinderella?"

"Afraid so, Prince Charming."

"Unless I… can stay with you… again?"

"My window's unlocked."

Don't make me spend another night with Twitch! His constant commotion could wake a comatose man!

"Is it?" Jesse teases. "Expectin' me at night now, are ya?"

"Just figured you'd want to stay again."

"Yikes. Am I that predictable?"

"Far from. I hate being alone, too."

BUZZ!

Mike reads Mom's text out loud. "'Say goodnight to Jesse!' Um… 'goodnight to Jesse.'"

Jesse chuckles. "I'll be waitin' in your room."

"You might die of old age."

"Ya say that like it's a bad thing," says Jesse and tosses Mike a dimpled smile. "It'll be worth the wait."

Goosebumps arise despite the mugginess as Mike smiles back, whispers, "I dunno where you came from, because you're too exceptional to be from this earth," then shuffles to his ineluctable discipline.

"Pronto," Mom brusquely says, pointing to the stairs, and we immediately pop a squat. "Why're you so muddy?"

"Went for a walk."

"Where?"

"The woods."

"At night?"

Mike's fingers rake through the locks Mom snipped, the fringes brushing his earlobes. "I know you're mad. I'm sorry. It won't happen again."

"Sweets, this has been a lot for you. I know you miss the house and Maddy. I miss her too."

She's halfway right. He missed how their house smelt like the fall foliage candles Mom burned, so her favorite season survived all year. They could condense Indigo's rooms into their First Avenue home three or four times. His feet raged at the textured carpet on their *new* floors, his toes longing for hardwood. He missed the woods, the lawn (that includes mowing it) and the chandelier in the open foyer. He didn't miss the haunting memories malingering in every nook and cranny, waiting for their opportunity to shock the flesh off of his bones.

He thought of school when he thought of the Golden Suburbs, and Cougar High would be Satan's first pick if he had to principal any school on the planet. Mike resented Mom for not homeschooling him. At home, his books wouldn't have been knocked out of his hands, and he wouldn't have gotten into fistfights defending himself and Maddy against erroneous rumors like being born addicted babies or selling crack downtown. How could he sell crack if he's never even seen it?

As for Maddy? Roads and miles will never steal the pieces of herself she left in Ohio, in his heart, and in his memories.

Unless I intervene.

"And Charlie," she continues. "I know she can be a bit...."

"Bitchy?"

"Not the term I would've chosen. She flaunted herself in front of Jesse, who's probably a minor—"

"He's nineteen."

"Oh. What I'm trying to say is, we've been—*you've* been—dealt with more than most. Your father—"

"I mean this in the nicest way possible, but can we cut to the chase and *not* talk about Dad? I'm glad he's out of my life. I want *nothing* to do with him. And I wasn't mad about Charlie hitting on Jesse. I was angry about the things she said to him."

"She'll be staying with your father until the semester starts."

"Good for her. She used her mental brother to get her way with Dad again."

"Michael, don't say that. You're more loved than you'll ever know," she says, snuggling up to him, her robe fluffing his forearm.

"Am I grounded?"

"I'm not going to ground you. You're technically an adult. But I'm calling Dr. Greene first thing in the morning."

"Therapy?!"

Mike's junior year of high school.

I deride therapists for evident reasons. Mike predicted Dr. Greene would be like the doctors portrayed in the movies: half-moon spectacles he'd have to keep pushing up his nose, a gray and white speckled beard set against wrinkles, maybe a casual suit and tie reeking of mothballs and aftershave.

Instead, we spend the year venting to a ginger man in his late thirties, his parchment-smelling office wreathed in motivational and mental awareness posters; posters about *me* nailed next to framed Marvel artworks.

Mike's swaddled in the plush sofa as he lies back to rant about his oh-so-shitty existence. I'm in the corner, scolding this Greene fella.

After two months of non-stop discord ("talk to me, Mike" and "I'd rather rot"), Dr. Greene surprises him with Prisma colored pencils, sharpeners, sketch diaries, and ink pens. He encourages most patients to write their feelings in a daily journal, but Mike's "special."

"Take an hour each day to draw out your thoughts or feelings. You don't have to show anyone the drawings, not even me."

The riveting temptation to slit Dr. Greene's throat with the hockey mask murderer's machete consumes me.

"My dad doesn't allow this stuff in the house. He raided my room last year and burned my sketchbooks and art supplies."

A win for me, surely, but for Mike? How would you feel if ten years' worth of work was reduced to ash within seconds?

"I spoke to your father, and he understands drawing will help you cope; let you process your feelings appropriately."

Leon didn't give two shits and a single piss about Mike's mental health and most likely consented to Dr. Greene's "art therapy" style to silence him, nor did he attend the monthly family sessions, which culminated in more heated words between his parents.

"It's not me who needs 'fixed,' Marie. Michael's broken. Not me, not you, or Charlie. I warned you! I told you Mike and Maddy spending all that time together would screw him up! You've coddled him! He doesn't need to be babied. He needs a solid ass-kicking!"

"You should be ashamed of yourself, Leon Sinclair! They're your *children!* Not stray animals you can just dump at the shelter because they pissed on your rug!"

"Some children they are! One's a junkie, and the other's a manic psycho!"

Leon's head snaps sidewards from Mom's blowing *SMACK!* Maddy pulls Mike further into their hiding spot (the corner of the living room and kitchen), Mom visibly trembling as Leon nurses his cheek.

"I swear, Marie, if you weren't my wife—"

"You'd *what?* Would you debase and neglect me as you've done your children? Wanna destroy my ego and leave me alone to suffer while going through withdrawals? Or would you rather wake me up at five in the morning to rearrange and dust over a thousand books, throw them on the ground, say it's not good enough, and refuse to let me sleep until your senseless standards are met?"

"You act as if I abuse him!"

"YOU DO! You do, Leon! Maybe not physically, but damn it, you wanna blame Maddy for Mike's behavior? Look at yourself! Michael works his *ass* off for your approval, and you throw him to the wolves. I've put up with a lot of your shit for twenty-one years. So, you know what? Wanna hit me? Push me? Y'go right ahead because come tomorrow, you won't have to worry about me being your wife any longer!"

Another *crack* to the Sinclair Family Levee.

Another hole.

Another gust of energy for me.

"Mike, tell me, did you recognize the person in there tonight?" She jabs her thumb at the front door. "Because I sure didn't. Care to explain?"

"I-I just snapped. If Charlie can't have what she wants, neither can I."

Don't discount Mom's ineffective suppression! Charlie instigated the situation yet underwent no consequence. What a crock of hogwash, Mike! You won't say anything. You never do. It did no good against

Leon, so why should Mom be any different? All you really want is motherly comfort, and don't fret; she'll give it to you. She's rubbing your neck just as she had when you were a little boy, and her love was the sword against the hibernating ghouls in your room.

I'll let you in on a secret about ghouls: they're imperishable. Mike's ghouls scuttled from their luxurious under-the-bed habitat and worked the streets as liquefied demons swimming in syringes and bloodstreams. Marie Sinclair: mother, hero, best friend—while she slew the imaginary monsters of a ten-year-old, she can't defend seventeen-year-old Mike against life's *real* goblins.

She can't protect him from me.

"I love you, Mike, and I trust you to depend on your instincts."

"But?"

"But I want you to be careful who you open up to. I think therapy can help with that."

Again, she's halfway right. Mike didn't recognize the person who lashed out at Charlie as *Michael Sinclair.* He identified him as *Leon Sinclair* and would rather be awkward, messy Michael than soulless Leon.

"I understand, Mom. I'll go to therapy."

Good for Mike...

...bad for me.

"Man, It's hot in here."

"S'alright. How'd it go?"

"Have to go back to therapy."

"*Ooof.* Brutal."

"It's alright. Not totally surprised, to be honest."

Jesse scooches in and tousles a leg between Mike's knees, the city lights outside the window gracing them.

"Wanna tell me why you were in therapy before?"

"Er..."

"I ain't gonna stop hangin' out with ya if that's what you're afraid of."

"How do I know that for sure?"

"We've all got demons, Mikey."

Mistrust built your backbone. You've been hoodwinked by so many "friends" like Timmy Crew and his star athlete clique spying on Charlie sunbathing by the pool. What about when Larry Townsend, his cousin Mark and Mark's girlfriend, Holly Jones, pretended to be your friend's senior year? Larry distracted you with video games while Mark and Holly broke into Maddy's room, stole her Suboxone, and read her diary.

A million sperms, and they received the gold medals? Your humanity is Hell bound.

"I'll tell ya a secret if you tell me one."

He peeps an eye at Jesse's proposition.

"I can see you're thinkin' 'bout it."

"Depends on who goes first and how good the secret is."

Music. It's been playing since he walked into the room.

About time you noticed, jackass! Jesse isn't like those other kids. The music is on for you. *He shot down Charlie for* you. *He doesn't even know Maddy's name. That alone should be enough, so why isn't it?*

Mike is dutifully holding his ground as they wait for the other to go first.

"Dang, you're stubborn. A'ight, the skatepark I took ya to? I've taken no one there. It sounds like a dumb secret, but it's a major one for me. I dated this chick off and on since freshman year, and I never took her or any of my other friends."

Girlfriend. How could you be so thick? Why wouldn't he have one?

Jesse naturally talks in a shout, but when they're alone, his mannerisms change to how Mike infers poets recited sonnets centuries ago. Outwards, he lives up to that "bad-boy" status girls gravitate to, and if you were to rip him open, you'd find a dynamic garden grown by sensitivity practically unfounded in the average Joe.

Do you think he speaks romantically to the chick? Probably. You're not that *special.*

"Why haven't you?"

"Taken anyone else? Daryl wasn't always the enemy. He became a father figure of sorts after Dad left. Y'know, took me school shoppin', to the movies, concerts. He drove me to and from school so I wouldn't have to take the bus. He taught me to skateboard when I was ten. That skatepark was our hideaway; a place to escape the chaos. Then he started doin' drugs and became *demonic.* I hated bein' 'round him. The place that was ours became my hideaway from him. Ain't it some shit how tables turn like that?"

Mike racks his brain for the enigmas he stowed away for everyone's sake.

It doesn't have to be a big secret—just an insignificantly significant one to appease him.

"I've shown no one my artwork. It's the same deal as your skatepark: an escape. My therapist encouraged me to draw at least once a day to keep my mind from going to its 'bad neighborhood.' I have about ten sketchbooks filled with work, and nobody's seen them."

I said small secrets! Not Mount Doom-sized!

TWITCH! Quit messing with the TV, or I'll blow your brains out!

He screeches at me like a fruit bat and sprints down the hall.

"Not even your ma?"

"Nope. Dr. Greene said they were my thoughts and feelings alone. Leon didn't allow art supplies in the house because,"—he satirizes Leon's arrogant demeanor—"'art is a useless, sissy hobby that'll get you nowhere in life.' I probably never would've started drawing again if not for Dr. Greene."

Don't remind me...

"You don't have to show me. That's far more personal than some skatepark."

"Not true. Why *did* you take me? You've known your girlfriend and friends for years. We've just met."

"*Ex*-girlfriend. My friends are, uh, simple? Not like dumb. They're not deep like you."

"You think I'm deep?"

"As an ocean. I still can't figure out what it is 'bout you. You're familiar to me, like we've known each other in another life. Shit... sorry if that sounds weird."

"It's not weird. You're familiar to me, too."

“Soulmates?”

“More like twin flames. A soulmate is your ‘perfect’ match and there’s no such thing as perfection. It’s dumb to think we need another person to ‘complete’ us. A twin flame is more like a reflection, so there’s more… more….”

“Equality?”

“Precisely.”

Mike walks his fingertips down Jesse’s arm and curls their fingers.

Careful. Love can be cataclysmic.

“Thanks for turning on the music.”

You may be afraid of the monsters, but Jesse isn’t.

“You should never have to suffer alone, Mikey.”

However, brazen knights have fears, too.

“Where do you suffer?”

“Darkness.”

“I’m there with you.”

“I know ya are, Mikey. G’night.”

“G’night, Jess.”

Before you flip the page, ask yourself:

where do *you* suffer?

ELEVEN
Iridescent

Gold-rose sunshine filters along their displayed bodies, the covers having been kicked off the bed overnight. Sweat and fresh leftover rain pervade the stuffy room, and Mike listens to Jesse's trickling snores as he supports himself on an elbow and skims two fingertips gently along the raised scar tissue on his left rib. Jesse stirs, and Mike jerks away, his heart plunging.

Good going, Mr. McTouchy, that wasn't creepy at all (insert eyeroll here).

Jesse lets out a lengthy yawn and molds his back to Mike's front. "It doesn't hurt much anymore. I got lucky. The bullet grazed me. Doc said I woulda died if it had gone through. Guess I'm kinda invincible."

"What'd it feel like?"

"Eh, it's hard to describe. It was more of a shock, and I was so outta my head 'cause of everythin' that happened before he shot me."

"Shit. Right. I'm sorry."

"Thank you. But I'll be alright. As I said, I'm invincible." He cranes his neck, his smile lazy, and says to Mike, "You should design a tattoo to cover the scar after it's healed."

"Me?"

"Yeah, *you.*"

His artwork permanently adorning Jesse would tote its own set of gains. Whenever he'd see it, he'd think of Mike, and whenever he'd see it, he'd think of Jesse.

Barf!

"What would you like?"

"Surprise me."

"It'd have to be colorful."

"Why colorful?"

"Because you're full of colors."

Jesse twists and pushes up into Mike's hand on his waist.

"Colors..."

"Mm-hm." Mike sighs dreamily. "*So many colors.*"

"I like colors."

"You should share them with me."

He's brought downward by Jesse's arm wrapping his neck, their eyelids shutting, the tip of his nose feeling out the shape of Jesse's.

"Mikey—"

"Don't talk."

"Okay."

Mom's knock on the door interrupts their semi-intimate wake-up call.

"You awake?"

They jolt to opposite sides of the bed, dormant and panicked.

"I'm awake!"

Jesse staying the night would be fine, but Mike's not in the mood to answer the questions if she were to find him. Why is he here? When did he get here? Why is he parked on Yellow Street and sneaking in when they have a perfectly functional front door and driveway? Why are they cuddling in Mike's bed? They'd be sensible questions. Perhaps Jesse sneaking into their home gave Mike his first taste of teenage rebellion.

"I'm going to the store. Need anything?"

"I'm good, thanks."

"Your appointment with Dr. Greene is at three."

Jesse mouths: *that was fast.*

"Uh… alright. I'll be ready."

"Call or text if you need me."

The front door shuts and they laugh madly. Twitch yelps his characteristic squeal while sprinting circles in the backyard. It'd be nice if that little shit would do the world a favor and *sleep!*

"Mind if I shower?" asks Jesse.

"No, dude, I don't want your sweaty ass defiling my clean shower."

"Don't be such a square."

"Don't be such an asshole."

"And your 'sweaty-ass-defilin'-my-clean-shower' remark makes you what? A square saint?"

Mike impishly elbows him. "You can even use my loofah."

"Clutch my pearls! Y'sure my sweaty ass won't ruin your

poofy, clean loofah?"

"Go take your damn shower, Jesse Harris."

"Ooo, look at you! So demandin'." Jesse heckles out of the room. "I'm shakin' in my smelly skin, Square!"

Twenty minutes later, Mike smells his woodsy body wash, the fragrance more sublime on Jesse than when it's on himself. He unlocks the drawer to his secondhand pine desk and hands Jesse three large sketchbooks.

Jesse sits on the foot of the bed and lays his hands flat on the matte-black hardcover journals.

"Seems like an unfair trade. It ain't just your life in these. It's your soul."

"Yeah, you're right, but you've told me so much about yourself. I'm not much of a talker. Never have been." He scratches the back of his head. "I'm gonna shower. I'll be back."

"Mike, y'sure you're cool with this?"

"I'm sure."

Twitch leaps through the windowpane and peeks over Jesse's shoulder at the sketches. I flick his ear. *Shoo! Scram!*

He gives me the finger.

Fine! You'll find out for yourself how injurious those sketches can be!

Mike's heartbeat's deafening as he envisions Jesse leafing through the pinnacles drawn in graphite and ink—secret thoughts, rampant desires, dreams in both day and night structures, Maddy's past, Jesse's face.

His fingerprints pruning is a crude reminder the shower isn't some timeless sinkhole that can swallow him whole, bones and all, and there's nowhere to run or hide. He dries off, changes into his clothes, and, back in his room, Jesse doesn't glance up even as the desk chair protests beneath Mike's mass.

"I'm in here."

"You are."

Is Jesse angry? He can't tell from his flat tone.

"I'm sorry, Jess."

"Sorry? Why're ya sorry? This is… flatterin'. But, uh"—he shows Mike the realistic piece he created the week they met—"I'm shit at guitar."

"I didn't know who you were. I had to guess."

"I look like a musician?"

"Rockstar, to be exact. Guess I'll just have to draw you skateboarding."

And for the late morning and mid-afternoon, relaxing underneath gray clouds and seafaring buttercream skies, Mike fleshes out speed-sketch after speed-sketch of Jesse rolling on the pavement, aerial, and "Concrete Surfing." Twitch backflips and lands on his board.

Show off.

During his timeout in the grass next to Mike, Jesse chucks his chin at his journal. "Y'mind?"

He half-nods, half-shrugs, and takes in the teal and metal park as Jesse takes in his sketches.

"Christ, dude, you have a legit gift."

"They're just doodles."

"Bullshit."

"You're the talented one. No way could I ever skate like you."

He wonders what they must look like to passers-by. What could this khaki-clad square and pierced skater possibly have in common? Opposites attract; they are scientific evidence.

"Sure, ya can!"

Jesse expertly demonstrates proper footing and balance, and Mike growls when Jesse exclaims, "You're goofy?! I mean no offense, just means you're a lefty. That's cool. You're one-of-a-kind. I mean, for a square."

"Screw you, Jess."

"In public? Wouldn't have taken ya for a kink, ya know, since you're a—"

"A square! Message received! Can we move on?"

All jokes aside (for now), he kicks off with Jesse's hands on his waist.

"Good, good. Just breathe. Stay calm"

Calm?! Calm our square ass! Jesse's not the one wobbling on the board, the vibrations from the wheels shooting up his feet and into his chest. As soon as he's told his balance is on point, they trip and fall into an unintentional jumble of tangled limbs and garish laughter, Mike atop Jesse, his hands in his damp, blonde hair.

"We should go back. Can't be late for my appointment."

"Time passes too fast when I'm with ya."

"Far too fast. Thanks for a good morning. It'll give me something to think about later."

"Sounds naughty, Sinclair. Ha! I love makin' ya blush! Yeah,

yeah, I'm an asshole. I know what you mean. I feel the same way. I had a good mornin', too."

They linger in the driveway, Twitch jumping on the car's roof and Mom supervising from the living room window.

"I swear, sometimes she acts like I'm still five."

"She's just lookin' out for ya. I pissed off her daughter and kept her *wittle Mikey* out late."

Mike whops at Jesse's pinch on his cheek.

"You better get goin'."

Their pinkies stroke on the center console.

"I don't wanna go back to therapy."

"Ya got this." Jesse hooks their fingers. "Dad texted me and said my apartment's ready."

"He's seriously leaving you by yourself after… after…."

"It is what it is. I'm better off bein' alone in an apartment than unwelcomed in his house. Anyway, I… I… er…."

BUZZ!

(Mom): Five minutes.

"Gotta go. What were you saying?"

"It ain't important, Mikey. I'll talk to ya later."

"I'll text you when I'm done."

"Sounds good."

Mike dreads the next two hours, knowing anywhere with Jesse is sunnier than his pandemic mind, and as much as I can't tolerate Dr. Greene, I, for one, can hardly wait to revisit Mike's "bad neighborhood."

TWELVE

Prismatic

Mike re-acquaints himself with the main lounge: beige, reflective tiled floors, tan-cotton and metal chairs, and if he were blindfolded, he'd be able to recite which posters about mental health, suicide prevention, and addiction hang on which wall.

Mrs. Harlem files papers at her desk to our right, humming a melody as lovely as her (according to Mike. Would I ever say such a thing?) She ran to him earlier in salutation, her saggy belly and breasts jiggling, and her hug chiropractic.

Her VERSION OF ME, a little girl sitting on the floor, chows down on a box of Milk Duds. Mike picks at his fingernails as Mom fills out the paperwork, the news channel on the TV in the upper left corner of the room as monotonous as she and Mrs. Harlem's work and weather gab.

(Mike): Save me.

BUZZ!

(Jesse): Be there in ten lol!

(Mike): Liar.

(Jesse): For real, I'll come get you.

(Mike): Mom would have my head in a vise. How's it going

on your end?

(Jesse): Dad's giving me a long-ass lecture about not having parties at the apartment.

(Jesse): Miss me yet?

(Mike): Very much. Miss me?

(Jesse): I bet you're exhausted.

(Mike): From skateboarding?

(Jesse): No. From running through my head all damn day ;-)

Mike snorts.

(Mike): LMAO! You gonna ask me if it hurt when I fell from heaven?

(Jesse): Haha! We both know you ascended out of Hell.

His blasting hysterics disrupts Mom and Mrs. Harlem's gossip.

"Sorry," he says, flashing them his phone. "Cat memes."

(Mike): Damn, I DO miss you. Thanks for cheering me up. TTYL.

(Jesse): My pleasure, Square. And just tell the doc what he wants to hear. You'll get out of there faster.

Mike triple-reads the text because *God forbid* Jesse advises him to *lie* to Dr. Greene.

Maddy always said, "Mikey, you couldn't tell a lie even if you were tortured with castration. Your voice gets stupid deep when you lie." Since then, he's paid close attention to his range whenever white lies, which are tiny, evaporating nothings, were needed.

As for *tremendous* lies, he supports the "spider web theory," where one falsehood interconnects with another until the truth is undetermined, and he can't lie to Dr. Greene just as he can't lie to Mom, Jesse, or Maddy.

With a toothy grin, Dr. Greene signals for Mike to come into his office.

Mike makes himself at home on the black pleather couch and puts his phone on silent (the doc doesn't tolerate disturbances). He's engulfed in the gushing familiarity of the room and Dr. Greene's gold and red diamond-patterned socks as he leans back in his chair and places his ankle on his knee.

Quick reminder: I'm in the corner grouchier than Oscar.

"I wish I could say it's nice to see you again because *it is* nice to see you bu—"

"There must be a not-so-good reason for it. I attacked Charlie. Mom freaked. Hence, here I am."

"Attacked in what way?"

Dr. Greene jots down Mike's description of his friendship with Jesse, the overall story outlandish and absurd when spoken aloud because what are the odds that he would save Jesse from a shooting?

Is Jesse aware, like Mike and Dr. Greene, that the likelihood of things self-destructing increases as they come to fruition? Their variances in look and temperament aren't the groundwork needing to be sorted. Timing's everything, and it swept into their lives like a Kansas tornado.

Mike concludes his narrative by describing how the friendly family dinner warped into sibling rivalry.

"I'm pleased to say it's been nearly a year since your last anger-outburst, but this isn't unusual behavior for you, Mike. Why do you think Charlie's remarks angered you?"

"I was embarrassed!"

"*Why* were you embarrassed?"

Mike knots and unknots his shoelaces. Dr. Greene, writing away, doesn't have a VERSION OF ME, shadows, or so much as a rake or a shovel! He just exists, and I never could find an explanation for it.

"You pushed me to make friends. I didn't want friends, so I figured I'd make them in college because I'll be around people with similar interests and have a clean slate."

"Jesse's an exception?"

The right corner of his mouth flinches. "Yes."

"Elaborate."

"He's... real. He doesn't sugarcoat things. We're a lot alike."

LIES!

"How so? Write me a list."

Our siblings were addicts
Our dad's left us for other women and families
We like the same music
We like to stargaze
Our favorite movie is *Donnie Darko*

"Quite a hefty list. Let's work from the bottom up. Why is *Donnie Darko* important? Friends and long-term partners have different movie preferences. Stargazing and sharing musical tastes aren't uncommon."

Mike cocks his head. "I... I don't know... maybe it has more to do with our pasts? It's like... tragedy brought us together."

"Tragedy? Interesting. If we're to push aside your backgrounds, your families, and how you met, what's left? How is he advancing your life?"

Dr. Greene's tricky tactics aren't new to him, yet he may as well throw a toaster into Mike's bathwater when he identifies their friendship as "unhealthy."

Good thing you didn't bring up that near-kiss from this morning, eh? Imagine the scrutiny!

Mom said Jesse was a sharp edge. If Mike's life is comparable to Jesse's, and they're bound by tragedy, doesn't that mean Mike's a sharp edge? One blade can't revoke the other if they're equivalent.

"You're doing what everyone else does. Do you know how it feels to be *that* person, Dr. Greene, who's whispered about and told to stay away from? *I've been that person.* I can make these decisions for myself."

Dr. Greene raises his hands in defense. "You're right. The choice is yours to make. I apologize if I was judging Jesse. I was trying to learn more about him."

Mike slouches. "Now you know."

"Our time is up for today." He smiles candidly and says, "I'd love to hear more about Jesse, so we'll continue this conversation in the next session. How're your medications? Are they helping you sleep?"

"Yes," Mike answers *honestly*.

"Are they still making you sick?"

"No."

"I'll keep your dosage where it is, but I'd like to get some blood work done to ensure your hormones are leveled. I'll set up an appointment at the clinic."

Mike quails. "Do I have to? I'd rather have my eyes gouged out."

"I know you hate needles, but it must be done. As for your outburst, Charlie should've known better than to push you, given your past circumstances. It *is* a moment, however, and an alarming one. Tell me how you feel about Charlie's provoking going unpunished."

"She could get away with genocide."

"Have you expressed these feelings to your mother?"

"I... I guess I can try."

He won't. He's doing what Jesse said to do: *lying*.

"Are you keeping up with your daily sketches?"

His pulse dances, recalling how his artwork had Jesse outshining the fireflies in their sacred beanfields.

"Everyday."

"Very nice. Be sure to ground yourself when you're feeling distressed. You remember how to do that?"

"Five things I can see. Four things I can touch. Three things I can hear. Two things I can smell. One thing I can taste."

Dr. Greene mutters, "Good, good," scribbling in his pad. "Blood work this week. Another meeting in two weeks. Have a good day, Mike."

"You, too."

Mom shuts her *Redbook* magazine and smiles back at him. On

the trip home, he messages Jesse to let him know he's *free at last* and to text him if he wants to hang out later. Mom never asks Mike about his sessions unless he discusses them of his own free will, and he isn't feeling willing. If she finds out about Dr. Greene's "unhealthy" opinion, she'll separate Mike and Jesse, and that's an outcome none of us want.

From the terrace, Mike watches Indigo's kids play tag and hoops. He taps his phone, the screen showing no new notifications.

(Mike): You'll love this. Gabe and Rachel are arguing over what to cook for dinner. She wants hamburgers. He wants chicken. Never thought food could cause such a fight.

Mike likens Indigo Street to a song by Maddy's favorite band, The Offspring, about how one street became the downfall of many bright, young lives. Ironic. Will the culprit behind Mike's downfall be

Indigo,

Jesse,

or will it be me?

THIRTEEN
Supernova

Now that we're Twitch-free, you'd think we'd get some decent rest, but Mike flips and flops, his bed too alienated without Jesse. He gives up, capitulates into his sketchpad, and I gradually slumber.

Having fallen asleep at his desk, Mike wakes with the birds, showers, and dresses for his shift at Blueberry Beans.

Sizzling bacon beckons us into the kitchen decorated in the same apple and tan motif we had in First Avenue's kitchen. Isn't it peculiar how something so familiar can feel so estranged?

Mom chirps, "good morning," and hands Mike his first of many cups of coffee for the day while a female broadcasts the daily news from the living room television.

"Police are still on the lookout for Daryl Harris. On July 15th, around midnight, Harris, age twenty-four, fled from his 245 Indigo Street residence after shooting Margaret Harris, aged forty-four, twice in the stomach and once in the he—"

Mom sets down the remote, the silence as ear-splitting as the news itself.

"Funeral's today."

"Are you going to miss it?" asks Mom.

"I'll make it to the burial after my shift."

"How're you getting there?"

"Jazz said she'd take me."

Mom nods and kisses his crown.

"Just keep in touch with me. We have to go. Can't be late for work."

His shift drags in slow-mo. He should be with Jesse, not steaming nonfat lattes for haughty housewives and corporate prigs. Jazz, who catches onto his moodiness despite his phony customer-service demeanor, is grateful he can stay attentive.

"Just another hour," she says.

Between customers, he texts Jesse, not expecting him to reply whatsoever.

(Mike): Thinking of you. Be there as soon as I can.

Five minutes later…

BUZZ!

(Jesse): Need you here. Everyone is so fake. Promising they'll be there for me if I need anything. Hugging me. Kissing me. Crying. These are the same assholes who gave her shit for Daryl. Hypocrites.

(Mike): Ignore them. They don't matter. I'll see you soon. Promise.

He waits and waits.

Silence.

Has he mentioned how much he detests it?

Normally, I'm stuck to Mike like Gorilla Glue, but I'm going to detach and switch it up a bit. I can't pass up a good funeral.

Earlier in the same morning, Jesse Harris couldn't remember the act of waking up, his throbbing head and boozy taste in his mouth the only telltale of the night before as he swished and brushed. He showered, slugged into his black suit and tie, black and white Converse shoes, and drove himself to the one place he never imagined seeing his mother for the last time: Wappner's Funeral Home.

The parking lot was packed, the facility hot and sticky inside and outside. I've been to my fair share of funerals and eased through the throng, but Jesse nudged and pushed throughout the mourning maze, embraced his Aunt Iris (Margaret's sister), chatted with the minister, and escaped outdoors to join his buddies in the dewy back lot.

To spare some time, I'll roll-call these guys and their VERSIONS OF ME:

TOBY ALEXANDER: short, stocky, and too smart for his own good.

HIS VERSION OF ME: CONRAD, a handsome young man (so attractive he'll have your ovaries spontaneously combusting or make your dick harder than Abstract Algebra). He's dressed to impress—Armani suits and Italian shoes, his blonde hair combed away from his Ken-doll face. He doesn't speak often and stands rightly postured, his arms behind his back and head held high.

BRAD STEPHENS: soft-spoken; lets his troubles melt off him like a pint of Ben & Jerry's Funky Monkey left on a burning stovetop.

HIS VERSION OF ME: the representative burnout zoning on a couch at someone's basement party; doesn't talk unless he's on an upper. He drips Visine into his eyes, and occasionally you'll hear—drip, drip, drip, *FUCK!*—because he always misses. We'll call him ZONE.

JAX FIELDS: a red-mohawk'd, septum-pierced, tattooed softy with a razor blade tongue.

HIS VERSION OF ME: SCOTTY: scrawny and the total works of "rock star"—tattoos out of the wazoo, chains, black jeans, spiked jewelry. He plays air guitar and brags about the number of girls he's banged and the lines of coke he's snorted.

ELI MILLER: brown-eyed, auburn hair, tall and athletic.

HIS VERSION OF ME: a meathead shooting steroids. You can hear him counting out his calisthenics. RICK never leaves the house without his dumbbells and power bars.

As they sat around before the funeral, Toby provided them, Jesse particularly, with drugs and consoling words.

"I'm sorry I'm a blubberin' mess," Jesse said after shouting how Daryl should be in the coffin, furious his brother couldn't have the decency to leave Margaret's face alone. There'd be no open casket today, just a shiny onyx box that could be empty for all he knew.

"You don't have to be tough all the damn time," said Jax. "If that were my mom, I'd be a psychotic, blabbering idiot."

Toby supplied him with two round blue pills.

"You can be high today. I think it's warranted."

The five formed a circle, pills and bottled water in their closed fists.

"To Margaret Harris, the most badass woman and mother," said Eli.

"To Margaret Harris," they echoed.

And with that, they tipped back their pills and prepped for the day ahead.

Jesse was sweating, and Brad was fidgety and scratching his arms. By the time the coffin sunk into the ground, Eli, the only sober one who drank water during the pill ceremony, was cool as a cucumber and had his arm around Jesse as he sprinkled dirt and roses onto the casket.

Jesse stood under the raging sun as neighbors, churchgoers, friends, and relatives queued up to bid him well, his lour darkening with every hug, kiss, and, "if you ever need me…" like parrots rehashing their owner's futile dinner party drivel.

Internally, he cursed the duplicity of it all. These couldn't be the same relatives, friends, and churchgoers who shunned Margaret for Daryl's street rep and her life choices? Every last one of them could shove off.

As the day continues, the burial five feet away, he wonders, *'where are you?'*

"I'm here," says Mike, ushering Jesse into his arms.

"Mi Sinclair."

"Got here as soon as I could. Stupid work."

"You're here now. That's enough. Come with me."

Mike's dragged across the lot where Jesse sits and delves into the chitchat, unaware Mike has braked outside the friend-made ring shaded by an apple tree.

"Hey! You!" shouts Jax, his red mohawk mismatching his dressy clothes. "Get lost! Friends only!"

Awkward.

"S-s-sorry. I'll just... just..."

Jesse approaches him, and his funeral outfit as well as his whispering, "C'mon, Mikey, it's fine," disarms his standard rebellious persona.

"No, really. I didn't mean to intrude. I'll leave."

Jesse's thumb lobs at the four other guys casting uranium glares. "Them? Nah, they're cool. Trust me."

He and Mike bridge the gap between Eli and Toby. Twitch pops out of thin air, panting, my hand on his head as his arms windmill.

Go on! GIT!

He jets into the visitors' building.

"This the guy who was there that night?" Brad asks, and Mike compares his lanky, bone-thin physique and four-inch-tall brown ringlets to a dandelion.

“Yes,” answers Jesse.

“Shit, dude, didn’t mean to yell atcha,” Jax apologizes.

“S’alright,” says Mike. “You didn’t know.”

They were preening to clobber Mike two minutes ago, and now they’re shaking his hand and thanking him for showing his support once they realize who he is and what he’s done for Jesse.

Mike tunes into their brotherly kinship.

He’s never had a brother…

Scotty jams on his air guitar.

Rick counts his crunches: *fifty… fifty-one… fifty-two…*

Conrad dusts invisible dirt off his blazer.

Twitch reappears and cartwheels.

Zone uncaps a bottle of Visine—Drip, drip, drip, *FUCK!*

This stuff never gets old, lemme tell ya.

“You should come to one of our shows sometime,” Jax says. “Eli and I are in a band, Jax and the Snax. Dumb name, I know, but our sound’s thrashy and heavy as hell.”

“Eli…” Mike snaps his fingers. “Jazz’s boyfriend?”

“The one and only.” He tips his imaginary hat. “Where is she?”

“Inside, cleanin' up some stuff,” says Jesse. “She texted me.”

Jax interrupts excitedly, “I mean it about the concert!”

His septum piercing glistens in the sunlight. He wears Converse. They all do. Mike tucks his shiny dress shoes out of sight.

Eli, chuckling, rolls his eyes. “Jax is always trying to recruit people to be our roadies.”

Mike laughs. “Just let me know when.”

"We'll go one night," Jesse assures. "They combine their sound with electronica, which I know is your favorite."

"How'd you know?" Mike asks, blushing from Jesse's wink.

"I pay attention, Square. Toby likes electronicore, too."

Toby and Conrad salute. "Affirmative."

Toby's a turnip amongst apples. He's "average,"—no piercings or crazy-colored hair. Mike wouldn't say he's "normal"—what's normal to the ant on the ground is aberrant to the fly in the sky. If not for Toby, Mike would be the turnip. Instead, he's a red apple amidst granny smiths.

"Any of you still in school?" asks Mike.

"We graduated last year," Eli answers. "I'll be going to the University of New York next year on a basketball scholarship."

Rick flips onto his feet, squats, and flexes. *'YEAH! BASKETBALL! GET SOME!'*

I'm surrounded by idiots!

"Impressive," Mike praises.

"Thanks, man. How 'bout you?"

"I—"

"He graduated early," Jesse boastfully butts in. "Mikey here is a baby. Seventeen."

"Nice!" says Brad.

"Thanks. It's not like I'm a genius or anything. I just started kindergarten a year early."

"You work at Blueberry Beans with Jazz, right?"

"She's my manager."

Jax groans. "I think I'd rather make coffee. My dad suckered me into the family business. He's a mechanic."

Scotty sticks out his tongue, his index and pinky pointed out like devil horns on his forehead. Twitch imitates him, and they head bang.

Conrad and I grumble.

It dawns on Mike where he's heard Jax's name. "Oh, yeah! Fields Automotive Repair out on Ashland Road!"

"That's us! It's an okay job, but definitely not what I had in mind."

"I don't think any of us are where we expected to be," says Jesse despairingly. "Whatta day."

Toby retrieves a sandwich baggie from his pocket and has everyone gather 'round. Mike capitalizes on the distraction and uses his shirt cuff to dry Jesse's tears.

"I got you."

"Thank you, Square."

Reverting to Toby, Mike's bludgeoned by déjà vu: his ten-year-old self sleuthing on Maddy and her girlfriends in the living room as Violet Ito opens a Ziploc—hushed dialogues about the drug in question. Ecstasy. The girls "rolling" while Pink Floyd's *Dark Side of the Moon* playing from the stereo pairs with *The Wizard of Oz* on the muted television.

The Sinclair Family Levee *cracking.*

Another hole dug.

My strength increasing.

Every VERSION OF ME scurries to their rightful persons, *whispering, whispering.*

Toby unties the plastic. "Got more goods from the Friendly Neighborhood Granny."

"God bless Widow Watson. I ain't had 30s in a hot minute," says Jesse, his eyes on the prize.

Twitch howls at the moonless sky as Jesse downs two more small, round Maya-blue pills they'd taken hours prior.

Toby distributes to three ravenous hands (Eli and Rick decline for the welfare of their pristine BMI).

"Ya good, buddy?" Toby asks, and Mike goes stiff.

"He's straight," says Jesse.

Straight as in *cool* or straight as in *square?*

"He ain't smoked weed 'til a few days ago."

You're such a DUD!

"For real? Well, just have half." Toby splits the pill in two. "Fuckers are strong for a first-timer. Don't want ya throwing up all over the place."

Twitch, Zone, and Scotty hover at Mike's left, Conrad and I on his right.

"What is it?"

Jesse answers, "Oxycodone."

"What'll it do to me?"

It'll make you happy, says Conrad.

And relaxed, Scotty adds.

Or it might wire you up, informs Zone. *You should see Brad on it. He can't stay in one place.*

Twitch hyperventilates.

Mike's become the powerless lab rat in their social

experiment, sightless to an escape route inside the labyrinth.

Years ago, months before they knew the extent of Maddy's addiction, Leon was prescribed Oxy after he'd burnt his hand, and when he couldn't find the bottle, he figured it'd been misplaced or accidentally thrown away. After a few Narcotics Anonymous meetings, Maddy confessed to having stolen the prescription.

An added *crack* to the Sinclair Family Levee.

A hole successfully shoveled.

Me soaring in the clouds.

"Don't feel like ya gotta, Mike," Jesse says to him.

He may come off sincere and sweet, but, c'mon, Mike, you know better. If you want to be accepted, you must earn their trust. Jesse won't love you if his friends hate you.

"What if he narcs on us?" Toby barks.

Jesse barks back, "He ain't gonna narc, ya paranoid ape!"

Twitch yowls. Conrad's upper lip tremors.

"I've known the kid for fifteen minutes!"

Look at them sparring, Mike. Who are you to crash in and muddle their brotherhood? You're not in the tribe just because Jesse says so. You can belong to a group that won't ask about "Maddy the Addy" or your cheerleader sister. You've waited for something greater than yourself, Maddy, and the Sinclair Family Levee.

It's sitting in the palm of your hand.

Do it, do it, do it! Show your worth! Show Jesse how much you love him! Isn't he beautiful?

"I'm not gonna narc," he claims to end the spar. "I'll try anything once."

"And twice if ya like it." Toby administers the half-pill to Mike.

My shrunken heart billows. *My boy, I'm so proud of you.*

"Anyone have water?" asks Jax.

Brad pulls a bottle from his book bag. "Way ahead of ya."

Conrad shakes my hand.

I give Mike an honorable slap on the back.

He cringes.

CRACK!

FOURTEEN
Spectrums

It's like we're in a time-jam. We could've been sitting on the mound for ten minutes or ten months. This high differs from the high in the Black Estates. The cannabis calmed him after being amped up from his fight with Charlie, and it was cooler that night. Now he's wedged between heat, drugs, his rumbling stomach, and the nagging urge to claw his flesh off.

So itchy!

The discussions, laughter, jokes, and playful insults intermingle. Jesse appears serene (or daydreaming?), and he and Mike fan themselves with the funeral pamphlets. He wasn't like this an hour ago; it must be the pills...

Or it might be the 90-degree high noon—just a thought.

Little by little, everyone departs to go to work or home. Eli and Jazz leave first, followed by Jax and Brad.

Mike vomits into the blackberry bush several feet away, Jesse on his heels and massaging his shoulders.

"Y'okay, buddy?"

"Bacon is *officially* ruined."

He hurls again… and again…

Looks like the drugs are working. Eat your heart out, sonny.

Jesse cleans Mike's mouth with his shirtsleeve.

"You must think I'm such a lightweight."

"You *are* a lightweight. Most get sick their first time tryin' Oxy, and it's worse if you're dehydrated. I shoulda given ya more water. M'bad."

"Why're *you* apologizing?"

"Y'did it so my friends would accept ya. I shoulda been smarter 'bout it. Shoulda said somethin'."

"That's not why I did it."

It's not?

"No?"

"No," Mike asserts. "And don't you *want* your friends to like me?"

"I don't give a damn what they think. *I* like you. You don't need to impress me or them hoodrats. Hear me?"

"Hear ya."

Jesse's smile has Mike feeling all-around fantastic, and the more I pester Twitch to careen his *ungrateful* ass this way and *help me*, the more he careens around the cemetery.

"So, uh… wanna… go back to my apartment?"

YES! LET'S GET HIGH!

"Does it have AC?"

"It does," says Jesse, snickering. "Ain't much else there *but* the AC."

"I'll take it."

Whew! What a relief! When Jesse didn't text back last night, Mike figured his going to therapy drove him away.

Stop being so negative.

Jesse straightens as Toby, Conrad, and the service preacher enter their spot. A VERSION OF ME rests his muscular arm on the preacher's shoulder, one iris blue, one brown, his tattered daisy dukes and crop top revealing his tanned legs and six-pack abs. He blows me a kiss.

Uhhh...

"You did good, son," the preacher tells Jesse. "Anything else I can do for you? We can meet on Tuesdays if you want some counseling?"

"That's nice of ya to offer, but no, thank you, Mr. Alexander."

Mike's head flings up.

'WHAT?!'

"I really appreciate ya doin' this for me. It was a beautiful service."

'WHAT?!'

"I'm sure Ma is smilin' down at us today."

'ALEXANDER?!'

"Yeah, Pops, you did a great job," Toby says to his *father!*

"Thank you, boys. It was an honor. Your mother was a wonderful woman and a substantial contributor to the church. She'll be missed, Jess, and always remembered."

Jesse's not the only watery-eyed one. Mike hadn't a clue he'd taken narcotics from the preacher's kid! I, indeed, did, and Mike's rueful reaction is *priceless!* To his credit, Toby's tanned complexion and dark hair doesn't resemble Mr. Alexander's slender build, freckled skin, rusty hairline, and nickel eyes.

You're going straight to Hell, my dude!

"You must be Michael Sinclair."

Mike dabs his palms on his thighs and prays (*ha!*) Mr. Alexander doesn't notice his shakes and sweats.

Jesus, Mike, don't throw up again. Not now.

"Yes, sir."

"Jesse mentioned you during our funeral discussions. It's a blessing you were there the night Maragret passed. People 'round here can be inconsiderate towards things they can't understand. You're a good person and, from what I've been told, a good friend."

'Baby Jesus in a bundle! Don't compliment me! I TOOK DRUGS FROM YOUR SON!'

Hold up...

Rewind...

Jesse talks about you! He. Talks. About. You! Damn, is it just me, or did it get hotter than a goat with a blowtorch out here?

"Thank you, sir."

"Well, we must be going. Jesse, if you need someone to talk to—*and I mean it*—my door is always open, and you're more than welcome to stay at the guest house if you want some privacy," says Mr. Alexander.

Toby gives Mike the one-armed hug he gave Jesse, their hands slapping and fingers sliding and snapping as they separate.

Mike immobilizes as Mr. Alexander steps right into his regurgitated piles. Jesse claps his hands over his lips and falls to one knee, laughing.

"At least you find this entertaining," Mike deadpans. "Why wasn't I told Toby's dad is a preacher?"

"'Cause it's *so much* more amusin' this way!"

"Bite me."

"Just say when!"

Mike shakes his head and grins.

Cars evacuate the parking lot, and Mike hands off a prelit cigarette to Jesse, their humor diminishing as they refocus on the burial ground. Mike visualizes virtual storm clouds winged overhead—fluffy and dreadfully glaucous.

"Should be Daryl in that damn coffin. She doesn't deserve to be in there; didn't deserve to die that way. Sick world we live in, man. Y'know them crazy evangelists who go on and on 'bout the second comin' of Jesus? I don't believe in all that biblical fuckery, but, dang, sometimes I wish it were true. All this corruption, murder,"—he smirks at Mike—"pollution."

"Ease up. Mother Nature takes care of us; we should take care of her."

"I know, Sinclair. You're so pure. Y'know who J. Robert Oppenheimer is?"

"No."

Jolly joy, it's Twitch...

He straddles Jesse's back and ruffles his hair.

"Oppenheimer was credited as one of the foundin' fathers of the atomic bomb durin' WWII when the US bombed Hiroshima and Nagasaki."

Jesse's spongy historical knowledge hits Mike like nostalgic riptides. His passionate gusto reminds him of Maddy's syrupy articulation, both characteristically loud until you ask their opinions regarding religion, politics, life, or love, at which point their loudness is reduced by two or three marks, as if doing so would compel others to *listen.*

"When they did the *Trinity Test* in New Mexico, Oppenheimer compared the experience to the *Bhagavad-Gita.* 'We knew the world would not be the same. Few people laughed. Few people cried. Most people were silent. I remember the line from the Hindu scripture, the *Bhagavad-Gita,* Vishnu, is tryin' to persuade the prince that he should do his duty and—'"

"'—to impress him, takes on his multi-armed form and says, "Now I am become death... the destroyer of worlds."'"

"Thought ya didn't know?"

"Sounded better coming from you."

Ick! That's just as tacky as when Jesse said it!

Jesse bites his lip. "He was right. *We* created mass destruction. *We* became death. We're *vicious*—destroyin' our own kind with nuclear bombs, mass destruction, weapons, wars, and all for what? Political and religious differences and sex and drugs. Why do ya think it's called the 'human race?'"

Mike scours his brain for a studious interpretation, and must be taking too long because Jesse says, "Humans can't stop racin'. We race to the cafés to be first in line for coffee 'cause we're racin' to get to work. We race for the trophies of success, riches, love, and some race towards death." He lays his cheek on Mike's head. "Why can't we just... *slow down?* Why this unquenchable thirst for the rush? The rush for the end, the outcome, the rush of the drugs? It's an endless marathon with no finish line. *Just slow down.*"

"We can slow down, Jess."

"No, we can't. It ain't in our DNA."

"Then we'll stop to marvel at the sights along the way."

Jesse flicks his spent cigarette into the wind. "Wanna know what I like most 'bout ya, Square?"

"Tell me."

"Your sugary impossibilities."

"They're not impossible, Jess. Doors will never stop closing, but new ones will always open. All we gotta do is find our way through the passageways first."

"*That,* Mike, *that's* what I mean. I can't talk to the guys like this. You don't make fun of my thoughts. Refreshin'. Just... y'know..."

"It's our secret."

"Thanks, Mikey."

Mike can count on twenty hands the number of times he's concealed Maddy's secrets from their parents and the public: slipping out of the house to meet her dealer, skipping class to score with her boyfriend, twenty-one-year-old degenerate Cody

Martin. Mike and Leon both despised Cody. He worked in a downtown porn shop, been to jail three times in a year for petty theft, and his greasy hair shined like kerosene under a heat lamp.

On the eve of Maddy's eighteenth birthday, Cody's mom, Lisa, called the Sinclairs. Cody hadn't come home, and Maddy told her he might've gone on a drug binge and passed out in an empty house where junkies hid to get high.

Maddy explained to Mike how she, Cody, and Violet broke into these anonymous houses, and since they nested in rundown neighborhoods, the cops were never notified. From there, they'd dial their dealers, who'd then tell their clients the house's address. By morning, a two-story facility was overrun with junkies sleeping or nodding out on the floors, in the basement and showers, bedrooms, and kitchens.

"I couldn't even walk down the stairs without stepping on someone," she said.

Addicts, including teenagers, often traveled with their lives stuffed into garbage bags, their clothes smelling of urine, sweat, shit, and covered in the filth of the streets. The preteens—runaways primarily—laid low in the houses to break away from their abusive foster families.

"It should've been enough to want to turn my life around, Mikey, but I swore I wouldn't end up like them; that I could stop whenever I wanted. Soon, those houses became home, and the addicts became my kin. They'd given up on being anything more than junkies. It's all they've ever known.

"I remembered my drug days, my high times, better than my

sober life. I think we—addicts—block out our lives before the drugs. If we didn't, we'd have to recognize what we've given up—the beauty, the comfort, no chasing dragons, no cravings. We would've purposely overdosed out of pure shame if we were to think back on our sober lives while shooting up."

She stocked the trap houses with tampons, toiletries, and donated clothing and spent half her paychecks on smack and the other half on food for the others that went to waste more often than not.

"I was a junkie, not a heartless bitch," she said. "Keep in mind, Mikey, that just because someone is homeless, or an addict, doesn't necessarily mean they're terrible people. They're lost souls in a world that's failed them."

Her statement felt like a paradox when she added how she left her credit cards at home and carried little cash because of her fellow addicts' sticky fingers. She'd go home to get her money if she needed a fix and use up her entire H load before nodding out in case anybody tried to nick her needles or stash.

Lisa called two hours later. A botched drug transaction that'd gone *horribly, horribly* wrong left Cody dead, two bullets to the head, in his vehicle at a gas station.

Maddy's VERSION OF ME resurfaced, and she relapsed from her three-month-long sobriety, overdosing for the third, fourth, and fifth time. Her addiction, her stories, her overdoses—*dreadful* secrets. Secrets Mike safeguarded to mislead others into believing the Sinclairs were "clean," but Mike knew they weren't any cleaner than the trap houses.

Mike's familial secrets were involuntary. He and Jesse's secrets aren't grubby. They're pocket-sized, gold-leafed delicacies. He likes their secrets.

Correction: he *loves* them and hopes they never expire.

FIFTEEN

Glimmer

As Jesse spends time alone at Margaret's grave, Mike basks on the hood of the Honda, his nimble pulse a giveaway that the drug's active. He tugs at his shirt adhered to his sweaty chest, the hankering for nicotine insatiable, and, if given a chance, he could talk someone into an indeterminate state.

Thirty minutes, and fifteen Camel Golds later, he slides off the car and hurls… *again.*

PULL YOURSELF TOGETHER, MAN!

He backtracks to the car, and Jesse, arms crossed, clucks his tongue.

"Tsk, tsk, Square. What did we learn 'bout chain-smokin'?"

Partway into the front seat, Mike snarls, "Shut up and drive."

Jesse fastens his seatbelt, cranks the AC, and hits the highway.

"I'm fixing to strip down and spread out in front of the vents."

"I won't stop ya. I encourage it," Jesse, friskily, says."Wanna stop by yours first so you can change?"

"I'm okay."

Red Street, messier than Indigo, stinks of garbage, and the residents socialize in their front yards—smoking, drinking, and gossiping. Children cool off in sprinklers and inflatable pools.

His apartment, a brown, shaggy two-story complex squished between two condos, hasn't seen upkeep in years, the lobby faintly lit by three flickering bulbs, the other three burnt black, and the Prussian blue carpet spoors of cat piss and mildew.

"Sorry 'bout the smell. The old landlady used to feed the stray cats, and they kinda squatted here. New landlord said he'll replace the carpet this month, but I doubt he will."

"No biggie."

Jesse unlocks APT 3, and new carpet and cleaning agents veto the cat piss. A periodic table tapestry above an umber, threadbare sofa flutters from the spinning ceiling fan, and, across from it, a flat-screen TV too wide for its stand. Jesse sets Margaret's photograph on display at the service below the double windows facing Red. Mike's blown away by Jesse's parallelism to her apricot skin, crooked nose, and straight teeth.

"She's pretty. You look like her."

"I've heard that my entire life. I take it as a compliment. Got my dad's eyes, though. Shame. Hers was like four-leaf clovers. She had beautiful eyes."

"So do you. They're like sunbursts."

Jesse, in the kitchen three paces from the living room, smiles. "Thanks. I like yours, too. They're like nightfall. Sunbursts and nightfall." His cheeks dimple. "Can't have one without the other."

Mike returns his smile, his cheeks rouged.

I find my place next to the window and Twitch springs on the couch.

Jesse opens the freezer and puts two glasses and a bottle of coconut rum on the white countertop.

"Drink?" he asks.

Do it!

"How are you able to buy alcohol? You know, don't answer that. Is drinking a smart idea?"

Don't be a candy-ass!

"'Cause of the Oxy? Eh, you'll be a'ight. One shot won't hurtchya."

They sit side by side on the floor in front of the coffee table, and Jesse connects his phone to the Bluetooth speakers.

"Any particular band ya wanna listen to?"

"I'm not picky," answers Mike.

Jesse sets his heavy metal playlist on shuffle.

"Download *Spotify*. We can create a playlist and add songs to it. We'll call it…." Jesse drums his fingers on his chin. "'*Jessike!*'"

"Did you *seriously* just give us a ship-name?"

Jesse wiggles his eyebrows and clinks their glasses; Mike's ears and face rosy. When the rum dam ruptures into his bloodstream, he asks Jesse where his stuff is.

"Stuff? Oh! I ain't gone to get it yet. Just haven't had the guts. I'll sleep on the couch or floor before I go back into that nightmare."

Jesse knocks back a second shot, unzips a pocket inside his backpack, and tosses baggies of weed and pills onto the table.

"Wanna roll?"

Mike blinks dumbly at the joint papers. He's seen Maddy do it, but never done it himself.

"Don't know how to."

"No problem. Can ya pick out the stems and seeds for me? Shouldn't be too many. Check this *dope* shit."

The weed nugget he chucks sticks to the wall.

"HOLY SHIT!" Mike hollers.

"TOLDJA!"

As Mike segregates the good leaves from the unneeded extras, Jesse pulls a glass chessboard from under the sofa and arranges a sheet of notebook paper over three blue pills, his Zippo *crunch, crunch, crunch*ing the Oxy.

"Ya don't gotta do this. Snortin' can be rough."

"You can *snort* those?"

"Whadja think I was doin' here? I prefer snortin', but to each their own."

"Is there a difference in high?"

"Sorta. It hits the brain and system almost instantly if ya snort, but the high lasts longer if ya eat them."

As an outsider who saw how Maddy's addiction whittled away at their family until they were but a caricature of what they'd once been, he swore he'd never try anything harder than alcohol, and snorting drugs would be *beyond* self-incriminating.

On my toes, I mosey over to Mike.

You're not Maddy. I won't trap you as I did her. And do you think your charisma *will woo Jesse?* Mercy! *A chalkboard without chalk isn't as dull as you.*

Mike sips the blue powder from the tail-end of a straw into his nasal cavity, and he slumps against the sofa, eyes closed and wholly immersed in a peacefulness he'll never, ever find again until Death whisks him off to... wherever he'll go in the afterlife.

Now you get it; get how Maddy tripped into her drug-laced catacomb. What do you feel, Mike? Pain? What pain? Physical? Emotional? Spiritual? Mental? No more pain in your domain. Your medications "stabilize" you, but I pull the rabbit out of the hat.

Jesse snorts his lines, fires up a joint, and lays out on the carpet with his head on Mike's lap.

Twitch is pounding on the living room window, barking like a mutt at the mailman.

You can't make this stuff up.

"Careful with the drip. Makes some people sick."

"Drip?" Mike asks, toking on a joint, and he sniffs *hard* then coughs on chemical-flavored snot.

"DRIP!"

Cackling, Jesse catches Mike's imposing hand, rests it on his breastbone, and they scrutinize each other like amateur mind readers, his fingers fondling Jesse's shirt buttons.

"When I was lookin' at your sketches the other day, there was a drawin' that really stuck with me."

"Really? Which one?"

"Some girl. She has this other girl comin' out of her chest, and they're... fightin'? One looks healthy, and the other looks exactly like her, but...."

Mike's blood pressure ascends.

"Monstrous?"

"Right," says Jesse.

Not *that* piece! He's not ready to give up the codes to his off-limited doorways. He's an abstract portrait buried by inches of black paint Jesse will have to chisel away one dried piece at a time to see any surviving colors.

"You're far away again. *Talk* to me. *Trust* me."

"It's... it's not you, Jess."

"Feels like it."

Twitch chugs the bottle of rum and sings off-key, "What Shall We Do with a Drunken Sailor?"

Sighing, Jesse sits up, refills the shot glasses, digs for two more Blues, and teaches Mike the crushing process, their intersecting hands rocking, the lighter *crunch*ing the pills into fine powder. Jesse removes the paper, and Mike scrapes off the residue with his pocketknife as Jesse grates the chessboard with a razor blade.

They snort their deviated piles, smoke, drink, and talk away the ticking clock, their personal lives and pasts circumvented. Jesse *must* be vexed: why isn't Michael Sinclair opening up?

Once Jesse knows about Maddy, he'll ditch you faster than one can say, "loser." Your story can't even touch hers. Do you think he'll keep boring ol' Mike around? Jesse's interest in you stumps me.

Twitch picks at the weed, and... is he... *eating* it?! *You're revolting, Twitch!*

Mike clears two fat lines in four snorts and retches.

“C’mere,” says Jesse, and they face each other, forehead to forehead, nose to nose. “I’m gonna…” He unbuttons Mike’s shirt. “All the way off, alright?” He waits for his nod and sheds off the polyester. “This is ‘groundin'.’” Fingernails dribble up and down Mike’s arms, shoulders, and wrists. “I do it to my friends sometimes.”

This *sensual* grounding is *nothing* like Dr. Greene’s *five things you can see, four things you can touch...* grounding.

“Am I hurtin' ya?”

“It feels nice.”

Too nice—his stomach and groin astir. He runs his hands up Jesse’s thighs, snags at his shirt, and exhales curtly. Mike could die a happy, drowning man in Jesse’s touch, and coconut rum, marijuana breath.

“Can I?” Mike asks.

“Yes.”

Mike helps Jesse peel out of his shirt, and they succumb to the sensation of Mike’s sights on his bare chest and their fingertips venturing along the geometric peaks and valleys of arms, necks, and collarbones.

Mike tussles with spirituality. He heard Mom pray for Maddy to get sober, Mike to get well, and Leon to step up, and although Maddy did get sober, praying to a “God” who didn’t care about his family was as beneficial as an atheist reading *The Book of Revelation*. If there’s no God, afterlife, or heaven, then the electricity from their fingertips must be caused by science.

They gasp, the lamp buzzing.

“Didja feel that, too?” Jesse asks.

“Y-y-yeah.”

Drugs. It’s just the drugs sharpening their senses—every hair follicle tingling, the two of them unable to quell their hunger for each other’s magnificent touch and skin.

Mike feels Jesse’s biceps as he conducts his own explorations along Mike’s stomach and the hair speckled below his navel. Sunbursts and nightfall collide, their breaths hitching as Jesse’s thumb brushes over his pecs.

“You ground all your friends like this?”

“Never.”

Jesse’s hauled in by the belt loops. Their heads slant as they inhale shared breaths, and Mom, *again,* disrupts what should’ve been Mike’s first kiss. He apologizes, answers the call, and half-listens to her.

His exhale shallow, Jesse goes into the kitchen, the shot glass overflowing from the trembling rum bottle in his hand.

Twitch rolls on the floor, giggling.

I’m… um… I’ll just… go over here to the… window.

“You’re at Jesse’s?” Mom reprises Mike’s reply. “It’d be nice if you’d tell me your plans, Michael. Are you coming home for dinner?”

“Um… I…”

“He shouldn’t be alone today. Why don’t I order a pizza, and you and Jesse can pick it up and eat here?”

“Dinner at my place?” he asks Jesse.

“Sure,” he mutters, the Oxy *crunch, crunch, crunch*ing.

"Text me the pickup time, Mom. We'll be home soon."

He ends the call, locates his shirt, and snorts his portion.

"You sober enough to drive?"

"Just gimme, like, ten or fifteen minutes."

Mike reckons there'd be traction because of their former physical correlations, but Jesse's raunchy jokes and their laughter iron the craters of their "almost-kiss," which Mike blames on them being hot-air-balloon-high and wonders if Jesse blames the drugs as well.

I don't know what or who's liable, yet I suspect it has *little* to do with me.

And *that* imposes a *critical* problem.

SIXTEEN

Starbursts & Distant Glows

Mike dazzles whenever Mom laughs at Jesse's jokes as they dine on Leaning Tower pizza and sugary sodas. His life has changed dramatically in only a few short weeks, with relationships exceeding his expectations. Even if he fumbles to keep up, it's the most significant obstacle he's ever achieved in his pursuit of... *happiness.*

Mom complains about exhaustion as Jesse and Mike clean the kitchen, her olive skin waxen. A specter in the corner, in his immature form, waves at me, and I bow.

"I'll take care of these," Jesse says, taking the leftover containers. "Go check on your ma."

She's on the couch, her arm covering her eyes and radish cheeks, her hair damp and frizzy. Mike moves the standing fan from his room in front of her after she mentions how humid it is tonight.

She kicks her feet onto the armrest. "Ah, much better. Thank you, Michael."

He kisses her balmy forehead. "Can I get you anything? Ice pack?"

“Don’t waste your worries on me, sweets. I’m going to lie here and read a book. Why don’t you and Jesse go play video games?”

“You sure you’re alright?”

“I’m fine. Go on, now.”

He and Jesse smoke their after-dinner cigarettes on the porch swing as Twitch sprints up and down the road.

“She okay?”

“I think the heat’s getting to her.”

Jesse seems unconvinced, probably because Mike doesn’t sound convincing.

“Wanna stay over tonight?”

“If ya go to the estates with me.”

“Not sure if Mom would be thrilled about me going out. I’ve burned a few bridges with her.”

“Sneak out.”

Mike tenses.

Jesse shoves his shoulder into his flippantly. “So, not only have ya never smoked weed, but you’ve never snuck outta your house either?”

He hasn’t, unless you count his and Maddy’s midnight swims…

Mike’s fifteen, and he’s grounded for disputing with Charlie over how, per Charlie, Maddy attending Narcotics Anonymous brought dishonor to the family.

“Your nose is so far up Dad’s ass you’ll be smelling shit for the next five lifetimes.”

Charlie told Leon what Mike said, and Leon practically fractured a brain vessel and, alas, the punishment.

Mike and Maddy creep downstairs in their bathing suits and float on their backs in the pool amid dank chlorine, speaking to the waning moon and twinkling stars suspended in the navy nighttime. I'm on the ladder, my feet in the water.

"What do you want most out of life, Mikey?"

"Uh... not sure. I think I'm too young to know."

"You're fifteen! You must have some idea."

"Ummm... I guess I want to go to an art college and work for, like, Disney or Pixar. You?"

"I can see that happening for you. I want..." Maddy's alto speech becomes a sparky soprano. "I want to be a bestselling author and travel the world doing book tours!"

He lauds her enthusiasm. Maddy is more likely to be seen flipping the pages of a book than flipping through the TV stations.

"What would you write about?"

"*Us.* I'd tell our story."

"Ha, wouldn't that be something?"

"Wouldn't it, though?"

He keeps his innermost desires reserved. He's too preoccupied armoring himself against the *snap, crackle,* and *pop* of the Sinclair Family Levee to plan his future. Right now, all he wants are the simple things: his family to reconnect, for Leon to accept his son for who he is and not for the son he conjured up in his head, and for Charlie to watch a movie with him without spit-balling insults. He wants Mom to smile again and for Maddy to be healthy.

Happiness, or what he defines *happiness* to be.

But we don't always get what we want, do we?

His desires now revolve around Jesse, and he'll do whatever it takes to fulfill them.

"Meet you at the cul-de-sac at eleven."

"I'll be waitin'. And I mean no offense, Sinclair, but I'd wear somethin'... *not so square* if ya don't want my buddies houndin' you all night."

At 10:40 PM, he grumbles to himself, "I *do not* dress like a square...."

Yes, you do, you flippin' straight edge!

"I wear what everyone else wears. Stupid, *not-so-square* bullshit...." He freezes, his shirts collared and pants either khakis or dressy. "*Aw, shit!* I *am* a square!"

The squarest of them all.

He decides on Jesse's blue jeans and black, DC sleeveless t-shirt he'd thrown into the hamper last night.

'Damn, they smell like him...'

He checks on his mother sleeping in her room, her hair wrapped in a towel, and sets her book on the bedside table. He turns the music on low in his dark room, climbs out the window and heads to the cul-de-sac.

Jesse screeches, "Holy crickets, man!"when Mike crops up in

the seat. "Scared the crap outta me! Little warnin' next time?"

Jesse's staidness deepens as Mike's voluminous hilarity enhances.

"I-I-I'm sorry, J-Jess! I had to get out while I could."

The following excursions have Twitch at the height of his hyperactivity, his hyena laugh testing my patience, but it's a small price to pay for Mike's besotted trip down Wonderland.

Keep chasing the white rabbit, Alice.

The thirty-minute junket to Olivesburg coasts by faster than the last time as songs and cigarette smoke craft *worthy* memories.

Mike's side of the car dips and Twitch shoots out of the backseat and dashes towards the woods, squawking joyfully the whole way.

Jesse digests the unlikely image on his right under the yellow floodlights.

"*Goddang.*"

"What?"

"Erm... you look... you... uh... you look—"

"*Un-square?*"

One of them blushes, and for once, it's not Mike.

"Was gonna say you look *damn fine* in my clothes."

Mike gnaws at his inner cheek and folds his hand into Jesse's on their woodland hike, the ground dry and the cloudless skies glitzy indigo-and-glitter. The Black Estates' architectural anatomy in eyeshot, they jog the rest of the way and skip every other rickety stair to the front doors.

Mike budges between Brad and Toby—weed smoke, music,

and hand-slap pleasantries bountiful. Jesse, across from them, completes the circle in the foyer illuminated by smartphones and flashlights.

Jax's Scotty rocks out with his air guitar; Toby's Conrad stands business-like behind Toby; Brad's Zone melts into the settee; Eli's Rick does pull-ups in the doorway: *twenty-three... twenty-four... twenty-five...*; Twitch slides down the banister (how the hell did he get up there?!)

"Hit?" Toby asks Mike, the water bong in rotation. "Or do you prefer shotguns from Jesse?"

Everyone laughs.

Mike lowers his head.

Splitting open a blunt, Jesse glares at Toby. "Can ya ever keep a secret?"

"M'bad."

"I think it's adorable!" Jazz says, and her spliff-toking, foot-tall imp in a jacket sewn together with marijuana leaves prances on her shoulder. What a quaint, wee creature…

"Is this even allowed?" Mike asks Jazz. "You're my manager."

She licks a joint shut. "We're off the clock. What're they gonna do?" She takes a drag, a thick smog unloading from her nose and mouth. "Fire me? I wish they would."

Maddy would approve of Jazz's attitude and punk aesthetic comprising black everything: fingernails, makeup, jean shorts, tank top, and knee-high boots. Her metal bracelets and chains jingle with her moving arms.

"Where'd Gemma go?" asks Brad.

"Probably off in the woods sacrificing virgins," Toby says, and Conrad snickers.

Jazz and Goblin give him the middle finger. "I think she went to take a leak. She'll be back in a few. My goodness!" She musses Mike's curls. "I never realized how cute you are outside of work! Jesse's been stingy with you!"

"Guilty as charrrrrged," croons Jesse, centered on his re-rolled blunt. "I'm selfish. Also, someone's gotta protect him. He just moved in across the street a few weeks ago."

"From where?" asks Jax.

Oh, no...

"Golden burbs."

Damn it, Jesse!

The others, excluding Mike and Jesse, whoop and whistle, and when Mike passes the joint to Brad, Toby exclaims—"Hey! He may be a yuppie, but at least he knows the Rule of the Left!"—and kills half the joint in a single drag.

Watch and learn, grasshopper.

Mike coughs. "The what?"

"Whenever you're in a circle, you always pass the joint to the left," Jesse explains.

"Oh. Right."

"Oh, my God," Jazz hollers, "you didn't know that! You should use this cuteness at work! You'd make some great tips from the ladies! Maybe tips *and* tits!"

"C'mon, Jazz, chill out," says Jesse. "He's not from Mars."

Could've fooled us. You're a freak in a three-ring circus. Jazz acts like she's never seen the opposite sex until tonight.

"Whadup, bitches?!"

Me-oh-my, is it my birthday?! The girl in the entryway, why, she hasn't *one* VERSION OF ME, but *two. TWO!* They guard her like she's Queen! The first is tall and sickly thin in her Louis Vuitton bedazzled dress and holier-than-thou diadem, and the second is an overweight, Plain Jane crybaby wearing a t-shirt and jeans. You may identify them as Mia and Ana. To us, they're Victoria and Baby.

Gemma shoves Jax sidewise, the circle shifting to conform to the plus-one.

Mike eats his heart when she plants a wet smooch onto Jesse's mouth and asks, "How's it going, babe?"

You honestly think you'll stand a chance up against her? She's gorgeous! *Sea-green eyes, hair like scarlet sage, divine sun-kissed skin.*

She and Mike's scowls typhoon-strong, Gemma asks, "And who is *this?*"

Will this ever end?

"I know, right? Isn't he adorable?" Jazz cups her mouth and whispers not-so-discreetly, "He's from the Golden Suburbs."

"Aww, that *is* adorable. Jesse's made a new friend."

Jesse skids away from Gemma's elbow prod.

"Yo, Gemma"—he mimes himself into a bubble—"stay out."

"You didn't mind me invading your bubble last night, *dickhead.*"

There it is! That's why he didn't answer your texts! They were at his apartment, getting high and screwing each other brainless. It irks you how she gets to see parts of Jesse you'll only see in your wildest, wet dreams. If you want him, make a move. Be bold! Nobody likes a prude.

"That was then, and this is now. People make mistakes."

Victoria *hmph*'s and Baby… bloody cries!

Blueberry smoke elevates.

"*MISTAKE?*"

"Can we not talk about this now?" Jazz gripes. "Shit's gettin' old. You two are *so* last year."

Aaaaa! Goblin chimes.

"Technically, we're *so* yesterday," Gemma says.

"I don't give a flaming sack of shit if you were two hours ago! Let it go! I can only handle so much of your squabbles."

"I concur," says Brad and passes the joint to Toby.

"You're just jealous because you want a piece of *this*." Gemma and Victoria wave over their figures. Baby… Baby cries.

"Sweetie, I wouldn't fuck you with Toby's dick."

Zone cackles. *Buuurrrn!*

"Hey!" Toby protests.

Conrad shudders.

"I'd get lost in that bush you call 'hair,'" Gemma fires at Brad.

"Low blow! My hair is *awesome!* I've been voted 'Best Hair' since—"

"Since the second grade! We know!" The gang and their VERSIONS OF ME finish.

"No reason to remind us every chance you get," Jax says.

Mike puffs on a tweezer-clipped joint, pawns it off to Brad, and, looking ahead, requites Jesse's flirty gaze.

“What’s on the agenda for tonight?” Brad asks. “Anyone got goodies?”

“Shit, man, do I ever show up empty-handed?” Toby recovers an orange prescription bottle from his messenger bag. The top *pops,* and, like the blunts and joints, it’s passed from the left.

“More Blues?” Jesse asks.

“And Percs.”

Jax takes two of each. “Man, you’re the shiz! How do you keep scorin'? This can’t all be from Widow Watson.”

The rotation skips Eli, and Mike blinks to keep his eyeballs inside their sockets, the bottle packed to the rim.

“I have my people. Just be easy. Stuff’s expensive. 'Cept you, Mike, you can have a little extra. Welcome to the gang.” Toby laughs at Mike’s gawp. “What, bro?”

“Pardon me, but—”

“How *formal!*” Gemma taunts.

Rude ass bitch! How’s that *for formal?*

“Gemma, shut your trap.”

“Shove it, Jess.”

“You both can shut it!” Jax snaps, and their mouths clamp. “What were you saying, Mike?”

“I, er, was going to ask how you can afford these? Aren’t they, like, thirty a head?” he asks Toby.

“Widow Watson charges me half-price, and I hook her up with reefer and mow her lawn, clean the gutters, go grocery shopping, etcetera, etcetera.”

“Half-price is still pricey as fuck.”

"Oh, shit, he *can* cuss!"

"SHUT UP, GEMMA!" They (omit Mike) yell.

"Damn, you're annoying tonight, Gems. Show off much?" Conrad's snarl stops Victoria from decking Toby. "I have a hefty allowance. Pops thinks I'm savin' for college."

"He's naïve as hell," Jax says, as if he's heard it all before.

"As I always say: being a preacher's son has its benefits. Really, Mike, no worries, take extra."

Here's the plan: pocket the stash and Jesse and spend the night in your room getting skull-stupid high!

What're you doing? Three?! THREE?! Don't give Toby the bottle! You're infuriating! You disappointing, useless, wea... wait.... OPEN YOUR HAND, MIKE!

Six Oxys?! Jesse? Jesse who? Toby's our new best friend!

Thank Toby, never mind Jesse's disapproving head shake (he dumped you for Gemma last night, you owe him squat), and find a way to crush these babies!

"Ya wanna bump? I got stuff you can use." Superhero, Jax!

He lays out a wooden slab, straws, and a *mortar and pestle?!*

Mike gasps. "*Brilliant!* Why haven't I thought of this? My sister left one behind after she moved."

"Fastest way I've found to crush. Want me to do it for you?" Jax asks.

We got this covered, you inbred blockhead!

"I can do it." *That's my boy. You, too, can be a sharp edge! Jesse may even choose you over Gemma.*

Mashing the pills with the grinder cuts Jesse's crushing

method in half, and he dumps and divides the powder onto the wooden slab.

"Tooters." Jax pitches at him a bag of straws.

"Thanks, Jax."

Jax and Eli plan out the next Jax and the Snax concert, and Jesse, glum, crawls to Mike's come-hither motion. While the group argues over the selected music, Jesse sighs, snorts his lines, scratches his nose, and lies down on the floor with his head on Mike's thigh. Mike's thankful for the musical distraction as he hunches in to bump the remaining Oxy. He's had enough of their potshots, even if they were harmless.

Mike places the board to the side and pushes his hand into Jesse's hair, his pinky caressing his forehead. He extends his touches over his jawline, and the pterodactyls in his stomach take flight as Jesse nuzzles into his hand, well-knowing Gemma's watching them.

Twitch, who's chatting up Victoria, yaps when her pointed-toe shoe assaults his shin. He limps to Baby, and she hugs him like a teddy bear, sobbing.

Within three rock songs, Mike's sour stomach and itchy, sweaty skin junction in with his heavy head and parched mouth.

Four hip-hop tunes in, he *crunch, crunch, crunch*es, snorts, and taps the straw to Jesse's nose.

Jesse opens an eye. "I'm comfy."

"You don't have to move."

"Can't snort lyin' down."

"Want me to getcha a crazy straw?"

"You're cute."

Jesse clears the board at an irregular twist to avoid disturbing his resting spot, and they're too eclipsed in their sunburst and midnight universe to see Toby abducting the spliff from Mike.

"Reached your limit?" asks Jesse.

Don't confess to him or, heavens to Betsy, any of the others you're sketched out of your mind! Be cool!

"Just taking a break."

Gemma and Jazz dance to the electronicore music. Goblin boogies on Jazz's head, and someone should purchase Victoria a stripper pole. Baby and Twitch are two swaying planks, his chest muffling her sobs.

Mike fans himself. "Damn, I'm sweating like a dominatrix in a rubber suit."

Jesse bursts out boisterously.

"I like when you laugh," says Mike. "You don't do it enough."

"I don't? I feel like I'm constantly laughin' when I'm with you."

"Is that a crack on my appearance?"

"No, dingbat. Ya make me laugh."

"Did you just call me a 'dingbat?'"

"C'mon, Square, would I do that? Get up. Somewhere I wanna take ya."

"Just us?"

"Just us. Up for it?"

"Fuck, yeah. One more before we go?"

Mike *crunch*es their pills and arranges their rails.

"Better take it easy," Jax forwarns, and Mike's fascinated by his red glow-in-the-dark mohawk. "Don't wantcha to get sick."

"He's got this," Jesse affirms.

"A'ight."

They hurry with their lines, and Jesse helps Mike to his feet.

"Where're you jerks going?"

Gemma? Jazz?

"None of your damn business!" Jesse retorts.

"Whatever, dipshit!"

Gemma.

Mike ingests mouthfuls of the clean night air as they travel down the west-side hill.

"What's the story there? You and Gemma. Can't tell if she loves you or hates you."

"Bit of both."

"Is she the ex you mentioned?"

"Yeah."

"She was at your apartment last night?"

"Um... yeah."

"Oh."

"Ya seem upset."

"I'm not upset," he immediately counters. "She's just...."

"Snooty." Jesse laughs. "She wasn't always like that. I guess I played a part in it. There's still some love there, just not the sort of love she wants. It's complicated. I worry 'bout her, so I stick 'round. Poor girl has a grisly eatin' disorder."

Twitch catches up with us and bestrides Jesse's back.

"How bad?"

“Pretty dang bad. I don’t know how much she weighed before it started 'cause ya never ask a girl her weight.”

“I get that. I grew up with sisters.”

“Exactly. If I had to guess, she was probably 'bout two hundred pounds in middle school. She was called ‘Gemma the Giant’ and mooed at. I stood up for her a lot, and nobody hassled me 'cause Daryl was known as a ‘Dealin' Boss,’ so, y’know, I was respected by default. Gemma clung to me, and we formed a tight bond.”

Maddy’s reputation ended in Mike becoming a bullying bullseye at Cougar High. At Richland High, Daryl pinned Jesse at the top of the popular food chain. Humankind is intricate like that.

“Gemma lost 'bout one hundred pounds durin' the summer of our freshman and sophomore year, *no joke.*“

Jesse says it was a darkly humorous circumstance. The same shallow goons who harassed Gemma suddenly wanted to date her, and when she snubbed them, choosing Jesse and his group over theirs, the anorexic puns arose. Girls stuck their fingers down their throats and fake gagged, and she earned a new nickname—

“Ana-Gemma?” Mike says. “That’s the best they could come up with?”

“Right? She’d always come to my house just bawlin' her eyes out.”

“She couldn’t win either way.”

“Nope. No one, not even the teachers, tried gettin' her help.

I'd take her to dinner, and she'd order this *enormous* meal and *smell* it the entire time. She'd bake me cookies and stuff but never ate them."

"Why didn't her parents help?"

"I never asked them. They didn't like me much; wasn't allowed at her house, and Gemma doesn't talk 'bout them often, but I know they took her to therapists and health doctors, but it did no good. What worries me most is her drug and vodka habit, which, to me, means a greater chance of an overdose or alcohol poisonin' since she's so tiny and malnourished."

"Is that why you guys broke up? The eating disorder?"

Mike latches onto Jesse as they leap across a miniature creek.

"Nah, that had nothin' to do with it. She wasn't a terrible girlfriend. She's fun, smart, and a talented painter. She's pretty."

Pretty. Jesse likes pretty. What guy doesn't?

"So, what's the problem?"

"Our two negatives couldn't make a positive. I'm too damaged for a relationship. I can't give her or anyone else the love they deserve."

They come upon a grassy shore, the cobalt horizon and lake blending, and moonlight mirrors off the glossy, calm surface.

"A lake?! I could kiss you right now!"

I bet you could.

Jesse strips out of his shirt.

"Figured ya like it. Open," Jesse whispers, placing an Oxy on his tongue, the chemical flavor hitting Mike's taste buds and lips traced by Jesse's fingertips.

Mike plays connect-the-dots with the stars as Jesse molts from his shoes and clothing, becoming nothing more than a naked moon child, and he and Twitch sprint to the lake.

SPLASH!

Mike undresses, folds their clothes into neat piles, and cannonballs as Jesse resurfaces, water flinging off his hair.

Mike breaks the surface. "This feels—"

Jesse pounces on him and they sink, the merry timestamp reversing them into two Benjamin Buttons. I observe the carefree souls play and swim until their lungs and limbs fatigue.

Their hands slice in and out of the water simultaneously as they float, the clustering stars and crescent moon keeping a watchful eye on them.

"This makes life worth wakin' up for," says Jesse.

Twitch dolphin dives a few feet away from where I stand barefoot at the shallow end.

"Jess?"

"Square?"

"What you said about being too damaged to love someone? I don't think that's true. You're damaged. She's damaged. Kinda works, don'tcha think?"

He'd sooner be nailed to the lake floor than see him with Gemma. However, Jesse should know he's 24-karat gold and deserving of love from the *right* person.

"If two people are damaged, how can they ever become undamaged? We all need someone to pick up our black, bleedin' hearts off the ground and shove them back into our chests. If she can't pick up my heart and I can't pick up hers, it won't work."

"What're you saying? You want someone who can fix you?"

"I'm unfixable. Nobody can save me."

"But someone can fix her?"

"I have no doubt."

Mike hesitates. "You think someone can save me?"

"Mikey,"—Jesse squints at him—"when're ya gonna realize that you're not the one who needs savin'? You're the one who saves."

Jesse's acclaimed commendation feels vaguely burdensome. Mike can't even save himself. Why would he want to play Clark Kent when the person he wants to fly off with is, in his words, "unfixable and damaged"? He sticks firmly to his genial faith that maybe, *maybe*, he *can* save Jesse.

"Hey, Jess?"

"Mm?"

"What do you want most out of life?"

Silence.

"This right here, Mikey. This is all I want. You?"

Silence.

"Same here, Jess."

SEVENTEEN

Dark Light

Exiting Olivesburg, Jesse's phone vibrates in the cup holder, and Mike, not trying to be nosy, looks over Gemma's messages.

"Goddang, she doesn't know when to take a hint!"

"She wants to stay with you tonight."

"Do you *want* me to go home tonight?" The question hovers as an asteroid aiming to extinguish their world or ascend into infinity.

I *whisper, whisper* in Mike's ear.

"I've already asked you to stay. We can get high and watch movies."

His forehead creased, Jesse switches lanes polar of the ROY G BIV and stays mute when Mike asks where they're going. Twitch howls out the window.

The Kroger shopping strip on Park Avenue is practically vacant at 2 AM. Twitch gets abnormally quiet. Jesse keeps the car running and lights a Salem Menthol.

"I'm gonna tell ya somethin'," he says, his face splashed with color from the storefront's blue K logo.

"Okay."

"It might change your entire perspective of me."

"Try me."

"You aware of the Ohio heroin epidemic? 'Course not. You're from the Golden burbs."

"Hey! Just beca—"

"I'm sorry, I'm sorry. I didn't... even people in the rough areas aren't aware of the 'epidemic.' It's been kept low-key. Ya heard 'bout the Oprah episode that took place in Shelby, right?"

Mike hasn't.

Jesse sighs. "It happened 'bout nine years ago. She wanted to bring awareness to our problem, interviewed and filmed some local addicts, and donated a crap load of money to the county to build affordable rehabs."

Mike scrunches his nose. Maddy's rehab was three hours away in Cincinnati.

"But... we haven't had any new rehabs in probably the last three or four years? So, where are they?"

"*PSSSH!* That's what I'd like to know! I don't see rehabs either, but I sure as shit see an ass ton of brand new, expensive cop cars! You do the math. Anyway, ain't it fucked how the 'epidemic' used to be a 'war on drugs' when cocaine, opioids, and heroin were in the ghettos and the inner-cities? Now that it's attackin' our upper-class, rich kids, it's suddenly an 'epidemic.' Screw 'em. Ghettos, suburbs—it's never been an epidemic; it's a *crisis.* In Middletown, they're tryin' to pass what's called a *Three Strikes*

Law. If you've overdosed three times, the paramedics are no longer required to give you Narcan—a drug that can reverse an overdose. Human life has become a game of baseball: three strikes and you're out. Messed up shit, man. Some people have fifty rock bottoms before they reach out for help."

Maddy overdosed five times, four times on heroin and once on a combination of Xanax, painkillers, and a full bottle of vodka.

Mike is thirteen.

Maddy's in the bathroom, chopping her long strands with shears, her hollow gaze staring nowhere and everywhere. She doesn't hear Mom shouting her name, nor the sound of the scissors skating along the tile or feel her fainting body hit the floor.

Mike carries her to Mom's car and buckles her in. His subteen mentality can't fathom the gravity of the situation as he stares stiffly at Maddy, also stiff.

Mom grabs his face. "Look at me." He does. "Go sweep the hair into a grocery bag. Hide it in your room. I'll throw it away on my way to work. For the love of God, Michael, do *not* tell your father. If he asks, I took Maddy to get her hair cut. If she needs to stay overnight, I'll take care of it, okay? Do you hear me?" She kisses his nodding forehead. "My brave, brave boy. I love you."

He loves her too.

He loves them both.

Maddy has her stomach pumped, and she'll be on a seventy-two-hour watch for the third time in the last two years.

Mom and Leon argue all night.

The Sinclair Family Levee *cracks* in half.

The hole is five and a half feet deep.

I'm evolving a voice.

Mike grits his teeth. *Horrifying* flashbacks: opening the door, seeing Maddy stooped on the bathroom floor, nearly dead, the screams from his throat sounding *nothing* like him. He hadn't known the paramedics revived Maddy with Narcan—he was just thankful to see proof of life in her blue eyes. If the *Three Strikes Law* was in existence at the time of her overdoses, he'd see her eyes only in photographs. She'd be underground and not in Florida, sober, volunteering her free time at a youth clinic for teenage addicts. She's made good of her fresh start—quit smoking weed and drinking, landed a decent-paying job, and rented an apartment with her friend and fellow waitress, Ryver Sutton.

"This parking lot had nine overdoses in the past month," says Jesse. "One victim was a mother with her two children in the back seat."

Death and I were with the "victims." I shook his hand with every demise: *stellar teamwork.*

"I know what you're thinkin': Why would a mother do that with her kids in the car? What a disgustin' piece of trash. She deserved to die."

"That's not what I'm thinking at all!"

"Y'really don't think that?" Jesse asks, his voice puny and eyebrows curved downward.

"No, Jess, I don't. Jesse... are you an addict?"

DING, DING, DING! Only took you seventeen chapters!

"When I was nine or ten, my anxiety was *extreme.* I had panic attacks at school, and the faculty had a meetin' with my 'rents, and—*wham!*—I'm seein' doctors and bein' pumped up with drugs. When puberty hit, the drugs must've altered my natural chemistry 'cause the anxiety worsened. I couldn't focus. I was depressed. I was still a straight-A student and involved in sports, but Ma was worried and sent me to another doctor who experimented with drugs on me to 'mask' my anxiety.

"I was thirteen when they put me on Xanax. It was too strong of a dose for someone my age, if ya ask me, but what did I know? I was just a kid. I couldn't take it durin' the day 'cause that shit knocked me out *cold.* You could punch me and... *nothin'.* I felt *nothin'.*

"One night 'round the time Daryl started dealin' and usin', he and his buddies were in the backyard havin' a bonfire. Ma was workin' a night shift, and I was 'bout ready to take my Xanax and go to sleep, but Daryl invited me to the party. You know how it is at that age. You wanna be cool and fit in. Daryl told me he had somethin' that would keep me awake, and I *hated* the Xanax blackouts. I didn't know what he was usin' at the time, and when I asked him, he said it was somethin' similar to a caffeine rush. Man, he was lyin' outta his ass. I took my first hit, and I ain't gonna go into detail 'bout what can happen to your dick when ya first try meth, so I'll just say there ain't anythin' in the world as euphoric as that first hit, and ya top it off with teenage hormones and ya got yourself an all-out jerk-off fest. My entire body was alive *and* numb, and I spent most of the night in my room by myself just givin' into my body's sexual needs. He wasn't wrong, though. I was awake for the entire night. I wasn't depressed no more. Every one of my senses was heightened. I was able to focus. My energy levels were *insane.* I was *unstoppable*. I smoked more with him in the mornin' and kept gettin' high everyday after that. One hit, and I was *done.*

"I spent hours at the skatepark 'cause I had all this pent-up energy, ya know? Since Daryl was dealin', we weren't ever low, sometimes gettin' batches at a time, and if we weren't meeting the quota, we'd sell shit 'round the house to repay the amount we took for ourselves.

"I ain't sure how I went from smokin' to slammin'. Daryl just happened to have needles, and we shot up together. Over time, it was gettin' difficult to find a vein. They were *fucked,* but smokin' or snortin' wasn't cuttin' it no more.

"Lookin' back on it, I realize I was tricked into tryin' meth. I ain't sayin' Daryl's fully to blame. I knew better. I knew repercussions came with tryin' any drug, but he was my brother. I trusted him. I dunno if he was tryin' to help me 'cause all the other prescription drugs were makin' me worse, not better. I didn't tell anyone—my ma, my friends, Gemma, they still don't know. They know 'bout my meth addiction, but not what started it."

"Why didn't you tell them? Your parents?"

"My *parents?* Dad was never 'round. As for Ma… there's somethin' 'bout her I haven't toldja. After her accident at the Mill, she was prescribed painkillers and got addicted. It doesn't take much. I read in an article that it can take three days to a week to become addicted to painkillers and that a small amount of drugs can alter the reward system in your brain, the uh… uh…" Jesse *snaps, snaps, snaps* his fingers… "Uh… *fuck,* what's it *called?*"

"Basal ganglia. It controls our ability to learn right from wrong."

He gleams at him. "I love your beautiful mind. So, when ya do drugs like opioids, meth, coke, or alcohol, dopamine is released, and it screws up the part of the brain that distinguishes risks from rewards. When you're withdrawin', the amount of dopamine decreases. The brain is so fuckin' hungry for that euphoria again, and when there ain't nothin' there to feed its food for learnin', it can lead to bad decision makin', like shootin' up, or stealin' from your 'rents or friends, or… or… noddin' out 'round your kid… gettin' your thirteen-year-old brother high on meth…."

"Jesse…"

"The doctors took her off the meds, and she was still in pain, and then the withdrawals kicked in. Daryl traded meth for money or painkillers, and once those became too costly and not strong enough…."

"Heroin."

"Heroin. All 'cause she got hurt at work. She'd never done a drug in her entire life. Took no time at all 'til she was hooked, and I lived with a tweaked-out brother and a strung-out mother for years. Our house was constantly littered with needles, cotton balls, and burnt spoons. It smelt of either chemicals or tar. I honestly dunno how she worked as much as she did while livin' that lifestyle. I dunno how she paid the rent or found the motivation to walk again.

"I'd go to Daryl's dealers' for dinner 'cause we never had food in the house. I'd sell my stuff to friends or kids in the neighborhood to afford new clothes and school supplies. I didn't dare tell Dad 'cause I was afraid he'd arrest Ma. And, like, yeah, my meth addiction started long before she got hooked on H, but I was thirteen and scared.

"Daryl and I got high and sold drugs together 'til I was almost sixteen. I'd stay up for days and days, sometimes a week, then sleep for days and days. I skipped school, and my friends cut me off; said they couldn't stand the monster I was. This one time, Jax pulled me out of the bathroom 'cause I stood in front of the mirror for *hours* pickin' at myself. Ma was never home, workin' her two or three jobs. Dad never saw us.

"When I was fifteen, Daryl shot me up with a dirty needle.

Stupid bastard. It started out as this massive red rash. Didn't think much of it. Then the veins 'round it began turnin' purple, then black, and next thing I know I got these damn little bubbles just poppin' outta my skin and they made this cracklin' noise if ya touched them. It was an infection I can't even describe. Smelled *rancid* like curdled fuckin' dairy creamer. I was always so tweaked that I didn't care. If I was in pain, I'd just get high.

"My homeroom teacher sent me to the nurse's office 'cause I kept leavin' to the bathroom to throw up, and I couldn't stop sweatin'. I was wearin' a hoodie and the nurse *still* smelled the infection and she drove me to the ER. They shot me up with morphine, which didn't do jack, and they was pokin' at the bubbles and last thing I remember before passin' out was this yellowish-green pus. Woke up in the hospital the next day with a bandage and a doctor tellin' me I was lucky he didn't have to amputate my arm. I didn't know the infection had gotten that bad.

"Then some lady came in and asked me a buncha questions like if I've ever attempted suicide or thought of it. She asked if I had an addiction to drugs other than meth. 'Course, the cat was outta the bag, and the 'rents sent me to a residential rehab. Daryl was arrested for possession and went away for 'bout three months. Dad pulled some strings with Children's Services 'cause if I was taken from Ma, I'd have to live with him and I'd be a nuisance. When Daryl was released, he came back to the house. Ma couldn't afford to kick him out.

"In group therapy, there were others who had stories similar to mine. It's messed up to think others went through it, too, but it was a relief to hear I wasn't alone, and eventually, I started talkin' to the other kids, which helped bring some closure."

"'Even in our solitude, we're never truly alone,'" Mike quotes Dr. Greene's "wisdom." "Is that when you got sober?"

"Nah, just detoxed. Don't know which was worse: detoxin' or the damn bubbles. Withdrawin' was hell. I was abusin' my Xanax so I could fall asleep after my meth benders, and I had a harder time detoxin' from the pills than from ice. I felt like I was on fire from vein to bone. I was pukin', sweatin', agitated, my anxiety and depression was off the charts, and I had a couple seizures. Benzos are no laughin' matter.

"Ma and Dad wouldn't let me outta rehab 'til the drugs were outta my system. I had to pass a series of tests and such, but... y'know, I lied to get free, and the counselors knew I was lyin'. One of them sold me cigarettes, for fucks sakes! And here's my opinion 'bout most hospitals and rehabs: I think they only care 'bout what happens to your body. They don't give a flyin' shit 'bout what happens in here." He touches Mike's temple. "The mental part of it? That's how you relapse. It's said it can take up to two years for the mental withdrawals to go away; sometimes a lifetime. Some say addiction can be maintained but not 'cured.'

Dunno how true it is. It's been a while, and I still struggle sometimes."

Mike scribbles a self-reminder to ask Maddy if she's over her mental withdrawals yet. I can assure him she isn't.

"When'd you finally stop?"

"On my seventeenth birthday when Ma became paralyzed. I couldn't take care of her if I was tweakin'. I was scared as fuck to go through withdraws again, but it wasn't as terrible as I thought it'd be. Just made me hungry 'cause the body loses its energetic fuel. I gained nearly ten pounds within two weeks, and my depression and anxiety came back full force, and damn, I won't lie, it was *exhaustin'* to stay sober. All the meth and heroin in the house... Guess my love for Ma was stronger than my love for crystal." Jesse twirls Mike's damp hair, the tresses crimping. "Wanna know why I'm tellin' ya this?"

"You know I'm gonna say yes," Mike replies, smiling.

Jesse's growing smile withers. "I don't wantcha to end up like me, Mike."

"Ain't nothing wrong with you."

"There's *a lot* wrong with me."

Mike rubs his thumb along the pulse in Jesse's wrist in place of his failing words because there are no waterproof idioms, phrases, or promises he can say.

I'm dizzy, too dizzy to punch Jesse, and Twitch is just listening, his head angled. *Don't you realize your kid is trying to save my kid?* I snap at him. *Do you* want *to die of starvation?*

"I get that you're experimentin'. I ain't gonna lecture ya, but you're so smart, Mike, and talented. Do you know how many addicts would kill to have whatcha have?"

"It's not like I'm rich or any—"

"I'm talkin' 'bout your art. Money, status, whatever, has *nothin'* to do with addiction. It can attack anyone, anywhere, anytime. You don't need drugs to escape from this... *wicked* world. Most junkies I know sit at home shootin' up and spend the rest of the day chasin' their next fix. They get high, go to sleep, wake up, and start all over the next day. It's a sick cycle. Most come from bad homes, abusive families, and others just have a hard time copin' with life. They're not bad people. They may do bad things, but even the godliest people are capable of doin' bad things. My point is, I'm sure if the junkies and tweaks I know had your skills, they wouldn't be addicts."

Is this why Dr. Greene pushed Mike into his art? Emotional release? Mental breaks? Or did it bypass straight into escapism?

Drawing, painting, pencil scratching paper, plain canvases birthed by colors—therapeutic? Sure. Escapism? Definitely. Do they give you the same rush as Oxy or weed? Drawing takes forrreverrr, Mike. Where's the instant gratification? And it's not like you're ever satisfied with your work. Jesse can't pick out the flaws, but you can. They're in every line. Every stroke. Flawed just like you.

Being with Jesse provides a rush stronger than anything else, and Mike knows to leave well enough alone. He won't allow himself to become an opioid addict, and he'll *never, ever, ever* touch heroin or meth.

Who says you can't have a bit of fun with the one you admire?

"Moderation," says Mike.

Moderation. Right on the nose.

"No such thing. You're too good for this lifestyle. And yes, Mike, it's a lifestyle. When ya start turnin' tricks to afford your next fix—"

"Turning tricks?"

"That's what I'm talkin' 'bout. Ya don't even know what that means. Sexual favors for drugs or money, and few people realize it happens right here in our *perfect*, midwestern, rural town."

He pauses to memorize the shapes and slenderness of Jesse's hands, needing to reassure himself that if he were to go senile, he'd be able to put his specific fingertip patterns to paper.

"Have you done it?"

Jesse grows rigid, hands and body, the artery in his wrist pulsating.

"Couple times. Does that... does that make me an awful person?"

"No."

"Gross?"

"Far from. What's the other reason you wanted to tell me this?"

Jesse bites down on his piercing. "God, I'm afraid you're gonna hate me."

"Jesse, look at me."

Jesse glances at the amatory gaze waiting for him and the

sturdy proclamation attached to it:

"I could never hate you. *Ever.*"

He releases an unbalanced breath. "After Ma died, I relapsed. When I came down, sick as hell, ashamed of myself, pissed at Daryl, pissed at the entire *fuckin'* world, my entire *fuckin'* life, I looked at that ice and… *needed* it; *needed* more. I spent three days tweaked to the max. Woke up on the fourth day, was walkin' to my dealers' house on Violet Street, passed Indigo, and saw ya sittin' outside."

Twitch plays out the storyboard of him and Jesse walking the neighborhood at night, Twitch frolicking triumphantly, rightfully fed and healthy.

Then, just as he said, Jesse saw Mike and stopped in the middle of the road.

Twitch sprang in front of him. *WHAT'RE YA DOIN', BRUH? LET'S GO! FEED ME! FORGET HIM!* He struck Jesse upside the head. *HE'S TRASH! FEED ME, FEED ME, FEED ME! METH! SWEET, DELICIOUS CRYSTAL, MAN! WHERE YA GOIN'?* He chased after Jesse. *YO! DUMBASS! VIOLET IS* THAT *WAY, YA DEADBEAT! FEED ME!*

Twitch nods after I stress to him, *we've got a major predicament on our hands.*

"I stood in the street for a minute, watchin' ya, and, *damn*, your light, Mike, it's… it's *unreal.* You're made of stardust, Mi Sinclair. Suddenly, I didn't wanna get high. I wanted to get to know you, talk to you, and thank you for helpin' me that night and for bein' brave. I couldn't do that if I was strung out or tweakin'. So, I headed back to my aunts to get your hoodie, bought your cigs at Langer's and the rest, as it's said, is history."

Maddy told him she saw a blue globe floating next to her during one of her withdrawals and swore it spread from wall to wall and ceiling to floor and transformed into an armor-plated angel bearing a shield and sword. Since that day, she's worn a silver pendant around her neck given to her by a sobriety companion.

"I now have two Michaels in my life: you and the archangel," she said.

Maddy clarified in a few words that Mike "saved her," and he believed it because she stuck with her sobriety after her "vision." Now Jesse is saying the same? Why? He hasn't a shield and sword to expel their demons. He's human. It's all he'll ever be.

"Not all saviors are saints," Maddy said. "Some are mere mortals fighting through life on this disastrous earth. But if you go outside at night and shut out the world, you can hear the angels sing and feel their arms around you. It's the safest you'll ever feel. You just gotta open up your soul."

Maddy's noble faith was handed down from Mom. Mike doesn't hold water to anything that isn't scientific and physical. Drawing allows him to typify what he's unable to see on a somatic plane, so why does he doubt his impact on Jesse? He's real. He's here. He can touch him, smell him, hear him, and yet...

"You would've been able to walk away with or without me."

"No, I don't think so. I dunno who you see when ya look at

me, but it ain't the Jesse I see."

"Who do you see?"

"I'm a shadow, Mikey. An empty, driftin' shadow. Faceless. Plain. Overseen. Emotionless."

"You're not a faceless shadow."

"If ya say so."

Mike buckles up and asks Jesse to take him home.

"Are ya mad at me?" Jesse asks while driving down the highway.

"No. I have an idea."

I have an idea of my own, I tell Twitch.

Sometimes we must work with our rivals if we want to win the war.

And I *never* lose.

EIGHTEEN
Neon, Neon

Mike hustles, collecting items from his untidy desk, and, arms full, he and Jesse sit on the bedroom floor, legs crossed and knees touching. Jesse chuckles at the sound of a battle cap unlatching and paint squirting. Twitch and I stay nearby, seething like a two-headed cobra.

"What're you doin'?"

Mike paints a stripe from Jesse's hairline to his nose and cupid's bow.

"Giving your shadow flesh."

Jesse, wide-eyed, stammers. "I... I..."

"Gotta be still." Mike borders his jawline in neon yellow. "You have a nice jaw."

"Th-thank you."

Mike vanishes into a trancelike state he finds himself in whenever he paints, only this time, he's brought a friend. Completing his face, he sets his brushes down, stands on his knees, and lifts Jesse's shirt.

"Uh... this okay?" Mike asks.

He raises his arms. "Yes."

Jesse tips his head back, the brush tickling his skin; the colors coating his throat and collarbone. Their gazes glint as Mike works the paint over his shoulders, arms, and wrists, the oxygen supply in the room depleting as he drags the brush across Jesse's chest, his nipple saluting beneath the hot pink pigment. Mike reasons it couldn't be cold—sections of his fleshy masterpiece beading like ice on a sunny window.

They don't move. They don't react.

"Y'alright?"

"Perfectly." Mike grins.

"You don't gotta keep goin' if you don't wanna."

Mike's fallen in lust with his Jesse-shaped opus. "I don't wanna stop. I just... um... I don't want to get paint in your... hair...." His *fingers* brush the lane of blonde ringlets flowing downstream on his torso.

Jesse nips his lip. "I don't mind."

Twitch and I smack our foreheads.

"I'm one lucky bastard."

Jesse smirks. "Ditto."

For the next hour, Jesse, his grip on Mike's knees, watches the artist complete his masterpiece. Mike takes a snapshot on his phone since there isn't a mirror in the room, his cheeks burning as Jesse smiles at the screen.

"Tidal waves."

"Should I have done something different?"

"Most badass, neon tidal wave I've ever seen. The foam's a nice touch. Looks like spray paint."

"Really?"

"Yes," Jesse ratifies. "Thank you, Mike. This is the coolest, most thoughtful thing anyone's ever done for me. Last time I told someone I felt like an empty shadow, I was told I was a selfish asshole who cares for nobody but himself."

"Gemma?"

"Mm-hm."

"We're all selfish by nature. We gotta be. As Layne Stanley once said, 'When everyone goes home, you're stuck with yourself.'" Mike recesses. "What's that look for?"

"How do you make sense of everythin'?"

Mike doesn't. If he excels in anything, it's cynically judging the world and voicing his thoughts in that sphere of time—a point of view which landed him in therapy. If it makes sense to Jesse or helps him, then who's Mike to contradict him?

As Mike and Jesse clean up the mess, I belt at Twitch—*Go! Now!*—and he races to disseminate his magical lingo.

Mike's summoned to the bed after he stores his supplies in the closet, confused by how Jesse went from being an anti-drug lecturer to *crunch, crunch crunch*ing six Oxy on the glass chessboard.

You're always the overthinker. He's preparing rails for you. He cares about you. He, like you, doesn't want to be alone. You think he's stunning, all painted up in your handiwork. Look at how he glows in the dark, his movements converting your tidal waves into currents.

There ya go, take the straw, snort it up.

Much better.

Look at that smile. He's smiling for you.

All because of you.

The plum horizon adapts into bright lavender and orange lateral crisscrosses while they talk, snort Oxy, and smoke cigarettes out the window, Mother Nature's hues unmatched against Jesse's neon-painted skin. The sun rises as they drift to sleep, the front door closing as Mom heads to morning mass.

I high-five Twitch. *Bravo, lad.*

NINETEEN
Fading Luminosity

Three weeks have passed, and you wouldn't find Mike without Jesse, or Jesse without Mike, not even after Jesse's hired at Wheelies, a skateboard shop five stores down from Indie Pages & Blueberry Beans Café. They spent their days in Jesse's apartment getting high, but since Mom wasn't comfortable with Jesse living alone in the worst part of town, they spent their nights sleeping in Mike's bedroom.

Mike knew Marie would come to see Jesse in the same awe and admiration he had for Jesse, and was thrilled to find his insights verified as he'd sloth in bed in the mornings and listen to Mom and Jesse discuss mechanics and physics over coffee.

He didn't, and still doesn't, understand a lick of their conversations. His brain isn't wired that way, but he's glad Jesse's is.

Raindrops, like hail, bounce off the roof. *Rain? Why today?* What *is* today? His eighteenth birthday. No more curfew. No more asking Mom or Jesse to buy his cigarettes. He's excited for Jesse's surprise present he's been dangling in front of him for days. Mom sings "Happy Birthday" while delivering his delicious birthday breakfast to him in bed.

He sits up to indulge in the crepes, bacon, sausage, and over-easy eggs and, doing so, comes the second unexpected inconvenience of the morning.

Mike feels sick, and he is, in a sense; his skin hot, his head like lead, and his sheets, clothes, and hair are sopping as if the rain gushed straight through the ceiling.

Withdrawals. Perfect. Jesse will be here shortly and fix you up good as new.

"You okay, sweets? You look peaked."

Mom will make him stay home if he doesn't eat, so he pushes past the sweats and vertigo, biting into his crepes, the sweet maple syrup fueling him for some ambiguous reason. He'd army crawl to the kitchen and down the entire bottle if he could.

"I'm great!"

"Good mornin', sweet Marie, Marie," Jesse cheeps and nicks a sausage link off Mike's plate. "Mornin', sunshine."

Mike smiles despite his broiling bones. Mom brings Jesse a breakfast platter and shuts the door on her way out.

Twitch and I pant in Jesse's ear.

Feed us, feed us, FEED US!

"Feel like shit?"

"Understatement," answers Mike.

Jesse places an Oxy on Mike's tongue.

"Happy birthday, Mi Sinclair."

They hug Mom, relieved the rain hasn't ruined Jesse's plans, and agree to meet her later for supper.

Wind and rain drizzle into the Honda from their cracked windows, releasing weed and cigarette smoke. An Oxy (triple dosed), food, a scalding shower, and Jesse: the supreme antidote. They sing and laugh, their hands grazing, and Mike reads the highway signs.

"Columbus?"

Jesse smirks his coy smirk. "The Columbus Museum of Fine Arts."

Mike jumps in his seat, exclaiming—"I can't believe you brought me here!"—on a continuous loop. "The tan building there with the triple-arched structure is the Sessions Mansion. The building to the right, the contemporary looking one,"—he signals to the blocky groundwork and window walls—"is the Margaret M. Walter wing built two years ago. She and her husband donated ten million dollars to the museum, so they made the wing."

Jesse's smile crumbles. "Dang. I'm bummed. I thought you'd never been here before?"

"Oh, shit! No, no, this is fantastic! I haven't been here before, I swear! Always wanted to go."

"Well, goddang, Square, you could give tours."

Yeah, yeah, Mike knows a buncha shit. Good for him. Can we please park so I can get out of this car?! Twitch spent the last hour and a half banging on the window and trying to get semi-drivers to honk their horns.

Twitch runs up the concrete stairs leading to the entrance and catapults into a gigantic, circular fountain with an outlandish bronze statue in the middle.

Behave! What on earth are you doing?

He looks at me, crazed.

Scuba diving for pennies? Groovy. It's gonna be a long day...

Sheltered from the rainfall and thunder, Mike beelines to the paintings in the lobby, and his ears perk at the kittenish female working the counter as Jesse purchases their passes. Jealousy is an unflattering color on anyone, yet he claims his stake, his thumb hooking Jesse's back pocket.

Jesse winks and hip-bumps him.

The monotone girl returns Jesse's debit card and tickets. "Enjoy."

Her VERSION OF ME boredom-checks her acrylic nails, her party dress three sizes too tight. She flips me off and tips back a bottle of Hpnotiq.

Coming into the first velvet-purple walled room, Jesse asks, "Why're ya laughin'?"

"That chick was *totally* hitting on you."

"Oh yeah? I mean, I *am* irresistible."

"You're so full of yourself."

"I bet ya wanna be full of me."

I'm laughing if you can believe it, and Mike's fever recurs, *not* from withdrawals.

Jesse casually leads them around the museum, their arms

linking every so often. Fingers drift fingers. Glances capture glances. We haven't seen Twitch and odds are he's trying on medieval armor or getting into some other mischief.

"What 'bout this one?" To test Mike's knowledge, Jesse creates a game where he covers the gold-plated information cards underneath random paintings. So far, he's gotten three out of five correct.

"*Carmela Bertagna* by John Singer Sargent. Oil on canvas, uh... I think 1878?"

Jesse uncovers the inscription about the young girl perpetuated in oil and realism, a scarlet ribbon capping her chestnut hair and a pink fur cloak swathing over one shoulder.

"Close. 1879."

"I still get a point."

Jesse chuckles. "Fine, but only 'cause it's your birthday. I won't be so givin' next time. She was young. His daughter?"

"His niece, I believe."

In the next room, he relishes Jesse in lieu of the Monet piece he's seen hundreds of times.

"I like this one," says Jesse. "Reminds me of your sugary impossibility."

"Which one?"

"The one where we take a Greyhound to California and live near the ocean. I imagine it'd be somethin' like this: clear, blue waters, pink skies, rollin' hills."

"Considering this painting is of the Cap d'Antibes in the

Mediterranean, you're not *too* far off."

"Smartass."

"We'll live somewhere like this someday."

He rests against Mike's shoulder. "I can hardly wait."

Jesse snaps a selfie of them in front of their futuristic landscape and allows Mike to type out the caption: *Took my Square to the C-bus Museum of Fine Arts for his birthday.*

Jesse posts it on his social media page and tags Mike to his own account Jesse set up for him.

"So glad you have a sense of humor. That's totally what I would've written."

"Yeah, I know. I'm used to being called a 'Square' by now."

PING!

Jesse unlocks his phone and doubles over.

"What?! What just happened?!"

He says in-between gasps, "Suzie Anderson still thinks you're hot as fuck!"

Mike grumbles.

They weave in and out of the rooms and document their day trip with photos and social media statuses. In the Egyptian exhibit, I spot Twitch doing the whole *Walk Like an Egyptian* dance. In the end, Mike's woozy from the Cassatt's, Renoir's, Homer's, Hartley's, and Demuth's.

An hour in, resting on a bench, they marvel at the artwork on the wall and its brush strokes and color-work.

"Your favorite."

"Le Brun has my heart."

"Who's the woman?"

"Varvara Turkestanova. Russian noblewoman."

"What's her story?"

"A tragic one. She had two lovers, Tsar Alexander, Emperor of Russia, and Prince Vladimir Golitsyn, and she wasn't sure which of the two was the father of her daughter. The scandal drove her to suicide. She poisoned herself."

"*Dang*. Ah, to be Royals."

For four hours in the museum, Mike lingered, looking at the paintings longer than most would, and Jesse let him. It's as if they spent the day touring an overseas continent, like France or Finland, while not leaving Ohio. They didn't have to worry about Daryl's WANTED posters spread over town, and the hallways had a flowery aroma as opposed to the cat-piss carpet smell in Jesse's apartment building.

Mike doesn't want to leave. Heading back to the car means reverting to the baneful ROY G BIV.

Sipping lattes at the black-iron table in the tiny, overpriced café, Jesse grins.

"Hey, Mikey?"

"Yeah?"

"Do ya feel that?"

"Feel what?"

"Somethin' is *definitely brewin'* between us."

Mike sighs. "Coffee is banned from here on out."

Jesse cackles. "Hey, Mikey?"

"No!"

“Are you Earl Grey? 'Cause you’re a *hot-tea!*’

Mike laughs. “Ridiculous.”

The ticket clerk gives them the stink eye on their way out and Mike, feeling gallant, tethers Jesse even closer.

“Thank you, Mea Harris.”

“Anythin' for you, Mi Sinclair.”

TWENTY

Chasing Sunshine

Mom and Jesse enlighten Mike's table talk at Logan's Steakhouse as he rambles and rambles and rambles on about all the outstanding paintings they saw. He talks fast and laughs garishly, faulting his offbeat personality on the rounds of Oxy he and Jesse did on their way to Richland.

Mike stabs his fork into his prime rib and baked potato, overwhelming remorse washing over him—he's high in front of Mom, her only son, a second Maddy, and she doesn't even notice! Why is he doing this to her?

Take another pill, and you'll forget all about the guilt.

"Are you not hungry?" she asks. "You've barely touched your baked potato."

He hasn't touched his baked potato because Mike *is* a baked potato.

"Still full from breakfast."

The fib would be credible if Twitch and Jesse weren't gorging themselves like two rats chowing down on nightly scraps a diner had thrown out. Mike will never grasp how Jesse can eat a three-course meal, intoxicated or not.

"Make a wish," he says in Mike's ear, nodding at the chocolate cupcake brought to the table by the waitstaff.

Mom's eyes make intervals from Mike to Jesse.

Staring at Jesse, he replies, "I've got all I'll ever need," and blows out the single-candle flame.

To Jesse's dismay, Mom wins their dispute over who's paying the tab.

Fine and dandy! More money for drugs!

Stalled at a four-way on the way to his apartment, Jesse asks if he had a good birthday.

"The best! Everything you did today, you did—"

"Didn't have to. I wanted to. I had fun too." He squeezes Mike's hand. "I have a favor to ask, and I hate to ask 'cause it's your day and all...."

"What is it?"

"The landlord at the old house is bein' a real prick 'bout gettin' my stuff outta there. Y'mind goin' with me tonight? I can call the dudes and make a party out of it."

"You don't even need to ask. I'll text Mom and let her know I'll be staying with you tonight."

Mom responds, "Okay, sweets," to his SMS, and he and Jesse walk upstairs past the cat urine and flickering lights.

On the living room floor, his feet laying on Jesse's crossed ankles, Mike drags on a joint and types back to the "Happy Birthday, little bro!" message from Maddy.

(Mike): Thanks, sis! Had a great day. My friend Jesse took

me to the Columbus Museum of Fine Arts!

(Maddy): That's great! He must like you a lot.

Working on crushing their pills, Jesse hums to himself, not noticing he's being looked at and talked about.

(Mike): You think so?

(Maddy): He wouldn't have done that for you if he didn't.

"Who's got ya cheesin' over there?"

Mike sets his phone screen-down. "My sister."

"Triple-A?!"

"No. The one in Florida."

"Oh. Maddy."

Mike's cigarette falls from his mouth, his lighter skidding across the table. He hasn't spoken her name *once* in over two months.

"Why didn't you tell me?" Mike asks.

"Why didn't *you* tell me?"

"Tell you what?" he snaps. "That my sister's a junkie?"

"And my brother's a junkie. What's the problem?"

"How long have you known?"

"A girl stayed with us for a month or two when I was eleven. She said her dad kicked her out. Beautiful girl. Ya kinda look like her 'cept for the eyes; never seen crazy blues like that in my life. She was nice to me and taught me how to play rummy. Daryl had the biggest crush on her."

What in blazes was she thinking, shacking up with someone with whom she had nothing positive to say? Maddy isn't here, and his hostility towards Jesse is unfairly misdirected.

"You know he grabbed her tits in the fifth grade, and someone told the teachers she was letting him? The teacher called her a slut for it. And you must've gone to school at Cougar if Daryl did. I never saw you. I'd remember someone like you."

"I did for a very short time. I kept gettin' into fights with the other students and was 'unruly', as the teachers said, so the 'rents sent me to a boardin' school in Tennessee halfway through kindergarten. They did the same to Daryl when he was my age. I don't think they knew how to raise us. They was young. But I was there 'til I was twelve and spent the summers in Ohio. That's why I talk a bit strangely. Twang and midwest. People always point it out, but I spent most of my youth with southerners and the other half here."

Mike smiles. "You're one-of-a-kind."

"I suppose I am," he says, smiling back. "When I came back to Ohio permanently, Ma was already on Indigo, so I ended up goin' to the Richland schools. Sorry 'bout Daryl. He's a dick. Mike, I've known for some time now 'bout Maddy. Her pictures are all over your home. It makes sense why you feel so familiar to me. I dunno why ya didn't just tell me."

Mike's attention strays to the blue lines on the glass chessboard.

"I think now would be the time to talk, don'tcha?" Jesse says, kneading Mike's shins.

They do a line.

"Mikey, it's okay."

It spews out like word-vomit. Better than *actual* vomit.

"Do you only hang out with me because you like her?"

"What does that have to do with us? Dang, dude, that came outta left field."

Mike pinches the bridge of his nose, exhales, lights a cigarette, and snorts another rail.

"She disappeared for so long that year. We never knew where she went. She never told us. God, man, the world can't be *this* small, can it?"

"Addicts find each other. If it helps, she was in good hands. Ma loved her. They watched Soaps and did crosswords."

'Probably shot up together, too,' he thinks with asperity.

Eighteen years on and he's still dusting off his sister's artifacts.

"What else is botherin' ya?"

"Did she do meth?"

"Dunno, honestly. If she did, it was never 'round me. I saw track marks on her arms, but she didn't act like a tweak. She talked *a lot,* though. I thought *I* was loud."

"Ha, yeah, give her a bottle of strawberry wine and a pack of Camel Golds, and she'll go on for hours about how the universe, people, and animals are all part of the same Tree of Life."

"Sounds like her."

"She's sober now. Has been for over two years."

"I've heard."

"I can't get anything past you." Mike stubs out his cigarette and snorts a line.

"Ya know, I've met a lot of junkies, more than I care to admit, and some—not all—were selfish assholes. Your sister wasn't one of them. She was soft. Like, it's as if she was drownin' while everyone 'round her breathed."

"Am I like that?"

"Sometimes. I didn't understand why at first, but now I do. I can relate to havin' an addicted siblin'. Growin' up 'round it ain't no cakewalk."

"I remember being in school and checking my phone every five minutes. My heart went into my ass whenever Mom texted me, or I'd miss a call; my first thought always being—"

"She's dead."

"Right. Every day was a struggle. Hours were weeks. I'd sneak down to her room and put my ear to the door just to hear her breathe to know she was still alive. I've written her eulogy in my head. Is that morbid?"

"Naw, I did the same with Daryl, the eulogy thing. Never thought I'd be writin' Ma's instead. Ugh, man. *Life*."

Two souls cloaked in darkness hold each other tenaciously, one striving diligently like the other to rekindle the tiniest spark.

"Y'think it'll always be this way?" asks Jesse. "I'm so tired of bein' sad all the damn time. It's like I keep waitin' on a light that's never gonna come."

"It's gotta get better. It *will* get better."

"How do ya know?"

"I don't. I just hope."

"Does Maddy know 'bout me?"

"Yes."

"By name?"

"Mm-hm."

"Last name?"

"Does it matter? You think she'll tell me to stay away from you?"

"I would if I were her."

"Luckily, you're not her. It'd be like your family telling you to keep away from me because of her. Nobody can keep me from you. No worries."

"Sure. No worries."

Finishing the Oxy, they prepare for the forthcoming night.

And what a night it'll be.

TWENTY-ONE

Fluorescent Whispers

At the Harris' property, the rain lets up on the ominous house as Mike's thumb eases the rapid pulse on Jesse's wrist while blood, cries, bullets, and the storm haunt Mike from that terrible night. His protectiveness for Jesse in July has increased tenfold, and he's left to smoke his cigarette at the end of the driveway when Mike volunteers to go first, Twitch whimpering behind us.

Finding the light switch, Mike's struck by the harsh bleach and paint smells, the blood and innards cleaned off the walls and carpeting, and he shuts the empty kitchen drawers and cabinets.

Jesse hangs back in the doorway and peeks at the couch in the living room.

"It used to be over there," he tells Mike, "on the other wall next to the kitchen. Aunt Iris wasn't exaggeratin' when she said they cleared the place."

"Where is everything?"

"Some at Iris's, some in storage. We donated just about everythin', though."

Headlights appear in the driveway, and two cars contain Jax,

Eli, Jazz, Toby, Brad, and (sumbitch) Gemma. They, along with their VERSIONS OF ME, talk and shout cluttered rubbish:

Sob.

Hmph!

Eighty-six, eighty-seven...

Rock N' Roll!

Nose in the air.

Lounging on a shoulder.

Drip... drip... drip... *FUCK!*

Gemma shoves between Mike and Jesse, her hips swaying and a thong outline visible under her miniskirt.

"Yo, Gems, thought you were here to help me pack?"

"I am."

"Then why're you dressed for the street corner?"

Mike resists laughing.

Gemma's neck miraculously stays intact as she shoots over her shoulder, "You used to like it!"

"Hey-o!" Jazz interferes. "Quit it! We're here for Jesse. Anyone have speakers for the music?"

"My room," Jesse answers.

Jazz, Goblin, Eli, and Rick vanish down the same hallway Twitch ran off to earlier and Toby slaps Mike's back with more force than necessary.

"Heard it's your big eighteen! I was planning on getting you a little treat, but money's tight."

"Whadja have in mind?" asks Jesse.

"White Girl," Toby says.

Twitch's feet patter up the hall, and in an instantaneous action, he skydives and dangles on Toby like he's a knotted rope hanging from a gymnasium beam. He growls as Conrad attempts to yank him off, and, tight-lipped, Conrad backs away, straightening out his Armani suit.

"Seriously?" pouts Jesse. "Man, whatta bummer."

Don't, Mike! Don't! Don't ask! Just roll with it!

"Da hell is 'White Girl?'"

Cue the laughter.

Have I taught you NOTHING? Stupid Square!

"You truly are from the burbs, aren't you? OW!" Toby rubs his punched bicep. "Damn, chill, Jess! I'm messin' with him!" He says to Mike, "Cocaine."

Twitch becomes a scarf around Toby's head, his coyote-howl uproarious.

"Why's it called 'White Girl?'"

"Beats me. It's difficult to find lately. My one dude scored a solid batch."

"Screw it. I got Oxy."

Me and Twitch salute Jesse the double-bird.

"It's not nearly on par with coke, and you know it. It's your favorite!"

"I just wanna get outta this damn house. Don't see the point wastin' my time chasin' after a dealer."

Twitch looks like he wants to shove Jesse's head into a deep fryer.

"He's on speed dial, bro. Anyone got funds?"

Mike stares at his Converse.

I'm in his ear.

Someone's gotta shut Twitch up.

Someone's gotta feed us.

We're *starving.*

Don't forget everything Jesse's given you: lack of judgment, money spent on your fixes and birthday, the clothing you borrow so you're not strutting around the ROY G BIV like an Old Navy representative. It's your turn.

Picture it: he might kiss you.

"Drop it, Tob—"

"I have money."

Atta boy!

Twitch hugs Mike's feet. Baby cries. Victoria and Gemma scour. Conrad waits patiently for the sealing deal.

Mike pays Toby and Jax three fifty-dollar bills Mom deposited into his birthday card, an amount he's certain took her months to save, and he's going to blow it on… *blow.*

The Son of the Year award goes to? *Not* Michael Sinclair.

"I can't take this from you."

"You'd take it from anyone else here."

Toby stuffs the bills in his pocket and gives Mike seven Oxy 30s stored in his left shoe.

"This is way above equal value," Mike says.

"No sweat. Happy birthday. Interested in coming along for the ride?"

"I don't do drug runs."

"Jess?"

"Gotta pack."

"A'ight. Let's roll, Jax."

Mike's awestruck, his toes leaving the floor, and Jesse spins him, his labret piercing making contact with his cheek.

Setting him back onto his feet, Jesse says, "You're spectacular, Square," and heads off to his room.

See? I make dreams come true.

Victoria and Gemma stride to Mike, their bony shoulders and chins raised. Baby, sitting near the unplugged refrigerator, wails.

"Golden Boy here to save the day."

Mike stops breathing, not because he's afraid of her but afraid she'll topple and shatter like tempered glass if he does.

Hmph!

Suck it, Vicki!

"The hell's your deal?"

She scans his face. "I don't like you."

"The feeling's mutual."

"That's not all we have in common."

Blood surges into his eardrums. "What're you talking about?"

"Don't play dumb."

"Gems! Get in here and help!" Jazz calls from the hall.

She folds her arms and swivels her hip to the side. It doesn't require much to send Mike into a myopic white rage, his fists compressed.

"We can be friends if you keep in mind *one* important thing, Mikey."

Friends? He'd rather play fetch with Leon, and that's saying a lot.

He asks anyhow, "And what's that?"

"Gemma! Let's go!" Jazz repeats.

They launch into silent warfare: chins to chests and eyebrows pinched.

Both girls snarl. "I *always* win."

Mike sneers, his comeback too daunting to be *Square Sinclair.*

"Game on."

Gemma appears as if she stepped into a grenade.

So proud of you! I cheer as we make our way to take part in the loud music and packing. Jazz waits outside the bedroom and smiles. Goblin and me fist-bump.

"Mi Sinclair." Jesse tracks his nose up Mike's neck and ear. "You smell nice. Ya good?"

"Never better, Mea Harris."

Gemma's and Victoria's glares burn in their direction.

What was it Maddy once told him?

"With every new friend comes a new enemy."

Stone the crows, she was right.

And Mike just found his.

TWENTY-TWO
Straining Sparks

Mike canvasses the surroundings and packages, tapes, and stores his VIP access into Jesse's private reservations—a life prior to Michael Sinclair—in his mental storage unit.

He thought their rooms would represent their diametrical personalities but was surprised to find they didn't differ all that much. A wooden desk close to the window is as deserted as the twin-sized bed (Mike abhors how Gemma titles it like she's Empress of Jesse Harris' room).

His belongings are stowed and arranged in suitable locations, the overall ambiance zen, notwithstanding the in-your-face knowledge of the persistent skeletons. It's no longer a secure room tucked inside a secure house, just as the First Avenue location no longer offers the safety it used to, although Mike spent his youth there.

Childhoods. Mike's wasn't ideal by any means, yet he's homesick for the simpler days when the most tremendous letdown meant the nasty weather kept him indoors. Did Jesse miss his childhood just as much?

Mike thinks it would be nice to freeze-frame our childhoods.

Life was easier in our infantile illiteracy, twined and netted with magical harmonies, and we didn't fear the ambushing family skeletons. On the contrary, we invited them to a game of ring-around-the-rosy.

One by one, we all fall down.

As teens, once the ashes have settled, we devise ways to dismember those bones, and that's how Mike and Jesse found themselves here, on the ground, distracting their family skeletons with cigarettes and conversations, unaware that the skeletons had the upper hand; they had closure.

Herein lies the real question: will Mike and Jesse ever get theirs?

Ever heard the trite, "cocaine's a helluva drug!"? By the night's end, Mike will attest: yes, yes, it is.

Jazz and Eli toss items from the desk drawers into totes and boxes. Brad rolls and secures posters with rubber bands. Mike and Jesse fold clothes. Gemma? She swigs from a flask and reads through magazines.

And then there's hyperactive-banshee-screeching Twitch. He's twice as jittery and howling twice as loudly, and he hasn't done a single line of cocaine yet.

Yay, me.

Mike wraps his lips around Jesse's cocaine-tipped finger, his amber, dilated pupils transmitting an expression difficult to understand since Mike's never encountered desire or longing, and the look passes by like an arrow trying to spear shatterproof glass.

"How is it?" Jesse asks, sucking on the *same finger* he had in Mike's mouth.

You two vulgar vultures make me *want to vomit.*

"The cocaine?" asks Mike, his ears pinkish.

"Er… yeah."

All things holy, please don't say, 'not as sweet as your skin.'

"Bitter."

Thank you.

"Woah, my tongue is numb."

"Toby was right," says Jesse and licks the powder off his teeth. "This is a *solid* batch. Ready for a bump?"

I've been patient for eighteen years. Stop flirting and let's GO!

"You first."

"Nuh-uh, birthday boy."

"If you insist."

Shit stockings! You mean I don't have to talk you into it? Who are you, and what have you done with goody-goody Michael? I'm beyond thrilled with the beast you've become!

Gemma and Victoria hawk in on him. "Doing that shit ain't gonna make you cool."

Mike snorts his line.

"You're gonna be a useless junkie like everyone else on this street."

"And what're you on right now, Gems? Xanax? Morphine? Molly?"

"Cram it, Jesse! You'd know I haven't touched that junk in months if you'd talk to me instead of using me for a good lay."

"Vodka counts." He points to her flask. "And when did I ever say it was 'good?' Mediocre at best."

Mine and Twitch's humoristic cries override Baby's sobs. Victoria, too, breaks into tears, begging Gemma to *stop drinking her calories.* Mike completes his line with incredible speed (*HALLELUJAH!*) and sits on his heels, gagging.

"Just wait it out," Jesse says to him.

"Can't be that bad. You get off every time. You can't avoid me forever," Gemma continues.

Jesse, a straw up his nostril, says, "A case of crabs is easier to avoid than you."

I can't breathe, my cheeks sore, and Twitch hugs his tummy.

"Why're you even here? This ain't a hang-out. Get the hell out if ya ain't gonna help." Jesse submerges to snort.

Mmmm, plastic grating glass: the anthem of our lives.

"You only want me to leave because you have *him* now."

"Ya mean *him?*" Jesse kisses Mike on the cheek for the second time, not that he's keeping score. "He's pretty great."

Mike glows.

Gemma flings the magazine to the floor.

"How're ya feelin' now?" Jesse asks him.

Cocaine isn't as gritty as Oxy, the drip smooth, the sudden need to vomit acute. As Jesse loosens the kinks in his neck muscles, Mike's never been more content. *Ever.* He isn't perturbed by Gemma's murderous, tapered vexation, and I'm not perturbed by Twitch kicking off the walls.

"*Swell,* as the squares would say," answers Mike.

Jesse, laughing, places his forehead on Mike's. "Goddang, you're perfect."

"Imperfectly so. Can't feel my throat. Or my teeth. That normal?"

"I don't think it's normal to feel your teeth in general. If ya have trouble swallowin', I'll getcha some water. Other than that, ya good?"

"Heart's racing, but I can't feel much else."

"The high won't last long. We'll do more when you're ready. Jax! Tobs! You're up!"

"YES!" Jax ambles to the bed, he and Scotty rubbing their hands.

They provide Jax and Toby access to the chessboard, and Mike wonders what purpose cocaine offers if he can't feel Jesse's touch as he plucks the Oxy from Mike's hand.

You're killing me, Smalls! You've spent years searching for ways not to feel!

"We shouldn't dry-swallow these," says Jesse. "And you're sniffin' like… like a coke fiend. Follow me."

Jesse unscrews a bottle of lukewarm Gatorade in the kitchen, the flavor tasteless, and fills water into the orange cap.

"Snort it. Gonna feel strange, but it'll unclog your sinuses."

"Are you asking me to… *snort* water?"

"Trust me, it works. Jussa drop."

Jesse's correct, and the high's still active, if not more active, now that he can properly breathe.

The dank night and their clammy skin vigorously grapple

outside. Jesse takes off his shirt and uses it to dab Mike's brow, their bashful glances flitting.

Mike drags on his Camel Gold. "Usually, we're on my porch looking at your house, and now we're on your porch looking at mine."

"That shit's hittin' ya *hard*."

"Naw, I feel great. Like a numb, floating square."

"You're hysterical when you're high."

"Only when I'm high?"

"You're *especially* hysterical when you're high." Cigarette crumbs land at his feet. "You were so uptight when we first met. Now you're all relaxed. And don't gimme that look! Didja ever think you'd be sneakin' out of windows to get high in abandoned mansions?"

"No. I was the outcast in the sandbox. Leon ran the house like a dictatorship, so it's not like I had much of a say."

"Now's your time for freedom." Jesse swings their interlocked hands and asks excitedly, "Ready for more?"

"Hell yes, Jess! Ha! See what I did there?"

"I saw, Shakespeare." Jesse says, sniggering. "We should finish this up and go to my apartment."

"*Dexter* and chill?" Mike inquires suggestively.

"Er... if that's whatcha really want."

"I just made you blush." He butts his forehead into Jesse's shoulder.

He mumbles, "Shut up, yo," smiling.

Midnight strikes, Jesse's room fitted into boxes piled next to the front door, and there's two blunts and a joint rotating in the circle formed in the middle of the living room.

Eli dials down the music. It's not as if the neighbors would report them, but they're teenagers possessing illegal narcotics, weed, and alcohol. We know Mike wouldn't survive in prison.

Mike lolls his head against Jesse's. "I'm so glad we're staying at your place, because I *cannot* go home this way."

"Yo, ya know you're talkin' like, *really, really* slow?"

Mike laughs, knowing he sounds just like Charlie Brown's parents. He's done an offensive quantity of cocaine (his words), and it's a miracle he's still vigilant.

"I need to sleep."

"Come with me to the room. You need another bump. Just gotta even out the weed."

Gemma obstructs the bedroom entryway. "Can we talk, Jess? *Alone?*"

Mike re-enters the family room, and within minutes, Gemma's squealing at Jesse like a pig on the way to the slaughter house.

"You're the most heartless lowlife I've ever met!"

"Back off! Ya really thought I'd want to do *that* in *this house?*"

"I've done *everything* for you and you treat me like a piece of meat!"

Victoria rolls her eyes at Baby weeping heavenwards.

"Ya bring it on yourself, girl. I've told ya we're done *more* than once."

"Yet you'll still screw me!"

"Pussy's pussy. S'long as it's wet, I don't care whose it is."

The crew's bombing laughter closes the lid on the argument, and Gemma zeros in on Mike as if *he* left her high and dry.

"Is this funny to you, Golden Boy?"

Jesse chortles.

"Just wait. You ain't special. Once he's done using you, we'll see who's laughing because that's what Jesse is: a user. He's always been and always will be a user!"

"Shut your trap, Gemma." Jesse doesn't sound miffed.

Who cares? You're a user too, Mike.

"You're a piece of shit!" she shrieks. "I don't even know why I bother with you!"

"Me either."

"You care about nobody but yourself!"

"Correct-o."

Eli hisses. "Will you two knock it off? You're gonna wake the entire street, and we're *fucked* if the cops show."

"Someone's gotta get fucked tonight because Gemma sure ain't gonna!" Toby says, and we recoil when Gemma slugs him in the jaw.

"OUT!" Jesse demands.

The humor curbs, her spit-wad landing between Jesse's eyes, and, having never seen Jesse angry, Mike's paralyzed and worried about how he'll respond to such disrespect.

He tactfully wipes off the spit and grabs Mike gently by the elbow. "Let's go home, Mikey."

Gemma's Ghostface is so unerring that Mike nearly tells her his favorite scary movie is *Nightmare on Elm Street.*

"Lock up for me, wouldja, buddy?" Jesse says, and Eli catches the house key.

"This ain't over, Jesse Harris!" yells Gemma. "Have fun with your freak!"

"He's better at suckin' dick than you'll *ever* be!"

"BURN IN HELL!"

Tears flowing, Twitch and I scamper into the backseat of the Honda. I haven't laughed this much in decades!

"Y'mind goin' to hell, Mi Sinclair?"

"Only if we take the scenic route."

"You're a man after my own heart."

Mike shines.

That makes two of them.

TWENTY-THREE

Symphonies of Light

Snorting Xanax to come down, they lay on the sofa, heads to toes, as *Dexter* plays on the TV. Twitch is balled up like a kitten below the window, snoring. Shocking. Cocaine must wear him out. I rest by the couch, feeling bleary as well.

"Can you answer something for me?" asks Mike.

Jesse peers at him.

"And be honest with me."

"A'ight."

"You hooked up with Gemma the night before the funeral, didn't you?"

"Yes, Mike, I did."

"So, why didn't you hook up with her tonight?"

He doesn't respond.

"Jesse?"

"Uh... well... There's several reasons. She treats the guys like scum and acts like she has some sort of title over me 'cause she's known me the longest, 'cept for Jax. I've known him since I was eleven. She treated Jazz like shit 'cause she thought she was after my dick when she was after Eli's. It's all a mess."

Mike picks at his fingernails, his tongue tussling to ask a question attaining an answer which might, inevitably, change everything.

"Just tell me."

"Tell ya what?"

"You know what."

Jesse wavers, then says, "Ya wanna know if you're the reason? How wouldja feel if it was?"

"Like I'm a barging inconvenience."

"You ain't an inconvenience, Mikey. We were finished long ago."

"Then why keep going back?"

"She's familiar. It's nice to be loved. Even nicer to be wanted."

We want you! Your drugs! Your hookups!

Mike wants more than that.

"Mikey... I guess... I guess I didn't wanna hurt ya."

"What makes you think fucking Gemma would hurt me?"

His posture disintegrates like a flakey croissant. "You tell me."

Don't lose him! We need him! Speak up!

"I just want you to be happy."

What a crummy confession!

Will you shut the fuck up already?!

Oh. **Oh.**

You can hear me?

Man, louder than a bell whistle! I'll handle this. I don't need your input.

Riiiiiii—

Stop it!

—iiiight.

"You make me happy," Jesse's soft reply is as spine-tingling as his fingernails trickling lightly up and down Mike's foot and ankle.

Jeepers! He means it. If you weren't manipulating him for validation, you could have something remarkable here.

What the hell do you know?

Michael, you're simply too unsuited for a committed relationship, and you'll shatter him if you give him what he truly *wants. You'll be thrown to the gully with the rest of the trash where you justifiably belong and isolated from the rest of the group because they'll opt for Jesse above you. You can't survive without Jesse or me, so pick your poison.*

Piss. Off.

Fine. Lose him. No skin off my teeth.

"Mikey, you're far away. Y'alright?"

"Just tired. The Xanax is kicking in."

"Same. I'll see you in the AM."

"G'night, Jesse."

"Sweet dreams, Mi Sinclair."

Your aching heart is an illusion. Don't let his dejected sigh cut you down. You made the right decision.

But I lov—

You love me and only me! I'm your only friend now, and I'll never *abandon you.*

You're right.

He *hears* me.

One step closer…

I'm one step closer.

TWENTY-FOUR

Light & Shelter

Mike's been taught to believe people don't get depressed for no reason.

What triggered it?

Did someone say something?

Did something happen?

Is it the gloomy weather?

What if reasoning isn't a factor? What if it *just is?* The saddened, fated darkness which prolongs no matter how marvelous life is.

Let's sack his most recent session with Dr. Greene. Mike couldn't care less about that brainless doctor. What had they done to have him categorize his and Jesse's relationship as an "unhealthy codependency"? Jesse isn't unhealthy. *Unhealthy* is the body's spent energy after wasting it on foiling from splitting open your chest to free the unexplainable desolation rotting away inside. *Unhealthy* is calling off work to sulk in bed for two days straight. *Unhealthy* is locking yourself into the fetal position, your hands muffling your ears to shut off the noises inside your head.

He might find some solace if he were to rip his flesh off his bones.

Shadows aren't brought on by triggers. Not always. It's not as if he lays down at night and thinks: *tomorrow, I'm going to wake up, not leave my bed, and wallow in self-misery and try not to kill myself! Yeah, that sounds fun!*

We're a package deal, **Mental Illness** and myself. By and large, you can't have one without the other, and we're misinterpreted; unforeseen. Just as Mike doesn't plan his episodes, addicts don't plan their addictions. Nobody *decides* it. I'm a devil you can't shake off. You won't see me coming, as Mike won't see his shadow coming for him, waiting for an endurable moment when he's content and untouchable. Then, we'll pull you back in by sleight of hand as if we've never left because we never truly did.

I remain close to him as he drifts off and awakens, the plain ceiling amplifying his even more emptier insides. He falls asleep and wakes up again, over and over, the sequence airtight. How long has it been since he's seen sunlight? What time is it? Lunch? Dinner? In-between? Mom occasionally checks on him and, as any devoted mother would, she worries about the devoid stare she isn't unaccustomed to. She reminds him she loves him and gives him space.

He gets up to use the restroom, a chore in and of itself, his head like concrete feeling seven hundred pounds overweight, and collapses back into bed.

The phone's been vibrating for hours, yet he hasn't got the drive to reach for it, much less communicate.

He scrolls through the messages from Jesse, asking if he's okay or wants to hang out or if he's mad at him. They haven't talked much since the Gemma situation.

Trigger?

Maybe.

BUZZ!

(Jesse): Come to your window. I know you're home. I hear music.

Jesse can't see him like... like *this!* His pajamas are wrinkled, his hair an untidy, knotty clump, and he hasn't showered or brushed his teeth.

I bet he's got the good stuff.

Pretty sure the "good stuff" is the reason I'm—

You are who you are. The drugs help aid you into forgetting Leon's your father or how it felt when Maddy overdosed. They help you suppress your... feelings *for Jesse. It's all one big ass lie. It's all in your head.* Literally.

Mike stumbles to the window and lifts the screen, almost slamming it shut on Jesse's down-turned smile. He'd give anything to cower in his blankets and hibernate the darkness away.

Sleep isn't the solution. Ask if he has Oxy. Ask. ASK!

He just got here! Rude much?

Why even come by if he doesn't have them?

He's more than drugs.

Nifty, but you must admit, they're a perk.

Mike braces himself for the things he's customarily told

during an episode:

What's wrong?

Just remember, every day's a blessing.

What do you have to be sad about?

"Hey, Mi Sinclair, I apologize for the intrusion, but, y'know, I was 'round these parts, so I figured I'd stop by and say hi."

He smiles the first genuine smile he's had in days. "Aren't you always 'round these parts?"

"Y'caught me. I just missed your handsome face."

Kill me.

Hush!

ASK!

"I took one of them Sortin' Hat tests on a Harry Potter website. Curious to know which house I was sorted into? Slytherin."

"And that's important because?"

"May I *slither in*to your room?"

Laughter spurts out of their tightened mouths.

"You're so lame."

"You love me." Jesse shuts the screen and draws Mike close to him, his voice dueting with his meek gaze. "Don't hate me for askin' but—"

"Then don't. Don't ask if I'm okay or need anything. I'm not mad at you. Why would I be? I'm just… having a day."

"C'mere, Mi Sinclair." Jesse's embrace supplies eternal lucidity, his breath on Mike's neck warmer than dispensed air.

I'm interrupting this scene to inform you Twitch is sprinting in the backyard. Eh, at least he's not *inside.*

As much as I'd like to describe how these two in-denial lovebirds are swaying to the music, I can't, and won't, be silent.

We get it. He cares for you. I bet the pills are in his pocket. Ask him. Ask him!

Stop badgering me!

Never! Ask! Ask! Ask! We need it!

"I'm sorry I've been ignoring you. I..."

"Shhh, it's alright, you don't gotta explain. Is it okay that I'm here? Should I go?"

He hugs Jesse breathlessly. "God, don't go."

"I'll stay for as long as you need me to."

"Forever."

"I don't think that'll be long enough."

Mike pulls him further in and snuggles into his chest and Jesse, humming a song, gently untangles his ebony curls.

Ask him!

Jesse's skin rises to an array of fleshy bubbles from Mike's fingertips as they tenderly map out shapes on his tailbone beneath his hoodie.

You're deceiving him. Remember when Leon referred to you as a "manic psycho"? You weren't troubled by the insult because it was true. Jesse won't understand if you tell him you're depressed, but if you tell him you're having withdrawals, he'll understand and *provide the remedy.*

It's obvious I'm depressed.

He's assuming. What's worse: fessing to your depression or asking for a fix? It's the drugs, not misery, that bond you.

I don't want to lose him, but I don't want to lie to him either.

It's one or the other, son.

"Mike, you're shakin', man." He taps his finger under his chin, their eyes meeting in the candlelight. "You need Oxy? You can tell me. I brought 'em."

Go with it.

I should tell him.

Not tonight. Maybe never.

"I think I do."

"I'll set up our stuff and we can watch *Dexter.* Can I turn the light on?"

Mike plugs the lamp in, finding himself sloppy adjacent to Jesse's white Vans t-shirt, black shorts, and skater shoes.

Jesse uses Maddy's mortar and pestle, the Oxy *crunch, crunch, crunch*ing.

"Hey, Mikey?"

Mike's mouth twitches. "What one-liner do you have for me today?"

"If you were coffee grounds, you'd be espresso 'cause you're *so fine.*"

"You have a never-ending supply of these, don't you?"

"It makes ya laugh and do that thing where ya roll your eyes like: *dang, you're stupid, Jesse.*"

They take turns bumping, and Jesse sets the board aside and tosses Mike's legs onto his lap.

"Wanna hear a funny story?" Jesse asks.

Mike tucks into the pillows, enjoying the muscular hands on his calves.

"When I was five or six, our family lived on Hammock Drive. Heard of it?"

"Mm-hm, by Lake Charles."

"It wasn't as ritzy as the Golden burbs, but we had a decent backyard, garage, pool, y'know, the works. Ma and Dad were outta town, and me and Daryl had a babysitter. Can't remember her name now. Her boyfriend came over so they could fool 'round, and she let us play outside so we wouldn't rat on her.

"I was *obsessed* with Pirates. I watched *Muppet Treasure Island,* and it just spun off from there. Don't laugh. I was young. But, I had pirate bed sheets, posters, books. I wore this Davy Jones shirt practically every day and refused to sleep in anythin' but my pirate pajamas."

They exchange a hearty laugh and Oxy.

This feels great!

Tell me about it.

"My neighbor Pete was just as into pirates, and we would pretend the treehouse his dad built was a pirate ship. Like any pirate, I wanted to find buried treasure, so I scrimmaged the house for jewelry, watches, cufflinks, loose change, *anythin'* shiny. I took the silverware!"

"No way!"

"No lie! I put it all in a shoebox and gave it to Pete to hide. He told me he buried it in the woods. Even drew me a map. I was *ecstatic!*

"I grabbed a shovel and set out for my adventure. Dude, I followed that map to the *T* and spent, like, three hours diggin' like mad! I couldn't find the damn loot! I ran to Pete's and asked him for help, and we're tearin' away at the ground, and he kept sayin', 'It's 'round here somewhere! It was next to this tree! No! Wait! That tree!'

"Ma and Dad got home, and I'm freakin' out 'cause I couldn't find the stupid box, and all their expensive shit's in it, and I didn't say anythin' 'cause I didn't wanna get in trouble. Welp, dinner time came 'round, and Ma goes to set the table and—"

"There's no silverware!"

"There's no silverware! Ma's geekin', thinkin' our babysitter stole it, and she was all, 'Why would the babysitter steal our silverware?' I came clean, and Dad was crackin' up, but Ma's pissed 'cause all her fine jewelry and family heirlooms are buried in the freakin' woods! Dad had a metal detector in the garage, and we were out 'til dark scopin' the area and still couldn't find the goddang treasure!"

Jesse secretly prides himself on being the light bearer of Mike's melancholy, his humorous reply auditory in the otherwise mellow room.

"I'm sure ya know what happened. Pete took it. Ma called Pete's Ma, and Pete returned the box, beyond scared shitless that Dad was gonna arrest him. I was grounded for the summer and not allowed to hang out with Pete no more. Oh, and my 'rents fired the babysitter."

"You were the *worst* pirate!"

Nodding, Jesse cries, "I know, I know!"

The humor fades like skipping stones into soft smiles, the chessboard spotless, and what Jesse says next destroys their upbeat mood.

"How 'bout you, Square?"

"My childhood was kinda shit."

"A memory, then. Any memory."

Jesse laces their fingers to keep Mike from tearing his fingernails to the quick and waits without pestering.

You can't get your fix if you keep pushing him away.

Gimme a second!

"I met this guy recently, and we got high with his friends in an abandoned mansion, then he took me someplace, just us two."

"Just you two, huh? Whadda fortunate fella." Jesse smirks. "And where'd this charmin' guy take ya?"

"To a lake. I'm not sure how this *charmin'* guy knew I loved the water. It's so peaceful. And we were floating, stargazing, talking about life and love. I could've stayed there for an eternity."

"I bet he could've, too."

My, how he glimmers! Ask for another line. ASK!

Relax!

Now's a perfect time!

Can't you see we're having a moment?!

Imagine how much better this moment would be if you were higher? I bet he'd lie down with you and hold you. Isn't that what you want?

"I'm glad you came over."

"I'm always glad to be here—*anywhere*—with you, Mike. Ya need more?"

"You… wouldn't mind?"

Please. He'd tar and feather his firstborn for you.

What a brash, dark statement.

"Not at all. But! Here's the dealio, Square: eat a couple of Oxy and take a hot shower."

"What are you implying? I know I'm gross right now, you don't gotta beat around the bush or—"

"If you're gross, then *gross* is the most beautiful thing in existence. I just wanna make sure ya get the best high possible. I hate seein' ya so down." He drops the pills into his hand and kisses his knuckles. "Trust me."

His energy's been so zilch all day that by the time Mike's finished bathing, brushing his teeth, and changing into clean pajama bottoms, it's as if he swam the seven seas in a twenty-four-hour period… *twice.*

Jesse's stretched stomach-down on the bed, his shirt and shoes scattered about the floor. Twitch (when did he get here?) laces and unlaces Jesse's DCs.

"Did that help?"

"A little."

"Ya want me to stay?"

"Yes."

"Y'sure?"

"Doubly."

I sit at the desk. Twitch paces in circles and throws clothes and objects out of the closet. Jesse clicks the lamp off and they shimmy under the sheets.

Mike shifts onto his side. "Wanna know what I like most about this show?"

Jesse looks away from Dexter Morgan. "Tell me."

"Dexter is aware of his darkness, but doesn't run from it. He uses it for the greater good and learns to control the monster rather than the monster controlling him. I like how he calls his urge to kill his 'Dark Passenger.' It's... hopelessly hopeful."

Jesse also moves onto his side and places a foot between Mike's.

"Dexter is quite the badass."

"You have a Dark Passenger, Jess?"

"For sure. I think everyone does." He strokes Mike's wet hair. "We're all made of scars. We're just not all serial killers. Ya don't have to face your Dark Passenger alone."

"I don't mean to shut you out."

Didn't I tell you the drugs would help? You wouldn't be saying these things sober.

"Don't apologize to me. Just promise you'll never forget that I'm here for you when ya need me. You've mentioned before your mind is a 'bad neighborhood?' I'm here, walkin' with ya, and I ain't scared of them dark streets."

"I wouldn't want anyone to walk with me in there, including

you."

"Who said I'm givin' ya a choice?" he rebuttals and, in the exact second, pledges, "I'm not leavin' ya. I know what it's like to feel trapped inside your own head. You have a 'bad neighborhood', and I have… I have rain in mine. I'll be your light; you'll be my shelter. Deal?"

"Deal."

Mike reacts instinctively to their curling bodies, his cheek nuzzling into Jesse's arm beneath him.

"You're rather comfy for a scrawny shit."

"Be nice." Jesse laughs. "You're 'bout the same size." He spins Mike's hair idly around his fingers. "You smell like apples."

"Had to use Mom's shampoo. Mine's out."

"I love apples," he says, his labret pressing against Mike's forehead. "Mi Sinclair, you're never alone." A kiss notarizes his declaration. "Tomorrow'll be better."

"And if it's not?"

"Then *we* will conquer your 'bad neighborhood.'"

Peacefully safe in each other's arms and in-tune breaths, the drugs coursing through their veins keep them awake for three episodes of *Dexter.* As for this abominable milestone? It'll happen again and again, and Jesse will be there to hold him and tell him silly stories because, as long as I'm here, the peace never lasts. I'm as permanent as a tattoo you agreed to in a drunken stupor.

I'm not *just* a Dark Passenger.

I *am* the darkness.

And I'll *always* snuff out your light.

The light will come, Michael.
I've crossed centuries of seas to arrive at this holiest time,
time,
time.

I'm strong.
Strong as tungsten.
You fed me well.
You built us a levee.
You dug a new hole.
A fleshy casing advances my bone-chilling form.

You don't become addiction.
Addiction becomes you.
I am, at long last...

MICHAEL

SINCLAIR

IN THE BEGINNING

FACT #1: BY THE TIME YOU'RE DONE READING THIS INTRODUCTION, FOUR PEOPLE WOULD'VE DIED FROM OVERDOSE.

I'M STANDING in the middle of the road.

I'm not sure why.

Self-torture?

Asphalt burns my heels. The climate is like a bubbling cauldron brewing spellbinding scents of moist earth swirling with sunflowers and lavenders Mrs. Jameson prunes and waters at 8 AM every morning, her stature feeble, her white, frizzy hair peeking over the fence dividing our properties. As I sketch her in my journal, I hum along to her singing "La Vie en Rose."

It's a song Mom sang while tucking me in as a boy, her operatic voice and lilac perfume cradling me to candy-land dreamscapes.

Years later, I'm no longer in my bed, and the beastly talons of this wicked world I'd somehow fallen victim to rob me of my lullabies.

I'm standing in the middle of the road.

I've no reason for it.

It's not a suicide mission.

It's not a busy street—a simple one-lane, narrow road curving into a cul-de-sac. I foretell the storm long before it overtakes the pearlescent skies. Rumbling clouds and a misty drizzle intrude on the calming afternoon, the harboring winds kidnapping the humidity.

I'm standing in the middle of the road.

I close my eyes, rain and wind filling my lungs, and for once—*for once!*—I feel serene. The world gets so loud sometimes here, inside my cluttered mind. I can't dust off the memories in my cerebral attic: the good, the bad, and the worst all crammed into oversized, imaginary boxes, stacking higher and higher, spreading further and further until there's no schism between the floor and ceiling. Piles among piles of boxes, each just as worn, torn, and mislabeled as the last.

I'm standing in the middle of the road.

It's not a death wish, not like it would've been ten months ago when I wasn't the person I am today. Ten months ago, I would've run onto a four-lane highway, arms spread eagle, *begging* for death, welcoming it as a long-lost relative I'd host a party for upon their homecoming.

I'm standing in the middle of the road.

Your front door slams shut, and our eyes immediately engage in the siring love affair established from day one. The silver Zippo flicks, and the menthol breeze travels in my direction. I skim the sloped, black skater shorts on your hips and your rain-shimmered naked feet and chest as you prop yourself against the wooden pillar. Your ankles crossed, your coy smirk speaks the words that aren't necessary to be said because I know *exactly* what you're thinking:

Get your ass inside, Square, before ya get run over or shot by a stray bullet! Dang, this ain't the burbs, yo!

We dawdle in our rightful places and continue to embark on the staring contest in which, for a minute, neither of us is a champion. Then your smirk transforms into your dimpled smile, and I lose the war without complaint—battle scars be damned.

I, too, smile because *you* know *exactly* what *I'm* thinking:

I can't help it, Jess. I'm irretrievably unraveled when it comes to the storm, the road, and the boy across the street.

AD-DIC-TION

/ə'dikSH(ə)n/

Noun

1. The fact or condition of being addicted to a particular substance, thing, or activity.

Synonyms: dependency, dependence, habit, problem.

"I don't have an addiction to oxycodone."

2. Devotion to, dedication to, obsession with, infatuation with, passion for, love of, mania for, enslavement to.

"I have a manic addiction to Jesse Harris."

Addiction's been slithering 'round since the dawn of time. Don't believe me? Who was it taunting Eve to bite the apple? Temptation, you say? The Devil? Temptation and Satan *had* to have been high. You can't tell me Jesus was only trying to make His point when He turned water into wine. Why wine? Why not tea? Was tea a thing back then?

If it's technicality you're seeking, I'll get technical.

In English, "drug" originated from an Old French word, *drogue*, and later into *droge-vate* from the Middle Dutch. It means "dry barrels" and refers to preserved medicinal plants.

Researchers discovered humans have been getting stoned since prehistoric times. Can you imagine cavemen high on opium, drunk on spirits, or tripping on shrooms? It couldn't have been all that bad—we have fire and wheels, don't we?

The earliest detection of alcohol started around 7,000-6,000 BC, first founded in ancient villages of Jiahu in China's Henan Province. Hallucinogens, as early as 8,600-5,600 BC, were brushed off fossil remains from San Pedro cactuses grown in Peru. Opium dates to the mid-sixth millennium BC, the fossil remains sighted in Italy less than twenty miles northwest of Rome. Prehistoric art reveals poppies were used in religious ceremonies. Humans chewed coca 8,000 years ago in South America. Pipes from 2,000 BC were dug up from the northwestern Argentina grounds, although it's unclear if their purpose had been for tobacco or hallucinogen use, but bits of nicotine in the pipes tells us tobacco's been smoked since at least 300 BC.

See, Temptation, perhaps even Adam and Eve, were possibly getting high and screwing like fleas in the Savage Garden. What if the apple was made into a bong? Nature with nature, am I right?

If you're asking yourself why this is relevant, give me a second to step onto my soapbox. It's important because when I watch the news or read articles and comments in the Ninth Circle of Hell that is social media, all I see and read are judgmental, unsympathetic assholes stating drug addiction's manmade. I don't disagree entirely, but denying its pre-Genesis existence is indisputable.

As Jesse once mentioned, and must be repeated for good measure: Addiction is ageless, sexless, classless, and raceless. Don't think it can't trap you in by its grubby net if it hasn't already, and you're just too vain, too self-righteous, to admit it.

We are all slightly arrogant in our personal contradictions.

Oh, and just so we're clear: I don't deserve to die. I'm not a bottom-feeding sewer rat, and I *do* accept responsibility for my actions. So, get off *your* high horse, slip on *your* soapbox, and straighten *your* halo.

I *don't* have a drug problem.

Okay...

I am *not* my addiction.

You're arrogant in your personal contradictions.

I am Michael Sinclair.

Whoop-dee-flipping-do.

And this is *my* story.

About *me*.

PART TWO

The entire galaxy would bear witness to our moment.
Thousands of stars were shining above us, every one of them shining as if the mouth of midnight was smiling.
We were wrapped in each other's embrace.
The stars were enchanting, but the majesty in your eyes was twice as powerful.
As we moved closer to each other, each star began to drop from the pitch-black sky, surrounding us as our lips began to touch.
At the very moment I felt your lips curve into a smile, all time had stopped.
I thought the universe was ours.
Little did I know the world just ended.

—David Porter

ONE

Covered In Darkness

FACT #2: DRUG ABUSE IS NOW THE NUMBER ONE CAUSE OF ACCIDENTAL DEATH IN THE UNITED STATES.

THERE'S A lot to unload here, and if I'm being honest, some bits of the last two months are hazy. Bear with me.

I'll start with Jesse.

I wish someone had warned me about his disappearing acts before they became real. It's not that he *ghosted* me per se, more like *half*-ghosted.

Two weeks after he came to my room during my depressive episode, he woke me up in the middle of the night, and I thought I was dreaming at first. I dream of him often. Sometimes we're at the estates floating in the lake. Sometimes we're in California amongst the beach tides and sea foam. Waking up to him speaking my name in that low timbre wasn't unordinary until I realized this was real life, not some seascape getaway.

"I have to go away for a bit," he said, knelt at my bedside. "I'll explain when I get back."

"What? Why? Where are you going?"

"I can't tell ya just yet. Gotta trust me."

"How long?"

"I dunno. I promise I'll be back, alright?" He kissed my forehead. "I'll be back."

I woke up, confident I dreamt it, but when I rolled over, my arm flopped onto the flat space next to me, and when there wasn't a text message asking if I wanted to chill or when I didn't hear him and Mom in the kitchen talking about science or whatnot, I realized it wasn't a dream at all. He really left. No calls. No texts. No social media posts. *Nadda.*

I should back up again and take you to the tragic event leading up to his disappearance. Our relationship really is built on tragedies.

How fucking tragic.

On the last day of August, I received a phone call on my work break. I hadn't heard from or seen Jesse for two days, and it's not as if we didn't go days without talking. We needed space just like anyone else; him being way more independent than me. I respected that independence and never asked questions. Jesse is Jesse. I wouldn't change him for all the Oxy in the world.

Liar.

My heart nearly imploded at the caller ID. I never thought the Richland Police Department would call Michael Square Sinclair—the straightest of all straight edges. I was afraid they'd show up at my house or job if I didn't answer.

On the other line was the second shock of the day. I'd met Paul Harris twice, the first time being the night Margaret was murdered and the second time at her funeral. His informal tone was frazzled as he told me Jesse was at the station, refusing to talk to anybody.

"I didn't know who else to call. What time are you off work?"

"Tw-two h-hours."

"I'll come get you. Look for the red Dodge truck outside the food court. He needs a friend right now."

"What happened?"

"I'd rather not tell you over the phone. We'll talk later."

He couldn't tell me over the phone but thought it appropriate to call me in the middle of my shift to tell me Jesse was at the police station? *Cool.*

It was just me working that day, and the following two hours felt similar to watching those boring educational videos in school. I messed up on multiple drink orders. My last Oxy was taken with my morning coffee. Nora, the closing barista, was fifteen minutes late, and she should thank her stars that I didn't impale her eyeballs with the milk steamer.

"Hey, Mikey," she greeted evenly, like arriving late was as average as blue jeans. She fluttered her eyelashes and swung her hips while tying her black apron. "You look nice today."

This was ludicrous, average behavior from her. I hadn't noticed she was flirting with me the entire two weeks we've been working together until Jazz pointed it out. Any other day I'd be flattered, even if I wasn't interested.

"Thanks. Bye."

I zipped by her, tossed my apron on the floor, and ran out of the mall, relieved *and* distressed, when I spotted Paul's truck next to the food court entrance. I got in, and all the questions spilled out of my mouth in the same juggling jumble they were in my head.

"Is he hurt? Where was–what was–where was-he-arrested–I don't–why didn't he–we—"

"Calm down, Mike." Jesse clearly had Paul's patience. "I don't know how else to say this…."

"What?!" I shouted. I clearly *don't* have patience.

Paul sighed. "Daryl passed away last night."

I wasn't shouting. Not anymore. My heartbeat stumbled over its own rhythm.

"Overdose?"

"No," he said, glancing from the road to me. "Murder."

I stared, inept, at the highway.

"He was there, wasn't he? With Daryl?"

Paul nodded.

The rest of the ride was vague and stifling, as if Daryl's death was a vampire who preyed on the world's brio and left it a bare-boned wilderness. I wrung my hands, plucked at the skin around my fingernails, and altered my seating. I'll never ask for time to slow down ever again. This time-vortex was *brutal.*

Coming into the station parking lot, Jesse was on the stairs, smoking a cigarette.

"What the fuck happened to him?" I was shouting again. "Is that… *blood?*"

I gave him no time to explain and jumped out of the moving truck. I slowed to a jog, took a knee, and landed a soft touch on Jesse's arm. He didn't look at me, but I knew he knew I was there because we're… *us.* It's like we were hashing out that dreadful gray and crimson night. I wish history didn't feel the need to repeat itself.

Paul stayed a few feet away, watching us. My father never showed concern, so I can't say if that's what I saw on his face.

"Mea Harris," I whispered, "tell me what I need to do."

Seeing his bruised, violet-green rimmed bloodshot eyes and the scab that had replaced his piercing sent my already achy stomach into a tailspin.

I smiled, an action achieved out of compulsion. "Hey, hot stuff."

His mouth twinged.

"Jesse, please tell me what you need. You wanna go home?"

He shook his head.

"You wanna come home with me?"

He nodded.

"Okay. C'mon."

We didn't touch or speak in the back seat of Paul's truck, and Jesse spent the ride gazing out the window. I wanted to hold his hand or wrap my arms around him, but I knew he didn't want affection. He probably didn't even want to be breathing. I recognized his absent, doleful energy. I felt it, too, when Maddy overdosed.

As we drove up, Mom was outside getting the mail. *Oh, boy.* She shouldn't have been home yet. She'd been leaving work earlier and earlier that month or calling off entirely. We'll tackle that later. I don't want to get off track here.

She brought Jesse to her bosom and rubbed the back of his neck, demanding to know why he was injured. Paul tried settling her down, but Mom was *brutish*—the Goliath to his David—a spectacle which could only be fully appreciated if seen firsthand, given he stood six inches over her 5'3" frame.

"What do you mean he got beat up by his brother's drug dealers?!" she blared at Paul.

I saw the meddlesome neighbors prying from their doorways or pressing their noses against windows. Who'da thought we'd someday fit into the ROY G BIV drama dynamic?

"Your young son not only lives in the worst part of town alone, but he just saw his brother die too?!"

Jesse shuddered.

"Where are these men? Are they arrested?"

"One of them, yes." Paul answered. "The other got away."

Mom moved Jesse aside and jabbed Paul's breastbone with every spoken, "*This. Is. Your. Fault!*"

"*ME?*"

"*You are his father!* I watched my son be berated and neglected by his father, and I did nothing about it until years later, and I won't let it happen to Jesse. You're cutting his lease, and he'll live here with us."

STANDING OVATION! BRAVO! BRAV—

SHUT UP!

Damn, Mike, I'm on *your* side!

Swords swung above us as I awaited Paul's rebuttal that she should mind her own family business, but was, instead, stupefied when he agreed.

"I'll cut the lease. I'll bring his stuff over later this week."

"No. You'll bring his stuff *now*."

"I'll bring it tonight."

"You will also set up house security and patrol the area until those thugs are behind bars! Do I make myself clear?"

Jesse stood next to me, our jaws dropped.

"Understood, ma'am."

"Good. And *you two,*"—she faced us, gentle yet agitated—"go inside and get Jesse cleaned up."

"I really wanted a cigarette, Mar—"

"Smoke in the bathroom. I don't care right now. You need to be tended to. You should go to the hospital."

"My wife is a nurse," said Paul. "She gave him a look-over."

Her shooting glare at him could've sent us all to our tombs. "A '*look-over'?* What if he has internal bleeding? His eyes are bloodshot!"

"I feel fine, Marie."

"Go inside, boys!"

We didn't budge. I'm pretty sure we were scared for Paul's life *and* livelihood if we left them unattended.

"*NOW!*"

We fumbled into the house, Jesse limping beside me, and he fell like a book onto the bathroom tile, his back to the tub.

"Damn, yo." He lit a Salem Menthol. "Your ma's *friggin' savage.*"

I noticed the sour-grape-colored, Saturn-sized bruise on his left shin.

"Jess... your leg. You should get this looked at."

"It's fine."

"You *limped* into the house."

"I said I'm fine, Mike! Jesus!"

"I'm sorry. I'm going to start the bath for you. You don't want to be covered in dirt and blood."

"Gettin' used to it." He flicks his ashes into the toilet.

My mental dictionary a thousand words short, I started the bathwater and left to grab some towels, clothes, and the first aid kit from the hall closet. Jesse lit another cigarette using the cherry from his first and eyed me as I sat down.

I dipped a washcloth into the water and carefully cleaned his fat lip.

"Did they rip your piercing out?"

"Naw, I took it out just in case me and Daryl got into it."

The white fluorescent fixtures emphasized his bruised and scarred inflictions as he ground his jaw. We heard Mom's wrath at Paul outside through the thin walls, and Jesse cracked a smile.

"Remind me to never piss her off."

"Softer than lace, but harder than stone. It takes a lot to rile her up. Shows how much she cares for you."

"Or pities me."

"No," I assured him. "She cares. One sec."

I left again to get an ice pack from the kitchen. He groaned as I brought it to his cheek, but held it in place so I could open the first aid kit, his hand muddy and unsteady.

"I must look like the ugliest POS right now."

"Shut up. You're... you're..."

He grinned. "I'm what, Sinclair?"

"Beautiful." I said it. I was powerless to stop it.

"Can dudes be beautiful?"

"You can." I dabbed peroxide onto his lip, needing to distract myself from saying more idiotic things that could ruin our friendship.

He seized my thigh, the liquid foaming white.

"Goddang, that burns."

"Sorry. Should've warned you."

I bit my lip, concentrating, and felt him relax.

"*Fuck*, Sinclair."

"Hm?"

"I'm lookin' at ya right now, and you're *insanely* beautiful."

My hand lowered. "Y'sure your swollen eye ain't messing up your vision?"

"Did I *fuckin' stutter?*"

I chuckled and finished cleaning his wounds, and when I asked him to remove his tattered shirt, I should've expected the response he gave, yet I tripped over my thoughts just as I'd done in Paul's truck.

"Couldja at least kiss me first before askin' me to strip for ya?"

"Shut it, Harris. Take it off."

"I think I like Dominant Mike."

"Jesse!"

"Fine, fine. Party pooper." He threw it in the trash. "That was my favorite shirt."

"We'll get you a new one."

I couldn't stress enough how fortunate he was to be alive, and he was bitching about a replaceable DC t-shirt? It wasn't the time to be sour, not while we were visited by the stampeding elephant in the room, and I reckoned he was as conscious of the serious scenario transgressing into a more... *sexual* one. How could he not? I was straddling him and had no choice but to touch him as I cleaned his body and rubbed the ointment into his gashes.

We weren't *talking*. We were *looking*. However, it didn't stray further than that, despite us creeping along carnal pins and needles. His palm was on my cheek, and I couldn't determine whether he was squinting at me because of his inflamed socket or if he was trying to decode an unspoken riddle.

“Why do ya do this?” he asked.

“What do you mean?”

“Take care of me? Why do you keep me in your life? I ain’t nothin' but bad luck, Mike, a catalyst for shitty karma. I destroy everythin' I touch. You’re better off without me.”

“God, Jesse, don’t talk like that. Whatever happened last night has *nothing* to do with us. You’re not bad luck or a shitty anything. You’re the best part of my life.”

I thought I was?

You, too, Envious Edward. Now shush.

“I’m fallin' apart, Mikey.”

My nose kissed his. “Then *we* fall apart. That was the deal, right? You fall, I fall. You’re my light; I’m your shelter.”

“I’m supposed to keep ya from drownin', not dunk your head underwater.”

“If I didn’t want you in my life, you wouldn’t be here. Got it?”

“Yeah.”

“Say it.”

His voice spasmed. “You want me in your life.”

I untied his shoes, and we undressed the rest of him, our laughter awkward as he graded into the watery suds and covered himself.

“I ain’t normally so modest.”

“Don’t I know it,” I said. “I’ll be in my room. Take your time.”

I stood, and he suddenly pulled me down from my half-rotation. My gaze latched onto his, mostly because I wasn’t sure what to look for. Wasn't it just an hour ago he was but a fragmented catastrophe, and now we're... we're...

My nerves convulsed, privy to his nudity, my shyness bolting straight to *holy shit!*—as I was brought in inch by inch by his wet hand on my chin, closer, closer, his short, metallic, outward breaths imprinting me. His thumb slipped from one corner of my mouth to the other, and I was self-confident for what was to follow.

Our heads didn't tilt, lips weren't licked in preparation, and his hand sank into the bubbles.

"Thanks for takin' care of me, Mikey. Sorry for snappin' atcha," he whispered, the shower wall far more interesting than the guy he *almost* kissed.

Addled, I replied, "You're welcome, Jess," and shut the door behind me.

TWO

Black Out

FACT #3: More than 10% of children in America live with an alcoholic parent.

Jesse didn't talk about Daryl's murder until the next day. We called off work and spent it high and day drinking. Paul brought Jesse's belongings to my place, and I helped him unpack and make his bed. We fell asleep in his *new* room while watching Dexter Morgan. He was officially moved in.

"You didn't have to listen to my mom and give up your apartment. You're a grown-ass man."

"And miss out livin' with a Square? Naw, it'd be foolish to turn down such an experience."

Not much of a Square anymore. You spend your paychecks on drugs and steal from Mom to buy more. You dress like Jesse. You talk like Jesse. You snap at your coworkers when you're out of Oxy. Jazz almost fired you for your piss-poor attitude. When was the last time you opened your sketchbook?

Don't listen to him. I stole from Mom *once*, and I'll explain later.

Jesse and I were sitting on the porch, the temperature frigid for September, and he was spaced out on what used to be his house across the street. I stubbed my cigarette in the ashtray and placed my hand on his bouncing knee. He inhaled nasally and, sullen, gave me the rundown.

Daryl contacted him from an unknown number and asked to meet at Junkies Playground. Daryl was tweaked and not making much sense. Jesse said they were yelling at each other, and he figured he'd have the chance to go off and let Daryl know what a piece of shit he was for ruining their family.

"He apologized for what he'd done, but I wouldn't hear it. Then, like... I ain't sure where they came from or how they found us, but Josh and Ethan, his dealin' partners, came outta nowhere. They wanted their money. Daryl didn't have it. Fights broke out, and I jumped in. Josh had me pinned, and Ethan was just... *slammin'* Daryl's head against the ground *over and over and over.* You don't forget a sound like that. Like a minefield. Louder than gunshots. I was beggin' for him to stop. Daryl's last words to me were, 'Sorry, bro,' and he was just..." he paused, sniffing and shaking his head. "I knew they were gonna kill me. They ganged up on me, and I fought back, but they was kickin' and punchin' and spittin'. Next thing I knew I was tastin' metal. Fuckin' gun between my teeth, Mike. Ain't ever been that scared or prepared to die. Ethan said I'd be no good to him dead; he wanted his money, and he'd let me go if I kept my mouth shut and found the funds.

"I got some saints watchin' over me, that's for damn sure, 'cause I dunno who'd done it. Called the cops, I mean. Five or six patrol cars. They caught Josh, but Ethan's still out there." Jesse let out a dead-reviving cry. "I tried, Mike!" He sobbed as I held him. "I swear to God, I tried! I didn't want him to die! I wanted him to suffer! Wh-wh-why does this keep happ-happenin' to me?"

"Shit, Mea Harris. I'm so sorry. I'm here. I got you."

Another funeral to attend. A second montage of friends, drugs, and alcohol on the back lawn, more false, "If you ever need anything..." promises followed by tearful, sleepless nights.

Jesse became quieter and aloof after Daryl died, and I clung to him to keep him from relapsing into his meth habit. As far as I knew, he stuck to Oxy and weed or the occasional cocaine and low-dose OxyContin the ER doctor prescribed once Jesse caved to Mom's nagging.

On my days off for the rest of September, I'd be in Wheelies with him and his boss, Max. He was stoned practically 24/7 and had thick, lime green dreadlocks, tattooed sleeves, and gauged earlobes, and he sold us weed and coke. Jesse would read graphic novels at the café corner table on his days off, sipping his upside down maple macchiato. If we were both working, we'd meet in the parking lot during my breaks (Max was more lenient than my boss, and Jesse corresponded his lunches and breaks to mine), and we'd get high in the Honda and talk about our days.

Living together, we established a routine, and he slept in his room for the first few nights, but spent the rest of them in mine. Mom never questioned it. Jesse demonstrated in his own way he didn't want to be alone and would hang out with her in the mornings until I awoke. We understood his need for companionship—to be loved and doted on.

He cooked dinners for us to repay Mom's generosity. I'm not talking about frozen dinners here. I'm talking roasted chicken, hand-mashed potatoes, homemade butter rolls, pies, cakes, and bread, which smelled and tasted like they came from a bakery or a top-tier restaurant.

We brushed our teeth in the tiny bathroom, swapped clothes (more like I took his), played video games, and had movie nights with Mom on certain evenings. At least twice a week, we disabled the alarm and snuck out of the house, meeting the Sharp Edges in the Black Estates to get high. He slept next to me no matter what we were doing, his snores filling the space on my left. It was the one time of day when his mind wasn't on autopilot, a time when he found peace.

In two instances, I found Jesse peering out the living room window. I spoke his name and his shoulders rose, but he didn't act like he was off-guarded.

"Go back to sleep, Mikey."

"Why are you up?"

"Couldn't sleep. I'm fine. Go back to bed."

He also looked over his shoulder, sped up whenever we were shopping at the mall or stores, and drove routes he ordinarily wouldn't. One day after work, while picking up takeout at Old Carolinas, he yanked the bag from the ladies' hands, hauled me outside by the elbow, and drove off without letting me get the other half of our order.

He blew me off if I asked about it.

"Just don't like bein' 'round people since Daryl died."

My intuition told me differently.

And my intuition was correct because in two more weeks, Jesse got up and left.

What I thought was a durable bond tying us together sifted through my fingers one brittle piece at a time, like an hourglass stapled to the floor. It was challenging keeping Zombie-Mike hidden from Mom while dealing with Disappearing-Act-Jesse. She believed me when I told her he needed to clear his head and was staying with relatives in Columbus.

My texts and calls went unanswered. As you may imagine, this confused me and left me emotionally, physically, and mentally dysfunctional. Toby said this was prevalent for Jesse after a crisis, and his MIA status had my drug/cigarette use at an all-time high (no pun intended). In my lock drawer, I kept his glass chessboard, a packet of straws, and the fifteen Oxy he left me lasted me three days. I purchased more from Toby, and getting high alone wasn't all unicorns and freakin' lollipops. It lacked a certain... *satisfaction*, like an immovable current of electricity.

I miss him, plain and simple, but it's not plain and simple. I miss his weight on the mattress, and the cologne and Snuggle fabric softener on his clothes. I miss his laughter, the stories he tells to brighten my "bad neighborhood," and the way he takes off his socks outside the front door after a rainstorm so he can feel the wet pavement on his feet.

He should be here with me where he belongs.

EVERY OTHER day, Toby swings by with my Oxy re-up, and I stuff money into his glove compartment for the drugs. We hang out on the porch to smoke a joint, our conversations along these lines:

"Still no word?"

"Nope. He hasn't answered my texts either."

"Has Jax heard from him?"

"No. I'm sorry, Mike, I wish I knew more."

1:48 AM

Our *Jessike* playlist shuffles, and Chester Bennington's lungs bleed into my eardrums as I drift in and out of space.

(Me): I miss you.

Butcher me and call me a hopeless romantic; I have faith he'll come back to me.

2:00 AM

(Me): You're an asshole.

Dashing.

You can shut up any day now.

I don't doublethink pushing SEND, nor do I doublethink snorting four Oxy in thirty minutes.

You're running out of ways to finance your drugs. Jesse doesn't charge you.

My neediness ran him off.

Fix it!

I'm trying!

Trying?! You called him an asshole!

What do you suggest I do, genius?

You know what to do, *coward.*

Sleep doesn't come, and time doesn't stop, not for you, me, or the child with a temper tantrum thrashing his fists inside my core. In attempts to become a halfway decent, functioning member of society, I shower, get ready for the day, and down enough caffeine to generate the ROY G BIV.

Mom left for work an hour ago, and I'm torn between going to work or back to bed. In the end, the responsible angel cannibalizes my conniving devil.

Toby's in the driveway in his 2013 bumblebee-yellow Mustang, courtesy of his preacher father who, I found out, sold ancestral land in Arizona for an outrageous amount. Let's just say the Alexanders sit pretty. The closest I'll ever get to a car this nice will be in a *Hot Wheels* package.

"Dude, you look like—"

"I know. I didn't sleep *at all.*"

Toby shakes his head. "Your brain's gonna be sludge if ya don't take it easy with them Oxy, man."

You wouldn't be self-medicating if Jesse would TALK TO US!

I open the glove box and make the trade.

"Ain't no way your petty paychecks pay for this shit."

"Been selling my Xbox games."

You pawned Mom's jewelry, too. Grandma's engagement ring was a half-carat diamond! Five hundred bucks? You got bamboozled!

SHUT! UP!

I eat two Blues, thank Toby for the refill and ride, and flump back into my seat when he grabs my arm.

"I get you're upset about Jesse."

I almost believe him.

"I really do. I swear I'll try to track him down."

"Alright."

"I'll be here at three to getcha."

I bid Nora good morning to be courteous and she, too ditzy and overenthusiastic, waves zealously.

"Hey, Mikey! Oh, my God, so last night, I was making this weird drink someone requested and...." She talks, but I can't hear what she's saying.

I can't focus.

I'm thinking about Jesse.

I'm *constantly* thinking about Jesse.

Too bad he isn't thinking about you. That's it. Take another pill. Nora thinks it's Aleve. She doesn't know...

Your secret's safe with me.

I WASTE my lunch and fifteen-minute break texting Jesse to text me back or, at the very least, to let me know he's not dead in a ditch or strung out on a bench.

I check my phone.

Nothing.

I clock out.

I've tripped over the source of heartbreak.

I sling on my backpack, say goodbye to the two booksellers and Jazz, and proceed to Ritzy Pretzels, but it's not Toby who's waiting for me.

We're four feet apart, the closest we've been in thirty-four days. He dons black skater shorts, a wallet chain, and a black muscle shirt, his hair impeccably spiked. It's unsettling the way his impression suggests tragedy hasn't afflicted him whatsoever.

He chews on his labret, his hands buried in his pockets.

This nimwit owes you a month's worth of Blues for his neglect!

SHHHHHHH!!!!!

Wait... you make a valid argument.

He toes the unseen line separating us, his mouth thin, and it's as if we've never met before, my heart balancing on a straight razor, another unsettling feeling, my heart novice in the "balancing" department. His head isn't hung and his coy smirk is amiss. I deserve an apology, a good ass excuse, *anything*. Seriously, I'm not asking for much here.

"Mi Sinclair."

"Don't call me that."

He winces. "You look tired."

"Do I? Huh, why the *fuck* is that, Jess?"

"You're angry, I know. Let's ditch this teenage slaughterhouse, and I'll explain everythin'."

He should put whatever lousy excuse he has for me so far up his ass that it'll dislodge his Adam's apple.

He's... he's Jesse, and I'm a shameless, lovesick doormat when it's shaved down to the stubble of our abrasive relationship, and after the month, year, *life* I've had, rejecting him isn't optional.

THREE

Love in Limbo

FACT#4: AMERICA MAKES UP 5% OF THE WORLD'S POPULATION AND CONSUMES APPROXIMATELY 80% OF THE WORLD'S PRESCRIPTION OPIOIDS.

I'M GIVEN an oblong capsule filled with tiny, piss-yellow balls in the Honda. Adderall.

"Perk ya right up."

Yessiree, you need to make amends. Suck his dick if you must. We all know you're dying to, anyway.

....

Go away.

Fat chance.

Fifteen minutes pass in complete silence, yet now and then, I'll glance at him and him at me, partaking in Who's Going To Speak First Russian Roulette, and you bet your sweet ass I won't be the dumbfuck pulling the trigger.

The heated altercation begins halfway to the Black Estates. It doesn't help that the only sounds we hear besides our clamorous outrage are the purring engine and the wind whistling through the windows. My shakes and sweats are contributed by three Americanos, Oxy, Adderall, and vexation towards Jesse.

"I toldja I was leavin'! It ain't like I just left! And why do you even care?"

"Why do I care?! WHY DO I CARE?! You really are an obnoxious, self-centered prick! My mother took you in!"

"I ain't a stray animal, Mike!"

The rage in the cramped space and his eerie shakiness cripples our framework. This isn't how we're supposed to be. This isn't us. I've had enough screaming fights for one lifetime, and I can't do it with him. It doesn't seem to matter. We're only becoming louder, and a lethal injection isn't as potent as our abusive jibes.

"Holy fuck! Totally ungrateful! You couldn't even tell me where you were or if you were—"

"Strung out on a park bench or dead in a ditch?" he mocks my text, glaring at the road. "Yeah, I guess that's fittin' for Jesse Harris."

I pound my fists against the dashboard and make some animalistic gurgles. The strength of fifty bodybuilders couldn't hold me back from socking him and pissing on his words. *Yikes.* Adderall makes me angry.

It's not the Adderall! It's Jesse!

"We need to chill," he says, his face like a watermelon jolly rancher. "This is *not* how I wanted this conversation to go."

I can't disagree; this isn't how I wanted our reunion, either. We arrive at the bend in the road, and Jesse kills the engine, the silence upstaging us again.

"You were dealing, weren't you?"

"What makes ya think that?" he asks the molting horizon on the orange and gold tree tops.

"It wasn't hard to figure out. I know some street rules, too, ya know. Daryl owed money he didn't have and if he's gone, that responsibility is on you. You didn't have the money, so it was deal or die."

Jesse rests his elbow on the door, and, head in hand, looks at me. "If ya already figured it out, why're ya so mad at me?"

"You ignored me for *weeks!* You left me hanging with no explanation! These disappearing acts are getting old! So excuse me for thinking you were dead."

"God! Everythin' I did was to protect you and Marie. I appreciate your ma more than you'll ever know. What do you want from me?"

"I didn't *want* to be *protected.* I *wanted* the truth! You were looking over your shoulder *everywhere* we went and *you* brushed it off *everytime* I brought it up!"

"Of course, I brushed it off! That drug ring is bigger than Josh and Ethan. They were followin' me! They know where you live. I'm sure they know where your ma works, where you work, our schedules. Ya think they can't get past the patrol cars? They know their schedules too. I had to do somethin' before they came after the two people who mean the world to me. I wasn't 'bout to let your ma and *especially* you pay for the debts and sins of my *lunatic* brother. I did what I had to do."

My brain can't compute. I'm sketched out of my skin—itchy, twitchy, tired, and wired.

"Where were you?"

"Cleveland."

"Jesus," I mutter, "I gotta get out of this car."

It's the first walk we've taken to the estates where we don't hold hands. We're better than this. We *had* to be better than this.

Is his limp temporary? He staggered at the mall, too, but I was too pissed off to care. Now I feel as insignificant as a jigsaw piece the cat pawed under the refrigerator. Jesse wouldn't dismiss my health as quickly as I had his if the shoe were on the other foot.

"Ya still mad?"

"I'm not mad. I'm… *hurt*. You don't trust me."

He comes to a dead halt, turns half-circle, and grabs my shoulders, the sunset reflecting off his honeyed irises.

"That's not true. When are ya gonna see it? Accept it, Michael?"

He's never addressed me by my full name. I know what he's insinuating; how he feels about me. I've known for some time. I realized it wasn't common for two friends—two guys—to be so touchy-feely and flirty if emotions weren't involved. He labeled me "hot" the first time we spoke. I'm not a moron.

Questionable.

Perhaps I am an idiot because I lack the necessary language to accommodate his statement, even if it's been on the tip of my tongue since mid-July, when I felt that incoming infatuation train disabling me like any other fever or withdrawal.

"You swore you were done dealing."

"Not only are ya changin' the subject, but you're missin' the point."

"*You* don't get to steer this conversation. You're the dumbest smart guy I've ever met. Your IQ is higher than Hawking's, and you—"

"His is 160. I'm no Hawking."

I'm seething.

He retracts. "Sorry."

"You just throw it away! What if you'd been caught? What then? You'd be in prison! Your entire life, your future—*BOOM!—gone!*"

"What future, Mike? I'm a useless deadbeat! I did what I did to protect us! Isn't that what you're always babblin' on 'bout? Bein' honest? I DID THAT! And you're wantin' to beat me into the ground 'cause of it?! Whadda buncha hypocritical bullshit!"

Minus the "useless deadbeat" and "hypocritical" remark, every morsel is true. Guilt hasn't yet sunk me, my incredulity and ire smothering what little compassion I have.

"You must have me twisted if you think I'm going to stand here and let you pin the blame on me!"

"Ain't blamin' ya, Square, but ya can't be angry at me when *you've* been *dishonest* from *the start!* Your sister, your feelin''s, your childhood. *Everythin'*."

I invade his territory and push, not wasting an ounce of my strength, his head colliding into the side of the Black Estates. I cage him in, my hands flat above his shoulders, close enough to parade my dominance but far enough to clearly counteract his narrowing glare.

"Go ahead," he browbeats. "Go ahead and *hit* me, Michael. I bet it'll make ya *feel so much better*."

If you punch him, he'll never see you again, and Toby will stop selling to you. Then what will you do? Go downtown and risk buying from an undercover? Don't be dense!

Lightheaded, my frustration dilutes to adoration. I'm not ready to forgive, but you'd have to put me on trial if I'm to refute the fervent tempestuous effect we have on each other, and when I look at him—I mean *really* look at him—I see the lost, unwanted, frayed and wounded parts of myself. In the darkest hour, two lost souls held the torches so they could see again. I don't have it in me to cast this aside, and for what reason? Jesse doing what Jesse does best? He's the sort to jump in front of a shotgun to defend the people he loves.

The three massive steps I'd taken forward reverse into three massive steps backward.

"I can't hurt you."

"I didn't leave to piss ya off or worry ya. It's over now. I had to do it."

"You should've just told me. I didn't think you'd come back; that you wanted nothing to do with me."

"I'm sorry," he apologizes and holds me as if the world's trying to tear us apart. "I missed you so much. Here, with you, I feel like I can breathe."

"I missed you more, but if you pull one more ghosting stunt, I'll make any beating you've ever had feel like puppy tongues."

He chuckles. "Noted."

We got high on Oxy and weed (strawberry flavored papers, that was new) that night, and when we got home, Mom was none the wiser. She hugged Jesse and asked how his family was, and he looked at me ambiguously, and I shrugged like *what else was I supposed to tell her?* He went along with it and made up a narrative about how thrilled his uncle and cousins were to see him, then added he was tired from the trip before she could pry for further details. We snorted Xanax, turned on *Dexter*, and we, like the sun, rose the next day refreshed.

Ethan was arrested on the Canadian border, and from what we've read and seen on the news, he outed the entire operation for a shorter sentence. It brought Mom some solace, yet she jumped ten feet when the Jehovah's Witnesses knocked on our door yesterday afternoon, spreading the good word. They had some serious moxie coming to our neck of the woods. Then again, the ROY G BIV needs God as much as Dexter Morgan needs a blood slide.

Jesse and I earned her trust, minding the house and our jobs. I canceled my Dr. Greene appointments (his "enabling" position about my relationship with Jesse was grinding my gears). Mom was obviously skeptical, but relented when I promised to take my ACTs and SATs and apply to universities to replace therapy.

The college topic brings us here in Jesse's car and the dusty lanes I've grown to love, our very own Yellow Brick road leading us to our home away from home. I'm higher than a UFO on Adderall and Oxy, chattering on about how we'll one day buy the estates and "repair that rundown piece of junk into a million-dollar kingdom."

"Sugary impossibilities."

"It wouldn't be if you'd get your head out of your ass."

"Da hell ya mean?"

I throw my hands up. "You could have a free ride to any college! And you'd rather glue yourself to the tracks instead of boarding the train!"

"Not this again! Are ya *ever* gonna let this down?"

"NO!"

Granted, we've had this spat numerous times. What choice do I have here? I can't sit back and let him toss his future into a TNT-filled barrel.

"I. Don't. Wanna. Go. To. Fuckin'. College!"

"Even if it means being in California with me?"

"It ain't 'bout that. It's just... ya keep talkin' 'bout the future, and I ain't a 'future' guy. I take life as it happens, and these plans you're makin' ain't guaranteed."

"Because you're not helping me out!"

"How're ya gonna pay for this move to Cali? Work three jobs? Where're we gonna live? Cali ain't like Ohio, where ya throw down six hundred a month for a two-story in the burbs."

"Pull the car over."

"What? Why?"

"Pull the damn car over!"

"A'ight, a'ight. Dang, man, no more Adderall for you."

He stands at the trunk and me at the hood like two rangers in the wild west. I'm waiting for the tumbleweed to roll by us.

"What is wrong with you?"

"Ya need to cool it."

"Look around us! What's here for you? For *us? Nothing!* Nothing but drugs (**Leave me out of this!**) and dead-end jobs and cornfields! Some would *kill* to touch your intelligence! You were Valedictorian!"

"They're just numbers!"

"They're a ticket out! You can be anything! A doctor! A lawyer! A—"

"I don't wanna be them things! I ain't like you!"

"I'm not asking you to be!"

The late afternoon prisms ricochets off his skin as he treads into my space. “That ain’t how it’s soundin'. You’ve this *insane* illusion where we ride off into the goddang sunset in a diamond carriage! You think it’s so easy! Well, buddy, it ain’t!”

“Life isn’t easy! It sucks balls! But we’ve got a chance here. Why won’t you take it? Do you seriously hate yourself that much? Do you hate *me* that much?”

“Oh, no, ya don’t. You don’t get to guilt trip me, Sinclair. I should kick your ass for even thinkin' I hate you!” He thaws as if he keeps a hidden switch inside himself. “You’re the only thing keepin' me goin'. Everythin'’s fallin' apart, 'cept what you and I have.”

“Then why are you making things difficult? What do you wanna be? A fucking junkie? Is that what you plan on being forever? Working some crap job and shooting up in a Kroger parking lot?”

“Watch yourself.”

“Christ, Jess, I’m just trying to understand you!”

“You’re goin' 'bout it the wrong way!”

“Then teach me! Show me which way I should go! I’m not a mind reader, and I can’t help you when you keep me in the dark!”

He’s yelling again. We both are.

“Who said I wanted your help?! Who said I needed you?!”

“YOU! YOU DID! Or was that all a lie? Just the drugs talking, Jesse?”

“Fuck you!”

We put distance between us, my teeth grating, and he rests against the vehicle, one arm wrapping around his waist and he chews at his thumbnail, our glances flinging side to side. Jesse sighs and steps forward, his hands reaching for my face on his way in.

"Mike," he says, his thumbs on my chin, "I'm nobody."

"No way is that IQ number accurate, because you're sounding dumber by the second."

"Mike, c'mon—"

"You're not a nobody. Right now, you're being a complete cock-bag for accusing me of thinking any less of you. You know I don't hate you. I don't care about what others think of you. I don't care what you've done. I care about the future. I care about *now*."

"I'm sorry too. I—"

"I'm going to say this one last time, alright?" I lay my forehead on his. "You're going to be someone great. You're going to write to colleges—"

"Mikey—"

"You're going to write to colleges and get a scholarship. We'll get our shit together, get out of this toxic wasteland, and do everything we've been talking about. Travel the west coast—"

"See the northern lights in Alaska."

"Stargaze Nevada skies."

"Buy the Black Estates."

"And be *happy*. When's the last time you've felt even *remotely* happy?" I ask.

He caresses my lower back. "Right now," he says. "I feel happy right now."

My smile impersonates his mild touch. "Then I guess we're well on our way, aren't we?"

"I'd say so, Mi Sinclair."

I hold our words in esteem, so why can't I terminate the tormenting voice inside my head?

You'll never be happy without me.

You're doomed.

And so is Jesse.

FOUR

Ecstatic Agony

FACT #5: THREE OUT OF FOUR NEW HEROIN USERS ABUSED OPIOIDS PRIOR TO USING HEROIN.

THE BLACK Estates manifests its authenticness in the daylight—moldy, ancient, and downright grotesque. If I'm to consider the last few trailing months, there's nowhere else I'd rather be—"Here, Mi Sinclair," Jesse says, lending me the chessboard and straw—and no one else I'd rather be with.

I gawk at the slim blue powder. "How many did you crush?"

"We've four left and two for tonight."

"Damn, didn't realize we were that low. My funds are on empty 'til Friday."

"S'okay, I got money."

Jesssee to the rescue!

When isn't he?

"And what happens when that runs out?"

"Dunno. Guess we start workin' them streets."

"Dude!" I punch his shoulder, and we laugh.

"Just messin'. We'll figure it out. We always do."

I smile at him, snorting the little amount we have. "Yeah, Jess, we do."

Eli, Jazz, and Jax file in after Toby, and he looks like a kid who left a candy store with a fruit basket.

Rolling a spliff, Jesse jokes, "Shit, who died?"

"Widow Watson," says Toby.

Jesse chokes on a cough, and we both yelp, "WHAT?!"

Toby sits, grunting. "She finally kicked the can, yo."

"Bucket. I think you mean 'bucket.'"

"Bucket, can, whatever the hell, Harris. She died in her sleep."

Satan's flaming testicles. This isn't good. Widow's our only supplier.

Thanks, Captain Obvious.

Jesse duplicates my overwrought gander and asks if Toby grabbed anything before she passed.

"Nah, man, I was set to see her this morning, and I tried getting into the house but couldn't get past Pops and the caretakers."

"You know anyone else?" I ask.

"They're on the down-low since Ethan ratted on all them dealers. It's gonna be dry for a bit. Sorry, guys. Didn't the doc write you a 'script for, like, seven months?" he asks Jesse.

"Were ya high that day? Nevermind. Dumb question. Three months and I can't refill for two more weeks."

"How much ya got now?" asks Jazz.

"Two."

"Between the two of you?!" Eli's finger wags from me to Jesse.

"Yep." Jesse passes Jax the spliff.

"Maybe this is a sign you guys should, oh, I dunno, *slow down?*" Jazz suggests. "It's a dangerous road you're heading down."

"Oxy's weak sauce compared to meth," Jesse says. "Wouldja rather me be tweaked out?"

"Hell, naw! You were a monster!"

"Yeah, you were terrifying," Toby agrees. "I'm surprised your face and teeth look as good as they do from all the picking and smoking." Smokey clouds pass through his own pearly whites. "Don't get me wrong, you're still ugly."

I threaten Toby, "I'll cut your dick off in your sleep and make you eat it," and wink at Jesse. "Your face is perfection."

Jesse's ears glow garnet. "You're such a cinnamon roll."

Jazz huffs. "Being cute doesn't take away how he was a complete and utter jackass on meth."

"Then quit your bitchin'."

"Back off!" Eli bolts at Jesse. "No reason for that!"

Jesse delivers a wet smacker to her cheek. "Sorry, toots, ya know you're my number one gal."

"I just worry about you."

"Don't worry 'bout me, Jazzlyn Fenstermacher."

Smoke vapors from my mouth and nostrils as I chuckle. "Your last name is *awesome*."

Jazz grins. "And you're high."

"That I am, Fenstermacher, that I am. Where's Brad?"

"Community service," answers Jax. "He beat the brains out of Isaac Caster our senior year, and Isaac's dad's a lawyer, and they pressed charges. Brad's *still* paying for it."

Jesse snorts. "Worth every hour of pickin' up highway trash."

"Why'd he beat him up?" I ask.

"Neal Lyons and his girlfriend, Courtney Redford—" Jax begins.

"Oh, shit, Mike, you're gonna love this!" Toby intrudes.

I reach for the blunt.

"They were always suckin' face in the halls," continues Jesse.

"And in the lunchroom," Jazz adds.

"And by the buses," Toby says.

"I think he gets the picture," Jax deadpans. "Isaac and his gang of scrotum-lickers filled a condom with mayo and put it in the hood of Courtney's sweater. Rumor was Courtney's friend, Dre Thomas, cement glued Isaac's locker shut to get back at him." Jax talks over our rib-aching fits and tears. "I felt awful for the janitor, who had to undo the glue, but it was *epic!* Isaac told Dre during lunch that he and his friends were gonna jump him by the end of the year. And, well, he may have used a certain… uh… *racist* term, and Brad just *went off!* He jumped up on his seat, ran from table to table, and started *bashing* on Issac!"

"How'd I miss that whole thing? I heard 'bout it but never saw it."

"You skipped lunch that day," Toby reminds Jesse.

"See what happens when you skip lunch?" I say, and Jesse sticks his tongue out at me. "Keep it up and I'll rip it out of your mouth."

"Don't tempt me with a good time," says Jesse, a hint of smut in his tone and eyes. "Gonna use your teeth?"

"Maybe."

"*Hot damn.*"

Jesse budges in closer to me, and his flirtatious grin has my body heat matching the Zippo flame at the end of my cigarette. I lay my head on his shoulder as his fingernails on my back send tingles up and down my spine.

"Your ass should be grateful you only got a slap on the wrist when you beat up Isaac," says Jazz.

"Geez!" I exclaim. "Didja all have a go at him?"

"He had it comin'. He pulled Gemma's skirt up in class and got off scot-free. Sumbitch has two fake teeth now. He literally ate them," Jesse flaunts.

"Mr. Reeves probably figured Jesse's ass-beating was punishment enough," says Toby, amusingly.

"Fuckin' waste because Gemma and Issac are now 'dating.'" Eli's fingers make air quotations. "I give it a week before she's used and tossed."

"Not that she'll mind. She enjoys being used and tossed." Jazz scours our gapes. "What? I'm supposed to support her *stupid* decision because she's my friend? *Puh-lease*. I'm over it."

Eli gives her a kiss after she finishes spit-sealing her joint, and he asks what we intend to do about our Oxy supply or lack thereof.

"I'm at a loss," says Toby. "I know a couple of dudes I could team up with. They've been trying to get me into their ring, but I keep backing out."

"Ya talkin' 'bout Ethan and Josh?"

"Not *them*. Just the ring."

"You're fuckin' with me? Not only will ya never get out of their drug circus, but... *look it! I'm FUCKIN' POPEYE!*"

"I like your limp," I tell Jesse.

"You would."

"You're not Popeye. You're Captain Jesse Sparrow."

"You're the one with the scar, so you're the pirate."

"But you have the limp."

"Scar."

"Limp."

"Scar."

"Limp."

"Scar."

"SHUT UP! You're both pirates!" Toby's hands—*thump!*—on the floor.

Jesse and I hunch over, laughing.

"This is serious, guys! I have nobody to revamp the supply, which means you two are SOL."

Jesse, drying his tears and snickering, asks, "Ya mean to tell me you don't have a *single* person who can score?"

"Do I need to say it slower for ya?"

"Percs?"

"Nope."

"Addy?"

"Just my personal 'script."

"How much?"

"Uh... one-fifty?"

"Fine." Jesse pulls out his wallet, and they do their deal. "*Any* painkillers?"

"I'm the preacher's son, Jess! It used to be an advantage 'til all these arrests. You have more connections than I do. Don't you have a guy for your guy, and that guy has a guy for another guy?"

"Main pill distributor went to prison for sellin' to an undercover, and his dude moved to Cincy. You're my Adderall guy. There's a few mall rats I could ask, but they never have anythin' stronger than

Hydros. I trust one other dude, but he's involved with meth and heroin, so I'd prefer not to ask."

Jazz rubs her forehead. "I'll say it again: don't you think this is a sign?"

Don't listen to her. What does she know?

Right on.

Jesse and Toby drone, eyes to the floor, and the rest of us shrug. I stand and announce I'm going outside for a walk.

"Sure, sure." Jesse waves his hand. "Be out in a few."

"Mind if I join you?"

"Not at all." I offer Jazz my arm. "M'lady."

"Don't be using your charm on my girl!" says Eli.

"Too late! He's got his white horse all saddled up and ready to whisk me away to his glass palace!"

"I'll throw rocks at it!"

We leave pattering laughter in our wake, our arms interlocked, her knee-high-laced military boots crunching dead vegetation.

"How're you doing, Mikey?"

"I'm... *doing*. It's been a day."

"Need to talk?"

Talking isn't on my agenda, yet I rave about the tussle me and Jesse had on our way to the estates. She listens closely, nods appropriately, and strokes my arm. Ending the tirade, we sit on the hilltop facing the lake. Superb oranges and reds sail to grant access for an inflowing amethystine ether.

"I hate to say it, but things between us changed after he and Gemma got into that fight."

"That's what I wanted to talk to you about. I've been biting my tongue for months. I know we talked at work about your up and down moods. That was Manager Jazz to her employee. Now it's Friend Jazz to her friend. I told you from day one to stay away from Jesse."

"You stopped with the warnings, though. Why? Afraid I'll tell the store manager you and I get high together outside work?"

"Don't be snarky, Mike. I've tried giving you two the benefit of the doubt. Jesse's like a brother to me, but he lives his life recklessly and without consequence. He's sucked you into his lifestyle. I can see how and why. You complement each other so well, but I'm afraid you're going way too fast and you're gonna burn out."

"There's more to Jesse than some guy who enjoys an occasional high."

Yeah, you tell her!

"*An occasional high? Seriously?* You *are* in deep. Ever since I've known him, he's either been high, withdrawing, dope sick, or chasing his next fix. I've *never* seen Jesse sober. You weren't there for the worst of it. I wasn't kidding when I said he was a monster on meth because he was! He's had fistfights with every one of them guys in there." She jolts her thumb to the estates. "He put Jax in the hospital! Jesse and Daryl would dress as homeless kids and panhandle the streets for drugs and money. They broke into houses and stole from their friends, their parents, from *us*. Did you know Jesse broke into my house and stole my parents' money, jewelry, and electronics? Jax told me. I never told my parents who'd done it because I wanted to protect him."

I hug my knees and pick at my fingernails.

"I'm just trying to help you understand, not upset you. I want him to get better. I thought… I thought he would grow up if he was around someone like you, but… it looks like you got tricked, too."

Ignore this drivel! Who does she think she is?

I've got this under control.

"He's not all bad," she resumes. "He has the biggest heart of anyone I know. He cared for Maggie when she was paralyzed, took over the household duties, and kept up with his grades on top of it, but, damn, Mike, he's… he's careless. He's—"

"*Human*, Jazz, he's human. And he's done with meth, so where're you going with this?"

"For now, sure. What about three months from now? Or a year? Trust me, I'm thrilled he dumped Tina, but I'm not stupid. I see it. I see it in his eyes sometimes—that starving addict. I see it consuming you."

Poppycock! You're not an addict! Whew, we could use a line right now… or five…

"I'm *not* an addict," I refute past clenched teeth. "I've *had* it with people telling me how I'm gonna end up. *I* make the choices for my future. Not you, not my parents, not Jesse. *Me*."

"How's your life with Jesse? Mike, you *are* Jesse. You're *never* sober. Have you researched what you've been snorting? Oxy is synthetic heroin. *Google it*. He's got you hooked."

Someone put a bullet in this bitch's mouth!

"Slow your roll, girlfriend. Jesse didn't put a gun to my head. Is it even possible for you to see the good in him, or do you just like to cherry-pick the negative?"

She folds her arms and stares down her nose at me. "Fine. I'm all ears. Tell me what I'm missing. Who is Jesse?"

I rifle for the proper descriptions, stating I see someone who's been shattered so many times he'll be fissured for life. He's lost and unglued, but who isn't? He's insightful, empathetic, funny, intelligent...

"Did you know his IQ is 145? I didn't know until recently, so there's another thing: he's full of surprises. He smiles and laughs with his entire body. And when I'm with him, I don't feel so... *alone*. He gets me, Jazz. He *just gets* me. If I wanted to ditch the drugs tomorrow, he'd back me up, no questions asked."

Her eyebrows arch and tears well up. "You... you... *damn*. I can't believe it. Eli was right."

"Right?"

Her smile enlarges—teeth and crinkled eyes.

"You're kinda freaking me out right now, Jazz."

Jesse gimps at an angle, planks down, and I steal the Salem Menthol from his mouth.

"Mine now."

He whispers, "You can have whatever ya want," his nose nuzzling my cheek.

Jazz keeps staring at us in that girlie manner I can't transcribe.

"Jazz," Jesse says, "you're kinda freakin' me out."

Her scowl ends our mirth. "Forget you two. It's getting late. I'm out."

She mumbles "stupidity" and "boys" uphill.

"What was *that* about?"

"Beats me," I say.

"Hm. Girls."

"You said it."

We drain our cigarettes to their filters and loaf in the twilight. Words can be murderous in these astral moments, his chin on my shoulder and nature’s melodies orbiting us.

“Ya good, Mi Sinclair?”

“Fantastic, Mea Harris. Y’good?”

His mouth skitters along my earlobe. “You’re here. Everythin'’s *perfect*.”

I stand corrected. Jesse’s lunar words shine brighter in my universe than nature ever could or would.

Enjoy it while it lasts.

FIVE

Chasing Ink

FACT #6: Top three prescription drugs used by high school seniors: Adderall (5.5%), tranquilizers (4.7%), other prescription opioids (4.2%).

Drug-free night #3.

Jesse and I finish our work shifts, and, at the house, he takes off to his room while I gently shake Mom, who's snoozing on the couch, to let her know we're home. Her eyelids flutter and she asks for the time.

"It's almost ten. Are you alright? You look... *yellow*."

"I'm fine, sweets. Just tired. How was your day?"

"Typical frappes and lattes. I'm gonna shower and go to bed."

"Okay, honey." She pats my arm. "I love you."

"I love you, too, Mom."

I kiss her cheek, shut the bathroom door, start the shower, and text Maddy.

(Me): Have you talked to Mom lately? Something's off. I'm worried about her.

Whenever I work up enough nerve to discuss her deteriorating health, she boots it away, saying she's "stressed" and "overworked."

Mind you, the seismic upheaval in our lives and the start of the semester for her had me sold, but when her olive complexion began developing a pallid tint (a color I blamed on bad lighting until it showed in the sunlight as well), my six-inch doubts grew six-feet tall.

Maddy and I haven't talked in months, so I'm not surprised she hasn't replied. Why own a phone if you won't answer it? Why have a brother you won't talk to?

Jesse, shirtless on my bed as I stomp in, looks up from scrolling through his phone and smiles.

"Hey, good lookin'. Why the long face?"

I open my closet. "Has Mom been looking a little... *rough?*"

"She has. I haven't said anythin' 'cause I didn't wanna worry ya. I'm sure she's just overwhelmed. She lost her house. Charlie hasn't spoken to her since that one night, and Leon never sees ya. I'm sure it's heavy."

"I guess."

I wiggle into my boxers under my towel, the damp cotton bundling at my feet, and Jesse springs off the bed and ransacks my clothes.

"Dude, it's bad enough you choose my outfits, and now you're choosing my pajamas?"

He spurns my satire and I look from him to the long-sleeved black shirt and black jeans he throws at me.

"Um... am I supposed to wear this tomorrow?"

"It's for tonight. We're goin' somewhere."

"We have work in the morning."

"Ya wanna score or not?"

Sit your ass down. We're *starving!*

I zip my jeans, save the shirt for later, and settle across from Jesse on the floor.

"Haven't seen ya draw for weeks," he says as I drag my sketchbook out from the desk. "You should paint."

"Yeah, you're right. What should I paint?"

"How 'bout the sketch of the girl fightin' herself?"

I snort the Oxy residue Jesse chipped off the chessboard and mortar. My dry, scaly nostrils burn. It won't stop me. Never does.

"Mike?"

"Jess?"

"Didja hear me?"

"I did."

"... and?"

I take a deep breath and recite to Jesse the time Maddy chopped her hair and overdosed on pills and vodka and how I carried her to Mom's car and hid her trimmings from Leon in a Walmart grocery bag.

"I was young. I didn't understand what was wrong with her; why she was always sick or staring into mirrors and cutting her hair. I spent two days on that sketch, made it into a painting and left it next to her bedroom door. The night she came home from the hospital, she woke me up and just... held me, crying and thanking me. So, um, the piece is Maddy's and Maddy's alone."

"I feel low. I didn't mean to bring up bad memories."

"You didn't know. It's cool. I'll think of something else to paint."

Like Jesse and his iconic profile. I immortalize it on parchment and ask him about tonight's plans.

"Not sure. Toby has an idea but didn't give specifics. Just said to make sure we're in black and have gloves."

That IQ test *has* to be rigged.

"It's obvious we're going to rob someone." Why does that sound normal coming out of my mouth?

"*Duh.* Just dunno who yet."

"Have you lost your mind?"

"Chill. We'll probably hit up Toby's."

"I… *what?*"

"We've done it *plenty* of times. His family's *loaded.*"

I slack against the wall, and Jesse's razor blade chips away at the tiny, blue shards in the mortar.

"You've robbed the Alexanders'?"

Jazz *wasn't* kidding.

"Toby's always been with me. I ain't *that* big of a dick."

"You've never been caught?"

"Nope." He's *scraping, scraping* at the Portland cement. "We'd wait 'til the 'rents were outta town and bust in the windows from the outside, unlock the door, whack shit over and flip the couch cushions. They live out in the boons, so nobody ever heard or saw us, and his family never suspected anythin' 'cause the entire town knows how rich they are, and a break-in wouldn't be unlikely."

"What about security alarms?"

Jesse shrugs. "We knew how much time we had 'til the cops showed."

"What's the benefit?"

"Money," he answers bluntly.

"What good is money if we don't have a dealer?"

"Dunno. Toby's plans never fail. I've stopped doubtin' him years ago. You can stay here or in the car with Jax if you don't wanna be too involved."

"Jax is in on it, too?"

"He's our getaway-man. He waits a few streets over. I toldja, Mike"—he smirks—"we've been doin' this since, like, freshman year."

We snort our pathetic, underweight rails, and I draw in my sketchbook as Jesse lies on the floor, his feet on mine, his arms behind his head. I continue to draft his jawline, neck, and salient hip bones.

"Like whatcha see?"

It's early October, yet the temperature in the room becomes a blistering hot August day.

"Who wouldn't?" I say.

"The view's pretty damn spectacular from where I'm at, too."

The pencil flips off my sketchpad, the music dissolving below the expanding blood in my eardrums as I touch his leg muscles to the pit of his knee, his rising chest hitching. He whispers my name, and I regress.

"Sorry."

He sits on his knees between mine, and mystifying soberness veils us like an opaque venereal haze, his gaze enslaving me.

"Mikey? How do I make ya feel?"

"You're my best friend."

"That ain't an emotion. How do I make ya *feel?*"

His fingernails scrawl up and down my forearm, and it's as if I'm a nomad wandering the amber landscape of his patient transfixion, wishing I could borrow even a third of his confidence. An internal earthquake vibrates in my bones as he raises our nervous, threaded fingers to our chins—a simple, motivating gesture.

"Remember when you said you thought Maddy was drowning while everyone around her breathed?"

"Yeah."

"And you said you feel like I'm drowning too?"

"Yes."

My lips graze the bridge of his nose. "You make me forget I'm drowning."

Could you be any cornier?

QUIET!

We're forehead to forehead, our fingers unraveling, raveling, unraveling, raveling...

I ask valorously, "How about you?"

His chuckle throws me off track, incapable of finding anything humorous about our conversation avowing to... *feelings*, a topic neither of us is dexterous with. Maybe he's just as self-conscious as I am when it's narrowed down to the nitty-gritty, and that's why he's laughing? Now *that's* a laugh. *Jesse? Insecure?*

"Sunflowers have this wicked ability called 'heliotropism,'" he says, his eyes staring directly into mine. "Their heads contain motor cells which allow them to spin in the sun's direction so, although they're stuck in one spot, there's always sunshine on their faces. I feel like... like when I'm with you, no matter what happens to me, even on the days I feel stuck, I'll never be stranded in the dark because *you* are the sun."

You two corn cobs were spun from the same husk.

"*Whoa*, Jess."

"Double *whoa.*"

How do I process this hurdle that's too tall and wide to leap or walk over? What choice is left for me than to confront my... *feelings,* his... *feelings,* my doubts and fears head-on? I'm not the "headfirst" type. Jesse lunges into the depths, and I test the waters.

"We don't need to decide anythin' right now."

It's like I've drunk my first sip of oxygen on earth. One of us had to say it. Better him than me.

"This is a lot."

"It's a big decision," he agrees.

"The biggest."

"Just know that I... that I... well, ya know..."

"That you what?" Honestly, I'm clueless.

"That I—" he then answers his chiming phone, "*What, Tobs?*"

He smiles as my thumb strokes his wrist.

"Uh-huh. Sure. Okay. Later." He hangs up. "Gotta go."

"Now?"

"Unless you wanna stay here?"

I swoop on my shirt to endorse my tribute. Jesse clothes himself entirely in black, his hair hidden inside a black beanie, and he snugs one onto my head as well.

"I'm a bad influence on ya."

"But there's never a dull moment."

"For sure. I deactivated the alarm, and your ma's fast asleep. Ready?"

"As I'll ever be."

Jesse kisses my cheek and mounts the windowpane, asking, "What's up? Changed your mind?"

"You were gonna tell me something?"

He delays. "It's nothin'."

"We don't keep secrets."

He sizes me from head to foot. "It ain't a secret, Square. It's pretty fuckin' clear."

"What's clear?"

"You're smart. You'll figure it out."

We run to Junkie's Playground, where Toby is waiting... and where Daryl died. Jesse goes inelastic, and my arm loops his waist. He gives me a smile; no words necessary. He knows I'm here for him, and I know he appreciates it.

I step back in protest as Toby attacks me with a lint roller.

"Can't risk spare hair in the car," he says.

He doesn't answer when I ask who owns the rusty Buick.

Jesse snags the lint roller before Toby's given a chance to harass him.

"Gloves?" Toby asks.

Jesse, not saying a word, lends me one of the two black pairs stowed in his pocket.

"Sweet," says Toby. "Make sure they're on before you get in or touch the car. Under no circumstances are you to take them off. Alright, let's ride."

Brad fist-bumps us from the front seat. Toby drives off onto the highway and lectures that we're not to leave behind cigarette butts or anything else of personal value.

What's his deal with the car? Is it his parents, and he's making sure there's no record of us "borrowing" it? Surely his family can afford a finer car than this Buick with a dangling piece underneath clapping in the breeze. The tape player has been removed (or stolen), and the upholstery stinks of gasoline, human urine, alcohol, and smoke (marijuana and cigarettes).

Highway 13 goes on and on. Jesse puffs his Salem Menthol and migrates to the middle seat and accepts my hand. He glimpses our gloved, woven fingers, his head on my shoulder.

Ten minutes.

Twenty.

Thirty.

I was a skittish teenager earlier, and now that teenager's searching for a time machine to go back to being the chastity boy camping out on the foot of his parents' bed. I need Oxy. I need to smooth the edges, because Jesse's hand in mine isn't doing me justice. I've been to Toby's. It's not this far out.

Toby slows down in a small, densely populated town, the houses scattered across acres, a lone stop sign proudly standing at the four-way, and there's a dollar store, two petrol stations, and an Elks Pharmacy.

He brakes. "Grab what you can, boys."

I stiffen.

Two duffels and two masks fly into the backseat.

"Put on the masks. Don't waste time reading labels—"

"Toby!" I shout.

"—five minutes and get the hell out."

I pull the ski mask over my cap and face. "How're we even getting in?"

Jesse's reach for the door handle extracts as Toby hightails it towards the pharmacy's window wall.

No.

No. Way.

This is *not* happening!

"Toby?! *What the fuck, dude?*" yells Jesse.

I'm a raccoon in a hunter's trap.

The elk on the pharmacy sign mutates into a prodigious blur.

Jesse isn't buckled in.

I toss myself onto him, staring ahead, flabbergasted.

Faster...

Faster...

Closer...

Closer...

I'm Jesse's human shield.

Glassy debris.

Trebling alarms.

I'm seeing red.

SIX

Sunny Disposition

FACT #7: FATAL DRUG OVERDOSES IN 1999–2016: 632, 331. NUMBER OF THOSE OVERDOSES CAUSED BY OPIOIDS: 351, 630.

"EVERYONE OUT! MOVE, MOVE, MOVE!"

Toby's lurid commands and the crash stun me from flesh to muscle to entrails. Jesse's face in my hands, I see my shocked consternation reflecting at me.

"Are you hurt?"

Glass shards volley from his shaking head and fear sidles in as we realize we're crushed beneath a beam spearing the rear window. He wriggles free, lifts the shaft, and I tumble out, Jesse urging me onwards, Toby and Brad ten paces ahead of us and laundering bottles off the shelves by the armfuls.

I'm not in my head. Apart from an imprudent lamb being led off the cliff by his shepherds, I don't recognize where I am or who I am. Me and Jesse vault over the pharmacist's counter and split up, him to the right, me to the left. The twelve aisles of five-level shelving seem kilometers long.

Mislaid in the bedlam of the flogging alarm like being at a Jax and the Snax concert, I dump various prescription boxes, bags, and bottles into my duffel, shelf after shelf. It's not Michael Sinclair stealing drugs. It's an inhuman monster.

IT'S ME!

"LET'S GET OUTTA HERE!"

Brad.

Jesse yanks on my wrist, and his limp has us tottering behind Brad and Toby, the distant trills of police sirens brewing bile in my throat as Toby navigates us to Jax's car parked on a side street.

I'm sandwiched between Jesse and Brad in the backseat and Jax steers out of the alley, so unperturbed, like a bus driver collecting school kids from a field trip, and he chooses the back roads away from the police. My guardian angel is undoubtedly hitting his forehead, and the voice in my head heehaws: **AGAIN! AGAIN! LET'S GO AGAIN!**

I struggle with my cigarette pack, and Jesse removes his gloves, both our masks, and grabs the box, the blue stereo light brightly showcasing the elevated blood pressure on his cheeks. I digest the smoke, and Jesse blows his out in several stout bursts.

Jesse's pissed-off glare could decapitate Toby, who's punching the air, shouting, "Holy shit! What a rush! Oh, my God!"

The rest of us are staring forward and zip-lipped. White, blocky letters spell out RICHLAND on a reflective green sign, and Jax notifies us his folks are gone for the weekend, and we can sort out the loot at his crib. Thank God. I need to wind down. I need a fix. I'd go for an aspirin at this point.

Jax pulls into the carport attached to a doublewide trailer across from Langer's Convenience Store. Duffels in hand, we wait for Jax to unlock the door to a home with chipped tables, a brown sofa, and a baby blue and white kitchen.

Toby yaps and yaps about the heist, and in a split second, Jesse drops his duffel, his fist *swishing*, the collision bone-cracking. Toby lands sideways on the duffel bags, his defensive elbow plowing into cartilage, and blood splatters from Jesse's nose.

We encroach at once. Jesse squiggles like a jellyfish in an overcrowded aquarium, trying to break free from my and Jax's clasp on his wrists, and Brad fastens his arms around Toby's midsection.

"I'm gonna *fuckin' kill you*, Alexander!"

"Jess, calm down," I order.

Toby spits crimson spittle. "The hell ya punch me for?"

"'Cause you're an actual idiot! It's one thing to rob your own house, but a pharmacy? A PHARMACY?! Are ya barkin' mad? What if there's cameras? We coulda died!"

"We made it, didn't we? We had masks! Gloves! I hot-wired the car from a junkyard, and it's unregistered!"

"And were ya *seen* in the junkyard?"

"Would we be here if I were?! I'm sorry I lied. I should've told you my plan from the get!"

"Ya coulda killed us! We coulda passed out! Then what, Tobs? Huh?"

"I grew up in that town and was familiar with the drugstore. The windows are thin, cheap glass. You could throw a pellet and it'd break!"

"Then why drive a car through it?"

"I don't know, man! It was a last-minute plan! Everything worked out. Have I ever let you down before?"

Jesse decompresses. "Nah, ya never have. I'm sorry. I'm in shock.

A pharmacy break-in was the last thing I expected to do tonight."

"I was scared shitless, too. I had to concentrate; make sure we didn't crash into anything fatal."

"Oh, your drivin' skills were spot on. I'm cool, guys," he says to us. "I'm cool. No more punchin'."

They hug it out, and I flop onto the couch and strip out of my shirt, pitching it... somewhere. Jesse discards his shirt, too, and takes a load off next to me with an "*oomph*," his bloody nose staining his upper lip.

"You're bleeding."

He dabs his nostrils and stares at his fingertips. "Ha! How 'bout that?"

"Where's the bathroom?"

Sweat collects on our foreheads in the last room on the left of a dark hallway as I apply balled-up tissues to the epistaxis.

"Don't put your head back. You'll swallow blood that way. Lean forward a bit. There ya go. Pinch your nostrils."

"How do ya know how to stop nosebleeds?"

"I got them a lot as a kid. Something about heights."

I search under the sink for medical supplies, leap onto the counter and motion Jesse in front of me, the scarlet-soaked tissue thrown away, and he jerks and digs his nails into my knees while I cleanse and disinfect the battered area.

"Almost done. Your friends are fucking crazy."

He laughs. "At times."

Papers rustle from the other room, and Toby declares, "Oxy 80s!"

TOUCHDOWN!

"Dude, no way!" Brad shouts.

"Bring four in here!"

I'll be damned if I don't get instant compensation for robbing a pharmacy.

Damn right!

"Gettin' feisty, Mi Sinclair."

I take the four pills from Jax and he runs his fingers through his deflated, neon-red mohawk.

"Sorry it's so hot in here," he says. "AC broke last night."

"All good. Thanks, man. I'll take the bottle too."

He sets the Jim Beam down next to the sink. "Never thought Toby could pack such a mean punch. Y'alright there, Jess?"

"*Peachy.*"

The door clicks shut, and my circulation welcomes the drugs we chase with liquor.

"I'm sorry 'bout tonight. I had no idea."

"You wouldn't have punched Toby if you had. You wouldn't have brought me along either."

"I ain't ever seen you that scared. If the cops catch on, I'll keep ya out of it. I'll talk to the guys later."

"Don't be dumb. I helped. I'm not gonna let you take the fall."

"But you have a future."

"And so do they! And so do you! You seriously need to quit your bullshit. I thought we solved this debate like… a *zillion* times?"

"I won't bring it up again."

My fingers receive kisses as they roam his smooth lips and scratchy stubble.

"Ya didn't have to cover me," he says.

"Yes, I did. We were speeding into a building. I kept imagining you flying through the windshield."

"I owe ya. I keep puttin' ya in danger."

"Consider this a freebie."

Jesse steps up to my eye level. "You know I'd take a bullet for ya."

"And I'd stitch you up afterward."

We barter a laugh and whiskey shots, our sticky chests melding after he stows the medical items back where they belong and helps me off the counter. He tickles my vertebrate, and the stubble I glorified blesses my forehead.

"Does it still hurt?" I ask as my hands gloss over the scar on his ribcage.

Goosebumps grow from my caresses, his breathing erratic.

"Not when ya touch me like that."

I dare to sneak a peek at him, his vamped fixation as intoxicating as Jim Beam, our swerving bodies like two ocean waves crashing into an amber whiskey horizon. The unrecognizable song he hums, the skin-on-skin contact, and the sweat and alcohol scents engulf my senses.

"Y'tired, Mikey?"

"I'm beat."

"Let's get our cut and go home."

"Not yet. You feel good."

"Are ya drunk already?"

"Shut up, Jess."

I judder, clawing the indentations on the small of his back with every nibble to my earlobe—his teeth slicker than his labret piercing—and the commotion in the living room is an afterthought as the guys sort out our stolen goods.

"If we don't stop right now, we're gonna end up fuckin' on the bathroom counter, and I don't think Jax or his toothbrush will appreciate that much." He laughs at my fallen jaw and kisses my forehead. "You're almost too easy to fluster."

"Jerk."

In the living room, Jax shoves empty, white bags postmarked by an elk logo into a black sack as Toby, a frozen bag of carrots on his swollen lip, auctions off the hundreds, if not more, orange bottles on the pea-green carpet.

"Five-milligram morphine. Going once... going twice..."

"Save 'em for Jazz," says Jesse. "They're 'bout the only thing she likes."

Jesse and I review the bottles in the gaps of our intersected legs.

"There's a shitload of people with high blood pressure and heart problems," I comment dryly. "Thinking this was a bust."

"Or you got a bad batch?" says Toby. "I have seven bottles of Oxycodone, two of which are 30s, three that are 10s, and one that's 5s, plus the 80s. Keep the 80s. I was an asshole. You're not used to this shit. You and Jesse split it."

"I can't take this."

Just accept it!

"Yes, you can. I can sell the 10s and 5s to the wannabe druggies at church and the high school kids at the mall; sell them for double their worth and make a nice profit."

"Sweet. Thanks."

"No problem."

"I got five bottles of Percocet," announces Jax.

"We'll take two of the 20s and you can have the rest," says Jesse.

I pinch my arm to convince myself I'm in Jax's trailer and not at some narcotics benefit.

"Oh, Jesssseeee." Brad chucks a bottle in his direction. "All yours, buddy."

Jesse muses and feeds me one of the Dilaudid 8s and whiskey.

"Adderall!" Jesse shouts happily.

"Blue or capsule?" asks Brad.

"Blue."

"Can we split?"

"Sure. I still have some from Toby."

This goes on for an hour; most of our theft throwaway junk: Zocor, Lipitor, OTC aspirin, cold medicine (not the fun kind), and antibiotics (which I keep because you'll never know). The opposite stockpile includes Morphine, Oxycodone, OxyContin, Percocet, Adderall, Codeine (liquid and pills), Dilaudid, and Hydrocodone. If Jesse and I plan smartly, we could spread it out for two months, though at our rate, it'll last one, maybe one and a half.

"I can't believe I'm sayin' this, but bravo, Alexander," says Jesse.

Toby curtsies. "I'm rather impressed with myself. I'm gonna bank off this pirated goldmine! We dried out that pharmacy."

"That may be so, but we're never doin' this again. It'll raise suspicion if we make a habit of crashin' into pharmacies."

"Agreed," says Brad, exhaling a long, rugged breath. "Once is enough."

"I'm good too. I already know I'll be on edge for months."

"We'll be fine, Mike." Toby flashes his blood-caked teeth.

"A'ight, we're out. You're gonna dispose of the evidence, right?" Jesse asks Jax. "Your 'rents won't hesitate to report us if they find the bottles."

Tremendous.

"Burning it as we speak, Jess, relax!" Jax tows the trash bags to the backdoor.

An ash, fire, and roasting plastic concoction stalk us home, our pockets bulging with embezzled narcotics.

"Don't stress too much, Mike. Toby's right—our faces were covered, and we were in and out. It'd take a lot of work to track us down. I promise we're good."

Drunk and high, we waddle down Indigo, and the amount of running we'd done has worsened Jesse's limp.

"Are you okay?"

"Kinda sore but"—he knocks his pocket, the pills jangling in their plastic lodgings—"that's what *these* are for."

"You should give it a rest for a couple of days."

"Yes, Nurse Mikey."

"Don't ever, *ever* call me that… *ever.*"

"M'bad… Nurse Mikey."

"I'll kill you."

"Ya wouldn't dare."

"Hop on my back. I'll carry you home."

I lift him off the ground.

"Ya gonna nay like a horse?"

"You're a dipshit."

"I'm sorry," he whispers against my neck. "You're amazin'."

"Just being me."

"Precisely."

"Not so bad yourself, Harris."

I let him off at the window, and he opens the screen, loses his footing, and the bed breaks our fall.

"Crap. Y'alright?" he asks, steadying himself above me.

"I told you that damn leg needs a rest."

"I hate this *damn* leg now. I won't be able to skate no more. Wish I could stomp the shit out of them fuckers and see how they like bein' permanent Popeyes."

"*Pirate.* Now get up. I can't breathe. You're too heavy."

"Now who's the dipshit?"

We empty our pockets and scratch our heads at the various drugs.

"Where are we supposed to hide this?" asks Jesse. "My room?"

"My desk drawer with the lock? I'll give you the spare key."

"That'll work. Wanna do some rails before we sleep?"

"Xanax?"

It'd be nice to sleep for once.

"Shit, yes," he assents. "I could use a good night's rest."

I change my clothes as Jesse arranges the chessboard and its fixings. Leaning on the wall, twisting and untwisting my flannel pajama bottoms, I lionize Jesse *crunch, crunch, crunch*ing the pills into chunk-free grains, and whether that's an effective and expedient talent is inapt.

Immersed in the *crunch*ing, he asks, "Y'ever thought of becomin' a photographer?"

"Not really. Why?"

"You're just standin' there starin' at me. Y'know what they say 'bout pictures."

My ears scorch, the rest of me immobile, and Jesse serves me the chessboard and straw like a dinner tray.

"Aw, c'mon, Mikey, I'm sorry I called ya out. Nothin' to be ashamed of. I know I'm sexy."

I sigh at the ceiling and situate myself on the bed. Jesse steadies the board for me, the drug causing gooey liquid to leak from my nose, and he uses his shirt to plug the blood.

"You'll start gettin' them childhood nosebleeds if ya don't lay off snortin' for a bit."

"Yes, Nurse Jesse."

"Touché."

The bleeding stops, and he drops the shirt into the hamper on his way to change. I never used to look away. This time, I do.

Outside on the porch, the Xanax kick-starts during my second cigarette, my cheek on Jesse's bicep and knuckles scrambling up and down his knee and thigh. Indigo's placid at night, and as our fingertips tap and palm-read, I reminisce.

"Penny for your faraway thoughts in that beautiful mind?"

I let him in on how Indigo Street's heartless residents didn't help him that mid-July rainy night. His mouth in my hair breathes in.

"You weren't heartless, Mikey."

"I'm like... one in seventy."

"That's what makes ya special. Why *didja* help me?"

"Why wouldn't I? I just knew you needed me. Intuition?"

"Fate? I guess it ain't worth questionin'. Who knows where we'd be if ya hadn't come to me? Do ya think we'd still be here right now?"

"I think you would've gained fifty pounds off maple macchiatos."

"Fifty?"

"That's how long it would've taken for one of us to break the ice."

More finger tapping.

"My coffee one-liners didn't break the ice? Just be glad I didn't say the original pickup line. Hey, Mikey?"

"Jesus, not again."

"Is that a steam wand in your pocket, or are ya just happy to see me?"

"I dunno, Jess, why don't you reach in and find out?"

The momentary clearing of shocked silence is filled by his robust laughter.

"Look at you, Sinclair! Catchin' *me* off guard."

"You're still ridiculous, but I wouldn't want you any other way. And I'll always find you," I promise, our palms flat and fingers interlacing.

"We'll always find *each other*, Mi Sinclair, even in our lifetimes after this one."

Jesse punches in the alarm numbers, and I follow his silhouette and lurching hips to the bedroom. He switches on *Spotify*, turns off the lights, and covers us with the bedsheet.

My head hits the pillow, and although I exhale jubilantly, things feel... *different*, for lack of a better term, lying here on our backs. It's never a big deal if our feet or arms come into contact or if our legs tangle by morning. Tonight, it's as if a partition protrudes from the mattress, and if one of us crosses it, the rubble will bury us, which scares the life out of me. While most people fear dying, I fear suffocation.

We don't budge.

We don't breathe.

And just when I think we're about to fall asleep to the inescapable tension, he finds my arm in the dark and guides me to his side of the bed, his chest taking the place of my pillow and his heartbeat replacing the music.

On the apex of sleep, in his ethereal arms, he twirls my hair, and his low tenor productively equips an extra gallop to my own beating heart.

"G'night, Mi Sinclair."

"Sweet dreams, Mea Harris."

"Only if you're in 'em."

SEVEN

Cyanide Sun

FACT #8: IN AMERICA, ONLY 10.9% OF INDIVIDUALS WHO REQUIRE TREATMENT IN A SPECIALIZED FACILITY FOR SUBSTANCE ABUSE ACTUALLY RECEIVE IT.

MY SHAKES on top of an operative smile dupe my boss, coworkers, and customers into believing I'm fine… *100% fine*; my actions, however, are too falsely chipper to be me. The headline on the front page of the local newspaper forces my bowling ball-sized heart down my garden hose-tight throat.

I call Jesse from the unoccupied breakroom.

"Mi Sinclair. I miss you."

"Did you see the paper?"

"Yes. It's all good. They're statin' there are no leads. It's fine. Stay calm."

"S-s-stay calm? It says, 'PHARMACY HEIST!'"

"It's the vaguest headline I've ever read, Mike. Whatever Toby crashed into that night disabled the cameras. We're good. I swear. Just breathe. Breathe with me."

Our coordinating breaths create static until my boiling nerves simmer.

"There ya go. I'll see ya after work."

"Thank you. I needed that. Oh, and Jess? I miss you too."

SUMMER STRAYS, and Ohio swaps its greenery for a tangerine, canary, and bronze collage Jesse and I spend time with. The foliate scent escorts serenity even to the putrid ROY G BIV, and, as you know, serenity is relatively infrequent these days.

A decent chunk of October was squandered with persistent looks out windows, reading newspapers and internet articles, and tuning into the news. A brain cell died with every passing police car, officer, or siren. Jazz and Eli weren't informed about what we'd done, and it only ignited another match to my full-blown anxiety gas tank. Jazz was already losing her patience with me, and God only knows what she'd do if she found out I partook in a burglary.

Without a single fingerprint or hair strand to work off of, the Elks Pharmacy dropped the investigation the week of Halloween.

Let's not flout Mom's health, her sluggish movements, and random naps that were becoming more and more prevalent. Jesse and I helped her grade papers and organize assignments. She claimed she consulted a doctor and blushed at the term *menopause*.

"I didn't want to have this conversation with you, but here it is, boys. Menopause is no picnic. Well, except for the hot flashes. They're hotter than a summer picnic."

I don't need to be well-versed in women's health to know menopause doesn't cause yellowish skin.

And then there's Jesse...

Jesse.

My lighthouse beacon.

The problem with beacons is that they're on a revolving

sequence granting you light every thirty seconds if you're fortunate, but if you're stranded in the eye of a tropical cyclone, the light is defective and provides little sanctuary, which brings us to...

Feelings. They're as flimsy as a house of cards. Jesse's my security blanket, and when he's not there to drape me, the devils gnash their fangs, terrorizing me within my dreams, awake or asleep. I flat-out loathed it when he slept in his room, which wasn't often, but I got pampered by his body warmth, and I adjusted to change as well as I acclimated to the move from Suburban Richland to Downtown Richland. And since we went from hot to cold in a span of days, I naturally blamed my indecisiveness on the drugs and that irritating voice:

You'll only break his heart. He'll leave you. Toby will stop selling to you. How will you get your fix? Choose, Mike: Jesse or drugs?

Why couldn't I have both?

On a lighter note, we've enough drugs to last another two weeks, give or take, although I couldn't tell you where we'll go from there. I scored high on my ACTs and SATs and applied to four art colleges in California. Jesse began teaching me to drive, a sight to behold, I assure you, never mind it's illegal to operate on a permit with a person under twenty-one, but I didn't trust anybody else. I nearly died of a stroke when I drove onto a curb. Jesse nearly died laughing.

Our days off were spent getting high with the Sharp Edges in the estates or at home playing Pictionary or other games with Mom. Paul and Jesse started a Friday tradition of having father-son nights together in town, allowing me and Mom to reconnect as well. I savored those nights because, hard as I tried, I couldn't seem to rise above the gravity of a forlorn future.

It's Halloween.

I end my afternoon shift by purchasing my fourth Americano and an upside down maple macchiato (extra maple, extra shot, light ice) for Jesse. Bent over the counter, Nora is meticulously flirting, her butt wagging, eyelashes fluttering, and breasts pushed together, forming a *V*.

Women.

She's not *that* obnoxious. She has iron-straight blonde hair and irises colored ice chips, and her legs are almost too long for her short figure. She dreams of being a photographer for *National Geographic*, and we have similar ambitions to head to California to live out the starving artist lifestyle.

Alright, she's cute, so sue me, but it's still off-putting when she bites her lip. Whenever Jesse does it, it's... *sexy*.

"So, Mikey, I've wanted to ask you for some time now, but you're always with Jesse."

I forgot to mention how she shuns Jesse at all costs, as if he's infected with the Black Plague, Ebola, or some other incurable disease.

"Would you like to... um... go to a party tonight? With me? As my date?"

I scratch the back of my neck. I've never been asked out on a date.

"Uh... well..."

"There ya are, Mi Sinclair!"

Thank you, Moses parting seas!

"This mine?" Jesse takes the macchiato. "Is there creamer in this? Or didja get enough of that last night?"

I mumble, "Dammit, Jess," laughing at the black checkered tile and scooting into him, his arm slinging my shoulders.

"Sup, Nors? Photography project comin' along?"

I can practically smell her grilling glare at Jesse. "*Splendidly.*" She then asks me, "How about it?"

"It's nice of you to ask, Nora, but I have plans. I'm sorry."

"Oh. Uh. Okay." She drags her words, her pupils swinging like a pendulum from me to Jesse. "Guess I'll see ya later."

His free hand flapping, Jesse shouts, "Bye, Nors!" and, in the parking lot, sings, "Mikey and Nora sittin' in a tree—"

"You fuckin' serious? Are we in kindergarten?"

An ion couldn't fit between us as I'm pegged to himself and the Honda.

"K-I-S-S-I-N-G."

I elevate an eyebrow. "Satisfied now?"

"What comes first, Mikey?"

"I'm *not* answering that."

"*What... comes... first?*" he asks again, deeply, slowly.

His daring scrutiny lances me—new and magnetic.

I give in. "Love."

Jesse bites his lip, and it's so far from gross that it's painfully delicious.

"*Love.* Ya love Nora?"

I snort. "You're a real jokester."

"Ya think she's cute?"

His hands are on my waist, his pelvis grating.

Sweet Mother…

Now *that's* gross.

"She's… not really my type."

"What's your type?"

"Not her."

"Y'got somethin' against blondes?"

This mother fucker has puns today. Skateboards double kickflip in my stomach at his devious grin. An eastern wind carts his cologne and natural musk that smells like 3 AM fog rising from damp earth after an April shower. I want to bottle it and reserve it for the nights he sleeps in his room.

I spin my fingers in his un-gelled, shaggy glacier hair. "I think blondes are *extremely* sexy."

"We do have more fun."

"What about you? Are you into blondes?"

He pushes his hand into my windswept curls. "Nah, more of a brunette man myself."

"You said blondes are fun."

"They are, but brunettes are *passionate*. And maybe it's just me, but I prefer passion over fun."

His tongue moistening his pierced lip and his hips seesawing on my motionless ones have me too preoccupied to notice wandering peers—the population being just us two.

"Are ya passionate, Sinclair?"

"I *am* a brunette."

Jesse just… Jesse Harris just *moaned*. Fuck me sideways twice to next Sunday!

He's… he's… he's walking to the driver's side! *What a dick!*

I get in the car, swallow an Oxy 80 and, our cigarettes lit, we blow smoke in more ways than one, neither of us uttering a syllable until—

"Are we just gonna keep turnin' a blind eye to this, Mike?"

"I... you just... back there... you..."

"I won't make a move if I don't hear ya say it. It doesn't work that way. If you wanna go with Nora, ya should."

"Are you *jealous?*"

He looks at me—"If I am?"—and back to the traffic.

"Why would you tell me to go? You *want* me to go?"

"*Fuck! No!* But, lemme ask, if you didn't know me, wouldja?"

BAH! This is outside my jurisdiction. *Feelings.* Nora lacks Jesse's mysterious, rebellious energy I'm sinfully attracted to. He's spontaneous. Raw. It's not his fault we're slow dancing in limbo—my insecurities, uncertainties... *feelings.* He's kind enough to let me lead the tango.

All you have to do is say the word. Wuss.

My intestines are as disorganized as yarn in an overstuffed pantry.

"I don't know, Jess."

EIGHT

Canticles of Ecstasy

FACT #9: THE RATE OF RELAPSE IN ADDICTION TREATMENTS IS 40-60% AND IS A RATE SIMILAR TO RATES OF OTHER CHRONIC DISEASES SUCH AS ASTHMA, TYPE ONE DIABETES, AND HYPERTENSION.

I SCOOP candy out of the plastic jack-o'-lantern while complimenting the neighborhood youngsters' costumes, ranging from ninjas, Batmans, princesses, witches, video game characters, musicians, and historical figures. Halloween has always been my favorite holiday, bar none, but I repel the candy bowl on my left, which ought to be Jesse's seat.

"You seem troubled, sweets," Mom says.

"Jesse should be here. He loves Halloween."

She smirks like Jazz had at the estates, and I ask the same question, "Why're you looking at me like that?"

"No reason."

Get this: she *giggles*, a full-on, giddy teenage girl giggle, not a short twitter.

"He's just having dinner with his dad," she reassures. "He'll be home soon."

When *soon* gets here, my head on his shoulder defrosts my

metallic anxieties into a material I can flake off and fling into an ultimate inferno. My nose in his gray sweatshirt absorbs the weed, Old Spice body wash, and fabric softener.

Plastic crinkles.

A Zippo flicks.

Weed, blueberries, and dried leaves substitute the previous fragrance, and if given a choice, I'd choose Jesse's aroma *every damn time.*

His fingernails dancing up and down my arm amplifies the gooseflesh on my skin from the October chill, and he whispers, "shotty," before I drink in the smoke he generously exchanges into my mouth.

"I missed you."

Making him smile will never be disbarred from the number one spot on my list of achievements.

"I missed ya too, Mi Sinclair."

Our legendary eye contact diverts to my hand on his knee. *How does that keep happening?*

"How wouldja spend your last night on earth if an asteroid was headin' towards us at this very second but wouldn't hit 'til mornin'?"

"With you," I answer instantly, my mind printing a picture book of us on my bed, listening to music and discussing art, science, and mythology. To die in his arms, to hear his heart pump its last thrum, would be an enthralling way to go out.

"What would we do?"

"It's our last night, right? So, we'd spend it getting… What's the saying? 'White girl wasted.'"

His laughter and intimate stare electrify my every neuron, the porch light zapping.

"Let's go to the estates."

"Jess, it's late."

"So, what?" His lips ghost mine. "The world's gonna implode by mornin'."

"You're nothing but trouble."

"Don't josh yourself, Mikey. I'm the kinda trouble you enjoy."

Zeroed in on his mouth singing in slow motion to our playlist in the car, the innovative *feeling* arises. He was never *just* a friend like the other Sharp Edges. *Feelings*. They're uncharted territories, unpolished and... *safe*. I feel *safe*, and that safety's confirmed on our nocturnal promenade done in small talk and held hands—the leafless backlands and odd bat signaling how alone we are.

In the cobweb-infested living room, our legs crossed and knees touching, dust and cigarette smoke waltzes as Jesse sticks an LSD tab on my tongue.

We lie in the tent we assemble on the lakeshore. The high boosting in, an oceanic cave sheathes the world I'm familiar with, the waves merging, ascending, and widening the further I gravitate into my hallucination.

The earth feels topsy-turvy, like I'm on a tightrope. Do I jump or freefall?

We sit up with our foreheads together, half for support and half for the thrill of the contact itself, and he gently scratches my arms, shoulders, and hands.

"Whatcha see?" he asks.

I illustrate *our* world: an ocean cave. Turquoise, sea green, gray waters spin in and out of riptides while fourteen-pointed stars sprout from his irises. Starbursts. *Beautiful starbursts.* Dried, chafing grass composes an orchestrated ditty of winds, cellos, and violins.

"Magnificent."

"How about you, Jesse? What do you see?"

"Your skin..." he whispers, caressing me from biceps to palms. "Your skin radiates like kaleidoscope prisms. Diamonds—pears, squares, spheres—drizzle from a galaxy sky. I swear I can see the Milky Way."

"I love galaxies. It's cold tonight, but your touch is... *sensational*; hot, like fire thawing me out of a block of ice."

"And your touch is like mocha icin'."

I scribble "mocha icin'" to my pitifully limited collection of praises for the sole purpose that it comes from Jesse.

I vomit out the tent door and Jesse rubs my back. Bottled water and a stick of gum aren't a cure-all, but they'll suffice.

It's Jesse's idea to go skinny dipping—one panned out to appease my water obsession. I no longer fraught over jumping or falling off my tightrope as I float next to him, the water deciding for me, our entwined fingers dunking in and out of the blackened surface. Weightless. Free. *Safe.*

"I'm shiverin' like a bird in a blizzard," Jesse says.

We swim back to shore, and I long to dive back in. I wouldn't mind us growing old on the water; crick joints, wrinkles, and white hair won't disrupt the sunlight I see whenever he looks at me.

Safe.

On dry land, we towel off our naked bodies, the harvest moon highlighting certain *features* of his physique. He buttons his shorts as he walks towards me, his mischievous grin spread ear to ear.

"My, my, Sinclair, ya sure got a habit of starin' at me."

"I think you're right. It's a habit I don't plan on breaking." Before I can stop myself, I just *keep blathering*. "Do you know what you are? When I look at you, you're a sunburn without the sting."

"Um..." Jesse lags. "Y'know, I think it's safe to say I'm a cheesy dude."

"Definitely."

"And I'd have somethin' equally romantic and sappy to say 'bout how I feel when I look at you?"

"Of course."

He grins, laughing with his nose. "You've left me speechless."

In disbelief, I smile. "Am I the first?"

"Yes. And you'll be the last."

"*Huzzah*."

We bump Oxy in the tent and, afterward, build a bonfire, a trivial task I don't recommend doing while tripping on LSD. Actually, I don't recommend doing LSD at all, but that point is moot. I have to physically *catch* the wiggling sticks, the strenuous quest worth the labor as we warm ourselves.

"The fire's screamin'," he says.

"It sounds like singing to me. Church choir."

"You're so bohemian."

I bite into my cigarette filter, flick my lighter, and the single flame performing a striptease for my nose snuffs as Jesse lowers my arm.

"Thing's gonna explode if ya keep it lit like that."

"Sorry."

"Don't be sorry. It's easy to get lost in a trip. Just stay with me. I'm right here."

Safe.

"Talk to me. What's goin' on in that beautiful brain?"

Sober Mike would hesitate and rip his fingernails to shreds. Brimming with LSD, ocean waves, and Jesse's divine, starburst irises, I'm anything but hesitant and say, "You're my reflection. Did you know that?"

In a literal sense, I can see our stress amassing a maelstrom.

"You can talk to me too, Jess."

"Can I, though?" The question purls upwards into our revolving sea.

I'd forego my LSD trip if it meant I could trip inside his head and hear what's left unsaid. I can only speculate he fears his feelings won't be reciprocated, and such speculation is soul crippling.

"Jesse—"

"Wait," he interrupts, sighing. "I need a second."

Seconds upon seconds upon seconds...

He eliminates the space between us, his thumbs rubbing my wrist in frequency to the spasmodic thudding inside my chest.

"I wanna try somethin' but... shit, don't... don't spaz," he says as his hands gliding up my arms declare homeland on my jaw.

I swallow. "Jesse?"

"Yes?"

"Are you going to kiss me?"

He blinks fast. "I... do ya *want* me to?"

My head's a feather swooping left and right into a flowering field of anticipation as I desperately try to solve Jesse's Rubik's cube-like visage showing... Uncertainty? Urgency?

"Do you really wanna know what I'm seein'? It's dark as fuck, Mikey, so dark I can't see an inch in front of me. But you? God, ya shine as brightly and beautifully as a stained-glass cathedral or a midnight quartz, and iridescent gems surround ya whenever ya talk or move." He drops to a whisper, "I ain't ever seen anythin' quite like it. Makes sense 'cause I ain't seen anyone or anythin' as exquisite as you in my entire life. And it ain't the drugs talkin'. Ya can't tell me there ain't *somethin'* here."

My eyebrows bunch. "Where?"

He slams my palm to his chest, stating, "*Here*," and his heart beating like a drumroll has me convinced it can live outside his body and inside my hands.

Safe. I'll keep your heart safe.

"Here, Mike," he repeats softly.

The stardust in his eyes covers him entirely then combusts into millions and purifies us in a sparkling, rainbow rain. Jesse places his own hand on my chest, says my name, and I come undone.

"Is it rainin' stars for you, too?"

"How're you seeing what I'm seeing?"

"Because I am you, and you are me." He kisses my knuckles. "Damn, you're beautiful. Everythin' 'bout ya, Mikey. In and out. Soul and bones."

"You're *literally* trippin'."

"No argument. But even in the slips, when I'm sober as sober can be, ya still shine. You shine, my crazy diamond. I know you've been beaten down. To hell with those douchebags who said you were nothin'. To hell with anyone who said you'd never amount to anythin'. You have this superman-like strength ragin' inside ya. I've seen it."

"Whatever, Jesse."

"Mikey, listen to me. *Listen...*"

He stares at me intently, and the electric-blue streak his tongue paints over his silver-hooped piercing transfers onto my thumb as it gently tugs his bottom lip.

"Say it first."

"Do it."

"Are ya sure?"

"Dammit, Jess!"

Our mouths fuse in a tizzy of groans, and my firm grip on his neck keeps him in place. We sigh accordingly, and as my lips feel his expanding smile, the artist in me sets his mollified portrait within a scene of briny tides and sea foam frames. I'm the first to depart, but he's the first to open his eyes.

"You're my reflection."

It needs to be restated, timestamped, dated, and stored in my mental attic. The only difference is this memory won't be moldy or forgotten. I'll keep it someplace clean and nontoxic, and it'll glow as a mound of clandestine wealth or become the Eighth Wonder of the World.

"And you're mine," he says. "My soulmate."

"My twin flame."

Mouths tackle. Heads twist, left, right, left, right. Teeth nibble lips. His hands are in my hair and mine are on his defined jaw. My weakness. All of him. My weakness. Stronger than drugs. As spirituous as alcohol.

Jesse retires this time—tiny, cotton candy sweet kisses on my lips, chin, and cheeks. I stay on his lap and share my cigarette with him. I ask why he stopped, and I'm an enamored imbecile as he pinches and pulls his labret.

"We gotta go slow."

"I thought this is what you wanted?"

"*Fuck, it is.* But you're new to this. You're my best friend. I can't screw this up. I ain't perfect."

"I don't *want* perfect." I kiss him. "Perfection is boring. I want what you already are, Jesse. Your flaws, your beautiful imperfections—*that's* where my weakness is."

I use my shirtsleeves to dry his teal tears circulating like sound waves.

"*I'm a pansy.*" He snickers. "LSD skyrockets my emotions like ya wouldn't believe."

"You're allowed to feel whatever you're feeling. We've had messed up lives, but they brought me to you, and I'd do it all again."

"Why're you here? You're too good for all the destructive shit I've dragged ya into, and all the destructive things I know will be in the future."

I'm a thief, pocketing a kiss, two kisses, three kisses… I've lost count.

"Jesse, I'm *exactly* where I need to be."

With Jesse between my knees and my chin on his shoulder, we watch the sun come up as we come down. As much as I miss our oceanic cave and Jesse's starry eyes, our sober world proves its radiance, the skyline radiating hot-pink, citrus, and mauve.

Jesse exhales.

I kiss his earlobe. "What's wrong, Mea Harris?"

"I know ya don't believe in *soulmates* 'cause of the 'not needin' another person to complete us' aspect, but you complete me."

"You've made me a believer."

His smile lasts but a blink.

"Why the doom and gloom?" I ask.

"I never wantcha to think ya don't make me happy, but, dang, I wish it wasn't always rainin' inside my head."

I kiss his temple, shoulder, neck, and cheek, sanguine in my touches and their healing abilities, as unfeasible as it may seem. I can't stop someone else's rain while trying to escape my hurricane.

"We'll be okay. *Someday*. I'm with you. You're not alone."

"You're here."

"Forever."

"Forever," he affirms, our lips folding, loving, tasting. "It'll never be long enough."

"Keep kissing me."

"Forever."

Forever kisses.

Forever branded.

Forever safe.

You hear me.

I'm here.

I'm not going away.

NINE

My Sweet Midnight

FACT #10: THOSE 18-25 USE METHAMPHETAMINES (375,000 PEOPLE/1.1% OF THE US POPULATION).

SIXTY MINUTES are misspent analyzing how we went from being on the primary verge of making out to getting home and parting to our individual rooms, and it tapers down to one explanation: the drugs. It *has* to be the drugs.

Blah, blah, blah, DENIAL!

I loiter outside his door, wide awake and detesting our separation.

"Come in, creeper," he says, peering up from the graphic novel he's reading, and his eyes follow me on the white and black bedspread as I place the opened *V for Vendetta* facedown on the table.

"Why are you keeping your space?" I ask.

"I thought you'd want it after last night."

"*Space? From you?*" I shake my head, saying, "You don't know me at all."

I turn off the lamp, the blackout curtains restraining the afternoon daylight, and dump my weight on him, our mouths two passing ships in the dark.

CURLED IN two *S* shapes, we sleep late into the day, his cheek on my chest. He wakes me up, and we shower (*separately, perv!*), snort and eat our Oxy, and smoke on the patio, all while warding off the *feelings* fluctuating like a Sword of Damocles.

Jesse cooks pineapple ham, homemade mac n' cheese, sweet carrots, and cornbread (from scratch!) for dinner. After gorging ourselves, Mom gets ready for bed, and Jesse and I pack overnight bags to stay at Toby's guesthouse.

On the way there, I reflect on how the world has lost part of its zing, a negative LSD side effect. The worst of it? The loss of Jesse's starry eyes. I keep my despairing thoughts to myself, not wanting to bring him down with me.

The Alexanders' meandering driveway is paved in white concrete, and the house is comparable to the Victorian-lace painted mansions in the Columbus district, with sleek pillars, a wraparound porch, three stories, and an elevator.

Jesse parks on the side of the road, and we walk through the spacious yard to a wing extruded from the south end of the main house. He leads me past an outdoor pool bordered by a garden trimmed in white and red wilting tulips.

I've been picked on for growing up in the suburbs, and here's Toby living the high life. Ain't that some bullshit.

"You have a key?"

"Mr. Alexander gave me a copy after Ma's funeral. I never felt the need to get away 'til now. I figured we could use a change of scenery."

I follow him into a dark corridor, and he flips the switch in the luxurious kitchen. As soon as I see the black, flat stovetop and four-door oven, I picture Jesse in a Kiss the Mother-Fuckin' Chef apron, singing to himself as he prepares sumptuous feasts.

Jesse stores our bags on the black and silver speckled countertop, opens the stainless-steel freezer, and swings a bottle of coconut rum.

"Your favorite."

"You planned this."

"'Course I did. Ya know as well as I do we need to talk 'bout this. You can't just come into my room and kiss me and then act like nothin' happened for the rest of the day."

"You mean like how you went to your room after kissing me at the estates?"

"See? We both suck. Why don'tcha sit down? You're burnin' a hole in the floor."

I select a seat at the round dining room table set for twelve. Jesse connects his phone to a computer and shuffles our playlist (there're speakers in all four corners of this place!). He picks the chair diagonally from me, arranges our cigarettes, two shot glasses, and coconut rum, folds his arms at his chest, and stretches out his gimp leg.

"We just gonna sit here and stare at each other all night?" he asks.

"When *aren't* we staring at each other? We're a young adult novel come to life."

"It ain't my fault you're sexy as fuck. Why do you get so nervous when I say things like that to ya? It ain't like this has been a secret."

I snatch the bottle and fill our glasses. He raises his for a toast, but I'm already helping myself to a second shot.

"Okay, maybe this wasn't a good idea. You're obviously uncomfortable, and I shouldn't push ya."

"I'm not uncomfortable," I object. "I'm... I'm *bad* at this. What are you expecting us to do? Confess our undying love and slam each other into the nearest wall and fuck?"

"I mean, now that you've mentioned it."

"Can you be serious for one *goddamn* second?"

"I joke when I'm nervous."

"You're nervous? *You?*"

He straightens his spine, his elbows on the table. "Why wouldn't I be nervous?"

"You're you."

"Meanin'?"

"You're certain and brash and so outrageous that if we did fuck, the entire town would know within the hour."

We laugh and go solemn in the same sentence.

"Shit, Jesse." I scrub my face.

"Let's back up. I'll set up some rails, and we can drink and see where this goes. How's that sound?"

"Like a cop-out."

"So... yes?"

"Why not."

Jesse returns to his seat with his bag containing our drugs and supplies, the friction in the room foam-board solid.

"What about a game?" I propose, the pills *crunch, crunch, crunch*ing.

"This should be interestin'. Whatcha got in mind?"

His eyebrows rise during and after my guidelines, his coy smirk showing me he's on board.

"Who goes first?" he asks.

I slide him the bottle and wink.

"Typical, Sinclair." His fingers skip on his chin and he says, as if deep in thought, "Lemme think…"

I kick off my shoes and wait (im)patiently.

"I'm guessin' Michael Sinclair's never watched porn."

"I'm a prude, Jess, not Amish."

He downs the rum. "Your go."

The joke's on me. No way in Hell will I benefit against someone who's likely done every thinkable and unthinkable subject in the book.

"I'm guessing Jesse Harris has never had a threesome."

"*Mike*, what kinda man do ya take me as?" He refills my glass. "It's on the bucket list if ya know anyone?"

"Fuck off, Jess," I snark, grinning.

I wait through two songs. It can't be *that* hard. I have a textbook of questions I'd ask myself in his position. I never ventured outside my bedroom until we met.

"I'm guessin' Michael Sinclair's never been suspended."

"*Whoo*, buddy! Twice!"

He ogles the tipping bottle.

"Seventh grade, Colby Fairborn told everyone on the bus Maddy fucked for drugs. When the bus stopped at the neighbors', I slammed his head into a window, put him in the hospital, and Mom and Leon put me in therapy because the principal said I had 'anger issues.' I do, for sure, you saw it for yourself, but I just didn't appreciate him talking trash about my sister."

"Did she?"

"I never asked and don't wanna know."

"Fair. Who knows what Daryl's done while dealin' and usin'. Second time?"

My teeth entrap my top lip. I may as well claim my burial hole and provide him the shovel.

"This wannabe gangster, Nathan Williams, followed me around in high school."

"*Obsessive.*"

"Not like that. He'd just call me names. Loser. Freak. Queer. I usually just ignored him. He meant squat to me, and everyone knew he was a punk-ass bitch, but it got out of hand my sophomore year. One day during study hall, I... uh...."

My tongue fails me as the *Titanic* failed her passengers. Jesse's chair scrapes on the tile and he lights my Camel, his kind gaze bewitching me out of my head.

"You don't gotta tell me. You shouldn't be afraid to, either. I'm not gonna judge ya."

"I know. I wanna tell you this. I wanna tell you *everything*. Well, these papers were passed around to other students, and they were staring at me, laughing, whispering, and pointing. It was like I was in some high school noir. I stole one from Lisa Marks and, just like... lost all feeling. Nathan hacked into my student email and wrote a very, er... *perverted* letter to Coach Martin.

"It's still a blur, but I guess I kicked his chair, and his head hit the floor hard enough that he passed out, but I didn't know he was passed out, and I was just *beating* him. His older brother punched me, and that, my friend, is how I got *this*." I point to the scar on my left eyebrow. "Got suspended for two weeks, and back to therapy I went."

"Lemme guess—this Nathan sleaze was in the closet?"

"Ah, yep, there's the kicker. Came out last year."

I save our rum from leaping off the table, his fists pounding.

"I knew it! *Fuckin'* rich!"

As badly as I want to laugh it off, I can't. Is it hilarious? A tad. However, it wasn't Nathan who had to explain to his parents and the school faculty that he and Mr. Martin hadn't done the hot beef injection on the wrestling mats after school. Yet, I almost felt bad that he was so insecure and saw no other choice than to use me as a scapegoat for his secretive sexuality.

Jesse picks up on my unamused gander because he recollects himself, and we grab our snorting straws, our heads bumping as we... bump.

"Why didn'tcha tell me?" he asks.

"Rejection."

"Rejection?"

"You're my first real friend. I didn't wanna lose that."

"What makes ya think I would've rejected ya? I mean, I think I came on pretty strong."

"You never made a move."

He sinks. "I was waitin' for *you*. I didn't wantcha to think I was tryin' to force ya into somethin' you weren't ready for. I threw ya some signs, but the line wasn't mine to cross."

"Yeah, the signs were there, but before last night, I never thought you'd want to kiss me or... do more than what we've been doing."

Jesse replenishes our shot glasses at the halfway point for my third Oxy line.

"Both?" I ask.

He snorts his two rails then lapses in his chair, his knee springing, his labret and teeth clinking. I guzzle my rum shots, my body scrunching as the twangy, coconut aftertaste streams into my belly; my head overloaded with the drugs, alcohol, and revelations.

"Your turn," I say.

"Ya don't need a game to ask me questions."

"It's fun."

"Fun? Or easy?"

I tear at my fingernails. Being high is the worst when affronting... *feelings*.

"We're gonna be blackout intoxicated at this rate, and that's not why I brought us here," says Jesse.

"Then just say what you need to say."

"I've done all the talkin' up to this point. You know *exactly* how I feel 'bout ya."

I breached tipsy two shots ago. His ankles cross, and in a *click*, I'm hot-blooded at the sight of his powerful legs. If it was negative thirty degrees outside, he'd still wear shorts instead of jeans, not that I'm criticizing. I've a soft spot for his legs, and I could identify his swagger from a crowded room simply by the rat-a-tat of his crooked limp.

I'll wager my life his wringing hands are itching to feel some part, or parts, of me because mine yearn to do the same to him. I lift from my chair and fall into those honey irises as I'm guided onto his lap.

"This ain't right," he says. "We're high."

"If we wait until we're sober, it'll never happen."

"Point taken."

"You wanna know how I feel? *This,*" I say, thrusting my arousal against his stomach, "doesn't even come *close* to happening when I think of Nora or *anybody else.* You enter the room and I'm on fire. I'm drunk. I'm high, but I also know how I feel when I look at you, touch you, smell you. 'Beautiful' doesn't cut it. You're *glorious.* And I'm sorry it's taken me so long to get to… *here.* And, fuck, it's been too long," I husk, and in a fluid motion, our teeth clank as my tongue raids his receiving mouth.

It's a "first kiss fairytale"—fireworks, sparks, stopped time—and then some. For the first time, sunshine's no longer a metaphor.

He hoists me onto the table, the rum spilling onto the floor, his grip under my knees desperately pulling me in, my thighs clasping his hips. Our greedy hands and mouth-bruising, tongue-swirling neediness heightens as our pelvises pivot on cue. He's just as hard as I am; the terrain unfamiliar, and I must rely on nature for supervision.

My instincts activate instantly. We're animals, are we not? I'm rocking against him as his skillful suckles and nips tasting every centimeter of my arched neck turns our bashful grinds into turbulent friction.

"I've waited months for this." Dainty kisses up my neck, jaw, cheek, and a growl in my ear, "I'd take ya right here if I could."

The pornographic phantasm leaves little room for modesty, and I work on undoing his shorts. "Why don't you?"

He restrains my wrists to my lower back.

"Damn, that's *hot*."

He laughs. "None of that. People eat at this table, for starters, and it's too soon for sex."

"*Too soon?!* You can't tell me this hasn't been building up?"

"'Course it's been buildin'. I jerked off less in middle school than I have these last few months. But I wanna do this right. You deserve more than a touch-and-go. I can't screw this up. You're Mi Sinclair."

"*Yours*."

The corners of his mouth flinch. "*Mine*."

"Yours. Mine."

"*Mine, mine, mine*," he sings, and the fumbling kiss detonates into further *clothed* bumps and grinds.

I suggest in a frisky trill, "I'm sure we can do *other* things?"

"Say no more. Hold on tight."

He carries me into the den and we crash onto the floor, missing the couch entirely, our bodies aligning and lips welding. Two soldiers in the core of a provocative battle combat over governance, a white flag I'd gladly surrender to my opponent. I sink my teeth into that sexy crescent shape where the neck and shoulder unite. I am, hands down, in the thicket of the *hottest* make-out session in history (if you don't believe me, I challenge you to find a better kisser than Jesse Harris, then we'll talk).

"You'll be sorry you ever met me if you stop kissing me. And *this*," I say, clinching his shirt, "needs to go."

"Well, which is it? I have to stop kissin' ya if ya want me to take it off."

"Jesse!"

"Shhh. Slowly, love."

He helms our pace to an easeful tempo, his hands in my hair and mine moving up his torso, and he says, "That feels *fantastic*," our shirts becoming fossils of yesteryear.

I've seen myself naked fewer times than I've seen him shirtless, and whatever inhibitions I may have had about staring at or touching him melt away as I flip him onto his back and let my palms and tongue feel and taste the patterns of his abdominal muscles.

I lick and blow my way up to his collarbone and neck, whisper, "You taste like the sea," and nibble his earlobe.

Jesse's piercing digs into my skin as his tongue creates looping designs and straight lines on the rounds and twists of my jugular.

"Ohhh, man, that's *awesome*. Kiss me."

He succumbs to my desires, my response to his yawning mouth spontaneous as we breathe into and in one another. I suck on the metal hoop in his bottom lip that's hexed my daydreams for months, and I'd dine on his saccharine moans to the peak of obesity.

Our hands and lips are competitive as if they're recreating the 100 Years War that's neither lost nor won. I grab two mighty handfuls of his toned backside, driving him down into my upward thrusts, his grip on my erection causing me to grumble obscenities my mother would backhand me for.

"You feel *huge*," he emphasizes the last syllable with a hoarse grouse, his talented hips teasing me.

"I'm fixing to bust a nut if you keep going."

"Maybe I should stop?"

"Maybe you shouldn't."

"What do ya want?" he asks and takes my index and middle finger knuckle-deep into his mouth, my answer muffled gibberish. "I didn't catch that, love."

He releases my saliva-glistening fingers, a drooping thread tying my fingertips to his lips.

"*I want you to touch me.*"

"Where?"

I ram our lips and hips together; the gasping and moaning engagements too coarse for romance. We convert into a shipwreck of stroking hands, teeth-marking bites and movements that'll result in carpet-burnt knees.

I'd commit unlawful deeds under his empire:

'Dive into the Arctic.' Yes, Jesse.

'Knock down that beehive and bring me the honey.' I'll feed it to you by the spoonful, Jesse.

'Assassinate the Kings and Queens and give me the world.' I'll give you the entire galaxy, Jesse.

No exaggeration. If he genuinely asked, I'd steal, murder, or lie if it meant I'd awake to his smile every morning and fall asleep flushed to his naked body every night.

"*Where*, Mike? Where do ya want me to touch you?"

Life couldn't be richer if Midas sculpted it in rhodium pearls and gold. I push my fingernails into his arms and whisper against his jawbone, "Mea Harris."

"Mi Sinclair."

I shiver from heel to crown. "I love when you call me that. Say it again."

"*Mi Sinclair.* Let me bring ya back to life. Tell me where...."

You're going to mess this up! All our hard work—*Gone!*—and for what? *Him?* You don't love him! You just love the attention. You're going to—

"*Anywhere.*"

TEN

Scream Me a Dream

FACT#11: CLOSE TO EIGHT MILLION ADULTS IN AMERICA SUFFER FROM BOTH A MENTAL ILLNESS AND ADDICTION OR CO-OCCURRING DISORDERS.

I WAKE up to clean, downy bedding after an exhilarating night of drinking (the bottle bone dry), an overabundance of pills, weed, and steamy foreplay. My bedroom is shrunken three times compared to this one, the outside blocked by royal blue blinds, the silver chain on the ceiling fan clanging with its whirls. Ocean scene photographs, anchors, and fish netting bedeck the steel and azure-colored walls.

My corneas adjust to the television's strobing lights, and Jesse stoops down for a morning breath and rum kiss.

"I think I like ya a smidge more when you're asleep. Like you're free. How do ya feel?"

"Heavy, but not nearly as heavy as your thoughts. What's going on?"

"You read me like a book," he says gravely. "I… why didn'tcha tell me you're on antidepressants?"

Ope! There it is! Why would he want to stay with a manic psycho?

My soul vacates my body.

"How did you—"

"You were too drunk to change last night. I went to your bag to get your flannels, and, yes, I dressed ya." He chuckles and continues thoughtfully, "I saw the bottle. I swear I wasn't snoopin'."

"I- I- I just assumed you knew. I see a therapist. We've talked about my 'bad neighborhood.' You've been there during my downtimes."

"I assumed, yes. You hid it well. I've never seen the bottles in your room."

"I keep them in a jacket pocket in the back of the closet."

"Ya didn't want me to know. Mike, it's *me*. Michael," he whispers, taking my hands hiding my eyes, and says sternly, "*it's me*. We've been playin' with fire. The drugs... the alcohol... how long?"

I'm hurting him... I'm such an asshole. I've been an expert secret keeper, but now I'm tangled in the web of my spinning lies, and there's only one way out.

"There's a sketchbook in my duffle. Outside right pocket. The green book, not the blue."

WHAT ARE YOU DOING? STUPID, STUPID, STUPID, STUPID!

SILENCE!

I swallow my spleen when he rolls out of bed, unzips my duffel, and plants himself across from me with the green sketchbook—my *therapy* book.

"Fifth page."

Dr. Greene requested I sketch myself in the rain, and Jesse's fingertips trace the black ink showing me standing in the middle of the road in a rainstorm without an umbrella.

"He said if you draw an umbrella, it means you're of a healthy mind," I explain.

"Mike..."

Five things I can see. Four things I can feel. Three things I can hear. Two things I can smell. One thing I can taste.

Inhale.

Exhale.

I un-spool my tangled web:

"The summer before my junior year, Maddy went to rehab for the sixth time, and Mom and Leon were fighting nightly. They would shove a blanket in the door, but I still heard them. Leon liked to shout. He was spitting my name like it was cyanide, and Mom just sobbed as he insulted me, calling me a damaged weakling. He caught me staring at the boy next door, Marshall Hendrix. I'll never forget what he said to Mom. 'He's a bastard child you should've aborted, Marie!' An object—a vase?—smashed into the door."

Jesse, glassy-eyed and unblinking, cradles my hands in his.

"Are you sure you wanna hear this?" I ask. "It's... it's um... triggering..."

I taste his supple lips.

"I can handle it if you can."

"Do I have you?"

"Mi Sinclair," he croaks and kisses me again, longer this time, passionately, "*forever*."

Inhale.

Exhale.

"The next day, I gave Marshall the baseball cards Leon put in my

Christmas stockings, knowing I hated baseball or any sport. Marshall was the star pitcher of Cougar High, and I figured he'd appreciate them more than I did. And, yeah, he was my first... 'crush,' I guess? I noticed him. I liked his brown skin; his long eyelashes.

"I'd had enough. I didn't feel safe at home or at school. I was bullied, spat at, and pushed around. Even Charlie and her friends harassed me. It's how she became popular: she disowned her siblings. I was... *tired.* Fuck, Jesse, I was *so fucking tired.* I was mad or not mad. There wasn't anything in-between.

"So, I shut myself in my room, the *only* place I felt safe, and I... I wanted to die in a safe place."

His caress on my ear glitches, and the tears he's been curbing race down his cheekbones, his head shaking *no, no, no.*

"I got a chair, a belt, went to my closet, and... shit, Jesse, I can't... I can't do this to you, don't make me say it...."

"Da fuck, Mike." He's sniveling and kissing my forehead, nose, cheeks, and lips. "A world without you? *No.* Why... how..."

"I was in *pain,* Jesse. I wanted to end my pain, not my life. I felt like I was disappointing everyone. Mom was always defending me against Leon, and it scared the shit outta me because he has a temper. And although I sympathized with Maddy, I hated her just as much for shutting me out and ruining her own life. This *perfect* suburban family hiding all these skeletons.

"I came up with this thing called 'The Sinclair Family Levee.' It's in the sketchpad with illustrations, like a mucked-up Dr. Seuss book: a series of events leading to the levee's destruction. Charlie heard the chair fall and cut me loose before any actual damage was done. I thought,"—I scoff—"I thought it was Maddy who broke the levee, but I can *still* hear Mom crying and screaming. I'd done it, Jess. *I* broke our levee."

"No, love, no. It wasn't you."

I'm in his arms like embers resurrecting the singed phoenix.

Safe.

"I'm sorry I didn't tell you." My ear to his naked chest, I count the heartbeats it loyally—mercifully—shelters. "I don't like to talk about it, and people treat you differently after a suicide attempt, like you can't function on your own, or if you're having a bad day, it automatically means you're going to try again. Leon told Mom I was seeking attention and couldn't even succeed in killing myself, which made things even worse.

"I've been to several therapists starting young. I didn't talk a whole lot as a kid. I felt like anything I said just pissed off Leon, so one day, I just stopped. Mom got worried and sent me to Dr. Stills, this troll of a woman. She'd munch on pork rinds and wore pigtails. I couldn't take her seriously, and I started talking again just so I wouldn't have to see her anymore. Then the fights began, first with Colby, and they kept going. I'd been in about ten fights between my seventh and junior years.

"When Nathan and I got into it, I was sent to Dr. Blackburn. This man wore too much aftershave and was sewing the lining in his coffin. That lasted about four months 'til we found Dr. Greene following the... the uh... ya know...."

I resist sleep while Jesse scratches my back. *Sleep.* Sleep's overrated when an attractive guy is holding you in an embrace that helps carry your luggage and kisses you in a way that erases your crestfallen blemishes.

"Were ya diagnosed?" he asks at the end of our mini makeout session.

"I have a major chemical imbalance, yes, manic depression. It sounds worse than it actually is. I don't have it as severe as others, but if I do spontaneous stuff like drink vodka in the middle of the night in a beanfield with someone I barely know, I'm definitely in an up episode. Ah, there's that smile I love." I kiss his dimples.

"Was that your first time drinkin'?"

"I've drunk wine with Maddy and had my first shot of tequila in the laundry room with her when I was fifteen."

Jesse chuckles and hugs eighteen years of my broken pieces back together. "Guess it's always rainin' in your head, too?" he whispers.

"Yeah," I say to him, "but I found my umbrella."

"... *damn*."

His breath shrouds my mouth, his hand on the back of my head, and I'm spellbound by an oxygen-stealing kiss giving me life. He adjusts on top of me, our mouths and hands testing each other, our lips standing still as if seeking permission to henceforth, and I let him in.

Our prudent start becomes possessive, his left leg sliding in between my knees, my spine bending upward to mold our sweaty stomachs.

I'm thirsty, dizzy, and jonesing for Oxy, but it pales in comparison to my longing for his bodily assets and for his touch as soft as the Egyptian linens entangling us. In efforts to integrate our damp skin, our fondling hands and desirous kisses grope at any and all body parts within reach, but the second I shove his hand into my boxers, the feverish exchange comes to an abrupt standstill.

"Y'sure?" he asks.

I buck my hips in reply.

"Shit, guess so."

Jesse's fast to undress us, our gazes fixed, and he's quicker to touch the hair below my navel, downwards. I struggle for air, grasping the scar tissue on his rib cage, and repay him with fervid petting.

I've never done this to another person, not even last night when kissing and a little dry humping (alright, alright, *a lot* of dry humping) was as far as we'd gone. Sexual participation isn't my speciality. Where do I put my hands? On his face? His back? Lower? Higher? The bed's doused in perspiration, our lips swelling and chests heaving, and we're nowhere near slicing into the meat of foreplay.

"*Together*," he tells me. "Do as I do. Give me a sign if ya like it. We have all day to get it right."

I don't mind that he gains control, his teeth biting and sucking my tongue in his mouth as my hair in his fist loosens and grips—the pattern looped. I lick the sheen dewdrops on his collarbone from end to end and nibble his shoulder.

We rotate onto our sides, our legs bundling and hands like wild scavengers incapable of stabilizing on one particular limb until...

"Oh, *fuck*." I hoist reflexively into his enclosed fingers, the sensation surreal. On impulse, I, too, replicate the surreal sensation, his eyes rolling backward and mine popping. "You've been hiding this AK-47 from me?" I say. "*Rude*."

The humorous comment survives a short lifespan.

"Eyes on mine," he instructs. "Don't look away from me."

That's a simple assignment—nothing and nowhere as striking as Jesse—his timid groans silencing the voices in my head. This foreign touch is eccentric. His fingers apply the right amount of pressure, and I follow his advice and imitate what he's doing to me. I attack his bridged neck, suckling, labeling him as *mine*, his baritone whimpers rumbling against my teeth.

"So good," he moans. "Faster."

His mewing noises are a newfangled addiction as we form a synchronized beat that could outdo our *Jessike* heavy metal playlist. He secures our lips to hydrate our mouths, and the occasional, "Is this okay?" is uttered, and I kiss him to say, '*Yes. God, yes.*'

Although our sexual exploits are anything but supersonic, they feel as such in the heat of the moment. Jesse's saliva-lubed hand jerks rhythmically to my hips, edging me ever-closer to that blissful brink until I shapeshift into a raucous fiend, and, losing all sense and sensibility, I ejaculate into his fist while gearing into the glittering cosmos of gratification.

He hungrily claims my outcries as his own, and once I'm flaccid and spent, he stares deeply into my eyes and licks my orgasm off his hand, one finger at a time.

How the *fuck* am I supposed to react to that?!

"*Holy Satan in a toaster.*"

"Pretty accurate," he says.

"Your turn, baby."

We spit into my palm and, my self-reliance rehabilitating, our lips lock as I assist Jesse to his glorious threshold, my name lobbying off his tongue, his toes on my ankle kinked. Jesse's jaw, his entire self, slacks as he curses the heavens.

"Look at me."

He hones in, then laughs with erotic enthusiasm at my copycatting his finger-licking.

Hot diggity!

"You taste *fantastic!*"

"Mmm. Holy Satan in a toaster."

More kisses.

"How're ya feelin', love?" he asks.

"Sticky."

"Same. I'll start a shower. Oh! But first!"

He unlocks his phone, the camera pointed at us.

"No. *Absolutely* not."

"But I just gave Michael Sinclair his first handjob. This is a historical moment!"

I flip him off.

"Say *jizz!*"

Click.

"Should I post it? Give it a status? '*Jessike Post-Foreplay. Be jealous. Hashtag: SCORE.*'"

"You're an asshole."

"But I'm *your* asshole."

"Gemma will strangle us."

"Only more reason to post it!" He chuckles. "I wouldn't do that, love," he says, gently pinching my chin and kissing me. "This is just for us."

"I'm holding you to that."

"That's not all you'll be holdin'," he purrs.

I pick my jaw up off the floor as he walks into the bathroom (*yowza*, his ass deserves the utmost respect!).

"C'mon, Sinclair, the water's hot enough to boil a lobster!"

We brush our teeth at the sink, and he winks at my reflection in the mirror.

"Enjoy your shower, sexy boy." He swats my ass. "I'll set up some lines."

I hold tight to his dilating pupils, stamp kisses on his shins, knees, and thighs, all five senses memorizing his masculine curvatures, salty skin, and groans. He does the same to me—feathery kisses, cordial touches—and in the steam, we eulogize each other's nakedness.

"How can one human possibly be *this* sexy?"

"You're blind. Have you *seen* yourself? You should be illegal."

He floats over to me. "Michael? Thank you."

"For what?"

Our mouths skim, tongues greeting in mid-air.

So many kisses. Don't ever stop kissing me.

"For bein' the sun chasin' away the rain."

I observe my Jesse Harris reflection—his stern jawline and defined cheekbones—and move inward as the reflection stays stationary. We've been *alert* (if you're picking up what I'm throwing down) since the second we wined and dined on the displayed naked flesh, and it's all I can do to not take him in every barbaric way possible, like a primate who knows little else than the process of procreation.

I'm *starving*. "Round two?"

"I've turned ya into a monster, but hell yes, baby."

We hobble and kiss our way into the shower. As keen as I am for the passionate stimuli we're providing, it's our extraordinary fire that brings me to my knees (both figuratively and physically), and it's a burn I'll personally reignite so we may perish and be reborn in the flames for the next thousand lifetimes.

Staring up at him, my hands take turns squeezing his ass, pumping his dick, and raking through his pubic hair. I'm given no instruction manual this time, but I must be doing something right because he's returning my gaze, tugging my hair, riding my mouth and throat, and chanting my name in a celebratory manner that nearly has me joining him in climax as he shoots his load onto my chest.

Breathlessly saying, "Goddang, Sinclair," he drops to his shaky knees, gathers the cum and water mixture onto two fingertips, and dips them in out of our smacking lips to exchange the salty flavor. "That was unexpected."

"You mean you *weren't* expecting the straight-edged Square to get *dirty* in the shower?" I ask, smirking.

"I *fuckin'* knew it," he rumbles, and lies atop me on the porcelain floor. "You *are* a kink. Don't stand up. Stay right here, *dirty boy*, and let me take care of ya."

If he says *dirty boy* one more time, my dick's gonna end up fucking his throat so hard it'll blow a hole through the back of his skull.

He dives in to repay me, and he's clearly way more experienced and skilled than I am, so much so that I find it impossible to focus on anything other than the starlit backdrop my sealed eyelids fabricate, my hands and hips rocking to the ebb and flow of his bobbing head.

My legs are propped over his shoulders to keep us from sliding, and the sound and feeling of the water and Jesse's tight, hot throat humming on my shaft delivers me to my second euphoric rush of the morning. Gasping deeply, I glance down at him just as he, unlike me, suctions and swallows, the sight leaving me a jumble of quivering bones and words.

Jesse gently lowers my legs to the ground, lavishes my body with additional kisses and, his fingers rounding my neck, probs his tongue into my awaiting mouth.

"That was fun," he declares, caressing me in all the optimal spots I've dreamed of him touching. "Definitely gonna have to take another selfie."

I roll my eyes. "You're the worst."

Invisible garlands connect our disbursed forms as we kiss, stroke, and wash off the aftermath, the apricot suds pooling at our feet as I hold him, his fingers brushing through my wet hair.

"Don't leave me, Sinclair."

"You'd have to kill me first."

Jesse sings to me some gushy love song. I think it's "Lego House". I'd poke fun at him for knowing the lyrics without missing a beat, but hell, I recognize the Ed Sheeran tune, so I'm just as guilty, and we sway until the water runs glacial.

We dress into boxers and boxer briefs, kissing in the foggy curtain, and makeout some more on the bed. Our hands, no matter where they rove, find their way back home to each other's faces.

"I want nothing more than to lock us in this room and suck your lips bloodless."

Jesse topples on top of me. "Doable."

"How long have you felt this way for me?"

"Since the night ya moved to Indigo. I saw ya sittin' outside, drawin', and I just knew."

"*Four months?* You should've told me."

"And risk losin' you? Michael, bein' friends with ya would've been enough for me. I just wanted ya in my life. It would've torn me up to see ya with someone else, but I'd keep carryin' this torch I have for you."

"Jesse, the only person I want is *you*."

Butterfly kisses? I like these.

"Mi Sinclair, I'm the luckiest guy in the world, and I'm gonna show ya just how lucky I am," he says, wetting his lips and watching me as he slides my boxers down my legs. "Any requests?"

"As a safety precaution, I wouldn't call me '*dirty boy*' if you wanna keep your brains inside your skull."

"Safety?" he asks, smirking and licking my inner thighs. "I live for danger, *dirty boy*."

Welp, we can't say I didn't warn him.

FOR THE rest of the day, we eat peanut butter and jelly pancakes in bed, watch cartoons, and sample various portions of skin, teaching what we do and don't like, albeit we keep a toe behind second and third base (I think this is the only time in my life where I don't mind sports idioms). I don't object to his "taking it slow" position. He's my first kiss, my first love, my first *feeling*, and he treats me as if I'm a novelty that's to be insured in an impermeable box.

I'm wrapped up in his enchanting kisses, how he looks as his back rockets off the bed whenever I touch him, and the unmistakable sated feedback he bestows while in the throes of sensual rapture, and how loved and secure I feel in his arms.

Safe.

Wearing nothing but our souls in the afterglow, he tells me, "You're my Polaris," while stroking my face. "My northern light guidin' me home."

GAG! ARE YOU DONE YET?!

Mushy, but that's Jesse for you, and I guzzle it like a basic bitch in Uggs slurping a pumpkin spice latte.

I ask how he re-stocked on Oxy, and he says his regular dealer, Kyle, the one who sold to an undercover cop over a year ago, is out of prison, and it's one less thing we have to worry about.

"You should sleep. You look tired."

"Michael Sinclair bein' all boyfriend-ish. I could get used to this."

Butterfly kisses (I still like these).

French kisses (I like these more).

Boyfriends? Are we tagged? We haven't talked about it. Do I bring it up? Wait for him? The connection we have is too exceptionally formal for labels. We respect our individual limits and are aware of how we feel, and the same can't be said for many so-called "couples."

Jesse nods off, his head on my stomach, and I twirl his hair and slip and revel with him in whatever dreamland he's in.

I hope there's butterfly kisses. **Doubts.**

And French kisses. **Insecurities.**

Love songs. **Death Rattles.**

Pancakes. **Drugs.**

Jesse. **Him.**

Me. **You.**

Safe. **For now.**

ELEVEN

Let's Paint Our Sorrows

FACT #12: Two main factors play an equal role in the onset of addiction: environment and genetics.

Jesse packs our stuff into our duffle bags and hurls clean clothes at me.

Groggy and annoyed, I sit up, asking, "What's up? You look like you've stepped through a poltergeist."

"Charlie's blowin' up your phone. I read the texts. Not sure what happened. She just kept sayin' she needs ya. She's at Leon's."

"She's in Athens."

"Not accordin' to the texts. Sounds urgent."

We're out the door in minutes, the sunlight blinding, and we down our morning cigarettes and Oxy. I dial Charlie repeatedly as Jesse speeds towards the Golden Suburbs.

"The fuck. She won't answer."

Jesse's thumb rubs my wrist. "We're almost there, love."

I'm confused to see Charlie's purple BMW parked by the garage, Leon's truck AWOL, but just as confused at the unlocked front door. We make a mad dash up the stairs, and she isn't in her girlhood room. Jesse races into the foyer and shouts my name.

My chest stresses. Charlie, naked and tear-stained, is next to the toilet like a roly-poly. I kneel and brush her hair away from her face and she looks at me like a doe clipped by a semi, asking to be put out of her misery.

"What happened?" I ask, and her sobs furnish the space.

Jesse taps my shoulder and chucks his chin to the blood-soaked towel under her.

"It hurts, Mikey! It hurts!" she cries in my arms, her tears seeping my collar.

Jesse swoops in with sweatpants and a shirt.

"We gotta go to the hospital, okay?" he says to her crucially. "Work with me here. Help us get ya dressed. Unless ya *wanna* go to the hospital in your birthday suit?"

Her laugh sputters, and we help her onto the edge of the tub and into her clothing. She lashes out as we lift her off the ground, her head thrashing this way and that, and she collapses like a wet noodle.

"I can't!"

"C'mon, Charlie, you're a bull! Ya got this!" Jesse's pep talk encourages her to stand, and we get her downstairs and into the backseat of his car, the twenty-minute drive to the hospital feeling longer than backstroking across the Atlantic.

He lets us off at the ER, and I carry her inside, bridal-fashioned. The front desk receptionist pages a nurse who helps Charlie into a wheelchair, and I'm stuck with paperwork on a clipboard, my writing ineligible. Jesse takes the pen, the clipboard, and my unsteady hand and coaxes me into an area where we sit and wait.

"I'll fill this out, love," he says. "Just tell me the information."

Jesse returns the clipboard to the front desk, and we twiddle our thumbs in the waiting room.

"What's wrong with her?"

"Miscarriage."

"How'd you know?"

"Ma had one when I was younger, 'bout a year before she and Dad split. She was further along than Charlie."

"How far?"

"Almost four months."

I slip my hand into his. "I'm sorry. You were fantastic. Thank you. I froze. If you hadn't been there, I... I'm a shitty brother."

"No, babe." He lays our hands on his thigh. "You were scared. Natural reaction. Ya did exactly what you were supposed to do. You're a *terrific* brother."

We sip coffee, and Jesse shifts, the woman across from us pursing her lips at our held hands and low-profile PDA (winks and knuckle-kisses).

"What?" I ask her, and she, startled, clutches her handbag. "Never seen two dudes kiss?" I grab his chin, smash my mouth to his with gusto, and say to the lady, "There ya go. You can use it for your spank bank later."

Jesse laughs theatrically, and she collects her things, her steps fast-paced.

"*Holy shit*, Square. I love it when you're bold."

It's confirmed Charlie has, in fact, miscarried, the doctor explaining the dilation and curettage procedure done to prevent any potential infections, and assures us she's fine and will be good to go home once the anesthesia wears off.

We knock on the door to Charlie's room on the maternity floor. She's reclined in the bed in a blue and white gown, the white blanket covering her from the waist down. She breaks down post-haste, and I soothe her as Mom would when we had chicken pox or the flu. Jesse stays in the corner, the toe of his shoe making circles on the laminate.

Her sobs peters out into hiccups, and those hiccups to hollow breaths, and those breaths into coherent words. She thanks me for helping her. *Charlie. Thanks. Me.* I should check to see if Christ is walking down Main Street or ask the Devil if he's freezing his dick off.

"Dad knows you're home?"

"Yeah, I came back on Tuesday. Told him I was sick and didn't want to give it to my roommate. He was *not* thrilled and said leaving college during my first semester was irresponsible, and I'm missing a few brain cells or some crazy shit like that."

"Sounds like Leon. How long have you known about...."

"Two weeks. The doctor said I was between five and seven."

"Does the father know?"

She pinches her lip. "Um... he would if I knew who the father was."

"Oh. Are you in pain?"

"A little." She shrugs. "Nothing like here, though," she says, her hand on her chest. "My heart hurts, Mikey. Pisses me off how people go on and on about how abortion is wrong because you're killing a human, but when a woman miscarries early on, they ask why you're sad over it because 'it's not like it was a baby yet.' I'm *designed* to do this, and the second I found out, I was in love. Terrified, but in love. I failed to protect it."

"You didn't fail. It's not your fault; you have every right to be sad. You just lost a precious thing, a part of you. Screw everyone else."

"Our family's cursed."

"Tell me 'bout it. There's a billboard sign on Highway 96 for a church that says, 'Why Did Jesus Create You?' and I always think: To pin needles into."

Charlie guffaws. "Truth!"

She dabs her eyes and extends her hand to Jesse. He stands next to me, and she pecks his cheek. "Thank you."

If she's anything like me, Jesse's smile has her heart melting in plasma lagoons.

"You're welcome, Charlie. I'm sorry for your loss."

"Me too. *Argh!* I can't possibly go back to Dad's."

I proclaim cynically, "Fuck no. He'll skin you alive."

"Or disown me."

"Naw, you're his favorite. We'd have a possible homicide if I came home knocked up."

Charlie belts out, "You'd make a beautiful pregnant man!"

Our buoyancy disbands, and Charlie looks me in the eye. "I'm sorry about everything. I don't want us to hate each other anymore. I never really hated you. I was, I guess, *jealous.* And I'm sorry for what I said to you, Jesse."

"No sweat."

"*You're* jealous of *me?*"

"Yes, Mikey. I know I've been an *awful, awful* person to you, to

Maddy, to *Mom!* I'm unforgivable, but, dammit, Mike, I pretended to be someone I'm not. I saw how Dad treated you and Maddy like you were shit on the bottom of his shoe, so disgusted he'd rather throw it away than wash it off. I didn't want that. I wouldn't have been able to handle it as you guys did. You're both *so strong*. You stayed true to yourselves, no matter what he said or did. You're the first person I thought to call this morning. I knew you'd help me and wouldn't judge me or be disappointed in me because that's who you are, Mikey. I have so many regrets. When I found you that night in your closet, I should've been better to you. I knew how much pain you were in, and I never... never...."

My winded sister cleaves to me and blatantly sobs and pleads for clemency.

"Charlie, you did what you had to do to survive. We all did, and it doesn't mean you're weaker than Maddy or me. In Leon's defense, you ended up *much* better than us."

Jesse hands her a tissue.

"Thanks, Jesse." She blows her nose. "Right, because getting pregnant your first year of college is *totally* five-star material."

Jesse scrunches his shoulders. "I mean," he remarks nonchalantly, "ya coulda caught the clap."

Charlie and I stare at him, then hoot hard and loud, even if it's reflexive. For now, we'll bluff our pain away and make believe Charlie and I didn't miss the chance to spoil a future niece or nephew. Moreover, I'm thankful for Jesse mopping up a dank, disastrous situation.

Once Charlie is discharged, we park at the pharmacy (we won't drive the car through this one) and wait for them to fill her prescription (antibiotics and 5-milligram hydrocodone—quite underwhelming).

Jesse's stomach grumbles. "Goddang, anyone else hungry? We should hit up a fast-food joint on the way home. Where ya wanna go, guys?"

"I don't care," I answer. "Wherever you want."

"Mikey!"

"Jesse!"

"What do you want?"

"I don't care!"

"Oh, my God!" carps Charlie from the backseat. "You two sound like an old married couple!"

I tear at my fingernails and Jesse sends me an air-kiss, his starry eyes revived.

Home (un)sweet home.

Mom welcomes us at the doorway, bags of burgers and fries in Jesse's arms, and milkshakes in mine.

Her exultant mien droops. "Charlie, what are you doing home, honey?"

Charlie squeaks, "Mama," her tears shedding, and Mom rushes to her.

Jesse closes the door, and Mom invites me into the huddle.

"You too, Jesse," says Mom, and he sets the bags on the kitchen table and binds in. "My babies. *All* my babies."

She's so… *tiny*. She's always been petite, but this is… she's… *waning*, like she'll snap easier than a wet popsicle stick if I hug too tightly.

"My babies. I love you all so much."

I detect hopelessness.

Screw it.

I hug with all my might because I feel her slipping away. The ice and snow will devastate our town shortly, frosting or killing every animated object, and the stats stab into me like fangs into raw pulp: while the earth's rotation controls the weather, I… I cannot.

TWELVE

Emptiness, My Home

FACT #13: 586,000 AMERICANS, AGES TWELVE AND UP, STRUGGLE WITH HEROIN ADDICTION.

BALLED fist.

Keep it tight.

Competent, reliable hands.

Cotton and burning spoons.

Brown sugar crystals boiling into liquid gilt.

A sweetened smell brews.

None of that sticky, tar bullshit tonight.

He got me the good stuff.

All for me.

Me, me, me.

Everything he does is for me. I believe him. I trust him. We trust *each other*. I'm trusting him to not blow the vein, and he's trusting me for trusting him not to. I trust him when he disinfects my skin with an alcohol pad, loads the liquid into a syringe, and taps my vein—*tap, tap.* I take a deep breath, let it out past my teeth, and it's but a microscopic pinprick solving every astronomical problem.

My love, pinpoint the poison.

Blood—ruby-slipper-red and buttery.

He slams it home, the difference between snorting and shooting like a tindering fire to a volcanic explosion.

Jesse emulates the procedure of tearing open the alcohol pad and needle. The Zippo flicks, the syringe sucks it up, and he tightens the tourniquet. I lie back—*ahhhh*—bringing my lover with me.

My numb hand can't feel his, but I know he's there.

He's the *Dark Side of the Moon* to my *Wizard of Oz.*

Adequately united.

Lovers.

Kindred.

Safe.

Jack Frost's barking winds fiercely break and enter my room via old, split windows and imperceptible cracks. It's too cold in this town. The magical elixir keeps me warm. Jesse's body keeps me warmer. Typically, "Golden Girl" can de-power my mind.

Not tonight.

Shooting up is a last resort when I'm particularly wayward and disordered, and such moments are becoming more customary.

Like tonight.

I liken the customs to an interstellar expressway paved exclusively for spaceships, since they're the only shuttles big enough to transport my memories. I grapple with the flashbacks from the previous month and a half as they whizz by. Like a slot machine, I push STOP to gamble which event ought to be evaluated first, which makes sense. Our brains don't keep track of memories like a well-planned shopping list or dally in any meticulous sequence. They shuffle in our heads like a game of blackjack...

WE'RE IN Toby's guest house.

Tan powder on our chessboard. It's bloodcurdling horrific. It doesn't burn going down. Pretty sure it's cut with a baby laxative. Multiple trips to the bathroom ratify it is. My drip's sugary; the euphoria as amative as Jesse's kisses, though not as mindblowing as I thought it'd be. I was expecting a rush to the head, but it's more of a stronger dose of Oxy, past 30s and 80s, as if someone pressed the pills into 300mgs and combined them into a single stockpile you can snort in one go.

A blatant:

BANG!

BANG!

BANG!

I've learned to differentiate gunshots as to if they're a street over—like the gang war that left three teenagers dead and two men injured on Yellow Street—or if they're on Indigo, like the afternoon when Rachel, strung out on crack, shot Gabe in the head. I didn't care about losing "the best sticky in town." We've found better and way stickier from other sources.

I worry about Rachel's children being taken by the state. Motherless. Alone. They may resort to drugs, tricks, or gangs. Hopefully, a sweet granny or aunt will nurture them with love, chewy cookies, and fluffy beds in a cozy home in a gated community.

BANG!

BANG!

BANG!

They're not gunshots. They're full-fisted knocks, but not on our door. We peep outside to find the main house surrounded, and get up, pack our narcotics into the duffle, and hurry out the window to the street and into Jesse's car.

"Fucking *SWAT?*"

"The hell'd Toby do?"

"Oh, Christ, do you think he'll confess to the pharmacy heist?" I light a Camel. "Is this *because* of the heist?"

"Babe, breathe. He'd never rat us out!"

Golden Girl's tenacious, my nerves seedy. Jesse can't slow down or stop the car, so I open my door and spew out onto the road.

"Toby's in a world of shit!" shouts Jesse, sucking in half a Salem. "*Fuck, man!*" He slaps the steering wheel.

I take his hand and count his fingers in my head as I give them each a kiss.

"Sorry, love," he calmly says.

Superfluity fog rises like dry ice. The lights of home. The puke in my mouth. Golden girl in my veins and head. Powder stuck inside my nostrils; itchy, burning. *Sniff. Sniff. Sniff.* Blood.

Someone's on the porch, a sunny-orange cigarette cherry glowing in the murky fog. I run towards her pixie blue eyes, hug her and put to memory her patchouli perfume and her healthy, sober body against my drug-infused thin one.

She studies me at arm's length. "Mikey, my gods, you look like *shit.*"

"Nice to see you too, Madds."

SHE PICKS me up from work.

Dining at Ninja's Sushi Steakhouse, she discusses work, her

roommate Ryver Sutton ("You'd love her! She does oil paintings of the night sky. I know how much you love your galaxies!") and the support groups she attends regardless of her sobriety ("I don't say 'clean.' Addicts aren't filthy.").

I don't contribute to the conversation. A kite on a limitless string in an unlimited stratosphere is *nowhere* near as high as me. I push my Volcano Rolls around with my chopsticks, then lay them down. I'll take them home to Jesse. Volcano Rolls are his favorite.

"Kiddo, you need to eat. I haven't seen you this skinny since you were ten."

"I had a big lunch," I lie.

Maddy closes in, and I avert my needle-head pupils staring back at me in the reflective, silver napkin holder. It's pointless. My pupils aren't the only dead giveaway to my strung out condition.

"How long, Mike?"

I slouch into the booth.

"I *swear* on Mother Nature's green earth, Michael, I'll ship your ass *right* off to rehab. Don't test me. I knew the second I saw you. Have you seen yourself? There's nothing to you! You're scratching and sniffing. You're fucking *snorting?*"

We're the only two on this side of the restaurant, but in my high mind, *everyone* can hear us.

"Not here."

"Well, we can't discuss it at home, can we? Dammit, Mike, I'm surprised Mom hasn't noticed. Whatever you're doing can block your antidepressants."

"I know."

"Then why are you doing it? I love you, kiddo, but you gotta snap the fuck out of it before you end up overdosing or worse. Have you learned *nothing* from my screw-ups?"

"I was a kid! I didn't know what was wrong with you! I just knew you were sick all the time."

"But you're old enough to know now. How'd this happen? How could you *allow* it to happen?"

"You're joking." My sweaty palms form condensation handprints on the acrylic tabletop. "You should know better than anyone, *Maddy!* I've watched *you* my entire life. *You* made it part of the family! *You* invited it in! I can't help that I'm fucked up!"

Idle chatting ends as people look up from their plates. They hear us now, and it's not Maddy's doing.

I mind my volume. "I'm messed up."

"You see a therapist. You have an advantage many would die for. *Use it.*"

"I ditched that useless doorknob. Why do I still wanna swallow a bullet if he's so *goddamn* great? Why do I still spend days in bed feeling miserable? Do you know who saves me on those days? Who walks with me in my 'bad neighborhood?'"

"I know you think Jesse's good for you, but he's toxic."

"Shut your mou—"

"No, *you* shut up. I'm calling it as I see it; what *I've learned.* Misery loves company. Neither of you is helping. You're both *enabling.* He's not a bad person. He's a good person who makes bad decisions. But Mikey, he *is* a bad decision. When you told me you were hanging out with Jesse, I told Mom to put a stop to it, but you know her. She's too trusting, and here we are."

"You don't know Jesse."

"No, but I knew Daryl, and he was one of the worst people I've ever met. He shot his mom, and then what? Took off to God knows where and got himself killed. Be cautious of the company you keep."

"*Jesse-isn't-Daryl.* Pretty chauvinistic of you to judge him based on who his family is. Charlie and I grew up in *your* shadow, so I'm sure you never had to deal with that shit, huh? He's *nothing* like Daryl."

"And you're *nothing* like me? Because from where I'm sitting, I'm staring *right* at my addiction. Use your head. Get sober. I'll help you. I'll go to NA with you."

"You dropped out of AA and NA!"

"Just because I'm against their God complex doesn't mean I'm against people using it to better their lives, and it's private and free. You can bring Jesse."

"*Fuck* NA. We're *not* addicts."

"Go *one day* without getting high, and we'll see if you're not an addict. I said the same bullshit: 'I don't have a problem. I'm a functioning drug user.' So, c'mon, Mike, prove me wrong."

Our lemonades spill as I stand up and bump into the table.

"Careful, Madds, your halo's slipping."

I storm out of Ninjas, cross the road to Meijer, call Jesse, and wait in the bathroom. Fifteen minutes later, I'm struck by his black and teal flannel jacket suiting his blonde hair. It's the first snowfall of the year and, you guessed it, he's wearing his black skater shorts and black and teal Vans.

"*Damn*, you look *hawt*."

His winter-wind blushed cheeks deepen in color, his mouth extending into a bashful grin.

Privately in the Honda, I recount my fall-out with Maddy, and as soon as I say, "And she said that you—" his hand shushes my mouth.

"Mikey, don't. Whatever she said 'bout me has you all unhinged, which means she said nothin' nice, and ya know what? She's probably right."

"How can you say that?"

"'Cause she knows what she's talkin' 'bout. She's been there, done that, and she loves you. She wants what's best for ya, baby, that's all."

"*You're* what's best for me. *You.* She has no right to lecture me, acting all high and mighty and better than everyone because she's *sober.*"

"She *is* better than everyone else. Gettin' sober ain't for the faint-hearted. She stared straight into the face of death and Satan, survived every circle of Hell, and came out stronger 'cause of it."

"We *don't* have a problem."

He hikes an eyebrow.

"*We don't!*"

His mouth on my wrist, he speaks softly and sincerely, "Okay, love. I know you're upset, but hear me out when I say to make amends with her. She's blood and ya know what's said 'bout blood and water. You may not always want me in your life, and there may come a day when I ain't there, but Maddy will *always* be there. And right now, you and your sisters need to stick together."

Maddy makes it home before us, and she's rocking on the porch swing wrapped in a fleece blanket, and I fill in the space next to her, ash my cigarette, and wait until Jesse's inside to say, "I'm sorry, Madds," and I mean it.

"Me too. I'm not trying to come off as self-righteous. I understand where you're at right now, but I'm going to lay it out for you, and I want you to *really* listen. There are only two outcomes to this, Mike.

"One: all your creativity will vanish. Everything you love to do—painting, creating—will disappear completely the longer you're an addict. You'll be so engrossed in your high that your desire to create will be taken away.

"Two: everyone you love, everything you care for, will slip away because you won't have time for anything or anyone other than the addiction. You will spend your days high, chasing your next fix, or dope sick.

"You're at a fork in the road, kid. Do you want to be the Mike who's sober, creating things, loving, and spending time with his friends and family? Or do you want to be Mike the Addict: the self-absorbed person not caring about anything or anyone other than his next fix? Is it more important to spend your time chasing down a high or chasing down more important things?"

"It's not like I'm doing heroin." Another fib.

"That's all you got to say?" She grunts, her head shaking. "Boy, smarten up! And you're not doing heroin *yet*. No matter what I say or do, you'll do what you want, anyway. I always did. And as much as I hate to do it, as risky as it is, I'm going to let you reach your own rock bottom. I won't force you into rehab or NA. I'm *definitely* not telling Mom. She's going through enough as it is. And I sure as shit don't approve of your relationship with Jesse or his living here.

I'll tolerate it. I'll be nice and give him a chance, but if I *ever* find a single track mark on your body, I'll kick Jesse out, lock you in your room, board your windows, and keep you there until you're back to the Michael I've always known."

When she looks at me, I know *exactly* what it is she's looking *for*:

Change in pupils.

Sweats.

Droopy eyelids.

I'm high now, and I'll be high later.

She's staring at me like she's just *waiting* for me to die.

At the bottom, guilt keeps me alive, as well as hatred, hunger and weakness.

"I'm sorry, Maddy," I say. "I don't mean to be this way."

It all comes 'round full circle.

THESE SONGFUL mementos signify how a once reserved kid transformed into a full-fledged, abominable addict, and such melodies make up the soundtrack to *The Tragic Downfall of Michael Sinclair.*

And no performance is complete without its encore.

ON THE day of Charlie's miscarriage, Jesse and I eat burgers and milkshakes at the kitchen table while Charlie and Mom talk in Mom's bedroom. Jesse looks behind him, side to side, and my insides somersault as I catch his smoldering gaze seconds before I'm enchanted with a tongue-stimulating kiss I could happily fester in.

He pulls away and breathes me in. "Mmmm, you taste like salty chocolate. Gimme more. I'm a greedy sumbitch."

"Mmmm, me too."

I drag him lustily from his chair, gripping his thighs as he straddles me, our make-out session sultry, and ketchup, chocolate, and salt tinge his organic flavor. His godforsaken piercing feels *outstanding* in my mouth, and I reposition myself, thinking back on how outstanding it felt on *other* things...

"Ya okay down there, *dirty boy?*" he asks cheekily.

No, I'm not okay! I'm an operational, walking, talking bag of testosterone, and Jesse's unfastened the strings to my hormonal flare-up. Staring at him, all I see is our naked bodies on that blue bed in that blue room and snorting blue powder.

I crash down hard (ha-ha, *hard*) from my risque whims, mumble, "You're the antichrist, Jesse Harris," and bite into my bland burger that started off flavorful.

Charlie cries in the next room, and curiously, I can't relate to her sadness, although I never had issues connecting to Maddy's addiction when I didn't have one myself.

Drugs, I conclude, can turn even the most empathetic persons into narcissists.

Jesse and I smoke on the patio and swallow four Oxy (my nosebleeds and nostril scabs are unmanageable, and I apologize for the TMI, but I haven't had a decent shit in weeks).

We head to my bedroom to finish what we initiated in the kitchen and catch up on some sleep, but Mom bids us into the living room, and we wind up on the loveseat diagonal from her and Charlie rather than my bed.

Her straight stance and crossed legs stem from her Catholic

upbringing, though she doesn't adjust her sweater hanging off one bony shoulder. I witnessed this posture after Grandma Sinclair passed away and the night she and Leon announced their divorce.

My head's fizzy. I clasp Jesse's knee, perceiving what's to come, and I've never been more unprepared.

THIRTEEN

Blooming Darkly

FACT #14: THE HOMELESS POPULATION IN THE US HAS AN ADJUSTED RISK RATE OF 1.8% OF OPIOID OVERDOSE THAN THOSE IN LOW-INCOME HOUSING (0.3%).

THERE ARE life events you virtually expunge as if they never blew in and turned your world inside out. You go on, partaking in the rites of passage; life like a mundane paint-by-number you fill in with the brushes of daily responsibility: bills, rent, school, relationships. Everyday distractions.

Is it the brain protecting the heart, or the other way around?

In any case, you're powerless until a stranger passes by with a glint in their eye, reminding you of home. You hear a titter in their laugh, reminding you of love. You see a polka dot dress, a diamond bracelet, and sense an emptiness not even time can restore. You smell hospital sheets, hear the beeping heart monitor, and your brain's bared. These little moments, like tidal waves, anchor you down. Not the neon-paint-on-a-beautiful-man's-chest waves, but genuine, breaking waves. You've suppressed these events and moments for so long that, once they're released, you're knocked off your feet and struggling under the roaring waters.

And you drown.

I'm splitting the wounds.

I'm fighting against the tides.

I'M STARING at a steel-colored wall.

Jesse massages my shoulders.

He kisses my neck.

It's like my veins are trying to wrestle my eyeballs into my skull.

They're dry, yet wet.

I'm perspiring, yet cold.

My mind's as blank as these steel-colored walls, yet one phrase spins like a demonic carousel:

Cancer.

Cancer.

Cancer.

"WHAT KIND?" Charlie asks.

"P-pan-pancreatic."

"What stage?"

Gulp. "F-four."

"How long do you have?"

"Six months... But some people have been told less and went for another two or three years. I'm going to fight this, kids. I've *been* fighting it. There's treatments and medications. We're going to beat this."

STEEL SUITS me effortlessly. My life. My *cursed* life.

Jesse has my back to his chest, skin on skin, his stubble like

Velcro on my shoulder blades. I don't mind. At least I'm able to feel *something.*

Cancer.

Six months.

Six months!

"Why don'tcha try to get some rest?" he says.

Silence. Staring.

"Ya wanna just sit here?"

Silence. Staring.

"Alright, love. We'll sit here."

I muster a 180-degree rotation and hug Jesse. I need to hear his heartbeat. I need confirmation he's still alive.

He kisses my hair.

He sings me love songs.

"HOW LONG have you known?" I ask.

Her fingers fiddle on her lap. "Since we moved here."

I jump up and yell at her, call her names, and point out her selfishness for not disclosing her fatal illness to her own damn children. Everyone's deaf with tears. Jesse tries to calm me. I shove him and run out the door.

I run.

And run.

Must outrace my hostile heartache.

Run...

Run...

Run...

Don't stop running...

I can't outrun fate.

I buckle inches from the ditch. Jesse pulls up in the car and scoops me into his arms. *Safe.* I pound my fists into his chest.

I scream at the dead Ohio sky.

Oxy's not cutting it.

"I need something stronger."

"I'm not helpin' ya down into that pit of Hell."

"I'm not *asking.* I'm *telling.* I've asked you for *nothing.* You can do this *one* thing for me."

"This ain't just a *thing* you're askin' of me. You're ask—"

"How'd you feel when your mom died?"

The corners of his mouth and eyebrows sag. He's hurt because of me. I hate how I've become this… *thing.* Am I even human?

"Get in the car," he says, undeniably crushed. "I know a dude."

The neighborhood he takes us to is one of the wealthiest in the county, with pothole-less roads and brick-red or colonial-white homes, their lawns manicured or fake—luxuriant and patchless.

He stops at an eggshell colored residence with taupe shutters, black doors, a spacious backyard, a mini-jungle gym with no missing pieces, and a tire swing hanging from a brawny oak tree. There's no misplaced toys or dead plants dangling from the wrought iron porch. The man who answers Jesse's knock is neither old nor young, late-forties, if I had to guess, and he's sharp in his three-piece tailored suit, white collar, and gold checkered tie.

Jesse goes inside.

I smoke a cigarette.

I put it out.

Jesse returns.

"He's an actual chemist," he explains, and I'd rather not know how they're acquainted, so I don't ask.

The Chemist takes "business trips" to Baltimore twice a month.

"Business," equals "heroin."

But I'm sure you worked that out for yourself.

"We ain't makin' a habit of this, sexy boy."

No. Of course not.

I'VE NO intention of leaving Toby's guest house. I've no plans to get out of bed. Golden Girl (heroin), Blue (Oxy), and Jesse (love) are all I need, and I despise him for saying we'll have to go home at some point or, at the very least, let Mom and Charlie know we're okay so they'll stop calling and texting in case they decide to call the cops. He doesn't want the other officers and Paul to find out where we are.

(Me): I'm safe. I'm with Jesse. I need space and time to let it soak in.

Soak it in. I'm not a sponge. I'm tinfoil in a monsoon.

(Mom): Take all the time you need. I love you.

I love her too. If I didn't, I wouldn't have this gaping hole the size of Jupiter in my chest. I wouldn't be crying myself to sleep in Jesse's arms if I didn't. If I didn't, I wouldn't be snorting heroin to annul this cremating pain.

I'm definite we're to stay in this blue and steel room for as long as it takes to glue myself back together. Then the SWAT team arrives and throws that dream down the gutter.

We've nowhere to go but home.

And that's when I find Maddy on the porch.

And that's when her patchouli perfume marks my dingy clothes.

The three of us chat at the kitchen table late into the night, Jesse and me flirting out of Maddy's view, playing footsie, holding hands, our fingertips tapping or caressing palms and knuckles.

She says to him, "Look at you, Harris, all grown up. The last time I saw you, you were six inches shorter, and your voice was changing. You've grown into a good-looking young man."

You can say that again.

Maddy's changed as well. She regained some weight, her elbow-length black, straight hair no longer stringy. She's always said she was "average" though, to me, she could be a movie star, her irises speckled like fairy dust with all the hues in the blue spectrum, and her complexion resembles a peach a day away from ripe when she's not on drugs.

"You can't run from this one, Mike. You need to be brave. You need to be strong."

Have I ever been brave and strong? I've forgotten.

"We're a family. Mom needs us and I'm here for you. I'd never let you face this alone. We'll take care of Mom together."

Something other than my heart needs to *crack*.

Where's the levee when you need it?

I KNOCK on Mom's door and follow the moonlight defining her frail form on the bed. I kick off my shoes, the eyes I inherited glancing up at me, and she spreads the duvet over us and, her arms encircling me in our secret cocoon, we cry. My apologies skid out like marbles on an ice rink.

"Apologies aren't necessary. It's okay to be scared. Just don't be angry."

"What else am I supposed to be?" I ask.

"*Thankful.*"

Her silky hands, like the bows she'd adorned Charlie's hair with when we were kids, dry my tears. "I'm going to let you in on a little secret. Keep it between us?"

"Okay."

"I've always wanted the American Dream: the hillside house in the country with the white picket fence, married to a wonderful man and *lots* of children. Life didn't go precisely to plan, but I had it all for a time. I wasn't sad when I left your father because I had Maddy, Charlie, and *you*.

"I adore your sisters more than life, but it was love at first sight when you were born. Gosh, you were the most beautiful baby. The nurses would come by on their breaks just to look at you. They called you 'The Baby with the Midnight Eyes.'

"I'm very proud of the kind, talented, sensitive man you've become. You had to grow up fast, and you took it all in stride. I did all I could to keep you safe from the world's evils, Michael, and I'm sorry I wasn't always there for you. Please forgive me for all the times I've let you down."

"Mom, you've *never* let us down. You were, are, and always will be the *greatest* mother in the world. Why do you think I'm all those things you said? We both know it's not because of Dad."

We laugh past our tears.

"Can I let you in on a secret?"

She tucks a cluster of hair behind my ear. "Always."

Jesse and I have yet to decide how or when to update others about our relationship. It's depressing to admit, but Mom's dying, and she's dying fast. She deserves to hear that her son has fallen in love for the first time. Her love, after all, taught me what love is supposed to be.

Her silence is dubious, and my anxiety is a noose.

"I'm your mother. You think I didn't notice?" she says after a long pause.

"What gave it away?"

"I was married to your father for twenty-one years, and *not once* did he ever look at me the way Jesse looks at you. That boy *loves you*."

"How does he look at me?"

"Like you're a song only he can hear."

My heart swells. "Do you think he's good for me?"

"Hmmm... I believe... I believe he's misled and had a difficult life he had zero control over, but he brings sunshine into the room, and I think he's given you that sunshine, or maybe you've given him yours? It worries me when any of my children fall in love. I don't want to see your hearts get broken, but heartbreak, like love, is all a part of life. I wouldn't say he's 'bad' for you, but I don't want you to lose sight of yourself, Michael. You don't need outside validation to appreciate who you are. Love Jesse with all your heart, but don't forget to love yourself just as much."

"I love you, Mom."

"I love you, sweets."

I stay with her until she drifts off.

Although I don't believe in God, I thank Him for having given me Marie Sinclair and, in the same prayer, smite him for wanting to take her away.

I GRAB a blanket on my way outside, and Jesse and I cuddle in the snowy night, his smoking arm placed on my knee. I graze my lips along the crook of his neck and he spins to accept my open-mouthed affection, our tongues tasting of snowflakes and tobacco.

"The house has been for rent for months," he says at the property across the street and its crooked FOR RENT sign. "No one wants to have family game night in a livin' room where a meth-head murdered his mother."

I'm the worst person to put my burdens on him. Sure, Mom's cancer is a link to our already impressive chain. Nonetheless, I have something Jesse didn't have regarding the death of our mothers: *closure*. Being the selfless badass he is, Jesse doesn't scorn me for it and has become my rock... my Polaris.

"I'm sorry you're hurtin'."

"I know you are, sweetheart."

"I'd take it all away for ya if I could."

"I know, Jess."

"Mi Sinclair?"

He looks up as I look down.

"I love you."

It's the first time he's said it.

"Likewise."

Kissing him upside down, I ponder over what Mom said. Have I lost myself in Jesse? Who *is* Michael Sinclair? An artist, a lost soul searching for somewhere he belongs, and his mother's dying, and he's in love, or so he thinks.

I am...

Bittersweet.

FOURTEEN

Sweet Talking Despair

FACT #15: IN ONE MONTH, 4.3 MILLION AMERICANS WILL USE PAIN MEDICATIONS FOR NON-MEDICAL REASONS.

IF THERE'S anything I want you to take away from this story, it's that time, my friends, is valuable.

The days X-ed off, it's the night before Christmas Eve, and November has been a ying-yang month of highs and lows:

Thanksgiving was unremarkable. Working, chasing down Golden Girl, Blues, and spazzing about Toby's arrest (a case with paper-thin facts) took precedence over holiday celebrations. According to the rest of the gang, Toby kept us out of it, which should've been our primary concern.

As for getting high? It took me three times the amount of *anything* to feel a quarter of what I felt six months ago.

"You've built up a tolerance," Jesse said. "You're maintainin'. That's why ya feel like shit when you're comin' down and a-okay once it's back in your system. I'm shocked it took ya this long, or are ya just now noticin'?"

I tried abstaining from the drugs like Jesse did, coercing myself into withdrawals. He could go days without it, and, dang, it's downright impressive and requires hardcore self-restraint. I'd last an hour before begging for a line, a bump, a taste.

"It's worth it in the end," he said during day four.

"Whatever," I said and snorted line four.

But soon, his self-restraint was lost on him, and that's when shooting up went from once a day to twice a day to as many times a day—after work, before bed, after oral sex, whenever time allowed. If time *didn't* allow, we *made* time and were careful to hide the marks beneath long sleeved flannels and hoodies.

I disliked drug runs as much as forced withdrawals, but we visited "The Chemist" every other day, and we'd be giddy on our way home knowing that the coveted baggie of sweet, brown goodness was securely nestled in Jesse's back pocket. He pinky-swore he'd take the hit if we got caught, and I appreciated his metaphorical sacrifice, even if he was an idiot for thinking I'd let him carry the can.

Except for Mom, we kept our relationship secret from those close to us. Jazz and Eli figured it out on their own; we just verified it. Aside from them, this delicate creation was ours and ours alone. Nobody to interfere. Nobody to tell us no.

Maddy's sermons surrounding my "addiction" stopped, though she hid Mom's medications and threw me a stony eagle eye if I sniffed and scratched like a coked-out character in a Katt Williams skit. Maddy had more important things to worry about than my so-called "drug abuse," like Mom's doctor appointments, meals, and sponge baths. Maddy's a saint. Period.

Speaking of Mom, she wasn't getting better or worse. I had dreary days, sunnier days, nights I slept peacefully, nights I cried into the morning, but I was always in Jesse's arms.

Safe.

Thanksgiving week, Mom loosened her headscarf, her ebony hair straggly and receding. She brushed her tears away as Maddy buzzed the last of her curls, per Mom's request.

Jesse and I were stacking plates into the dishwasher when Mom burrowed herself underneath the blankets on the sofa. He vanished and was gone for a while, and I found him shaving his hair in the bathroom. He set the razor down and dipped his head.

"Don't be mad."

I whispered, "Baby," as I stroked his freshly shaved hair, hugged and thanked him a million times, then handed him the razor.

"Y'sure? You love your hair."

"Showing Mom she's loved is more important."

He kissed my forehead. "I love you, Sinclair."

I couldn't say it out loud, but I realized I loved Jesse Harris more than I ever thought possible.

"Likewise."

Seeing our peach-fuzzed heads, my sisters, who hugged and thanked Jesse as well, chopped off their ponytails and shaved the rest.

As a family, we marched into the living room, formed a line, and comforted Mom—hugs, kisses, tears—as she sobbed.

JESSE DEVOTED his leisure time to Mom, and I could tell she enjoyed his company and his jokes, her laughter brightening the grimness pushing us down like an invisible, heavy hand.

They were playing bridge, and Jesse exclaimed, "Marie! You're kickin' my ass, woman! Good thing this ain't strip poker!"

She hadn't laughed like that in... *forever*. It was contagious, and Maddy, Charlie, and I joined in. Jesse was our comedic relief, but I knew it was a gambit because the decaying wormhole in his soul shone in his forlorn, distant gaze.

Now we're here at the cemetery because of that wormhole—Margaret Lily Harris and two cherubs blowing trumpets inscribed in black on the rectangular headstone. The two dozen roses we bought from Langer's stand out on the snowy flatland like crimson footprints.

I step to the side, and he dusts snow off the stone.

"Hey, Ma, sorry it's been so long. Life's been crazy lately, as I'm sure ya already know. Work's okay, Dad and I are gettin' along, somethin' I know you've always wanted, and I'm sorry I couldn't give it to ya when you were still here.

"Ya always said I should fall in love with my best friend. I did. His name's Mike. You'd love him too. He wants us to move to California. Can ya believe this punk?"

"You'd be happy there."

"It's his sugary impossibilities I love most 'bout him. I wish you were here, Ma. I took our Christmas tradition for granted. Who's gonna stay up 'til midnight with me eatin' homemade caramel popcorn, drinkin' hot chocolate, and watchin' *It's A Wonderful Life*? We didn't get to do it last year, either. Daryl blew our Christmas funds on friggin' meth. I'm sorry I didn't do more to help him. I miss him too, even if he made our lives a livin' Hell. Shit, we should've given ya an easier life. I swear I'll make you proud someday. I love you, Ma, never forget it. I think of ya every second of every day." He kisses her engraved name. "Merry Christmas."

I assist him to his feet and immediately embrace him as if my arms and body will wash away his sufferings, and if they *can* heal him, I'll hold on forever.

"She's already proud of you."

"I hope so."

On our way to the store to pick up our Christmas ham and cheesecake ingredients (Charlie's request, Margaret Harris' recipe), I text Maddy and kiss Jesse from his fingertips to his wrist and back again.

"I love you, Sinclair."

"Likewise."

Meijer is packed, so we park nearby at Best Buy and, arm in arm, trek through the sleet and snow.

Trying to track down items for a Christmas feast is comical. We make fun of ourselves as we revisit the same aisles, which turns an otherwise humdrum activity into an adventure, and it transpires once more how much I love Jesse Harris.

We meet up with Eli and Jazz so Eli can buy a bag of weed for his older brother, Marcus, and Jazz gives him a hard time for forgetting about Christmas, their cart stuffed with wrapping paper, bows, toys, and other knick-knacks.

"You forgot too!" Eli claps back.

"Yeah, yeah."

"Anyone heard from Tobs?" I ask.

"No. I spoke to his dad last week, but he told me to forget it happened. I'm sure he's going away for a long time. He was working for a *huge* drug ring. They found an entire storage unit of marijuana plants and, like, *loads* of heroin and cocaine. He's *beyond* screwed," says Eli.

Jesse asks, "How'd he even get involved?"

Jazz glances around aimlessly.

"Spit it out, Jazz," says Jesse.

She groans, stomping her foot. "Toby wanted to help you pay off Daryl's debts, and he started dealing for… whoever he was dealing for—never told me who—and it kinda just spiraled out of control."

Four pairs of eyes look at four pairs of shoes.

"I know what you're thinking, Jess," says Eli. "You can't blame yourself for Toby's choices. It doesn't take much to get duped into the business. Cash is king."

"But he already had a shit ton of money," says Jesse.

"In a trust fund he can't access until he's twenty-five. You know Toby. He's a greedy mofo. Anyway, you got the *pizza*, right?"

"Stuffed crust." He winks at me. "Be right back, hot stuff."

My cheeks overheat, my stomach homing a family of bats, and when they venture off, Jazz grins at me as if she just had her first kiss.

"Seriously, why do you women do that?"

She ignores my sarcasm and blurts, "Has it happened yet?"

"Has *what* happened?"

Her glee disperses. "C'mon, dude! What're you waiting for?"

"Ugh! I dunno!" I clean the sleep from the corner of my eyes. "I'm tired and it's hard to think straight when I'm high."

"News flash: you're *always* high."

"Bullshit."

Jazz stands straight, leering. "You're high right now, motherfucker."

"Guilty."

"I hate public exchanges."

"Same, but, eh, what can ya do?"

She sneers lewdly. "You can make *sweet, sweet* boy love to Jesse."

"Shut it, Jazz."

"Wow, Mikey!" She rascally punches my arm. "You're blushing brighter than that chick's Santa hat. But for real, what're you waiting for?"

"The perfect moment?"

"That's Hallmark channel crap."

"How did you and Eli know it was the right time?"

"Not sure." Her smile hints at nostalgia. "We just did. It wasn't planned. We were watching TV, and, well, next thing you know..."

"How was it?"

"Not like what you see in the movies. We were nervous and laughing a lot, and we didn't come out from under the blankets even though we'd already seen each other naked. And I was bleeding."

"*Bleeding?*"

"Oh, bro, Eli is *huge*. Like,"—she swings one of those oversized plastic candy canes filled with other smaller pieces of candy—"*this* is *spot on.*"

"Okay! Okay! We're done here!"

"And his *girth! Whoo!*"

"Done! Ew, ew, ew! My brain! I need bleach!"

"Why do we need bleach? I didn't see it on the list." Jesse bends his arm around my neck and stares bugged-eyed at Jazz, her profuse frenzies having shoppers rubbernecking us. "Man, da hell I miss?"

Doubled-over, Jazz holds the candy cane aloft, her merriment so robust she could deafen a deaf man.

"We're gonna go before she faints." Eli pushes her along. "C'mon, sexy lady."

"Yes, man-slave."

Jesse grimaces. "Nasty."

"You're just jealous!" she hollers.

"Woman, please! I have Michael Sinclair. It is *you* who should be jealous!"

"Alright," Eli repeats, "and we're off. Merry Christmas, guys."

"You, too!" we shout.

I glance at him. "Get out of my head."

"Never," Jesse says. "I love your beautiful mind. Or have ya forgotten?"

"Never."

Stopped at the end of Indigo, our caressing lips forge into a romantic, fulfilling, tonguing choreography. *Long. Soft. Kisses.* I'll never get enough. He blows out a content sigh and strokes my cheeks with eight fingertips.

"What're you thinking?" I ask.

"I wanna carbon freeze this car so time can't affect us."

"Now who's poetic?" I whisper and moan as his mouth on my neck travels to my cheekbone, nose, and ear, my hand on his breastbone rising with his sharp inhalation.

"I love you, Sinclair."

"Likewise."

He frowns. "Ya never say it back."

I've got an intense animosity towards myself for causing his frowns. Why can't I say it? I *want* to say it... I *think*. I *think* I love him. I love how he shimmers after we're done fooling around in bed. I love his swag walk. I love how he saves his caring, passionate, foolish side *just* for me when it's *just us*. I love how he makes me feel...

Safe.

"I feel it.".

"That's better than words, Mi Sinclair."

I admire him from my peripheral as he pulls into the driveway. Here's my formal statement: nothing in life exceeds riding in a car with a sexy man; drugs in his pocket, his hand in yours, his flavor—a delicacy that can't be store-bought—rewarding your taste buds.

Bittersweet.

FIFTEEN

Flatliner/Heartkiller

FACT #16: In the past ten years, heroin addiction in young adults (ages 18-25) has doubled.

Mom's asleep in her room, and my sisters are out shopping. Jesse and I snort Golden Girl, smoke a cigarette, and prepare Christmas dinner. He measures out what he needs for the cheesecake into a mixing bowl, and we peel, cut and boil potatoes, and our playlist, subjected to love songs (Jesse's handiwork), plays from a mini-speaker.

A song by The Script describes an unwavering love that can only be rationalized by faith, not science. Jesse spins me, and I laugh because it's somewhat girly, and he sings as we twirl and dip, dancing as old-fashioned gentlemen, none of that Frankenstein nonsense.

We remain attached, the song fading into a thrashing tune, and I translate the hieroglyphics of his hips grinding against mine and the sincerity in his proclaimed, "*You're the best thing about me.*"

The trillions of atoms in my body come alive as we probe and kiss at any exposed skin our lips and fingers can reach. Wrapped up in our private galaxy—our actions borderline sexually explicit—the front door opening and closing goes unnoticed.

The music stops, and grocery bags—*KAH-THUMP!*—onto the counter.

Maddy tilts her head, Charlie's winter-bitten cheeks swell like apples behind her gloved hands, and Jesse's a stuttering, sexy stud.

"Uh… I was… erm… just checkin' him for cavities. Y'know… holiday sweets and… I… I'm gonna go smoke…."

You're more likely to see spotted zebras than an embarrassed Jesse running out of the house.

"Jess!" Charlie yells after him in a giggling fit. "Come back, man, it's fine!"

Maddy, a hand on her hip, raises her eyebrows. "So, uh, anything you'd like to tell us, Mike?"

I sneer. "I'm *totally* cavity-free."

Charlie folds at the waist and slaps the table, wheezing.

Maddy smiles and shoos me away. "Go to your dentist."

"Did you get the stuff?" I ask her.

"Sure did. Gift wrapped, too."

"Best sister ever."

"You'll love me even more after I bake you some snickerdoodles."

I smooch her cheek. "*Best sister ever.*"

I put the bag on my bed, grab a quilt, and go outside to rescue Jesse from the cold and shame. I hug and kiss his neck.

"I didn't think it was possible to embarrass you. They don't care. Hell, I think Charlie's *still* busting a gut in there."

"I wasn't embarrassed 'cause of the kissin'," he mumbles.

"Why then?"

"You have a dick too, sweetheart. Do I *really* gotta spell it out for ya?"

"Huh?"

His cigarette arrows to his crotch.

"Oh. *OH!*" I swear I try to hold it in, but I laugh harder than Charlie.

Jesse thumps his foot on the stairs. "I'm thrilled ya think me havin' a *ragin'* boner in front of your sisters is *so* hilarious."

"I-I-I'm sorry, it's-it's just of all the ways we co-could-could've told them!"

"Laugh it up, Square."

"Ooo, 'Square!' You *are* mad."

He giggles, twisting left to right. "Stop ticklin' me, ya evil shit!"

"I'm sorry, babe."

"I'll believe ya when you stop laughin'."

"But you're—" Hiccup! "You're laug—" Hiccup! "Dang it! I gave myself the hiccups!"

"Karma."

"You're laughing too!"

"Only because you won't keep your hands to yourself!"

"Is that what you want? Okay then."

He gropes my ass and slides me over to his side.

"I take it back," he says.

"Thought you might."

"You're such a—"

"Square," we say collectively.

"But I still love you."

"Likewise."

We finish our cigarettes and Jesse races to my room to avoid my sisters.

“What’s this?” he asks at the foot of the bed.

I shut the door. “For you. Open it.”

I’m overcome with pterodactyls and fireworks and stopped-time as he unwraps the DVD copy of *It’s A Wonderful Life* and a bag of caramel popcorn.

“Next year we’ll make homemade caramel popcorn together.”

“You’re incredible.” He runs his hands up my arms. “I’ll never understand how I landed you.”

“*I* landed *you*. I may even let you stay up past midnight.”

“God, you’re amazin'.” He kisses me. “I got ya somethin' too.” He slinks to his room and then, back in mine, gives me a small box.

I remove the penguin wrapping paper and smile.

“It’s engraved,” he says, flicking the black and silver Zippo. “I got one too.”

I hold it up to the television light. “*Mi Sinclair & Mea Harris: The Ultimate Sugary Possibility.* You’re perfect.”

“Imperfectly so,” he reciprocates, his lips a portal transporting us into that secluded, cosmic vault of heaven only we have the password to.

In bed, we drink hot chocolate, feed each other popcorn, and snort Golden Girl as his favorite Christmas film plays out on the screen.

High on drugs and emotions, we exchange premium presents—butterfly kisses, French kisses, sentimental touches.

“Every time Michael Sinclair kisses me, an angel gets his wings.”

“Let’s not leave them wingless then,” I whisper as our mouths reconnect. “And, also, we’re alone.”

"I am well aware, my love," he says, thrusting himself into me, his arousal from the kitchen back full-throttle.

Jesse forms an alternating pattern between dropping kisses on and inhaling my skin. My tongue flips his lip ring, licks his neck, and lingers at the spot below his earlobe.

I've difficulty catching up to my breaths, and his heartbeat on my chest falters over its barreling tempo. He looks *spectacular* on my white sheets. I want to strip away the layers which make him human and become one with his interstellar soul.

We're trembling. If we keep this up...

I *want* to keep this up.

"Jesse? Remember when you asked me how I'd want to spend my last night on earth?"

He nods.

"My answer is still the same: *with you.* But... it's changed, hasn't it? You and me?"

A second nod.

"I *want* you."

Lips. Tongues. Teeth. Bites.

"I want *all* of you."

"Are ya sure?"

The kiss I give him is an endless-deep, and it flips the script, him playing out the nervous character and me as the dauntless one.

"I feel so incomplete sometimes," I say. "You're the only thing in my life that makes sense."

Tears sneak in-between our mouths.

"Don't cry, Mi Sinclair."

"*Complete* me. My twin flame."

“My celestial. ‘Do you want the moon? If ya want, I’ll throw a lasso 'round it and pull it down for you. Hey, that’s a pretty good idea. I’ll give ya the moon.’”

“Mea Harris,” I whisper in his mouth, “I’ll give you the stars.”

On our knees, we undress each other in the shy of the moon, our eye contact dignifying mutual trust. I welcome his weight on me, our lips responding affectionately as I feel his back muscles and the velvet changes in our typical avid exploitations as we give and receive permission to *touch here* and *kiss there*.

“Don’t be nervous. I’ll walk ya through it,” Jesse oaths and switches our positions.

I lock into the love written on his face beneath me.

And he walks me through it.

And it’s far from perfect.

Our hands do most of the talking and encouraging kisses are swapped back and forth. It’s painful and passionate and klutzy… *bittersweet*. Most of all, best of all, it’s—

“*Just us*, baby,” he vows.

Thereafter, he loads two needles, and Golden Girl, as she often does, donates to the adrenaline and completeness we just created, setting the cinders off into a blaze. We drink in the nirvana, curled up on our sides, gazing into honey and oil irises and confining ourselves in sugary words of endearment.

And if you’re to ask me about love, here’s what I’d tell you: love is only love until you put forth the labor to make it into a commitment, and a boy is just a boy until you help him grow into a man. Love hasn’t a single image. There’s a mother’s love, a lover’s love, a greedy love, a lustful love, and a dark love. There’s black-and-white love, and there's multicolored, high-definition love.

Then there's *our* love: gibbous, starlit, constellation, moonbeam love—a love without bounds, eternally flying beyond the universe and into an opened door on a distant planet where we'll await the next life and rediscover our love all over again.

That, to me, is the grandest love of all.

FACT #17:

All good things come to an end...

fucking always.

PART THREE

Art by Matthew Keeton Lyrics by Scooter Ward

My lungs are screaming for air and the surface is only getting farther away.

On the other side of the mirror, it's raining.

I step into the rain, and I sip a full breath of air into my lungs, and I feel alive.

The drops dampen my hair, but then it slows, and I feel sun on my back.

The rain stops and warm rays of light hold me until I'm dry. I breathe.

"It stops only for you," he says. "But there are dark clouds coming from over there."

Glancing up, I only see blue sky, but no, that's not sky anymore.

I see water, and I blink, and he's gone, and I'm falling, falling, falling below the surface of a bottomless ocean.

I can't breathe.

I try to scream, but only bubbles boil out of my throat.

I feel his hand grab mine, and I can breathe, just for a second.

The mirror blurs into my vision and shatters, the sharp pieces skim my skin. I forget the stinging of the wounds and I focus on keeping a grip on his hand.

"Let go," someone else whispers.

"No", I insist. "Never."

—Kayla Guerrero

ONE

The Dark, The Light

FACT: Michael Sinclair is a straight-up disgrace.

You're eighteen! Stop acting like a child!

But he's gone! He's gone!

You thought he'd stick around? For who? For you?! You're hysterical!

He said he loved me.

Nobody loves you. You never said it back. The fault is your own, Mike. You should've said it.

I should've said it.

He wanted more than this semi-charmed life with you.

Puffy eyes. Dry lips.

A dignified man wearing a dapper penguin tuxedo loiters closely. He's clean-shaven, with slicked-back black hair and eyes like a haunted playhouse.

You see me.

Uh-oh...

We'll backpedal.

Mike's in his bedroom.

An entire month's gone by.

Maybe Jesse *doesn't* love him.

He's clung to this damn metallic-gold origami heart like a life jacket.

Why are you holding that stupid thing?

It's all he left behind. He said it belongs to me and always will.

It's a useless piece of paper. That's not all he left behind for you. Look at it, Mike. I SAID LOOK AT IT, DAMN IT!

I direct him to the desk and the baggie containing fifteen 80-milligram Oxys and a fat stack of Golden Girl.

Now that's *love.* That's *worth leaving behind.*

Lost in the sight of the drugs, the folded heart falls sideways to his feet. I make room for the shadowy hand pushing out of his left socket; the phantom spawning from his pupils—hands first, then arms, head, chest, and legs. **Mental Illness** vaults off the desk and faces me like a mouse to a gomphothere, the shadowed figure featureless, the ceiling squishing his head. He crouches as I bow, the two devils on his shoulders,

whispering... **whispering...**

He never loved you.

You're unlovable.

Your Mom's dead...

...she didn't want to be with you either.

No one wants you here.

You're a bottom-feeding junkie.

Do it, Mike.

What's left for you here?

Everyone's better off without you.

You're not worth coming back for.

Mike clamps his eyes shut and covers his ears.

Just do it.

It'll be quick.

Painless.

Like falling asleep.

No more agony.

No more rain.

No more darkness.

Defeat your "dark passenger."

Don't be a burden.

Just do it.

Do it! Do it!

DO IT! DO IT!

He grabs the baggies.

He drops to the floor.

He searches for…

He looks at me.

I cater to him, the chessboard balanced on my white-gloved fingertips.

What was it you once called me? Ah, yes, I'm your doting, patient Stalking Butler. I have what you've sought. You haven't time for the mortar and pestle, and the dimwitted, disappearing bastard took all the syringes! Fine! A straw will do. Here, have some water. Down the pills first...

That's my boy.

Excellent!

Snort your beloved
Golden Girl.

She's your lover now.

There ya go.

Straight out of the bag.

More.

More.

Until it's gone.

Until *you're* gone.

Mike melts into the carpet, hands on his chest, the chessboard propped halfway on the floor and his hip, the fan blades *whomp, whomp, whomp*ing like the bass guitar he heard at a Jax and the Snax concert at CD Jungle.

Jax…

Brad…

Toby…

Eli…

Jazz…

We're wrong.

This isn't quick.

It's slower than a snail on a sizzling sidewalk.

Life, as it's been said, flashes before his eyes.

It's okay.

We aren't on borrowed time.

What's the rush?

You're as good as dead anyway.

Go on, Mike.

Remember…

Remember when:

You celebrate and ring in the new year with Jesse, your sisters, and Mom.

Jesse spins you 'round and 'round, and fireworks explode on

the television and inside your veins as he kisses you because that's the effect he has.

Jesse's phone rings.

Eli's dead.

He overdosed.

You and Jesse weren't aware of his heroin addiction.

Marcus explains Eli tore his shoulder muscle during a workout in mid-November. The doctors said he may never play basketball professionally and was prescribed painkillers to dull the sprain.

I convince him Jazz will drop him on a dime if he's not a successful NBA star. How will they afford an apartment in NYC if he loses his scholarship?

Eli heated the spoon.

He terminated his pain.

He's happy, Mike.

And you will be, too.

Very, very soon.

Remember when:

Jazz throws her lit cigarette at Jesse, holds him accountable for Eli's death as he's the one who initially brought heroin and drugs into the group, and sends you packing from the funeral. Toby's in prison because of Jesse. You're a junkie because of Jesse. Daryl's dead because of Jesse.

She tells you to go to Hell.

You may just end up there.

The Good Book says that's where suicide victims go.

You'll never be cold again.

Remember when:

You tear open the The Otis College of Art and Design acceptance letter.

Mom cries joyful tears.

"Ya got in." Jesse sweeps you off the floor. "I'm so proud of you, Mi Sinclair."

"Our future's now, Mea Harris. I can't wait to experience Los Angeles with you. One sugary possibility down, a lifetime more to go."

"I love you."

"Likewise."

You don't say it.

Why don't you say it?

Remember when:

Fuming, you and Jesse drive to the Shelby Reservoir after he vanished for a week following Eli's funeral. Twitch has lost his spunk, and he nods off in the backseat, dirty and hollow-eyed. He's a living corpse, and, observing Jesse, so is he.

You hold his needle injected-abused arms and cry for him to get sober; you guys *need* to get sober. You have goals to accomplish *together.*

He talks over your pleas. "I'm too far gone. I'm just too far gone."

You deliver him to his car at the skatepark.

"I'm sorry, Michael."

You should let him go, but you're a hopeless romantic who can't let go or take no for an answer, so you kiss him like it's the last kiss you'll ever share, and it will be.

"I love being with you. You're my light and my best friend. A portion of me has been afraid to be with you because of these voices in my head: every insult, every bad name they've ever called me, Leon telling my mother she could keep me after the divorce as long as he got Charlie. All those damn voices, Jesse, saying I'm worthless and we don't really love each other. I know it's not true, but I've never had a sober second to figure out if I love you or if I've been... *using* you to feel good about myself."

"Mikey—"

Hard kisses. Supplicant, hard kisses.

"I want you. I *need* you. *Please* get better, Jesse. *Please* be with me."

You'll never see him again. No explanation. No reasons. No goodbyes. No more kisses. The firework display has come to a close. Paul goes by the house to pack Jesse's things, and he knows where he is, but is sworn to secrecy. He promises you he's safe.

All he left you was history, drugs and a gold, origami heart on your pillow.

And that's not the worst of it...

Presenting:

DEATH

But he's not here for you.

Not yet.

TWO

Draining Sunshine

Remember when:

"Mikey, wake up."

Your tired eyes adjust to Charlie standing in the dark.

"Why? I'm exhausted."

"Mikey… it's Mom…."

No. No. NO!

You're not ready for this.

It was coming, but you're *still not ready for this.*

The signs were foreshadowed: dementia, hallucinations, jaundice, and her daily consumption of half a grapefruit. You hired hospice because it was too much for the Sinclair siblings, and Jenny and Abigail, two nurses, rotated shifts, assisted you and your sisters in caring for Mom, and provided a hospital bed for her room and the apparatus accessories.

You and your sisters camped out in Mom's room for two months. She was unresponsive, yet you talked to her as if she were lucid. You told stories, shared memories, laughed and cried.

"She's so crafty," Charlie said. "Remember when she hand-sewed that fairy costume when I was in the second grade? She put my hair into an updo and did my face in bright green eyeshadow. I won first prize for 'Most Beautiful Costume.'"

"Yeah," you said, "and it snowed that Halloween and you couldn't wear the fairy costume."

Maddy chuckled. "You were *so* pissed, but she put you in your pajamas and drew freckles on your cheeks and you carried your teddy bear. You cried the entire way to Shelby, but—"

"When I got home, I kissed her because everyone said I was *'cute.'*"

You never left her side, and neither did **Death**. Even now, he stands committed by her sickbed. His cornflower-blue eyes are earnest, his tiny hand atop hers, and he never speaks. He doesn't have to. He's ageless, but his appearance is that of a five-year-old blonde child clad in his Sunday best.

You regret having left her tonight, but Jesse's absence led to an affair with Golden Girl, and **Death's** fingers graze what's left of Mom's hair when you stagger from your room to hers. Why does it seem like there's no end to this freeway? You manage it and kneel at the side of the bed between your sobbing sisters.

"Is she in pain?" you ask.

"No," Jenny reassures, "she isn't. But she doesn't have long, I'm afraid."

You three say your last goodbyes:

"Let go, Mom. It's okay. Your kids are survivors, thanks to your strength. I'll watch over Mike and Charlotte. *Let go, Mom.* We're here, and we're telling you *it's okay.*"

"Mommy, I'm sorry I've been such a pain in the ass, and I'm even more sorry I never told you just how special you are to me.

You're my inspiration; my hero. I hope to be half the woman you are. I love you *so, so much.*"

You place her hand, her skin like tissue paper, to your heart. The Marie Sinclair you remember fondly was healthy, her hair styled in luscious, black curls, and thick in the hips. She supported you through good times and bad, stood up against Leon for you, and cooked tremendous breakfast feasts for eighteen birthdays. This unrecognizable, hairless Marie Sinclair is shrunken down five sizes; her cheeks gaunt and eyebrows pencil thin.

And yet... and yet...

"You're the most beautiful woman I've ever seen. I love you. You can let go, Mom. Go be with God. He's waiting."

She's kissed by **Death**, and you hear his rattle. You'll never *unhear* the Death Rattle. It'll become an affixed, patronizing ghost gunning you down for the rest of your young life.

You don't see, hear, or feel it, but as you and your sisters grieve, Marie gives each of you a kiss on the top of the head and whispers, "I love you, my sweets."

Hand in hand, she and **Death** fade away into the sparkling, iridescent, white twilight.

You're *so damn cold.*

"I love you," you tell your sisters.

They love you too, Michael.

Remember when:

Sensory overload. Raised voices. Charlie's grip on your arm cuts off your circulation. Poor eye contact, yours and Leon's, demonstrates a lack of respect. Fresh mental photographs of the funeral home taking Mom, the house now stale without her.

And where the *fuck* is Jesse?!

The one voice you need to hear is absent in a room of voices.

Tragic.

Maddy's *pissed.* She and Leon have been going at it for the last hour. At the head of the table, Mr. Matthews, the funeral director not much older than Maddy, tunes into the father-daughter disunity.

"It's stated right here in her will!" Maddy proclaims for the umpteenth time. "She wants to be buried next to Grandma and Grandpa! Her casket is bought and paid for! Why are you making this so difficult? Why's it so hard for you to understand? Cremation goes against her religious beliefs!"

"Marie never *once* spoke of being buried in our twenty-one years of marriage! She wanted to be cremated!"

"It's here and black and white! This is *not* a debate. We lost our *mother,* and your number one priority is *yourself, as usual!*"

"How *dare* you speak to me this way! You lost all credibility after the turmoil you caused this family with your drug habit and going in and out of rehab like it was a revolving door! Who footed the bill for those clinics? When you came home passed out on the lawn, who brought you inside from the rain and snow?!"

"You changed the fucking locks on me! Mike and Mom did more for me than you *ever* did!"

"Alright, alright, everyone, calm down," Mr. Matthews intercepts, and even *I'm* turned off by his lovely, female corpse

VERSION OF ME. “Madeline, is it okay to call you Madeline?”

“Maddy.”

“Maddy is correct, Mr. Sinclair. Marie Sinclair had her funeral pre-planned for five months.” He flips the papers in a binder Maddy provided. “Flower preferences, bible verses and hymns, and Maddy’s to write her eulogy.”

“Butt-out of our family matters, Mr. Matthews.”

“With all due respect, sir, we’re dealing with notarized law. Looks like she wrote you out of her will when the divorce was finalized. Now, either compose yourself or get out of my facility because I have the authority to kick your family out, and I’d hate for your children to have to find an alternative on such short notice.”

Leon’s the deer to Mr. Matthews’ headlights, and Leon nearly gives himself whiplash as you snicker under your breath.

“Keep it up, Michael, and I’ll *purposely* remove your mother from here.”

Mr. Matthews, with a hindering sigh, shuts the folder. “I’m going to make an exception. You can stay,” he addresses the three of you. “As for you, Mr. Sinclair, I’m gonna have to ask you to leave.”

“No, wait, I have something to say.”

“Very well, Michael.”

Your chest expands.

Leon sneers. “Feeling like a big man, son?”

Charlie’s already mighty grip on your arm intensifies.

“Actually, yes.”

"Is that so?"

Your blood, the drugs, pump.

"Where the fuck were you for the last eight months? While you were off screwing your twenty-one-year-old *bimbo,* Maddy dedicated her life to tending to Mom. She changed the sheets, gave her sponge baths, made sure she got her meds, and had a healthy dinner every night."

"And Maddy didn't have to. I paid for home care."

Your clobbering fists *wallop* on the tabletop, everyone jumping except for Leon.

"You're *unbelievable! We're a family!* We didn't need or want strangers looking after her! We were honored to do it! You didn't visit her when she was sick, so what makes you think you can make decisions now that she's dead?"

"I'm the father of her kids!"

"*Father?!* You were an abusive, neglectful, heartless cockroach!"

He stands. You stand. You're leaned in so close that you're cross-eyed.

"You're as ungrateful and useless as your sister! You two have been and always will be a mistake! You've caused me more grief than joy!"

"I can say the same about you! Fuck this noise. I'm outta here."

"That's right, Michael," he ridicules smugly, "run from your problems like you did your junior year! Let's hope Charlie won't be there to save you this time!"

"That's uncalled for!" yelps Charlie, on her feet.

"Raising a queer was uncalled for!"

“Dad!” Maddy also shoots from her seat. “You—”

“Y’know, Leon, you’re right,” you interrupt. “I *loooooove* suckin' cock, but at least I ain’t one!”

“Get the hell out of my face!” he shouts, slapping the funeral papers off the table.

“Get the hell out of my life!”

The double doors crash into the sides of the gray stone building as you charge to the family SUV and take off, the tires squealing and your screams penetrating your eardrums as you punch the steering wheel.

Tossing your jacket onto the patio, you plonk down on the stairs, swallow four Oxys 80s (they don’t make even so much as a dent anymore, but there's comfort in the habit) and chain-smoke.

Indigo Street in the springtime bustles with yard games, cookouts, and the blending smells of smokey mesquite, daffodils and mud. Children ride their bikes around the cul-de-sac in their bathing suits, shouting and giggling. You wish you could be them or, at the very least, join them—to be a kid again, liberated and unscathed.

Time couldn’t heal Jesse, and you now understand why. Time doesn’t heal all wounds. Time’s as interchangeable as the Death Rattle, shredding your sanity in this lackluster, vacuous world.

You refuse to go into the place she was last alive, where her clothes are packed away to be donated and worn by strangers. Her lilac perfume seeps through the vents, but without her to attach to, it’s just air. Meaningless air.

You refuse to look at the sorrowful house across the street, yet you can't shake off its despairing ghouls, the blood and brain on the walls and carpet, and the ashen-blue motherly ghost.

You can bleach the walls and floors, confiscate the bodies, but you can't eliminate the remnants, not really.

Remember when:

"Mikey, people are waiting to see you. Why don't you talk to a few of them?"

"I don't wanna, Madds. I wanna go home."

Home. Mom was your home. Jesse was your home, and now you're homeless, so where do you go? You want to be with Jesse, wherever he is, but you can't. You're an undesirable, nameless orphan.

"I know, kiddo. Can you at least come in and sit down?"

"Leon in there?"

"He's greeting the visitors. Today isn't about him. Be strong for Mom. Celebrate her life."

You stub your cigarette butt into the potted ashtray and follow the sound of Maddy's heels *click-clacking* on the concrete.

You're three drained dominos, Charlie's head on your shoulder and yours on Maddy's, and she nudges you when the priest at the pulpit directs the congregation into hymns and prayers.

You, your sisters, Leon, and your uncle Joe transport the casket into the back of the hearse you follow to the cemetery. A blonde-haired guy crosses the car at a stoplight, and your pulse fluctuates. You novelize a scenario where Jesse's doppelgänger turns around and buckles himself into the passenger's seat.

"I gotchu, Mi Sinclair, let it out," he'll say, and you'll weep in his galactic embrace, which has restored you, the supernova, in every alternate reality and lifetime before and after this one.

Safe.

Mom's lowered into the ground.

The Sinclair siblings drizzle earth onto the seashell-pearly coffin.

Leon focuses on you.

You're tall; your head up and shoulders back.

You dig a hole for the levee,

and bury it in an unmarked grave.

Remember when:

The Sharp Edges, what's left of them, surround you, and they aren't *hmph*ing, dripping Visine into their eyes, dancing on shoulders, or strumming an air guitar. They are crying with Baby.

Brad pats your shoulder.

"She's always with you," says Jazz.

"And Eli's with you."

She squeezes your hand, and you open and close her car door for her, watching as she merges into the line of traffic exiting the cemetery.

You and Gemma sit on the hood of the SUV, her company neither displeasing nor inconvenient. If anything, you now have a partner with whom to vent your resentment towards Jesse.

"Mike, I'm sorry about everything."

"No need, Gemma."

"I need to say this. I admit I was angry when you came along. Jesse was my rock. He loved me when I was at my heaviest and when my self-esteem was nil. He was my first for many things. I loved him." She sniffles. "I still do. But something was always missing between us, and I couldn't figure out what it was until I saw him with you. The way he looks at you... *God,* the love there... it's—"

"He doesn't love me," you say bitterly.

"That's not true."

"You don't leave the people you love. You leave the people you use."

"You may not believe me, but he left *because* he loves you. He ran off to God knows where for a few weeks in our senior year. He never told me where he went, but I think he checked himself into a rehab because when he came back, he was sober for the first time in a *long* time. This could be another one of those situations. You have to understand, Jesse's always felt like a burden. He believes everyone around him ends up dead or addicted. He'll come back for you, Mike." She touches your arm. "Don't give up on him."

"I never do. Damn, I'm so sick of looking at the burial grounds."

"Same here. It's been a shitty year, that's for sure."

"So much for fairytale endings, huh?" You flick your cigarette at the venomous plantation. "I had a friend in the eighth grade, Brett Howser. He was a loner like me, and we never hung out outside of school. I found out later he came from an abusive home, and he wore long sleeves everyday to try to hide it, but I saw his bruises in the locker room.

"He told me his older sister—Brittany?—was in a mental hospital. She tried cutting her fat off with a knife."

"*Shit.*"

"Brett vanished in the middle of our freshman year. I read in the papers his dad was arrested for domestic violence. I'm not sure if his mom moved him away or if he was sent to foster care."

"What about his sister?"

"Dunno. I'd like to think she overcame her demons."

Baby sobs.

Gemma, smiling, says, "Me too," and Victoria appears terror-stricken.

"You're beautiful, Gemma. Your body doesn't define you. Your weight has nothing to do with who you are inside. Go out into the world and burn it down with a vengeance, girl."

"My God,"—she blinks away her waterworks—"no wonder Jesse fell for you. You're not half-bad, Golden Boy."

"Ditto."

Remember when:

The engine *click, click, clicks...*

Have you been sitting here for minutes? Hours? Days?

Tears drain into your ears as you speak to the saints. "I can't, Mom. I can't do this. I'm... so... *broken.* I died with you. I'm dead inside. *DEAD INSIDE!*"

"Sweets," her voice as a figment of your imagination rings as genuine as your own, "this is just a bump on your journey. You'll run into more ditches, stop signs, and dead ends. You must keep going, Michael. Otherwise, you'll never get to live out the surprises a new route offers, and how boring would that be?"

"But, Mom, I'm so... *tired.*"

The devil bent your ear that day:

I have magical elixirs that'll take away the memories.

And here we are, Mike.

Everything's dripping ink.

No fears here.

If the darkness taught you anything,
it's how to prosper inside it.

THREE

Lux Nostra

Mental Illness, his giant shadowy form on my right side, crouches beside Mike. ***Death*** approaches *us* when he *should* be approaching Mike.

The past ten months unfold like a picture show:

Cookie-cutter houses… Dirt and alleyway ash… Indigo Street… Maple macchiatos… Jesse on a bloody porch… Beanfields, stars, and vodka… Shotguns from Jesse's mouth in the Black Estates… Mom's hugs… Her fingers rubbing the back of his neck… Cat piss, flickering lights, snorting Blues in an empty apartment… Jesse "grounding" him, touching him… Mom singing "Happy Birthday"… Art museums… Cocaine numbness… Daryl's death… Disappearing acts… LSD, oceanic waves, diamonds… First kisses… Coconut rum, foreplay… Charlie in a hospital gown… Cancer… Needle biting vein… Christmas lights, dancing, having sex for the first, second, third, hundredth time… Driving tests, posing for his license… Jesse's unanswered texts… Nightmares… Mom's last breath… Every blonde head in his crossing never Jesse…

"Don't give up on me, Mi Sinclair," you hear him say.

'I never do.'

You've given up.

'Mom, I'm coming. I won't leave you lonely.'

Death declines our handshakes, his tiny fingers counting down:

5...

4...

3...

2...

The bedroom door kicks in.

BLOODY HELL!

Maddy and Charlie fall to their knees, and Maddy pinches his earlobe, listens to his chest, then flips him onto his side. She shoves her fingers down his throat, and pills and heroin dissolve in acidic bile.

"What else did you take, Mike?" Maddy cries. "WHAT ELSE DID YOU TAKE!"

"Fuck you!"

"I told you, Michael! I told you if I saw a *single* track mark on your body, I'd do this! Didn't think to unroll your sleeves at the funeral, didja?"

"NO!" he shouts, vomiting, and striking the floor. "NO! *NO, NO, NO!* Why did you bring me back?! *FUCK!* NO!"

Mental Illness shrugs and spreads thin from wall to ceiling to floor, downsizes into two lines, and jets back into Mike's eyes—*his midnight eyes.*

"NO!" He pushes Maddy to the ground. "DON'T *FUCKING TOUCH ME!* I WAS HAPPY! I WAS..." He collapses, panting. "I was... *free.*"

Maddy crawls over him for the leftover Oxy and heroin, and when she stands, he yanks her ankles, Charlie yipping as Maddy rams face-first into the floor and is dragged across the carpet. In an all-out brawl, Maddy and Mike fumble and kick, and she successfully keeps the narcotics out of his reach despite his grueling efforts.

"Charlie! Take the junk!" Maddy yells. "*Charlie! Take it!*"

Mike locks Maddy's wrists to the ground and warns Charlie in a snarling growl, "Touch it, and I'll *fucking kill you!*"

Maddy launches her knees into his gut, knocking him sideways. She pounces, restrains him, and Charlie, baggies in hand, bolts out of the room. Mike, listening to the toilet flush, belts out a string of profanities.

Using his last energetic surge, he uppercuts Maddy, then turns over, his projectile spew staining the floors and walls. Charlie kneels in the middle of them, and tears stream from her and Maddy's eyes as slanderous insults spill from his mouth.

Maddy skitters out and back into the room, and a vial of Narcan nasal spray bowls in Mike's direction. "Is *this* the life you want?! You want your sister to revive you from an overdose?! You wanna continue going through this cycle?! You think that shit's your friend, Michael?" Maddy shouts, pointing in the bathroom's direction where his last saving grace wastes away in a septic tank. "You think *that's* your answer? It's *dirt!* Nothing but *disgusting dirt!* We lost Mom. We're not losing you too!"

"I HATE YOU!"

"I don't give a *flying fuck* if you hate me! It stops here, Mike! It *ends* with *you!*"

"I was free!"

"That ain't freedom! It's a prison!"

Mike surrenders, gulping in oxygen, his palms pressed into his eyes, the back of his shirt and carpet sodden with vomit.

He wipes his snotty nose and faintly murmurs, "I just wanted to be with Mom," his chin quivering.

Maddy and Charlie lay next to him, hugging him from opposite sides, the three drained dominos mourning for the second time in the same day.

Madame's aged fifty years, her jade dress crinkled and red lipstick chapped, her paper fan moth-eaten.

Death, unreadable, glides by the VERSION OF ME coming into the room I've shunned since the night she re-emerged. What a doormat she's become. There was a time when I put her on a pedestal. Amazonian. Ferocious. Our past interactions in the Sinclair household were seldom as she was mostly *inside* Maddy, and I was fascinated by her booming screams at Maddy whenever she fought her withdrawals.

She wheels over to me, her chair squeaking, and her irises—sapphires sunken in wrinkled meadows—hunt me down. She's older than Madame, older than prehistoric dirt, and her white hair sticks out in haphazard directions. Swimming in her long-sleeved, black, dingy dress, she hasn't wolfed on a decent, fattening meal in ages. *Pitiful.*

Her warped finger points at me, and her piddling croak

declares, *You're next.*

Mike writhes on the ground, and Maddy tries soothing him from a safe distance and declines his demands to be left alone, not wanting to take the risk of him escaping out the window.

He goes in and out of a cold and hot sweat. Unable to control his bowels, his boxers are soiled, the pail next to him bulging at the seams with foamy vomit.

He needs a fix. He needs Golden Girl. He needs Mom. He needs Jesse. His restless legs and his cluttered thoughts won't let him sleep.

My chalky, tickly throat shouts, *GET THE FUCK UP! GET UP, YOU PANSY, LITTLE BITCH! VISIT THE CHEMIST! IF HE DOESN'T HAVE SMACK, I'M SURE THE DUDES HANGING AROUND THE BISSMAN BUILDING WILL!*

His arms shield his ears. "Leave me alone, leave me alone, leave me alone!"

I'M NOT GOING ANYWHERE! I'LL ALWAYS BE HERE! THE BUG IN YOUR EAR! THE GRIEVOUS WHISPER IN YOUR SPARSE FLASHES OF SERENITY! I'M NOT LEAVING! EVER! NOW GET UP AND FEED ME!

"Stop, stop, stop! Please! Go away!"

GET UP, MANIC BITCH! GET. UP. NOW!

"I CAN'T!"

JUNKIE! USELESS ADDICT! YOU DID THIS TO YOURSELF! YOU DESERVE TO DIE! YOU'RE NOT HUMAN! YOU'LL NEVER BE ANYTHING MORE THAN A JUNKIE! LEON HATES YOU!

JESSE HATES YOU! HE ONLY FUCKED YOU BECAUSE HE FELT SORRY FOR YOU!

"No! That's not true!"

DO YOU SEE HIM HERE? YOU DIDN'T HEED MY WARNINGS! I TOLD YOU HE'D LEAVE IF YOU GOT ROMANTICALLY INVOLVED, AND NOW YOU'RE SHITTING AND PUKING ON YOURSELF! HOW DOES ONE FAIL AT KILLING THEMSELVES... TWICE?! *FAILURE, FAILURE, FAILURE!*

"STOP!"

Maddy and Charlie nurture him like a teething infant. Maddy's VERSION OF ME, Sister Hazel, she dubbed her, tuts her tongue from the doorway and wheels off. Madame's able to see us from her rocking chair in the living room, but she stares into nothingness.

The glass chessboard shatters on the wall over Charlie's head. Mike crumbles, apologizing. Tears. Hugs. More apologies. Shakes. More tears. Sneezing. *Oh, God, the sneezing!* Random electrical shocks in his brain. Yawn, yawn, yawn.

GET THE HELL UP! JUMP OUT THE WINDOW! GO DOWNTOWN! GO ANYWHERE!

Sisters hold their brother protectively. Tears. Apologies. Hugs. Sneezes. Tears. Apologies. Hugs. Yawn, yawn, yawn. Sneeze, sneeze, sneeze.

These vile sneezes!

3 AM

A week of *pure* hell.

Charlie's sleeping soundly on the bed. Maddy, exhausted but refusing to rest until he does, sits on the floor across from Mike. They both held up their ends of the bargain: she didn't force him into the hospital as long as he complied with her conditions: no leaving the bedroom unless to piss, puke, or shit, and no sugar or caffeine.

"Why'd you do it?" she asks.

He picks at his fingernails. "Why do you think? Jesse's gone. Mom's dead. Leon's still a dick and a half. I feel so… *alone. I'm so alone,* Madds."

"Listen, kid, I'm gonna get real with you. You know why I carry Narcan?"

Mike shakes his head.

"I never told you the entire story about Violet. We were on a three-day binge, doing nothing but shooting up speedballs—a cocaine and heroin mix—and drinking. The batch of smack we got was laced with fentanyl, an opioid a hundred times stronger than morphine. It took no time for her to…" Her voice cracks. "Michael, she died right next to me, practically in my arms, and I was too strung out to do shit about it.

"Her mother was so distraught that she had a heart attack in the middle of the funeral service. She survived, thankfully. I thought of Mom and how it would've destroyed her if it'd been me instead, and I didn't want Violet's death to be in vain.

"I made an oath to get sober, educate myself, and buy Narcan underground if I had to, so I'd be prepared in case *anything* like that happened again to someone else. I just… *dammit,* Mike, I *never* in a *million years* thought it'd be *you,* and *thank God* I got to you in time."

"How *did* you know?"

"You're my brother. My blood," she says, her lips tugging into a Marie Sinclair, motherly smile. "The look in your eyes told me everything I needed to know. It's the same look you had the day you tried taking your own life. I rushed out of that cemetery as fast as I could the *second* I realized you were gone."

"First Charlie, and now you." Mike grunts sourly, slumping into the wall behind him and stretching out his legs. "I'm sorry I keep putting you through my bullshit. You don't deserve it."

"We're each other's keepers. I've always got your back, little brother, just as you've always had mine, even in the moments when I was less than deserving of it, and you're *more than* deserving. I love you, kiddo, and love knows no bounds."

I grimace, and Sister Hazel clicks her crude tongue again. *You're going to lose,* she heckles.

"I see it," Mike says, looking at me brooding in the doorway. "I see my addiction as if he's an actual… *person.* He's been with me since my childhood, growing stronger and waiting to strike."

Maddy chuckles. "I've seen mine as well. She's a crippled old bitch now, and yours will be a crippled old bitch, too."

"Maddy? What led to your addiction?"

She mulls for a second. "For a long time, I thought it was because of the people I associated with. They weren't to blame.

You said your addiction's been with you since your childhood? I think mine's been with me since my birth. You know Dad forced Mom into a c-section because I was taking too long to come out? It had to do with *control.* I wanted *control.* I hate authority, and you know how Dad controlled everything, but not Dad, or anyone else, could control my drug habit. Addiction became another uncontrollable part of my life, and I was too deep in the hole to see it."

"I'm sorry you suffered for so long, Madds. I'm sorry I wasn't there for you."

"But you were. *You were.*" She wipes her tear-stained cheeks. "I wanted to be better for you, for myself, for everybody."

"Will I always be this way?"

Maddy fondles her two-inch long hair. "I hope not. The whole 'once an addict, always an addict' is true for some. I had this dream once where I was in a hospital—blinding, white lights, sea-green walls—and I passed by a vending machine stocked with syringes, tourniquets, and every brand of smack imaginable. I looked at it, said, 'Huh, that's weird,' and kept going. I wasn't tempted by it. I just kept on walking. That's when I realized it was over for me. You could give me an entire, whole ass vending machine of heroin, and I'd walk away. It's not my life anymore, Mike. You just need some time. I have faith in you, but you must also have faith in yourself. And, Mikey, you're *never* alone."

Sister Hazel's wheelchair bumps my leg. She directs her stupid, knotted finger at me, opens her mouth, her words unspoken and lips frozen in a capital *O.* She shrivels, and her solid form, like a desert floor, breaks apart into sand drizzling on the carpet and chair.

RIP, Sister Hazel.

Tick-tock, tick-tock, tick-tock.

Let's not go off half-cocked.

There's some fight in me, yet.

"Who'd like to speak next?" Colored tattoos bejewel Fred's arms from wrists to biceps, FAST LIFE spelled out on his knuckles. His VERSION OF ME stables himself on a metal walker. He's a twiggy man in a fishnet shirt, black leather pants, chains and a balding, peacock-green mullet.

Maddy's next to Mike, her legs crossed and right foot swinging. They're in a circle with five others, their VERSIONS OF ME varying in age and rank:

A female VERSION—her eyeliner as sharp as the razor blade in her hand, slashing her arm one slit after the next—is high, high, high on Benzos.

The second female VERSION, a child, dangles her feet from the chair, her strawberry-blonde tendrils framing her round face. She pushes her flora skirt over her knees and avoids eye contact with the boys. A lurching, faceless man heats her glass pipe. Chemicals swirl.

Three male VERSIONS:

The first bangs his head to the music blasting from his headphones while he boils heroin in a rusty spoon. The second—tweaking and nose bleeding—whispers in his human's ear. The third slurs incoherently and toys with his wiry, brassy-colored beard, his stained shirt barely covering his overhanging beer belly.

Pathetic, the lot of you. This is ridiculous. Why're you here, Mike? You don't have a problem and are far superior to them!

Mike opens his snapped eyelids.

Silence.

Bitch.

The girl beside Mike scratches at her arms like an angry cat shredding her owner's furniture because her food bowl is half-empty. He glances at the thin boy on the other end of the circle, dressed in black from his clothes to his wavy hair and sneakers. I'll leave it up to you to determine which VERSION OF ME he belongs to.

Maddy elbows Mike. "Go ahead."

You better not!

Five things he can see… four things he can touch…

YOU CAN'T IGNORE ME!

… three things he can hear… two things he can smell…

I'M RIGHT HERE!

… one thing he can taste.

"I'm Mic—"

"Speak up," she presses.

He fixes his slouched posture. "I'm Michael, and I'm an opioid addict."

You're barking mad!

"Hello, Michael," they say robotically.

“I’ve been sober for two months.”

“Do you mind sharing why you decided to get sober?” Fred asks, his fern-green eyes friendly and harmonizing with his auburn goatee and buzz cut.

“Well…” he says, tearing at his fingernails. “It’s a long story.”

“We have time.”

Maddy encouragingly nods.

Inhale.

STOP!

Exhale.

MICHAEL!

“It all started in mid-July….”

EPILOGUE

A Light that Never Comes

FACT #18: 10% of Americans ages 18 and up are in recovery from either alcohol or drug addiction.

I'm standing in the middle of the road.

Summer's here—cigarette ash, lavenders, and wet soil accompany a wafting scent of sunflowers Mrs. Jameson tends to every morning. Did you know sunflowers have "heliotropism," which allows them to steer their heads in the sun's direction?

You should.

You taught me that.

If only humans had motor cells...

I hear Mom singing "La Vie En Rose".

I'm standing in the middle of the road.

I've a reason for it.

It's not a suicide mission.

It's not a busy street—a two-lane, straight and narrow road veering into a cul-de-sac. I sense the storm long before gray clouds overcast azure skies. I breathe in the rain, and for once—*at last!*—there's hope. A future.

I'm standing in the middle of the road, and you're here. Not in front of me, nor behind me. *Beside me. Equals.* Your lopsided smile is sincere despite its informal coyness, and I'm glad it's a quirk you never could control because your coy smirk flipped me heels over head from the beginning.

"You're standin' in the middle of the road."

"So are you," I say, matter-of-factly.

"So I am."

Thunder trundles, and misty rain turns into a downpour.

I close your opened umbrella. "Let's feel the rain."

Soaked to the marrow, I reach out to touch the watery rhinestones on your porcelain chest and my face is held steady in your tender hands.

"I'd never let ya face the storms alone, Mi Sinclair."

"You're here."

"Forever."

"Will never be long enough."

We stand in the middle of the road in the rain, unaffected by the lightning's crackling impressions slashing the violet clouds against the dull, silver backdrop.

Our feet are shoeless, your breath is light, and dewy beads percolate off your eyelashes bordering unfiltered-honey irises. Under your gaze, my soul, my whole self, my hopes, fears, desires, and unsaid declarations are laid vulnerable for your taking.

What's the cliché? Moth to a flame? You're the heated flame, and I'm the charred, wingless moth committed to decomposing in your fire.

How'd we get here? Who said what first? Who made the first move? Had it been mutual? Perhaps nothing needed to be said or done to advance us over that delicate line in the sand dividing friends from lovers. Maddy calls it "fate." Mom would've said it's "destiny." Others, those who don't matter and never will, would classify it as "sinful."

With our naked toes on the road and my wet face in your wet hands, I drown in you, and all of a sudden, spiteful people and their malicious jabs become irrelevant.

I see *you*.

I hear *your* inner thoughts.

I am *yours*.

We step in, and our mild, dancing lips have us gasping.

Our feet pitter-patter across watered potholes, and I bring you into the house, our childish glees but a sweet remembrance.

We're alone.

We debrief every empty room.

The living room, where we decorated the Christmas tree and played cards with Mom.

The kitchen, where you ran your foot along mine under the table and brought me back to earth the night of that sibling-rivalry.

My bedroom, our sanctuary from the ugly, outer world, where you snuck in through the window and, in my bed, we shared kept secrets, laughed at jokes only we knew the punch lines to; where we got high, confessed love in the dark, and had sex for the first time.

"I finally figured out who I really am."

"And who are ya, love?"

"I'm Michael Sinclair, son of Marie Sinclair, younger brother to Charlotte and Madeline Sinclair. I'm an artist, a dreamer, and a recovering addict. I love pineapple on pizza, storms, stargazing, and the wind on my face. I love the smell of oil paint and canvas. But do you know what I love most of all?"

"What, baby?"

You already know the answer. You're enlightening me.

I kiss your forehead. "*You. I love you.*"

Your lips press against me as well. Sensible: my third eye kissed by my muse. It's poetic and whatnot, but not all muses are meant to withstand the test of time, and art is nothing if not substantial.

We peel off our damp clothing. I'm tipsy on your deep stare and the smell of cigarettes, fabric softener, and cologne. Laying you beneath me, I crawl into your body.

"We shouldn't, Mike. I can't promise you anythin' after today. It wouldn't be right."

"You're not a 'future' guy, remember? Live in the *now*, with *me*."

Hungry kisses. Whimpering moans. Sharp inhalations, scrunched eyelids, exposed throats from flung heads, and conjoined bodies.

No awkwardness.

No clumsiness.

We've mastered the art of our pleasure.

I crave for the darkness we've made into our home. It was in the darkness where I found myself inside your galactic, interstellar aura. In the darkness, we're unified, untouchable twin flames. Kindred spirits.

Nonetheless, sometimes the pieces are too splintered for reconstruction, and it's those pieces where, the sun you can't prevent from rising, breaks in.

Am I being too pessimistic?

Instead of fearing the sun, why not rise with it?

After petting in the limelight of our intimate encounter, we dress and continue on.

To your room, a space we spent little time in and cleared out in late January. I slept in your bed to feel you somehow, smelling you on the sheets you left behind solely for this purpose I'm sure.

In Mom's room, her lilac perfume, clothes, shoes, and makeup brushes are gone and forgotten. Her love, however, is evergreen. I feel her hugging me to her bosom and her hand rubbing the nape of my neck.

The bathroom concludes the tour, and the royal blue towel I use to dry you contrasts elegantly with your glacier-blonde hair. I watch as my hands drag the fabric along your keen jawline and protruding Adam's apple. My fingertips feel your stomach and the oxygen becomes scarce. Has your flesh absorbed it?

"Mi Sinclair," you whisper on my neck, your lips straying, "don't cry."

I'm crying?

"It's rain."

"You've never been good at lyin'."

That makes one of us, I think to myself. I can't be gruff, not when we're hurting. The hair on my arms tingle—a sure inkling of impending doom.

"It's gonna be okay, Mi Sinclair. I'm here. I'm with you."

But you're not here, are you, Jess? You've become a memory—white noise and static, the prickling numbness in your feet when they fall asleep, and you stand up only to fall right back down.

You're not really here.

I'm alone.

I'm empty.

And I've never felt so alive.

Maddy whines, "I don't see why you have to take the bus. It's such a long trip," but brightens when I say:

"It's an adventure."

Jax, Jazz, Brad, and Gemma, glum and teary, form a circumference. Jax will work towards a music degree at Richland Community College. Jazz will move to the city she and Eli dreamed of living in. Gemma's going to Cleveland to study nursing. Brad leaves next month to backpack through Europe. Maddy signed up for English classes at Ashland University, and maybe someday she'll write that book about us she mentioned. Charlie will trade her law degree for fashion.

Gemma ruffles my hair. "See you later, Golden Boy."

"I can only think of one person who'd do something like this," says Jazz, handing me a cardboard box, my name listed above her address.

As can I.

My sisters kiss my cheek.

Starting from the left, I hug the Sharp Edges, our hands slapping and fingers sliding and snapping as they separate.

The Greyhound bus hisses to a stop.

I step up the stairs, give the driver my ticket, zigzag to the very back, and place the box on my knees. The bus rolls forward, and I wave back to the people who mean the most to me but must be left behind in order to thrive.

"You can't stay healthy in the environment that made you sick," Maddy said. "Why else would I move to Florida? I hate the heat!"

Heavy metal blasts in my headphones.

Cutting the tape on the box with my pocketknife, I use my phone flashlight to unveil the awaiting treasures:

Jesse's silver Zippo.

A stack of photographs—some of just us, others of the gang.

Paintbrushes tipped in neon paint.

Ticket stubs from our first date at the paintball park.

An unopened pack of Salem Menthols and Camel Golds.

A silver, metallic origami heart, and written in black ink: Read Me.

Hands shaking, I unfold it:

My Sugary Impossibility,

Don't forget our story. I know I won't. I love our story—it's pure, raw, and, at times, uncomfortable, but that's what makes it enthralling and truthful. You, me, us, and everything in-between, that's where we are, stuck in the minefield separating life and death, love and hate, desire and danger. When you see the ocean for the first time and hear its roaring waves kissing the shore, that's where you'll find me. That's where I'll be waiting for you.

I love you, Mi Sinclair, without expectation and without limit.

Love,

Tuum Harris

Tears. He wouldn't want tears. There were things I didn't want either, so I set them free.

Seated across from me is an old man. We'll call him Stalking Butler. His sordid penguin suit and tie hang loosely off his ailing skin and bones; a glass tray and stainless-steel dome lid held up on display. What's he got for me? Syringes? Tourniquets? Golden Girl? White Girl? Blue Sacrament?

He lifts the lid.

"Not today, Butler. I choose to live."

He sets the empty tray aside and mopes. He'll always be here. He's not going away. He'll mill about in shadow, his tray in one hand, his other behind his back. Doting. Patient. He'll never stop demanding to be fed. Does he not realize I've learned to drown out the voices *inside* me by drowning in the sounds *surrounding* me?

I prop my head on the window.

Jesse.

I hear him. I feel him. In the orange waxing moon, I see him. Wherever he may be, in my mind, he's overlooking a lake on a grassy hillside, and he walks further, on and on, until he's floating along the surface and singing sugary tunes to the cosmos.

His smell is stuck to me as that of a second layer and will enrich rooms, street corners, and buildings he's never walked into a day in his life because he's become me, and I've become him, an unconditional nexus that'll never dismantle in any rate of space or time.

Twin flames.

Forever branded.

Safe.

Somehow, somewhere, in some perplexing alternative universe, a Michael Sinclair is lying on a distant planet in the multicolored beanfields, stargazing and holding,

loving,

kissing,

Jesse Harris.

Bittersweet.

(Author's Note: Listen to "Overpass Graffiti" by Ed Sheeran to complete this novel.)

"FACT" CITATIONS

Fact #1: Math

Fact #2: *American Society of Addiction Medicine* opioid-addiction-disease-facts-figures.pdf (asam.org) 2016

Fact #3: *National Institute on Alcohol Abuse and Alcoholism* Alcohol Facts and Statistics Fact Sheet (nih.gov), updated 2020

Fact #4: *Prevent Opioid Abuse. Org* Americans make up 5% of the world population. But we consume 80% of its opioid supply. – Prevent Opioid Abuse, 2019

Fact #5: *Heroin Alert: A 3-Part Response*, Rebecca Smallwood, RN, MBA, Heroin Alert: A 3-Part Response | Relias, 2018

Fact #6: *Prescription Drug Take Back Day: Let's Build Healthy Communities Together, PowerPoint Script, U.S. National Library of Medicine* https://lor.nnlm.gov/op/op.Download_Share.php?documentid=795, 2017

Fact #7: *Overdose Deaths Involving Opioids, Cocaine, and Psychostimulants—United States, 2015-2016* Overdose Deaths Involving Opioids, Cocaine, and Psychostimulants — United States, 2015–2016 | MMWR (cdc.gov), 2018

Fact #8: *90% of who need substance-use disorder treatment don't get it*, Kevin B. O' Reilly 90% who need substance-use disorder treatment don't get it | American Medical Association (ama-assn.org), 2019

Fact #9: *Understanding and Avoiding a Relapse into Addiction, The*

Hazelden Betty Ford Foundation Understanding Relapse and The Risks | Hazelden Betty Ford, 2021

Fact #10: *Meth Addiction Statics, Sunshine Behavioral Health* Meth Abuse Statistics - Sunshine Behavioral Health, 2023

Fact #11: *Alcohol and Drug Abuse Statistics (Facts about Addiction), American Addiction Centers* Alcohol and Drug Abuse Statistics (Facts About Addiction) (americanaddictioncenters.org), 2023

Fact #12: *Genetics and Epigenetics of Addiction DrugFacts, National Institute on Drug Abuse* Genetics and Epigenetics of Addiction DrugFacts | National Institute on Drug Abuse (NIDA) (nih.gov), 2019

Fact #13: *Stats and Figures: Drug Addiction in America, Alvarado Parkway Institute Behavioral Health System* Stats and Figures: Drug Addiction in America - San Diego | API (apibhs.com), 2017

Fact #14: *Substance Abuse & Homelessness: Statistics & Rehab Treatment, Stacy Mosel LMSW, American Addiction Centers Substance Abuse & Homelessness: Statistics & Rehab Treatment (americanaddictioncenters.org), 2022*

Fact #15: *Can mindfulness medication offer drug-free pain relief? Mary Brophy Marcus* Can mindfulness meditation offer drug-free pain relief? - CBS News, 2016

Fact #16: *Today's Heroin Epidemic, More people at risk, multiple drugs abused,* Today's Heroin Epidemic | VitalSigns | CDC, 2015

Fact #17: Hard-Knock-Fact-of-Life

Fact #18: *Alcohol and Drug Abuse Statistics (Facts about Addiction),* American and Addiction Centers, 2023, Alcohol and Drug Abuse Statistics (Facts About Addiction) (americanaddictioncenters.org)

FURTHER READING

American Fix by Ryan Hampton
American Overdose by Chris McGreal
Beautiful Boy by David Sheff
Chasing the Scream by Johann Hari
Dopesick by Beth Macy
Dopeworld: Adventures in the Global Drug Trade by Niko Vorobyov
Dreamland: The True Tale of America's Drug Epidemic by Sam Quinones
Fentanyl, Inc. by Ben Westhoff
Ohio by Stephen Markley
One by One by Nicholas Bush
Pain Killer by Barry Meier
Recovery: Freedom from Our Addictions by Russell Brand
Refuge Recovery by Noah Levine
Smack by Melvin Burgess
The Least of Us by Sam Quinones
This is Ohio by Jack Shuler
Tweak by Nic Sheff
We All Fall Down by Nic Sheff
White Market Drugs by David Herzberg

ABOUT THE AUTHOR

Jessica enjoys spending time with her friends and family, writing, painting, and creating. She loves the smell of oil paint, canvas, pineapple on pizza, and the wind on her face. She's a recovering addict, barista, sister, lover, wife, daughter, friend, and cat mom living in the heart of Ohio—a state she's grown to be protective of—and she hopes to make a positive, changing ripple in the opioid crisis someday. You can follow her on IG, TikTok, and Facebook @JKirschAuthor

Printed in the USA
CPSIA information can be obtained
at www.ICGtesting.com
LVHW012305111024
793580LV00002B/313

9 798218 186234